SCAPEGOAT:
THE HOUNDED

SCAPEGOAT: THE HOUNDED

A NOVEL BY

RAE RICHEN

Back Beat Publications
And imprint of Lloyd Court Press

Scapegoat: The Hounded

A Novel by Rae Richen
Copyright@ 2016, re-issued 2024 by Rae Richen
All rights reserved.
Published in the United States of America by

Back Beat Publications
an imprint of Lloyd Court Press
3034 N.E. 32nd Avenue
Portland, Oregon, 97212
www.lloydcourtpress.org

Cover art by Diana Kolsky, Cover design by Diana Kolsky
Book Design by Amit Dey
Chapter Silhouettes by Carol Sand

ISBN: 978-0-9832242-5-9, Paperback
ISBN: 978-0-9832242-6-6, E-Book

Publisher's Cataloging-In-Publication Data
(Prepared by The Donohue Group, Inc.)
Names: Richen, Rae.
Title: Scapegoat. [Volume 2], The Hounded : a novel / by Rae Richen.
Other Titles: Hounded : a novel
Description: Portland, Oregon : Back Beat Publications, an imprint of Lloyd Court Press, [2016, reissued 2024] | Interest age level: 13 and up. | Includes classroom and book club discussion questions. | Summary: "In The Hounded, Alexander (Xander) Lloyd is on the brink of adulthood, living in a multi-ethnic community on the border of Pakistan and Afghanistan. After a 2006 terrorist attack on the hospital and school kills his parents and friends, Xander lives in Portland, Oregon with his grandfather. Haunted by guilt, Xander avoids friends until Haroon, a Kurdish boy, coaxes him into playing soccer. When Haroon's father, Nasdar, is accused of supporting terrorism, Xander and Haroon pursue justice."--Publisher's website.
Identifiers: ISBN 978-0-9832242-5-9 (print) | ISBN 978-0-9832242-6-6 (ebook)
Subjects: LCSH: Teenage boys--Juvenile fiction. | Terrorism--Pakistan--History--21st century--Juvenile fiction. | Terrorism--Oregon--Portland--History--21st century--Juvenile fiction. | Political culture--Oregon--Portland--History--21st century--Juvenile fiction. | Prejudices--Oregon--Portland--Juvenile fiction. | Historical fiction. CYAC: Teenage boys--Fiction. | Terrorism--Pakistan--History--21st century--Fiction. | Terrorism--Oregon--Portland--History--21st century--Fiction. | Political culture--Oregon--Portland--History--21st century--Fiction. | Prejudices--Oregon--Portland--Fiction.
Classification: LCC PS3618.I34 S332 2016 (print) | LCC PS3618.I34 (ebook) | DDC 813/.6--dc23

"Fear is the cheapest room in the house.
I'd rather see you living in better Conditions."

The Persian Poet and Sufi Master, Hafiz,
Shams-ud-din Muhammad

1320–1389

Translation, Daniel Ladinsky, The Gift

CHAPTER ONE

SPRING 2006, IN THE SOUTHWEST OF PAKISTAN

Seventeen-year-old Alexander Evans-Lloyd stared through the darkness, trying to see why the school gate stood open – the gate between the boy's school and the wheat field near Tiri, Pakistan. A shiver slithered up his neck. Outside the gate, the acacia trees rattled in a breeze and the wheat seeds scraped against each other.

His friend, Mohammed whispered, "Where's Mr. Tallan? He's the guard, on this side of the school."

"Out there?" Xander whispered, pointing out the open gate.

"He's supposed to be in here until four in the morning."

"Yes," Xander said, his voice barely audible even to him. "And the gate…"

"We have to close it."

"What if Mr. Tallan saw something?" Xander whispered.

"Closed. That's what they taught us. If he went out into the wheat field, he had a key."

"What if he's in danger from the Taliban? They bombed the market in Quetta last week."

"We have to . . ." Mohammed said.

Xander started toward the double iron gates. Mohammed put a hand on his shoulder. "This may be a trap."

They moved to either side of the two halves of gate, each boy hidden by the brick wall and the darkness. Separately, they inched toward the heavy filigree of iron – the deeper blackness against the vast stars of the night sky, a sky in the dark of the moon.

Beyond the wall, Xander could hear only the whish of leaves in a breeze. He listened for footsteps, either Mr. Tallan's or some unwanted footstep. No sound came to him but the rasp of summer-wheat.

He glanced across the emptiness toward the shadow that was his friend. Mohammed's arm reached out. Xander reached at the same time. Each of them grabbed their half of the gate and yanked toward himself. The gate-halves swung closed, clanging. Xander thrust the key into the lock.

They could see through the filigree of iron. Outside, no one rose from the wheat. No one moved. No voice protested being locked out.

Both boys backed away. They moved to where possible invaders outside the gate couldn't see them, or shoot at them – in the yard near the chicken house. Awakened by their footsteps, Shazada, the red hen, strolled out of the coop without a worry in her head.

Stupid hen, Xander thought.

Next to him, Xander heard Mohammed's quick breathing. His friend had been as frightened as he. An open gate at night was a deep breech.

"This is the second time Mr. Tallan hasn't been here when we've come out," Xander whispered.

"Last time he claimed to have missed his alarm. But someone opened that gate tonight. If not Tallan, then who?"

"We should have guns," Xander said.

"So, we shoot into the darkness and kill a friend by accident?" Mohammed said.

"How can we protect the boys and the girls? It's crazy what they voted."

"You were at the meeting. You know how every adult there decided. Guns will do nothing but invite bloodshed and then revenge."

"So, we become the targets of Taliban guns? And we have nothing?" Xander asked.

"Xander, my boyo. I hate to be arguing the Quaker teaching with you, but I want nothing to do with changing a situation by killing others. My Muslim faith will not forgive my murder of another just because I am afraid."

"We need to have guns."

"My friend, 'Fear is the cheapest room in the house. I'd rather see you living in better Conditions.'"

Xander stared at Mohammed. "What the hell are you talking about?"

"Hafiz, the poet."

"Yeah, sure. Look, Mohammed, we need something – some kind of protection to slow down invaders."

"Roadside bombs? Think your Grandpa Gilbert will send us bombs?"

Xander frowned, exasperated with Mohammed's naïve jokes. This hospital, their boys' school and the girls' school across the field was an experiment in communal living, Muslims, Quakers, Catholics living in peace in Pakistan, and much of it funded by his Grandfather's U. S. foundation, and Catholic, Quaker and Muslim fundraising. Even Shazada and the other hens, a gift from Heifer International thanks to the tireless work of his Grandfather Gilbert.

An experiment in peaceful living, so there was funding for walls and gates for all the buildings, even a brick wall around the wheat field.

But guns, never.

Xander bent down next to the side wall of the hen house and picked up a long, stout stick. "We could practice with this," he said.

"Where'd that come from?"

Xander pointed west, toward the other end of the field. "I took it from the dead acacia tree between the girl's school and the hospital."

Mohammed touched the stick. "Strong wood."

"Watch this." Xander whirled. He thrust out his leg with a flash of his white shalwar trousers. His powerful kick thudded into his imagined opponent's gut. The huge man doubled over. Xander's blue kameez shirt was loose enough to allow his arms full power, so Xander finished the big fellow with a smack of his acacia stick to the head.

The man crumpled into the chicken manure, never to rise again. Xander thumped the end of his stick into the ground and stood at attention, as if saluting the dead.

Frightened, Shazada squawked and flew at the compound wall. She flailed her wings, fluttered to the ground, and pecked at pebbles.

Mohammed, clapped softly. "Excellent, Xander! You dance exceeding well."

"That's not dancing," Xander growled. "Can't you see? My man is dead in a pile of bird shit."

"Ah! Fighting." Mohammed smirked. "I never thought you so vicious."

Xander twirled his stick toward his teasing friend. For a moment, the fear of the open gate faded from their minds. He and Mohammed had played like this since they were seven.

"Yiee!" Mohammed backed up, hands out in mock surrender.

Xander took one last thrust. Mohammed jumped out of the way, whispering. "Your poor mother – her son just another violent boyo," he said.

Xander sobered, and glanced once more toward the gate. "Why was it open?"

Mohammed grew quiet. "And where is Tallan?"

"The sun rises," Xander said. "We should check to see if he is out there."

"Not by ourselves."

"I hate this. If they let us have weapons, we could practice every day, and get really good. No one would dare to attack us."

Mohammed grinned. "We can advertise our mighty powers – become famous American gunslingers – like old movies." He pointed at Xander, "*Butch Cassidy*" Mohammed thumped his own chest, "*and the Pakistani Kid.*"

Xander's snort of laughter stopped short. They both heard squeaky door hinges from the cottage next to their boys' school. Xander dropped his stick in the dust. Mohammed kicked it toward a pile of straw.

They turned their backs to the stick and faced Xander's parents coming out of the cottage – doctors, Daniel and Rebecca Lloyd – Dad, with hair as dark as Xander's, and Mom, with a swinging braid that reminded Xander of the braided seed-heads in the wheat field.

His parents always woke early to work at the hospital. Xander glanced out toward their dark hospital building which stood further west, beyond the girls' school.

Mom and Dad carried freshly-washed scrubs, ready for a day in the operating room. Dad waved a greeting, then picked up his briefcase.

"Hi," Xander said, as cool as possible, trying not to glance at his stick, which he hoped looked like nothing important.

Mohammed bowed slightly toward Xander's mother, "Mrs. Lloyd, doctor, ma'am."

Xander's mother smiled. "Good morning, Mohammed. What are you boys up to today?"

"Guard duty in fifteen minutes," Mohammed said, shading his eyes in morning's low sun.

Xander's mother frowned and turned to Dad. "Daniel, I thought we were going to stop using boys as guards."

"Seventeen is not boys," Xander said.

Dad nudged the rooster away from nibbling his pant leg. "Honey, these fellows guard only during breakfast preparation."

"Yeah, Mom, we guard one hour in the morning," Xander said. "We could do more if we didn't have to finish the chimney and the tunnels." He waved toward the boys' class and dormitory building. The community had been working on it for two years, two levels of dormitory and one floor of classrooms constructed on top of the tunneled foundations of a ruined palace and an invaders' Christian church.

Mom looked around. "What guard are you replacing?"

"Um . . ., on this side of the school, we replace Mr. Tallan," Mohammed said.

Dad leveled his gaze at Mohammed. "Mr. Tallan wasn't here when you came, was he?"

Mohammed looked Dad in the eye. "No, sir."

Dad studied both of them. "And you weren't going to report that, right?"

"No, sir."

"If he cannot protect us, we all need to know that."

"Yes, sir," Mohammed said. "When we came out, the gate was open."

Dad and Mom both looked toward the wheat field and then to the girls' school.

Dad said, "We need to check the gates between here and the hospital. Rebecca, you and Mohammed stay here so you can warn Mr. Bhatti if anything is wrong. Xander, you come with me around the perimeter."

Xander and Dad unlocked the gate and stepped outside. After a moment, Dad pointed at a bottle. Xander didn't recognize it.

"Whiskey," Dad said, picking it up. "Tallan drinks whiskey when he's off his program."

"And here's his shoe print," Xander pointed out. Mr. Tallan was the only member of the school staff who wore American athletic shoes. "I think he's gone back inside and just left the gate open."

Dad studied the prints. "I think you're right, son."

"What do we do?"

"You and Mohammed did the right things. But that's all you need to do," Dad said. "Mr. Bhatti and the other teachers will have to deal with this at meeting tonight. Right now, we need to check the other gates."

They moved swiftly across the irrigation ditch and toward the gate from the wheat field that led into the girls' compound. It was shut tight. Dad waved at one of the teachers who guarded the girls' school. Xander and Dad then strode further west, behind the girls' class and dorm rooms. They checked the gate in the continuation of the brick wall that also surrounded the hospital.

"All's well," Dad said as they walked back to meet Mom and Mohammed.

Dad spoke to Mom. "I'm going to call Mr. Bhatti when we get to the hospital. Tallan's absences can't be ignored."

Xander knew that the last time, Mr. Tallan had been found drunk in his bed.

Mom coughed, probably to get Dad off the subject of Mr. Tallan and why he frequently went missing. Dad glanced at her and shifted his tone to ask Xander, "Where is your buddy, Manzur?"

Relieved to move on, Xander said, "It's his turn to get the boys dressed." Patient Manzur always enjoyed the little kids' antics.

"Who will guard the east side?" Mom asked.

"Mohammed will. I take this side today," Xander said. He glanced at his stick, and then saw his father's gaze go in that direction. Dad stared at him, and raised his eyebrows in the way he did when he wanted Xander to be a better person.

Mohammed spoke quickly. "I'll meet you in an hour, Xander."

Dad glanced again at the stick. "We love you boys. Watch carefully."

"We will," Mohammed said, and hurried off to relieve Doctor Branson on the east side.

With Mohammed gone, Xander expected Dad to say something about the stick, but Dad took Mom's hand and said, "All is safe. Rebecca, the boys will be fine. We have many patients, and should get going."

Xander's mother glanced off to the west, beyond the wide wheat field, beyond the girls' school and the hospital. She seemed to be staring at the looming hills of Afghanistan where the Taliban were known to hide out.

For a second, Xander saw a frown tighten her eyelids. Then, she pulled back her shoulders and said, "Take care, son."

Xander stood tall. "I do, Mom."

Mom walked out the wrought-iron western gate. After they passed through, Dad closed and relocked it. Xander watched them through the filigree design. On the other side of the gate, Dad seemed to be checking again for signs of Mr. Tallan. Mom finally took Dad's hand and pulled him toward the hospital.

Xander could see them walking down the path that skirted the wheat field. Three years ago, that field had been part of the boys' soccer pitch. Now, the wheat fed the community and it helped pay for material to build and maintain the hospital and two schools.

All of the buildings had been built since Xander turned seven. The first was the hospital. The Quaker, Muslim and Christian doctors provided goodwill and safety. The families of the farms surrounding the village of Tiri learned to trust them. They had asked for a school to educate their children.

So, with Grandfather Gilbert's foundation and other help, the community built a school for boys on top of the ruins of an early palace built by Indian invaders. Soon after the boys' school, they began the girls' school on top of the ruins of an old Christian church. The girls' school stood at the far side of the soccer field full of wheat. Even further west, toward the Afghan hills, stood the original hospital. Each building had its protective wall and gate.

There was always a construction project going on here. Most recent was the chimney repair on the boys' school and a tunnel to connect the girls' school with the boys' tunnels under the ancient palace and the catacombs under the old church. The tunnel was already three quarters finished.

All of the buildings and the wheat field were within one hundred yards of each other – the length of a soccer field. Friends Welcome Schools and Hospital was a small community in a vast country.

Xander retreated to slightly higher ground where he could see over the fence around the boy's school. From there, he saw Mom and Dad approach the side of the girls' school. A girl came out the front door. She replaced her teacher as the girls' guard. Xander's mother waved to her,

Sophia.

Sophia's father was the hospital's anesthetist, Ali Gohary. Sophia wore a head scarf and the long-skirted version of her school's blue and white checked uniform. Xander, watched her and thought, *Wisdom, grace. Just like her name.*

Near the edge of the wheat field, Dad took Mom's hand and helped her jump across the irrigation ditch. After she jumped, Dad still held her hand.

Xander glanced again at Sophia. She looked away. He hoped she pretended disinterest because she didn't want to be caught looking.

Xander smiled, glad that she was outside on his guard morning. He might see Sophia at Friday prayers in the mosque, and then again at Quaker Meeting on Sunday or at Catholic Vespers. Everyone at *Friends Welcome Schools and Hospital* celebrated God and Allah together. It was the adults' way of supporting each other. Xander liked the services. It gave him more chances to visit after prayers with Sophia.

Before he turned to his job of guarding, he studied his father's hand in Mom's. Xander decided not to pick up his fighting stick.

CHAPTER TWO

Half an hour later, Xander patrolled the dusty yard, watching the area while trying not to look at Sophia's rose and blue head scarf. Instead, he studied his sides of his mission school while Mohammed guarded the east and the north. Xander watched for motion in the farm fields of Tiri. He watched the border beyond the hospital, where the shadowed Afghan hills and dry mountains hunkered over their valley.

During the past summer, fanatics from those hills had attacked other towns in Pakistan. On the radio, he'd heard about a bomb in the music market of the nearby town of Quetta. The very next day, Mother turned off the radio after the announcer said something about a hand grenade on the Jail Road in Quetta. A few days later, in a town closer to the border, someone shot rockets into the home of a tribal elder, missing him. Instead a rocket murdered a twelve-year-old girl.

On that day, the mood in Friends School and Hospital changed. At the Monthly Meeting, the faculty and the doctors debated the best way to care for the community. After many hours, the unanimous vote of the adults – Muslims, Catholics, and Quakers together – decided that weapons invited violence and negated their witness for peace.

"Guards," they said, "need to warn of attack and lead others to shelter. We have the tunnels under the old palace for our defense. And soon, the girl's school will be connected to them."

Mr. Din, the old gardener had asked, "So we have tunnels, then what?"

"When the attack is over," Headmaster Bhatti had said, "then we come out, either in the school and hospital compound, or out in the fields beyond Tiri."

Xander shifted his gaze from the hills to those fields beyond the town. Maybe that was a safe place to come up. Maybe not.

He studied the hospital, the girls' school and Sophia, then the wheat field. Nothing seemed to move in the heat of morning, nothing but a small breeze rippling the wheat. Xander worked to remain alert. He felt like an easy target. The memory of the one open gate jazzed his nerves.

He tossed grain to Big Buster, their American rooster. Shazada, the red hen, pecked Buster's wing feathers, chasing him off. Xander stopped her rush by tossing a trail of grain away from her enemy – a distracting tactic he'd learned from his friend. Mohammed also used this distraction method with any squabbling little boys in their school dormitory. Mohammed and Manzur had a talent for getting boys and chickens to stop fighting.

As Xander's gaze returned to the hills and fields, he listened to his friends in the dormitory behind him. In their chatter, he recognized each one by his accent or his dialect. He heard his friend, Manzur, talking to one of the little boys in their native Kurmanji. Manzur didn't think the little guy had really brushed his teeth. Xander laughed.

Two other boys spoke Persian Dari as they argued about whose turn it was to set the table for breakfast. One of them sounded like

Mohammed's little brother. Other kids talked about homework. Some spoke English, the language they all shared. Others spoke Pashto or, like Sophia and her father, Gorani.

Seven-year-old Edmund Branson searched for his sandals, as usual. Edmund spoke broad Yorkshire English sprinkled with *thee* and *thine*. He'd learned that talk from his English Quaker mom and dad, who were doctors with Xander's and Sophia's parents.

He glanced again toward Sophia.

She suddenly moved to the south side of her building. Something made her body tense. Xander followed her gaze toward the west. Beyond the girls' academy, and beyond the tan walls of the hospital, a small white cloud gathered over Afghanistan's barren humps and cliffs.

He grew certain that was no cloud. It billowed too fast.

He strode toward the gate of the compound, followed by the scolding hen. That was smoke, near the hospital, but it couldn't be from the incinerator which stood on the other side of the building.

Sophia ran to the front door of her school, pointing at the cloud as she yelled into her dormitory. Suddenly, orange and yellow flickers followed the cloud upwards, licking at the scrub acacia trees by the hospital wall. Xander tried to blink the cloud away. Instead, it grew dark and large. It was the hospital's western wall, and the acacia trees nearby carried the flames toward the second story.

"Fire! Fire!" He yelled toward the boys' in the dormitory. He raced along the compound wall to gather buckets for the fired line they had practiced.

Across the wheat field, Sophia yanked open the double wooden doors of the girls' school, yelling at her friends, "Hurry. Hurry!"

Girls in blue and white-checked uniforms spilled out. Women carried little girls. Girls ran alone. Older girls pulled little ones.

He heard a loud pop, and a scream. Sophia seemed to deflate, and then she crumpled face down on the steps of the school. One of the other girls stopped and shook Sophia's shoulder. A teacher yelled at the girl. She straightened and rushed on. As the other girls ran past her, Sophia's body didn't move.

Teachers and girls ran across their school's open courtyard. They disappeared into the field. Wheat swayed and leaned, and then closed up around them, but the line of their movement snaked toward him. Xander dropped the buckets and ran back to the open gate of the boy's compound to get to Sophia.

The sharp smack and recoil of another rifle sounded from the wall north of the girls' school. In the tall wheat, a woman shrieked. Her arms rose as she fell, throwing the child she carried. The child's body hung in the air, her small hands opened toward the sky. Her blue and white-checked dress became a sail as she floated.

Bile rose in Xander's throat. A sudden drum of shots sounded fifty yards away. Xander's mind froze. Men with stubby guns climbed the walls surrounding the girl's building. They aimed at the women. Their volleys raked the field. Screams rose from many parts of the wheat. The grains swayed and fell. On the steps, Sophia's body seemed a zone of quiet in chaos.

Behind the girls' school, flames flashed ever higher, suddenly covering the western wall of the hospital.

Xander's numb mind awakened. "Mom," he shouted. "Dad." He grabbed at the wrought-iron gate, but in that moment, a long arm whipped over his chest, yanked the fabric of his kameez, and pulled him to the ground, a crash that sent air from his lungs.

Mohammed's voice whispered in his ear. "Go that way, you'll be shot. We must save others."

Xander could barely breathe.

"Crawl to the side door," Mohammed said. "Manzur holds it."

Xander shook his head. "But Sophia, and the hospital."

"We can't help them. Boys and teachers we can help. Go." Mohammed gave him a shove toward the side door, ten feet away. Behind them, shots and shrieks mingled.

Xander shoved the gate closed. Mohammed reached up and yanked the lock shut. Bullets hit the iron. Mohammed belly flopped, joining Xander working toward the side door.

As he crawled, Xander gulped on fear. They had practiced for this day, but prayed it would never come. He could still hear shooting – lots of shooting, but few screams.

They moved below the level of the bullets that hit their building. Both crawled up the side dormitory steps. From the doorsill, Xander glanced once more at the stillness that was Sophia, then he pushed on the wood. Manzur pulled it open from inside. Behind Manzur, the little boys huddled, wide-eyed.

"To the basement and the tunnels," Xander called. He and Mohammed rushed in, shoving the heavy door closed behind them and pulling down the bar to keep it closed. Xander took young Edmund by the shoulders and turned him toward the basement stairs. "Manzur and Mohammed will take care of you."

"Will thee come also?" Edmund's voice quivered.

"Soon. But I must find the teachers."

Outside, the girls' cries had stopped. Xander choked down vomit and ran toward the teachers' wing of the dormitory.

Why didn't we work faster on the girls' tunnel?

The cedar dining room door swung open. All five teachers pushed into the hall, each carrying food from the larder, ready for a siege.

The gardener, Mr. Din, was not with them. Nor Mr. Tallan, the custodian.

"The basement," Mr. Bhatti called. "Go to the basement."

"Manzur and Mohammed have taken the boys there," Xander said.

"Tallan?"

Xander shook his head. "He left the gate open this morning. Where is Mr. Din?"

Mr. Bhatti frowned. "At the tool shed, minutes ago."

The shed sat behind the kitchen on the classroom side of the building. The old man was hard of hearing and might not have seen what was happening.

"I'll find him." Xander hunched his shoulder, pushed the heavy dining door open and swung through.

Mr. Bhatti's voice followed him. "Bring him to the tunnels."

Stopping at the kitchen window, Xander saw Mr. Din outside. The old man raised a rake above him as he shouted in Pashto. The tops of black headscarves appeared on the other side of the compound wall.

Glancing to the right, Xander saw Mohammed stand in the chicken yard, arms over his head.

But Mohammed is in the basement . . .

Xander jerked open the kitchen door. He ran toward Mr. Din, while yelling at Mohammed. "The boys need you. Go inside."

Old Mr. Din pivoted and swung his rake, narrowly missing Xander, who ducked away. Mr. Din's eyes widened with shock. The rake finished its low arc. Its weight toppled Mr. Din into Xander's arms.

"Boy!" Mr. Din's yell muffled into Xander's chest. "Go back. Go back."

A high-pitched whistle passed over Xander's head. *A bullet.*

As he turned toward the kitchen door, Xander yelled again. "Get inside!"

Mohammed still didn't move.

A man in a black kameez swung himself up on the wall and aimed his gun toward Mr. Din. Xander pulled the gardener into the wooden tool shed. A bullet smacked into the shed doorframe. As they dove inside, Mr. Din grabbed a single-headed axe from the wall. The blade of the axe shone in the sun. The shed door slammed behind them.

Xander yanked Mr. Din behind the wheel barrow that stood on its blunt nose. He crouched in the shadow of the barrow with the gardener in his arms. Shots whistled through the shed walls as if through a cardboard box. Each bullet that hit the hanging shovels or the upended wheel barrow rang with steel strength.

Outside, he heard Mohammed's voice sing out. "Allaahu Akbar." *God is greatest . . .* as if beginning his morning prayer.

The shooting stopped. In Xander's imagination, Mohammed bowed to the ground in the chicken yard. Xander tried to shut down his mental movie, but the reel stuttered on, showing men in black who circled and debated, their guns aimed at Mohammed. Mohammed continued his prayers.

"God eees great," muttered Mr. Din. "Mohammed eees a fool Quaker."

Xander heard the squawl of the red hen. Mr. Din wrenched himself from Xander's arms.

"So sorry," Mr. Din said. A sudden thud rocked the side of Xander's head. As his muscles collapsed and his back hit the floor, he thought crazily that the wizened old man had hit him with the butt of the axe. Stunned, he sank into growing darkness, listening to Mr. Din's bare feet smack the floor as he ran from the shed.

Mr. Din screamed in Pashto, "For Allah and my children."

"Go back!" Mohammed yelled from the yard.

Bullets rang out against the wheelbarrow. Hot searing sharpened Xander's senses for a moment. He realized one bullet had crashed into his out-flung arm, but his mind spun away from pain.

What will Grandpa Gilbert do when we're all dead?

CHAPTER THREE

PORTLAND, OREGON, U. S. A.
THE SAME DAY, 2006

Grandpa Gilbert Evans, editor-in-chief of the *Journal of the Americas* and partner-owner of Evans International Media sat, rigid with alarm. He gripped the arms of his office chair and leaned forward in a darkness broken only by the flicker of light on this computer screen. Outside, the lights of Portland night life shone through a warm rain.

Gilbert Evans considered himself a rational man, a man of business, a man who easily ran ten regional newspapers, five west coast television stations, an online news source, and one radio station in every large west coast town.

But tonight, his mind froze. His attention focused on the raw film arriving from the Afghan-Pakistan border. The film came live from his television crew.

Through their clear feed, he could almost smell what his daughter, Rebecca, described in her letters – wind from the northern mountains as it blows across the plains, the pungence of pine and acacia forests and tough grasses.

The crew chief, Ted Oxnard, and his men retreated from rifle shots. But they continued filming the band of men who descended the Afghan hills into Western Pakistan.

On film, Oxnard said, "Tonight, I've been in contact with other reporters. They've seen many groups pouring into this southwestern area of Pakistan, but I don't know how far into the region they have penetrated.

"The invaders dress in black, their faces masked. They seem to know about our camera crew, and shoot toward us as if in boredom." Oxnard kept whispering into the microphone. "We believe these men want our news team to follow them, and broadcast their power across the world."

Gilbert leaned forward to see more detail in the film. The invaders halted outside a compound containing dormitories and a hospital. Oxnard's telephoto lens showed a sign over the door of the hospital. An Arabic script flowed. Underneath it, English words proclaimed: "In the name of Allah, the Compassionate, the Merciful" – a Muslim Hospital.

As the film stuttered on, and even as Oxnard used a bullhorn to blare out a warning to hospital staff, the invaders scaled the compound walls and spread out. At a signal from their leader, each team invading the Muslim hospital kicked in a door. The first scream in the night ripped from Gilbert Evans' own throat.

As soon as he understood the men and their purpose, Gilbert stood up, kicked back his chair, grabbed the desk phone and punched in the number for the hospital near Tiri, Pakistan, and for his daughter, Rebecca. But his phone call to the far side of the world brought static-laden sound and frustration. The nurse who answered, yelled across the transmission noise. "I can't connect you with Doctor Rebecca, or with Daniel. They're performing cataract operations." Suddenly, she screamed, "No! God! No!"

The phone went silent.

With growing fear, Gilbert punched in the number for *Friend's Welcome School*, near the hospital. He recognized the voice that answered. Gilbert shouted, "Headmaster Bhatti, my reporters are filming a series of invasions. Now, the nurse at your hospital is screaming. Get the boys to safety."

Gilbert heard Bhatti drop the phone on a wooden table and run off. Then, that line also went dead. Gilbert redialed. Nothing.

In a sweat, he called and woke his staff members, warning that Oxnard's team needed rescue. His next call found President Musharraf's secretary. The President and his government already had sent armed help to twenty schools and hospitals, and were on the phone with U.S. military, pleading for assistance.

Over the next few calls, Gilbert put together a team that included fresh reporters, translators and security guards already in Pakistan to aid Oxnard, the hospitals and schools.

His sleep-deprived secretary worked out airline arrangements. Gilbert talked to a contact at the Pentagon, and then the ambassador's aide in Pakistan, Tony Hilling. He dialed and yelled orders, limping madly about, tossing things in a briefcase. Finally, he called his own sister, Justine.

While her phone rang, he checked his watch: barely five in the morning in their Pacific Coast time zone.

"Juss? You awake?" he asked.

"Am now, Brother."

"I'm going to Pakistan. Things are very wrong there."

"You read that? Or saw it?"

"Ted Oxnard sent film – while being shot at."

"But Rebecca and Daniel say life becomes safer. The fanatical groups lose control."

"I know what I saw. I could practically smell the hate."

His sister remained silent.

He added, "Justine, I called Tiri. The phones went dead. There is danger."

"Yes, but . . ."

"Men strike out when they lose control."

He heard her feet hit the floor, then a fumbling sound.

"This was vivid, Justine. Real men. Real guns. Real scrub acacias with seed pods that rattled in the breeze."

"Oh, Gilbert . . ." He heard worry in her voice. "You run off into those mountains at your age, and . . . ."

"Rebecca needs me."

"What do we do?" she asked. She'd never sounded old before.

"I've lined up the Evans jet to New York, then on to Karachi."

"Us alone?" she asked.

"Tony Hilling and a support team will meet us in Karachi." In his suit pocket, Gilbert kept his fingers crossed, hoping for her help, her strength. "Can you make it?" he asked.

"Look, Bubba, I always have my jail-house suitcase packed. I'll pick you up."

"Great. Go by the house and grab me a change of clothes, will you?"

"Sure. And you raid the cafeteria for breakfast," she said.

As Justine's phone clacked shut, he leaned on his cane and slumped. Then he straightened. He needed her, his little sister, his sparring partner. He could not think about his fear.

CHAPTER FOUR

PAKISTAN, 24 HOURS LATER

Two men lifted Xander onto a pallet. He cringed against the pain in his arm. Somewhere near, he heard a woman wailing. "Aye. Aye. Mohammed."

Tears slid from his closed eyes.

The men strapped Xander's body into a kind of metal platform. Hot sun weighed on him, making breath and thought difficult. He faded into deep oblivion.

Later, he awoke. Something lulling-loud vibrated through him. A helicopter engine revving up, he thought.

"Where'd they find this one?" A high, tense voice asked from the front of the helicopter.

"In the garden shed behind the wheel barrow." The voice that answered seemed deep and calm, and close-by.

Next, the deep voice spoke to Xander directly.

"Son, you've been bleeding a long time. Dehydrated, too. Got to get a saline hooked up, so here comes a small prick of needle."

Something poked into Xander's arm.

"Weren't there other boys in that school?" the far away voice asked.

"Shut up and get us in the air," the near and deep voice replied.

"But," the other man said, "They found bodies, girls, women, but no boys except the one in the chicken . . ."

"You are out of line," Deep Voice said. "Stop talking and fly this thing."

Mohammed, Mr. Din, Sophia.

Xander tried to tell the man next to him about the boys. *They're in the basement. The ancient palace, and its tunnels.* But he could not open his mouth to talk, couldn't feel anything in his body but his sadness.

What seemed like many minutes later, he woke again to hear the pilot's voice from up front, "How come this victim gets VIP soldier transport?"

"Grandson of Evans International Media."

"What the shit was Evans' grandson doing in that lack-water way-station?"

"Going to school," the deep voice said, "and you need to stay on task. Get us to Karachi."

Heat raced through Xander's body. He opened his eyes and found a big black man in an American service uniform watching his face – a medic.

When the medic realized Xander looked at him, he glanced down at Xander's arm and at the needle he had inserted into a tube. He said, "You need to sleep, Alexander. We've got to get to Karachi and then get you a lot closer to home."

"Mom? Dad?" Xander whispered.

The medic closed his eyes. After a moment, he looked at Xander again. Touching his shoulder, the man held Xander's gaze, and then shook his head.

An image of waving wheat and waving blond hair mixed in Xander's mind. His mother's hand in his father's. His throat burned. Searing tears ran down his cheeks and into his ears.

The medic whispered to himself, "Wolves. Nothin' but a vicious pack of wolves."

* *

TO NEUSTAT BEI ALPEN, GERMANY

Gilbert and Justine Evans halted at a shout from halfway across the terminal at John F. Kennedy Airport, New York. They stopped near the exit for the Evans' private plane. Someone shouted Gilbert's name.

Gib used his cane to help him swivel about, searching for the source of the yell. He spotted the woman across the hangar space.

"Isn't that Martha Boyden?" Justine asked.

Gilbert nodded, recognizing one of his reporters at the New York office. Boyden ran. As soon as Gilbert saw her, he knew the woman brought bad news. The young reporter breathed hard as she caught up to them.

"Sir," Boyden said, "Saadik Barzani called from Western Pakistan. He had very bad news. Your daughter's hospital has been attacked. Your ... Rebecca and Daniel Lloyd have died. Alexander, is wounded."

Gilbert closed his eyes. Beside him, he heard Justine gasp and then sob. He glanced up quickly and saw her back against a nearby garbage can where she grabbed the lid for support.

"Xander wounded?" she asked.

"Yes, but alive."

Alive, Gilbert thought.

"There were other attacks, weren't there." Gilbert said.

Boyden nodded. "Hundreds of fighters down from the Afghan hills. They attacked several border hospitals and schools."

"Rebecca is dead?" Gilbert asked again, trying to focus. "They are certain?"

Boyden nodded. "And Daniel, as well. I'm so sorry, Mr. Evans. They were afraid . . . the ambassador and Saadik feared for you, too. Saadik heard there were some who planned to kidnap Rebecca and Daniel. They were killed by mistake."

Justine sank to the floor. Gilbert leaned on his cane with a heavy ache.

"The attackers didn't find Xander," Ms. Boyden said. "After we broke the siege of the school, our Air Force medics discovered him in the tool shed. He's on his way by helicopter to Karachi right now."

So much ugliness since the news film of last night. He should have forced Rebecca and Daniel to come home months ago.

As if that would have worked . . .

*   *

The erupting situation in Pakistan brought a U.S. Army colonel to the airport, sent at the urging of John Hamilton, the Evans Media contact in the Pentagon. The colonel came to confer with them about transporting Xander, and the bodies of Rebecca and Daniel. They decided to meet Xander in Germany.

"Please," Gilbert said, "Bring them to the base at Neustat bei Alpen."

"Sir?" the colonel asked.

"I . . . we know that base. We once lived near there."

He didn't mention that he and Justine had lived there as children. He needed something familiar to stop his world from slamming out of control. Justine took his hand. He gripped her fingers – a warmth that meant sanity in chaos.

Late that afternoon, the government of the United States hustled Gilbert and Justine onto a military flight to Berlin and then to the U.S. Army hospital near Neustat bei Alpen, Germany.

*   *

Several hours later, they sat in the unnatural hush of a base hospital in Germany. Occasional cries and mutterings broke the quiet. The smell of antiseptic crept into their clothes. Wounded men and women suffered here – soldiers who had served their country in Iraq and Afghanistan.

They were told that Xander's transport had arrived in Karachi, Pakistan. He had been transferred to a military flight and would arrive at the base airport in a few hours. From the cargo bay, Gilbert also would claim the bodies of Rebecca and Daniel.

It was now about forty hours since Gilbert watched the film from Ted Oxnard's crew. He and Justine had been in the air for twelve hours since Portland. No one yet had told them much about the attack except that it had taken most of a day to break the siege, an hour after that to find Rebecca's and Daniel's bodies in the hospital operating room amidst many bodies. After another hour, they found Xander who'd been bleeding all that time.

Many girls and women had died. Only one old man and one other boy had been found. The boy, Mohammed, was shot dead, in the entry yard while kneeling, face to the ground, as if in prayer.

"Mohammed," Justine said. "Mohammed and Manzur – Xander wrote about them."

Gilbert's head bowed. Boys. Mere boys, and all those girls.

When the military flight brought Xander, the boy would need all their understanding and their energy, but Gilbert felt all his sixty-seven years. His grandson needed more than a dazed old man.

Next to him, Justine whispered, "He will blame himself for living still."

Gilbert slumped in the chair. "I know."

How well I know.

CHAPTER FIVE

Early summer, four weeks after the attack on his school, Xander stood on a hill in Portland, Oregon. He and Grandpa and Aunt Justine were at Lincoln Memorial Cemetery, attending a service for his mom and dad. But Xander tried to keep his mind somewhere else. The members of East-Bank Friends surrounded them, as well as strangers can do for strangers. They'd been bringing food and comfort to Grandpa's house ever since the return from the hospital in Germany. Among them stood a strong-faced woman dressed in western clothes, but to Xander it was clear, from her whispered prayers, that she was Kurdish and Muslim.

Xander didn't remember any of these people, but they remembered Mom and Dad.

His arm ached inside its bandages. His mind studied two stacked rectangles of green turf. Not far away, lay two piles of dirt covered with straw to keep them from collapsing into the graves. His attention followed a beetle crawling in the straw. Behind him, he heard the song of a stupid bird that didn't care about death.

And then he heard a familiar, soft, grieving cry. He closed his eyes, expecting to hear Mohammed's name, but the name of the lost one didn't come from the crying man. Xander glanced across the lush green grass and saw a family. At the bottom of the cemetery hill stood a row of women wearing long dresses. They had covered their hair in saffron-yellow scarves. The men in the group climbed the hill, carrying a shrouded body laid out on a platform – a Muslim family – a family probably from the mosque he'd noticed at the bottom of the cemetery hill. Masjid Maryam – Mosque Maryam.

The women awaited the men. Xander had seen this in Pakistan. The men bury. The women wait. Dark-eyed men wept as they carried the small platform on their shoulders. A tall boy, dignified, quiet and lonely, stood near the open grave. Next to him, another pile of straw-covered dirt waited.

For a moment, Xander thought he had flown back to Pakistan and the boy was his friend, Manzur.

His grandfather's hand rested on Xander's shoulder. He glanced up at Grandpa who also gazed at the boy across the hill. Then Grandpa's attention moved across the space between the two funerals and stopped to study a man standing among nearby graves. Grandpa's jaw tensed. His eyes flashed dark suspicion.

"No," Grandpa whispered, as if some weight were piled onto the weight of his grief.

Xander looked at the man. Beyond the circle of Friends, under the drooping branches of an old Douglas fir tree, the man stood, not with the Friends, but clearly watching them, and watching the other funeral as well. The man had dark hair, turning white at the edges. Wide shoulders filled his suit and were out of proportion to his short legs. Xander had the impression of a man who lifted weights. His dark suit and brown shoes seemed out of place, neither part of the Muslim men's white kameez and shalwar pants, nor the sandals, chinos and open necked shirts of the Friends. There was no sign of sadness in the man, only awareness and wariness.

Xander took his grandfather's hand where it lay on his shoulder. "Who is that, Grandpa?" he whispered.

"Just a stranger," Grandpa said. Then, his attention returned to Xander, to the two graves in front of them, and the people who surrounded them.

Xander tried to listen to the people speaking at the grave site. He decided after all to be present as members of Friends' Meeting testified to their memories of his mother and father. The short, strong man in the suit had nothing to do with his parents, or with this day.

One woman spoke softly. "Rebecca and I were buddies in medical school. We studied together. She knew the chemistry out of wanting to know it. I learned it because we had to"

"Yes," an older woman said, "Rebecca and Daniel shared that. Wanting to know."

These people, these Friends, knew things that happened before he was born. They understood his parents in a way he never would.

"I remember when they met," a man said. "Such intense discussions about right and wrong. Such a commitment to causes. I don't think they realized they were falling in love until that first election campaign came to an end."

Xander struggled to pay close attention for the rest of the short service. *They fell in love*, he thought. *They held hands even after she jumped the irrigation ditch.*

Listening to their stories tore at his gut. His heart followed the other funeral and the boy near the other grave.

His heart also thought of Manzur, Edmund and of Mohammed's little brother. At the hospital in Germany, he'd barely been able to tell Grandpa where the searchers should look. But even after Grandpa understood him and called someone in Tiri to explain, the boys were not found. The school and dormitory above their tunnels had been destroyed by the mortar fire of the siege. Their bodies were not in the rubble. No one knew what had happened to them.

*   *

That night, after the funerals, Xander watched Aunt Justine choose one casserole from among the many that Friends had left in Grandpa's freezer. Xander knew he couldn't eat.

"Can't," Grandpa said to her. "Neither of us wants food, it looks like."

Aunt Justine hugged Xander and fussed with his hair while she crooned. Then she whispered, "God, I loved your mama. She was my darling, too."

He glanced at his aunt's strong-jawed face and realized he saw tears in her big blue eyes. Her nose grew red with the effort to keep her tears from spilling.

She coughed, and said, "Good night, boys," threw her long cape over her shoulders, hurried out into the dark, and ran down the sidewalk to her home. He and Grandpa watched from the porch until they saw her open her door on the duplex she owned in the next block.

Grandpa shook his head slowly. "Invincible Justine," he whispered. Then he saw Xander watching him. "Your Aunt Justine loved to play games with your mama when she was little. Used to play Hangman with her during silent meeting. Penciled their guesses on the Xeroxed hymn sheets or the Monthly Meeting Minutes. Finally, your Grandma Elizabeth had to sit between them."

Xander's knees gave out. He collapsed to a sudden sit on the front porch steps. His mama used to play word games with him during boring meetings, too.

Grandpa stared at him a moment. "I expect you're tired. Let's hit the hay."

In his mind, Xander saw the straw at the cemetery covering the piles of dirt that waited to fill the graves.

Grandpa looked at Xander and said. "It is a sad day for more than you and me, Xander. A sad day." Then he began the trudge upstairs.

"Grandpa," Xander said, "who was the Kurdish lady at the funeral?"

Lifting his eyebrows in surprise, Grandpa said, "I forgot, you probably know how to tell who is Kurdish and who is Afghani and ..."

"And the man by the tree?" Xander asked.

Silence, a long moment of silence, and then his grandfather said, "She is Nazneen Qubadi – a good friend. Her husband and I work together, but he is in Iraq to arrange his sister's wedding. Nazneen came to support us all."

"The man?" Xander repeated.

"A troublemaker, a suspicious son-of-a . . . a fellow I don't trust."

"Shouldn't I know his name? If you don't trust him, then . . ."

"Mr. Guy Saurus. Right now, Saurus is off my radar. I have to sleep."

Grandpa stepped up the stairs with a sharp clip of dress shoes and determination. Xander thought for a moment about all the reasons Grandpa might not trust someone, a bad reporter, maybe, someone he had fired once, or maybe . . . He had to get Grandpa to tell him more. The old man had silent habits, silent and closed. Xander saw him staring at walls, sometimes. What was he seeing? Mama playing the piano in the music room? Grandma in the kitchen? Did he see Dad?

He followed Grandpa upstairs and said goodnight before walking into the room that once belonged to his mother. He folded back his sheets and touched the pillowcases where crocheted lace shells surrounded the edges. Grandma Elizabeth always added this crochet pattern to linen. He ran his finger over the cool cotton fabric.

Shell-edged linen had traveled with them to Pakistan, too. In the hospital cupboards, pink, blue and yellow shells probably smoldered in neat stacks as the hospital burned to the ground. Burned, collapsed and killed many bedridden patients. Yet, as he had learned from the chatty helicopter pilot, the fire miraculously didn't touch the bodies of his mother and father where they lay dead on the floor of the separate, tiled, operating room.

He sat hard, his fists grabbing at the pillowcase until he heard stitches pop.

* *

Five weeks after the attack, Xander again sat fully clothed on the side of his bed trying to make himself do something. He noticed the radio on the night stand. He'd been in Pakistan since early grade school days. Now he was seventeen years old and knew nothing about being an American. He hadn't even tried to listen to American radio since he came here to Portland. Maybe he should see what kind of music kids listened to.

He punched the *On* button. The middle of *Tannhauser*. He recognized the chords and partial tune. It reminded him of the radio station his Dad liked in Pakistan. A German opera. Not American, and probably not a high school favorite. Rolling the dial from right to left, he stopped at the sound of a soft voice. A woman's voice. Mom's voice. Almost.

"You can know God's love," she said, "and know the love of your fellow members by becoming an elder in the *Church of the Master*. This is your opportunity to serve God. He needs you to pass his love to those not as fortunate as you, those who have not yet received the Word."

A man's voice broke in. "Call 1-800- 555- 5282. Remember God loves you. That number for your service opportunity for God, your eldership in the *Church of the Master* is 1-800-555-5282. And now," the man said in a hushed voice, "The Reverend Pastor Lori Gotamere will bring us the message from scripture."

Xander waited for her voice. Was it really like Mom's voice?

"And God said unto his chosen people *'Thou shalt not bow down to their Gods.'* My friends, this is God's command to Moses. And it is God's command to us."

Xander leaned closer to the speaker. Very soft, very soft, he thought, but under the softness, a tone of brittle certainty.

"And God speaks unto Moses 'Thou shalt utterly overthrow them and break down their images'. God wants our obedience."

The voice of Pastor Gotamere continued. "It is an abomination to God that we turn a deaf ear and a blind eye to the existence of temples among us – temples that worship Mammon . . ."

Xander sat up. He feared what might follow.

". . . Temples that worship Buddha, temples for those who bow to the vicious commands of Allah. God promises 'I will send hornets before thee, which will drive out the Hivite, the Canaanite, and the Hittite from before thee.'"

Xander slammed the *Off* button and stared at the radio. Pastor Lori Gotamere used Mother's caring voice.

Xander folded himself onto his bed and covered his ears, trying to hear nothing. But what he heard was the whisper of the black medic in the helicopter. "Wolves. Nothin' but a vicious pack of Wolves."

He lay there remembering that ride, playing in his mind the shake of the man's head when he asked about Mom and Dad, and then that whispered curse at the attackers from Afghanistan.

But Pastor Gotamere called for a wolf attack right here in the United States.

She's nothing like Mom.

"Xander?" Grandpa called from downstairs. "Want to go for a walk?"

Grandpa's voice jarred him out of his memory.

No, he didn't want to go for a walk, but he knew what would follow. If he didn't answer, Grandpa would climb the stairs, sit on the side of the bed and not have any idea what to say. Xander forced himself to get up. He pushed himself to open the door and willed his voice to sound strong, or at least normal.

"Coming, Grandpa. Coming."

"Great!"

They were both forcing it.

*   *

Six weeks after the attack on his school, Xander stood in the bathroom of his grandfather's Portland house – a bathroom of hexagonal tiled flooring, a tub surrounded by pebbly glass to create a shower, a porcelain sink, a toilet and the damned mirrors – a very American room. He listened to the rain of a warm August afternoon. Water dripped off the roof, drumbeats on the outside sill. He missed the sun of Pakistan.

He turned away from his looming shadow where it hovered along the glass shower walls. He pulled open the mirrored door above the sink so he wouldn't have to look at himself or at the bullet wound on his upper arm – the arm that had been flung from behind the wheel barrow when Mr. Din knocked him out.

He leaned on the porcelain sink. Mr. Din died in the dusty chicken yard.

Xander turned on water and reached for soap, meaning just to keep doing the next dumb thing until pain and loneliness became easier to bear. Then he wet the soap bar. Too late he recognized his mother's scent – lilacs in glycerin. The smell made him drag in a sob. He had known details of the attack for weeks, but still he couldn't take them in.

One image stayed with him night and day – a little girl in a blue and white checked dress floating through the air as her teacher crumpled to the ground with a bullet in her back. In his dreams, the child floated still.

Xander stood in the bathroom and tried to make sense of it all. Sophia, Mohammed, Mr. Din . . . so many children. Sophia. And the teachers. All gone. The patients in the hospital. Nurses, doctors. Mom and Dad and Ali, their anesthetist who was Sophia's father, and Edmund's parents – all dead.

Xander closed his eyes and leaned against the frame of the medicine cabinet. His wounded right hand swung the mirrored door near to his right ear and away again as if his arm were the only part of his body capable of rocking in grief.

Grandpa was a good guy, but he wasn't making it, either. Almost everyone Grandpa loved had died. And he'd been left with a big responsibility – this mess of a grandson.

Aunt Justine would be okay. She was a tough little bird. Like Shazada . . .

Xander stared into the medicine cabinet. A bottle faced him. "Elizabeth Evans, take as indicated for heart pain."

Heart pain.

Xander emptied the bottle into his palm.

CHAPTER SIX

"Xander?" Gilbert called. "Peanut butter and strawberry jam for lunch," As soon as he said it, Gilbert's throat dried. Doc Adam said they had to eat, hungry or not, but both of them avoided meals. The kid had been reading a book or been in bed most of the time since Rebecca and Daniel's memorial service.

Gilbert started gimping his way up the steps to figure out where Xander had holed up this time. As he rounded the corner at the first stair landing, a tremendous crash of glass came from the second floor.

The shower wall. He knew it by the ringing sound. Xander must have slipped and fallen. The crash echoed stomach-deep and endless. Gilbert rushed up the rest of the stairs, yelling. "Xander. Xander."

He tried the doorknob and beat on the wooden door. Locked. And Xander wouldn't, or couldn't open it.

Cold raced through him as he stumbled down stairs and out back of the house to the woodpile by the garage. He grabbed a hatchet. Upstairs again, he splintered the bathroom door, reached in and flipped the lock. He fell into the bathroom and gathered his bleeding grandson from the floor, brushing glass from his hair and ears and ....

He saw the pill bottle on the floor. *Nitroglycerine.*

"Xan. Wake up, Xan." Xander didn't respond. Gilbert lifted him out of the glass, hoisting him in his arms like a long baby.

Lots of pills on the floor, he thought as he carried Xander into the bedroom. Lots of pills, but not enough.

He lay Xander on the bed and jerked the phone from the nightstand to call nine-one-one.

"Yes," he heard himself saying, and knew he must have seemed calm. "Yes, that's the correct address. I think he took my wife's nitroglycerine. And he's bleeding . . . bleeding from all these places..."

The woman said she had dispatched an ambulance and told him to be ready to let them into the house. Ignoring the pain in his knee, he ran downstairs, unlocked the door and then left it wide open. Grimacing, he raced upstairs again and grabbed a towel from the bathroom rack.

In the bedroom, as he daubed blood off of Xander's face, he realized he'd seen no shards, no stabbing, jagged pieces, only these small pellets. All the blood he'd found so far, came from surface wounds. He hoped he saw the outside damage correctly.

But what toxic damage ran through his system?

"Xander? Xander, please wake up."

Xander didn't even moan. Gilbert grabbed up the phone again and called Justine. She promised to be right over. He bent to push at his gimpy knee, but instead, collapsed onto the bed next to Xander. He picked glass from the boy's t-shirt, the fold of his elbow, his eyelid.

His eyelid, for Cripe's Sake.

Toweling away blood and picking glass became important. He didn't want any more cuts. Nothing left to harm his boy.

Vaguely, he realized his own bum leg had worked for him without pain. His leg muscles jumped, but they worked. The wait for the ambulance seemed to stretch. His grandson shivered. Gilbert pulled the bedspread over him, cradled him, tried to warm him without scraping glass pebbles into him. Xander lay on his side in Gilbert's arms.

Long minutes later, the wailing ambulance blared into the driveway. He heard Justine at the door, and then her footsteps.

"This way," she said. He heard her sturdy shoes thump up the stairs.

Justine pushed herself out of the way against the wallpaper. Two men and a young woman followed her into the room. The young woman's nametag said *Angela*.

Gilbert rose from the bed. "Please," was all he could get out. One of the men opened the stretcher they had brought. The other, a young black man with the thick eyebrows checked Xander's back for glass, then rolled him gently from his side onto his back and began checking his vital signs with stuff he pulled from a bag. Gilbert recognized the blood pressure armband and its pump.

After a moment, the man said, "Blood pressure's high."

Angela, looked at Gilbert. "Nitroglycerine, you said?"

"I think so. On the bathroom floor."

She stepped into the hallway. He heard the crunch of pebbles he'd tracked through the hall.

"Glass. Don't . . ." he said.

"I'll be careful," she called. A few moments later she returned, carrying the bottle. She'd been on the cell phone with someone and clicked the call off.

"Jim," she said, to the black man, "the emergency room doc says do the IV fluids."

The man, Jim, said, "We can start it right away."

The other medic, whose name tag said 'Ron', whispered, "Geez. Glass everywhere."

"Tempered glass," Gilbert said. "How hard do you have to hit it for this . . .?"

Angela held up the pill bottle. "Was this full?"

Gilbert shook his head. "I don't know."

By the time he glanced back at Xander, the two men had him strapped on the low gurney, its wheels folded up to make it easy to carry downstairs. They lifted the frame.

As the men carried Xander toward the stairs, Angela put out an arm to keep Justine from grabbing one corner of the gurney. "They're trained to do it together," She said. "You help, it goes kitty-wampus."

Justine looked helpless, and suddenly old. Gilbert put an arm around her shoulders.

"What will the IV do?" Justine asked.

"Encourage his blood pressure to come down." Angela rattled the pill bottle. "Nitroglycerine sends his blood pressure right up there, but we'll get it under control as we drive."

"Whe . . .whe . . .Where?" Gilbert managed to stammer out as he pulled car keys from his pocket.

Angela shook her head. "You're coming with us. Don't want either of you driving right now. The dispatcher is sending us to Emanuel Hospital." She held up the bottle, pointing to where the doctor's name was printed. "Your Doc Adam Whitney is on his way there, too," she said. "So, climb into the ambulance as soon as Jim and Ron have the gurney locked down. But once inside, stay out of the way."

By the time they were downstairs and outside, Justine breathed like an old lady who'd been running, but she waved off Gilbert's help and climbed into the ambulance. Gilbert followed, but Angela had to pull his arm to get him up. His basketball knee had stopped cooperating.

Jim and Angela, set up the IV and attached it to a needle in Xander's arm. As Ron drove them north and west toward Emanuel Hospital, Gilbert stared at his pale grandson and found himself praying – something he didn't manage often, even in Silent Meeting. He wasn't really talking to God, he knew. He was talking to Elizabeth.

God will listen to wise, gentle Elizabeth.

For the first time, Gilbert realized that Xander looked like Rebecca with Daniel's dark hair. The thought comforted him. He went back to talking to Elizabeth – his ombudswoman in the heavens. *Did you see that? He's a beautiful kid.*

I wish . . .

* *

"But we need a parent to fill this out," the receptionist said.

"I am the parent. His parents died."

"Do you have papers proving your guardianship?"

Gilbert leaned over her desk, knuckles on her stack of papers. "I do not carry around my parent card. Do you carry yours?"

He saw a security guard moving toward them. Justine pushed at Gilbert's shoulder and stepped up to the desk in his place. "I'm sorry that my brother is yelling," she said softly. "He's been through a lot since his daughter died only a few weeks ago."

The guard hesitated. Gilbert decided to sit down and let Justine deal with hospital inanities.

"Doctor Adam Whitney will vouch for Mr. Evans' guardianship of Alexander Evans Lloyd," Justine said.

The receptionist glanced at him, took their doctor's name and helped Justine fill out the blasted forms.

Afterward, Gib and Justine fidgeted with every sound they heard from behind any closed door. Finally, Doc Adam came out.

"Alexander did take nitroglycerine, but he's conscious now, and his blood pressure is almost back to normal."

Justine sank into a chair. Gilbert stared down at her, realizing that the glitter in her spiky hair was glass. He reached over and pulled it out. Doc Adam went on talking and talking. Gilbert heard something about the need to observe Xander for a few days.

Then, Doc recommended the psychiatric unit for evaluation. The man never used the words 'attempted suicide', but Gilbert knew.

He said, "Yes." "Yes." And "Yes", all the time thinking I've got to get people in to rebuild that shower before he comes home.

Even when they finally hailed a cab and went home, Justine never once said, "You should have tossed the stuff."

*   *

Five days later, political cartoonist, Mike Halverson, pushed open the glass and oak door and barged into Gilbert's twelfth floor office at *The Journal of the Americas.* The big man dropped a stack of drawings on the wide oak desk. Gilbert stood and started to reach for them, thinking they must be Mike's ideas for the next editorial page, but Mike put his hand on top of Gilbert's, stopping him.

"Gib," Mike said, "You can't treat that kid like he's got an On-Off button for sadness."

Gilbert felt the hairs on his neck rise. "What are you talking about?"

"I've been in here when you're talking to him on the phone. 'Stop thinking about it,' you say. 'Wipe that from your mind,' you say." Mike took a breath. "And I'm here to tell you memories and sadness don't work that way. You've tried it all your life. You should know it doesn't work."

"Stay out of our business, Mike," Gilbert said, as coldly as he could.

"I'm not through, my friend." Mike leaned over the desk. "Better sit down for the rest of it."

Gilbert glared and did not sit. To anyone glancing through the glass door, Gilbert knew they would seem to be publisher and political cartoonist, squared off across a heavy desk, arguing news policy. The truth was they were lifelong friends, but Mike had crossed a line. Friends were friends. Xander's business was family.

"Admit it, Gilbert," Mike said. "You're scared spitless. Think about what he feels. Think. Imagine. Feel."

Gilbert glanced away, refusing Mike's craziness. His office and conference room spread across one quarter of *The Journal of the Americas'* twelfth floor. Beyond Mike's hulking figure, his windows gave a view of the sweeping curve of the Willamette River. Gilbert tried not to let his glance go out there. Directly across the river was the heli-pad for Emanuel Hospital. He gripped the edge of his oak desk to steady himself.

"I see you avoiding the view," Mike said. "Right now you're trying to forget last Sunday night, the hospital, the whole thing. Is it working?"

"He's so moody," Gilbert said. "It's like he's dragging sorrow after him – a sack of rocks being pulled through the halls of the hospital's psychiatric ward."

"I know Doc Adam said he would come home soon."

"I'll have to watch him all the time."

"And you're terrified," Mike said. "I would be, too." Mike reached into his pile of drawings and held out a sketch of a teenager surrounded by jagged fear lines – a cartoonist's shorthand symbol. The kid stood on a Persian rug. The rug humped and bumped all over the sweep of crayon that meant floor. Clearly, big stuff hid underneath that carpet. But the man at the edge of the carpet had turned his back on the kid.

The drawing needed no caption. Gilbert stared angrily over his half glasses. Mike fiddled with his pencil, making doodles on desk stationery.

Famous cartoonist, Gilbert let the thought distract him. *Every squiggle worth hundreds of dollars.* Mike's silence made Gilbert even angrier than his stupid talk.

"So, you're saying I'm no good for him?"

"Idiot. I'm saying lift the rug and look at the uglies with him."

"But if he continues to focus on that, he'll succeed in killing himself."

Mike's voice softened. "He needs you to hear his grief."

"No! It's grief that weighs him down."

Mike's pencil lead snapped. "Hell, Gib, you don't even listen to your own grief. Both of you need help."

Gilbert walked away from his desk. "So, I find him a psychiatrist?"

"The hospital is doing that. But he needs you, present and listening. Not explaining how to move on. Not hiding the hell of their deaths behind polite conversation and busywork."

Gilbert strode toward his office window staring at a helicopter taking off from that wind-blown landing pad. He said, "I can't just let Xander rant about what he should have done. First off, he couldn't have gotten near his mother and dad. He couldn't save Mohammed, or the gardener, or those poor girls."

"Just like you and Brendan O'Connor."

As if struck, Gilbert reeled forward. He caught hold of the window jamb and leaned his head against cold, thick glass. When, after pained moments, he opened his eyes, he was staring across the river at the spot where freight trains come down Sullivan's Gulch, where he'd first met Brendan O'Connor, and, later, later, a day more than fifty years ago, a time when fear turned humans into slobbering monsters.

CHAPTER SEVEN

The whole time Xander stayed in the hospital, he felt guilty about how worn his grandfather looked. Grandpa had lost Mom, too. And Dad. He'd loved Dad, Xander knew that from all their visits over the years. Grandpa had lost everyone, but he didn't try to take pills to die.

Xander often watched Grandpa Gilbert's face as he stared off into space, tears hovering in his old eyes. Sometimes Grandpa sat heavy into some hospital chair. The sigh that came out of him wasn't about his bum knee, but if he realized Xander watched him, he rubbed that knee.

If Grandpa thought he was by himself in the waiting room, he leaned his elbows on his knees and put his face in both hands as if holding up his head was too much work.

Then, moments later, he would get up and find something to do, some mindless chore like fixing the waiting room shade cords so the shades worked correctly.

One day, Aunt Justine came to see him without Grandpa. "Xander," she said. "My brother is a guy from a generation when guys do not let on that they are hurting."

"I didn't think about taking those pills. I just didn't want to feel…"

"I know. Feeling is tough."

"I didn't want to leave Grandpa. I just … "

"You ever get to feeling like it's all too much, you call me. We can talk. Gilbert doesn't know how to talk, he's been closed in on himself for a lot of years. Only your mama and your grandma could get beyond his wall."

"You mean he didn't get this way just because Grandma died?"

"Oh no. It's old stuff. Way back stuff."

Xander listened and pretended to believe Aunt Justine, yet he knew she only said that about old stuff to make him feel less guilty about Grandpa's worries. He shouldn't have taken those damned pills.

One day, as Xander dragged himself from his room in the psych ward to the waiting room, he overheard Aunt Justine talking to Grandpa.

"You were fourteen years old, Gilbert. Fourteen! And you were not God then. Not any more than you are God now, no matter how many TV stations you buy."

That was when Xander realized something from long ago really did have hold of Grandpa. *Of course. There's lots more important than me to drag Grandpa down,* he thought, and the idea hurt.

When Xander told his therapist about this new hurt, he ended the confession by saying, "Pretty nuts, huh?"

"Alexander," Dr. Webster said, "You are going to get well."

"How do you figure?" Xander asked.

"You care if your grandpa loves you. Two weeks ago, you were afraid to love."

*   *

September fourth, three weeks out of the hospital ward for guys and girls who try to kill themselves, Xander was down to once a week with the psychiatrist, Dr. Webster, who wasn't a bad sort of guy. And he and Grandpa had a silent accommodation: *I don't talk about it. You don't talk about it. We can make it through the day.*

They weren't talking in anything but grunts and gestures as they drove to the first day of American high school. As Xander leaned forward to crank up the heater in the Subaru, Grandpa raised an eyebrow. The September air was wet on the best of days, and the best of days never got over seventy degrees.

Starting American high school as a junior seemed like climbing a rock wall barefoot. He'd lived in Pakistan since he was seven years old. Nine years and several languages later he knew nothing about being an American.

Praise be to God-Allah that the sun shone on this first morning, if weakly. The front of the school looked like a huge sandstone castle – *Friends' Welcome School* could have fit inside its walls six times over.

Xander climbed out of the Subaru, but ducked his head back inside for a moment. "Nice car, Grandpa, but bio-diesel is the new wave. You don't have to wait for Shell and Exxon to find oil in somebody else's country."

Grandfather smiled at him. "Want to write a news story on bio-diesel?"

"You're kidding."

"Might as well start with something you're interested in. I hope you learned how to do research in your mission school."

"Sure did." Xander smiled. "Manzur and I are building an engine to run on goat dung. And Mohammed is creating a fuel . . . he's . . . Oh damn."

"Well," Grandpa said, "Mohammed needs you to write about it, Xander. He needs you to do that for him."

Xander straightened. "Yeah. Sure." But he thought of Mohammed's laughter when he dodged Xander's stick that morning. *The Pakistani Kid.* He could never do justice to Mohammed's cool ideas.

Mr. Din's words came into his memory. "*Mohammed ees a fool Quaker.*" Mohammed was no fool and no Quaker. What did the old man mean? Why was Mohammed praying in that chicken yard anyway?

Xander yanked his backpack onto his shoulders, closed the car door and slapped it with a goodbye to his grandpa. He heard the car move off as he strode down the sidewalk.

Toward him shuffled several guys his age – a bunch of kids with dragging drawers – all colors of guys, but all wearing blue or black pants and t-shirts with various designs and sayings, almost a uniform. One tee-shirt caught Xander's eye. It had a drawing of an old torpedo. On the cylinder of the torpedo were printed the words "Louder than Terrorists".

Xander froze.

The boys stared at him as he stared at them. He made himself stop looking at the torpedo and glanced down at his pressed shirt and gray slacks. He bet these guys could tell he had gone clothes shopping with his Great Aunt Justine. Good first impression, foreigner.

At *Friends' School* in Pakistan, nobody wore tee-shirts with messages. All the kids wore uniforms – blue kameez top, white or gray shalwar pants for boys. Some boys wore hats in winter, a couple of Sikh kids wore turbans all the time – headgear depended on religion or family habit. If somebody sent a fellow a fancy shirt, it was saved for holy days – anybody's holy days. If a guy dressed up for his friend's holy days too, he had a better chance of wearing out his fancy shirt before he outgrew it.

Girls at *Friends' School* all wore the blue-checked school dress. The older girls, like Sophia, wore the blue and rose head scarf, a long blue skirt and blue checked blouse.

Sophia. Xander caught his breath and fought down the memory of her body on the steps.

He stepped aside to let the group of guys hurry past him, but one of them, the guy whose tee shirt said "Louder than Terrorists" stopped and turned back.

"Hey, you're that guy from Pakistan I read about, aren't you?" The fellow looked at Xander's shirt and then down at his black shoes. Xander felt more alien than ever.

"You read about me?" he asked.

"Sure. School news. Talon writes stuff up for the first day – welcome new students and that shit."

"I wasn't aware anybody…"

Another boy, laughed. "Aware? You always talk like that, or just showing off?"

"I mean no one interviewed me or…"

"Who would interview you?" the first boy asked.

"Think you're big guns?" the other asked.

"No I merely . . ."

"God!" laughed the guy in the torpedo tee shirt. "Merely . . . Bet he always talks like some English prick."

The other guy started walking with his knees together, mincing about as if he were a girl. "Ooh, isn't he sooo cute?"

They back-slapped each other as they all pranced like girls up the stairs and into the double front doors of the school.

Xander stood there, stupid, and fully aware for the first time that he didn't even speak like an American. This place was a big mistake. He didn't want to go in. He figured he still had ten minutes until he was due in the office to work out his schedule with the vice-principal – some guy named Mr. Talon.

Grandpa told him the other kids had received their schedules in the mail two weeks before. Only new students would be in the office.

He stood on the walkway and stared at the words carved into the sandstone over the oak doors. *"Linus Pauling Junior High and High School"*. Pauling – a big scientist, Xander had heard. Discovered what? He'd have to Google him – when his new computer arrived.

In this school, kids from sixth through twelfth grade were in the same building. Grandpa said the high school used the upper two floors. The place seemed to be a huge version of school at home in Pakistan – except for the name. Friends believed in science, but they rarely named things after scientists, and never after politicians.

As he stared upwards, Xander heard someone push hard on the panic bar inside the doors. He glanced over in time to see the left door swing open.

A young girl in long pants and a blue and white checked blouse ran down the steps toward him, shrieking.

An older boy in baggy shorts and dark t-shirt chased her, yelling, "Tekla, give me back my notebook."

Xander understood nothing more than the image of blue and white check. He stepped between the boy and his prey. Crouched, he gave a shoulder slam to the kid who chased her.

"Hey!" the kid yelled as he flew backwards. He landed on his rear end, a look of complete surprise and then pain on his face.

Behind Xander, the girl yelled, "Don't hit my brother!"

He felt a whack on his back as he turned. The girl smacked him once more with a black notebook. Small folds of paper flew out of it, floating through the air like wheat chaff in a breeze. Xander's chest tightened. He couldn't breathe. He backed up from her angry face and her checked blouse, nearly tripping over the boy who crawled around gathering together his folded notes.

"Gonna get you for this, Tekla," the kid growled. Then he glanced up at Xander who was peddling fast to keep from falling.

"Gonna get you, too," the boy said to him.

Xander stumbled backwards until he landed under the rhododendrons near the front door. He turned over and threw up his breakfast at the base of the bushes. After long moments, when he thought he was empty, he felt a hand on his back.

"You okay?" the girl asked.

He turned his head, and there she was next to him. Her hand came around to his forehead, just as Mom's would have done. But she pulled it back as if surprised at herself.

He tossed more breakfast into the dirt.

"You're pretty sick," she said. "You should go to the school nurse."

Behind them, her brother's voice said, "Tekla, help me catch all these notes. I got to write a paper with them."

Xander felt her standing near, but she didn't touch his head again.

"Those aren't homework notes," she said to her brother. "Those are love notes to Jenny Cartwright and Susan Tolevan. Get 'em yourself."

Xander snorted, pushed away from his used breakfast and sat on his haunches. He wiped his mouth and looked up at the girl. Her dark hair curled near her tan face. She looked like one of the younger Kurdish girls at *Friends School*. He guessed she was a junior high student, but he couldn't be certain. He didn't know the clues for age here, especially for girls.

She stared at him. "You better?"

He nodded. "Sorry I busted your brother. I thought he was trying to . . . to hurt you."

"Really?"

He nodded.

"Well, you were right," she said, "but Denny can't hurt me much because I fight back."

Denny stood up, surveying the ground for any missed notes. He turned on Xander. "What the fuck were you doing?"

"He was saving me from you," the girl said.

"Sorry, man," Xander said. "I thought you were going to. . ." he didn't want to say *kill her*.

"Yeah?" Denny said. "Well, mind your own business."

The school bell rang three times. The boy stomped into the building carrying his notebook in one hand and his love notes, if that's what they were, in the other.

Xander looked at the girl.

She gazed at him. "How come you do something brave, and then you throw up?"

He stared at her checked blouse with its red ribbons at the neck and sleeve edges, and her dark blue slacks. He wished he'd noticed how different it all was from the girls' school uniform. "I guess you're right," he said. "I feel kind of sick."

"Thought so," she said. "Now, you're a mess."

He looked at the vomit on the front of his shirt. "I'll go home and get cleaned up."

"Tomorrow can be your first day of school."

He smiled at her. "Yeah? By then all your brother's friends will know what a wuss I am."

She laughed. "But all my friends will run to you when their brothers chase them." She reached a hand out, as if to pull him up.

He started to reach, looked at the garden dirt on his hand and pulled it back. "Too mucky," he said. "I'm Xander Lloyd, in case you need to tell someone why you're late."

She glanced at the door. "That was only the warning bell," she said. "I'll be on time because the seventh grade homeroom is on the first floor near the office".

A dark-haired young teacher pushed partway out the front door. "Tekla, aren't you coming to class?"

"Sure, Mrs. Price." She smiled at the teacher and left Xander without glancing back.

As Tekla bounded up the stairs, Xander stood, brushed grass and dirt from his pant knees, then straightened. After Tekla passed her, the teacher still stared at him. She frowned.

"You need help?" she asked.

"No, thank you, Ma'am." He thought, *Too formal, foreigner.*

"Best get to class then." She held the door for him.

"I, um…Okay," he said.

Somebody inside distracted her, and she let the door close.

Xander reached into his pocket. With relief, he felt his copy of the house key still there.

Thank God Grandpa's gone to the newspaper office, he thought. He took off at a jog, smelling vomit in the wind. Jeez, I gotta get ahead of my own stench.

As he tried to run and not to breathe, he planned, I'll wash my shirt in the sink and hang it in the shower – the new shower.

He sure wasn't going to explain any of this morning's events to anybody – certainly not to his grandfather or the shrink he had to visit this afternoon.

How could he have gone so crazy about a little chasing game?

When he let himself into the house, his grandfather was standing there, keys in hand, about to go out. He said, "The school called. What happened between you and that girl?"

Xander stood there, dumb. His grandfather glanced at his shirt. "What's been going on?"

CHAPTER EIGHT

Gilbert Evans felt every one of his sixty-seven years. He sat on an overstuffed chair in the waiting room, rubbing his knee. There was no real pain from his old basketball injury. He used this habitual gesture to ignore his present worry.

He felt damned lucky to get this appointment. After finding Xander a clean shirt, he'd been afraid to leave him at the house, or take him back to the school, which is what Xander insisted he should do. Instead, he brought him to Dr. Webster's.

On the other side of the paneled oak door to the psychiatrist's office sat his only grandson. Gilbert imagined Xander, in the next room, slouched, saying nothing, and no doubt he refused even to look at the athletic and graying doctor.

Yesterday, he too had sat in that office – part of what the hospital called 'family work'. Looking back on the hour he'd spent with Dr. Webster, Gilbert had to shake his head. He hadn't been much more receptive to the man's probing questions than Xander would be. In fact, he'd been downright testy with the good doctor. But in the long run, Gilbert recognized that Dr. Webster echoed the sentiments of Mike Halverson.

"He needs you to listen to his grief," Mike had said.

Gilbert always struggled to avoid what Mike and Dr. Webster wanted him to face. But it hadn't worked. Thoughts of Rebecca and Daniel intruded. He was pretty sure they intruded all the time for Xander as well.

At the thought of his beloved daughter, Gilbert stiffened his back, hauled his briefcase into his lap and started to pull out some work. The office door opened. Xander stood there, hesitating. Gilbert dropped the papers back into his briefcase.

"Grandpa?" Xander's Adam's apple worked up and down.

Gilbert blinked to clear his eyes.

"Grandpa?" Xander said again, but then, he dragged in a ragged breath and turned his face toward the doorjamb.

Gilbert dropped the briefcase as he stood. He strode toward the door. Xander nearly fell into his arms, his voice strangled by sobs.

"Why?" Xander cried.

Gilbert started to give a logical answer, something about war and tribal factions. Then he thought what his wife would have said. "I miss them too, son."

"It's not fair!" his grandson cried.

"No. It's damned unfair."

Over Xander's head, Gilbert was aware of the doctor, but he didn't care who was there. He stroked Xander's dark hair, so much like Daniel's. He felt the strength of his shoulders, and the boy-thinness of his wiry arms.

Xander pulled into his grandfather's chest, whispering, "So many girls and Mama. Bullets. The wheat flattened and turned red"

"God" Gilbert whispered.

"Like Mama on the floor. Daddy – they said Daddy tried to use her hair to pull her and crawl into a closet."

"No!" Gilbert's mind shut down, but he held to Xander as if holding would take it all back.

"And then they shot him again."

Xander's images poured out. His tears penetrated his grandfather's stiff shirtfront and his denial. All of the attack ripped into his imagination. Someone had described their murders to Xander. Gilbert would find that idiot and clobber him.

But now, as Mike had said, Xander needed Gilbert. He held his grandson close and whispered, "Yes, Xander. It was very bad."

"And where are the boys? Where?"

Gilbert shook his head. "Friends are still searching for them . . . No one . . ."

And suddenly, they were both crying.

Dr. Webster nudged them into the room, closed the door and left them alone. And for minutes, only their reluctant sobs filled the room. After a time, Xander pulled back and looked up at his grandfather.

"I shouldn't be alive," he said.

Gilbert's heart jerked in his chest. He thought, "But you can't", or "killing yourself won't bring them back."

Instead, he searched his own mind and heart, and said at last, "Don't leave me, Xander."

Xander blinked. "Here is too hard."

"I understand," Gilbert whispered. "I also wonder 'what's the point?' But then I think about Grandma Elizabeth, and about your mama and daddy. What would they want us to do?"

Xander jerked away. He turned his back on Gilbert and began to pace the room. His fist flung out, hitting Webster's wall, then his desk, a sofa back. In the moment before Xander swung at the window, Gilbert had him in his arms again. Into his mind came the firm voice of his wife, Elizabeth, and the softer voice of his daughter. "Cry, *Cry with me . . .* with me." Thoughts of them colored his next move.

He pulled his grandson away from the glass. They fell together against the wall. "It hurts," Gilbert sighed. "It is hell on earth that they are dead and we are left here."

"Grandpa," Xander's muffled voice warmed his heart. "Don't send me back to the hospital. I won't kill myself."

Over Xander's shoulder, Gilbert saw Doc Webster's silhouette in the doorway, probably brought in by Xander's whacking. He waved the doctor away.

"I want you home," he said to Xander. "But I'm afraid of that moment you might decide to try again."

Xander stood up and looked his grandfather in the eye. "I can't sleep. I see Mohammed praying. Mr. Din running toward those men. I see the girls screaming. I see it all every night, and every night I try to run out to help, but Mr. Din chases me with that damned hatchet."

Gilbert nodded. "And I bet the old man gets faster and faster each time."

"How'd you know?"

"My own dreams," Gilbert said. "My plane never gets off the ground. I know I'd be in time to take you all, and I mean all of you, to safety, but my plane won't wind up."

Through his tears, Xander snorted. "Won't wind up?"

Gilbert shrugged. "Did you ever notice that in our dreams, we are either the most powerful person, or the most helpless? In my dreams, I get this balsa-wood, rubber-band, wind-up plane, and on the other side of the world, you all need me."

Xander cracked a sad smile at him, nodded slowly, then lowered his head to lean on Gilbert again. They stood together a long time, arms around each other, tears messing up any pretense at being strong.

CHAPTER NINE

They drove home in worn-out silence, opened the front door and felt the cold of fall in the house. Gilbert started a fire in the woodstove. The chill fell away, but Gilbert knew his mind was crawling back into its hiding place. He couldn't force himself to talk anymore.

Xander pulled out dishes and set the table as if doing a well-learned and very slow dance. Forks left. Knives right. Glass up top. Napkin folded in a triangle.

Gilbert watched his grandson's robotic motions. He believed there was something he needed to say, something to make the next moment easier. He wished Justine would show up, spontaneous and forthright. But he vowed to get through this on his own.

Besides Justine probably had chained herself to the Federal Courthouse as a protest. Blustery politicians had taken up sabre rattling because of the attacks on mission schools. People, important people were claiming that Iran stood behind all the violence.

Gilbert worried. Expanding war into Iran would ruin Xander's recovery. The kid already had nightmares about the friends he'd lost in Pakistan. The boy would be very aware of innocents on the ground in both countries.

As he watched Xander's slow work, Gilbert thought,

Foot slog. Foot slog.

Marching up and down again.

There ain't no end to the war.

Gilbert had learned the soldier's chant from Mike Halverson's dad, the gray and solid old World War II sergeant. The chant was a soldier's despair – any man's despair. His own slog of grief after Elizabeth's death. Of Rebecca and Daniel's death in Pakistan.

Move the next mud-caked boot forward.

Gilbert had known this despair when he was even younger than Xander. And he'd talked about grief enough for one day.

He hauled out a fry pan and began making dinner.

*   *

Xander watched Grandpa Gilbert go through the motions of frying chicken wings, cooking, as if food mattered. Xander wished Aunt Justine would breeze through the door. Their silence was heavy and dark. He searched in the refrigerator, found what should have been the drawer for salad greens and realized it contained sodden potato chips.

Potato chips in the fridge? That must have been one of Grandpa's really bum days.

He glanced around the room and remembered from before his hospital stay. The house always was neat, but in the kitchen, Grandma's kitchen, Grandpa seemed out of place. He needed help.

Xander had helped Mr. Din cook for the kids at Friends School. The gardener grew the vegetables and fruit. Mr. Din had never been willing to let go of the produce until he knew they were on the table, cooked perfectly with all their vitamins still intact.

Xander touched the side of his head. The hatchet bruise had faded weeks ago.

In the freezer compartment, he found an ancient box of frozen peas. He plopped them in a sauce pan with a little water, turned the heat on under the pan and then set out in search of edible cheese. Cheese might disguise that the peas looked older than Grandpa.

He found a brick of fontina, cut off the green outer layer and shaved the cheese with the potato peeler because the cheese grater was rusty. Peas gooped with cheese went into a glass dish and into the microwave oven for one minute.

And still, only silence between them. Xander felt wrung out from his morning at the school and the talk at Dr. Webster's. He needed to sleep.

He walked off into the music room next to the kitchen, the room with the piano and the desk where Grandpa's dad used to compose music. In this room, when they came to visit, his mother loved to play the piano and sing with her mom and dad, Grandma Elizabeth and Grandpa Gilbert. He never looked at the piano bench without seeing his mom there.

For a moment, Xander stood, remembering the Christmas three years ago when they were home on leave from Pakistan. He'd been fourteen years old and uncomfortable in the cold and rain of Oregon, uncomfortable walking down a street in his stateside-clothes and stiff shoes. But Mom and Dad had been happy.

Mom had played Christmas songs with Grandma Elizabeth, Grandpa sat in the oak side chair, one elbow on the desk as he watched his daughter and wife make music. Dad sat over there on the window bench, humming along and thumbing through old photo albums.

Xander sat down where his dad had been, in the very same place, trying to absorb the lost heat of his family. He put one hand on the leathery book lying next to him, then glanced at it – a red photo album. Dad had been looking through it that last night. And it still sat near the other albums.

Xander picked up the album and dusted it off. Inside, he found photos of Grandpa as a kid, maybe about fourteen years old, freckles on his nose, thick brown hair, a quizzical look in the rise of his eyebrows, as if he didn't believe something. Within a few pages, Xander found an eighth grade class photo with three rows of students, Gilbert proudly front and center, the girl who became Grandma Elizabeth stood in the back row on the end, dignified and watching, her gaze on the back of Gilbert's head. Off to one side as if forced to participate in the photo, stood a tall man, probably their teacher, but much blurred by motion. It looked as if, when the lights flashed, the man had ducked and raised one hand to ward off a blow.

Maybe the fellow didn't want his photo taken.

The bell on the microwave rang, but Xander decided to let the peas sit for a moment.

Later in the album, Xander found teenaged Gilbert Evans in a soccer uniform with long shorts – a sadness in the downward turn of his mouth. Xander realized that sadness had been a part of his grandfather ever since those days.

Xander had been told that kids in the United States didn't really play soccer until his mom's generation, but this photo proved that information wrong. In later pages, after the prom pictures of Gilbert and Elizabeth, there were college photos from Ohio State basketball games – and articles about that national winning team. The articles puzzled Xander. Why include them? Then he read a photo caption and discovered that Grandpa had played on that team – a guard, number twelve – the big guy with thick hair had no more freckles.

Ohio? Why did Grandpa go to college so far from Oregon?

Maybe a scholarship accounted for the choice of schools. The news stories made it clear that Grandpa had been a great player.

Time and the camera moved on through wedding photos, followed by baby and childhood photos of Xander's mother, Rebecca. Then his father, Daniel, became part of the family, and then, baby Xander himself. The caption on the sleeping baby said, "Alexander Evans Lloyd". There followed a few snaps of himself. The last photo showed him hiking with his mom and dad, Mohammed and Manzur in the hills east of Tiri – the hills farthest from Afghanistan.

He stared at the laughing people in that photo.

Gone. All that laughter, gone.

He turned the last page. Out fell a photo that must have been tucked into the pocket of the back cover. Xander bent down to pick it up and turn it over. The photo had been framed with matte board. Around the matte edges were the holly and berry design Xander recognized as Grandma Elizabeth's pen and ink drawing.

The man in the photo was big, with light colored eyes, no eyebrows and little hair. He smiled, but crookedly. Xander held the photo into the waning light of sunset and saw that the man's face had been scarred, badly scarred. One of the man's hands had only three fingers.

And then, a thought came to him. He turned back to the class photo, the blurred man. He looked at his hand closely – the one that seemed to ward off danger. Yes. The same hand.

He heard his Grandfather's footstep and looked up. Grandpa stood in the doorway to the kitchen and stared at what Xander held in his hand.

"Who is he?"

Grandpa moved over to Xander, took the photo, touching only the outer edges with his fingertips. He gazed at the man for a time before he said, "He was my first coach, and a great teacher. Brendan O'Connor."

* *

Gilbert stared at the photo remembering that first day of eighth grade, the new teacher's scars, his baldness, as if he'd never had any hair, his crooked smile, his three-fingered hand, his care for every student. That day Mr. O'Connor had started the soccer team at a time when no one in the United States played soccer. Gilbert remembered this man's life with pain.

He shifted his gaze to the portrait of his wife. Thank God for Elizabeth, he thought. After that year, I needed her patience and her tough core.

Elizabeth, I need you now. We need you.

He handed the photo back to Xander. "Brendan O'Connor was a great man. I hope you have at least one teacher like him."

CHAPTER TEN

Xander watched his tall, stooped-shouldered grandfather stare at the photo for what seemed way too long. He was about to wave a hand in front of Grandpa's old eyes when Grandpa's gaze shifted to a portrait on the music-room wall – Grandma Elizabeth. He wondered if the coach, Brendan O'Connor, had something to do with all the sadness in Grandpa – sadness that went way back to high school days, if the photos were a way to judge.

Maybe someday he'll tell.

Then Grandpa seemed to shake himself out of a daydream and focus on Xander. He braced himself for his grandfather's daily question.

"After dinner, d'you want to come to Cleary Park with me?" Grandpa asked. "Get some exercise?"

Xander had maxed out on ways to say 'No thanks'. But, no way was he going to go out where he would have to be with other people, especially not tonight.

He spoke more sharply than he meant to. "Actually, I'm not hungry. I'm just going to bed."

"Okay, Xan," Grandpa said, "The peas don't look all that great to me, either. But tomorrow I'm taking you to school, and this time, you stay the course."

"Grandpa, we just spent two hours with a psychiatrist. Are we going to go back to pretending normal?"

"How else are we going to get over it?"

"I'm going to sleep and you're going for a walk. At breakfast tomorrow we won't talk and at dinner tomorrow we'll get poor Aunt Justine to tell us how the protests went today, and we won't have to talk for another twenty-four hours."

Grandpa sat heavily in the oak chair. "Yes, we can talk. But we also have to eat and live and put one foot in front of the other."

"Oh, the excitement!"

"Xander, it will get better. Over time . . ."

Xander snorted. "I don't think I can stand the suspense." Hearing the harsh sarcasm in his voice surprised him, but that didn't stop him from mouthing off. "Until it does get better, I'll be asleep."

Grandpa Gilbert stared over his glasses at Xander. "Eat something before you hibernate."

Xander turned his back on his grandfather and walked upstairs. One thing he'd learned at Dr. Webster's. Grandpa was as lost after Mom and Dad's death as he felt. He'd figure out tomorrow how to get through tomorrow. He needed to search for the boys, Manzur, Edmund and all. They hadn't been found in the rubble. They had to be alive.

He remembered the feel of little Edmund's thin shoulders as he turned him toward the stairs to the tunnels. "Will thee come also?" Edmund had asked him.

Searching, and begging others to search, the boys and teachers needed him to do that.

As the front door closed and his grandfather's footsteps receded down the front stairs, Xander sighed. He felt mean inside. His grandpa didn't deserve mean. But moments ago, he couldn't seem to stop the mean from spilling out.

* *

The next morning, Xander walked up to the front of Linus Pauling High School for the second time.

Fine. Step one.

He met with Vice-Principal Talon, a guy who couldn't button his coat over his belly, but insisted that every kid should take a gym class. Xander accepted whatever he got as his class assignments. Step Two.

He sat in each class and looked like he was taking notes. Step three.

Then came lunch. He found himself a spot at the back of the cafeteria away from all others. He hauled out his sandwich and hunched over it.

"You're Alexander Lloyd, yes?"

The voice interrupted Xander's bite of turkey. He didn't look up. The guy would go away soon.

"My name is Haroon Qubadi," the voice said. "Haroon as in tune. Qubadi as in the Kurdish poet. I'm in your English class."

Xander hunched down closer to his sandwich and behind his lunch sack.

Haroon as in tune, I've never read Qubadi. Wonder how Mr. Bhatti skipped that Kurdish poet.

He saw one leg swing over the long bench, felt the weight of a hand leaning on the long table, heard the smack of a lunch tray on the Formica, and knew he couldn't get rid of this character so easily.

"You ever play soccer?" Haroon asked.

Xander made the mistake of jerking his head up. He loved soccer, in the dust, in the mud, in Pakistan with Mohammed and Manzur, and all the little kids. He would never play soccer again.

"My team could use a good striker," Haroon said, "and you look like a striker to me."

Xander refused to ask 'why?' out loud.

"Eyes down. Attention on the sandwich," Haroon said. "Nearly impossible to distract. All good skills for a striker."

Is the guy nuts?

Xander glanced up again, looking for giveaway signs of craziness. What he saw was too much like Manzur, curling brown hair, dark eyes, thin face, straight nose, and a mouth waiting to smile.

"I don't play soccer," he said.

Haroon's near smile opened up into a grin. "I hear otherwise."

"Heard where?" *Mistake to ask.*

"Rumor," Haroon said, waving an arm at the cafeteria crowd. "In fact, I hear you're so good the Simon Benson High School soccer coach already has his recruiting letter written. Wants your kicking foot to attend his school instead of this one, with or without your mind."

Outrageous, Xander thought. *Like Manzur.* "Yeah? Well, he'll have to wait," Xander said in a tone that he hoped sounded final.

"Dang-bet you he'll wait," Haroon said. "And by the time you bother to answer his letter, The Pauling Rats will have won the state tournament. By then he'll be offering you a BMW and plenty of ice cream to play for Benson High."

Xander chuckled. He couldn't stop himself. "BMW? That the best you can do?"

Haroon nodded. "Yeah. But the steering wheel is heated and the sun roof stores sun for rainy days."

Dangerously close to a laugh, Xander said, "Can't do it." He looked down at his sandwich again.

"We practice on Monday, Wednesday and Friday. So, how about tonight after school?" Haroon asked.

"No." Xander said. He'd already leaned away from Haroon and started to swing his leg off the bench when he noticed a silence in the whole cafeteria.

He looked around and saw several guys a few tables away. He recognized one of them from gym class– Rob Palmquist, a big kid with wide shoulders. Rob and the other two guys watched him and Haroon closely, and then one of them whispered something very loudly.

"Terrorist."

Xander realized the whisperer was the blond and athletic Denny, brother of the seventh-grade girl, Tekla – the brother he'd knocked to the ground that first day. He didn't look the same in a strutting position as he did flat on his ga-wumpus.

In a low voice, Haroon said, "I guess it wouldn't be good for your rep to be seen with me."

Xander turned to Haroon. "I'm the one he thinks is a terrorist."

"Just because you head-butted him on your first day?" Haroon gathered his lunch. "Don't be too flattered by the thought," he said. "Rob Palmquist and Denny Jones have been calling me a terrorist ever since Nine-one-one, back when we were eleven years old."

"You're kidding me. Why?"

"Their folks listen to Fox News and Lawrence Fafner on radio. Somebody's gotta be a terrorist and I'm the nearest Muslim."

"They don't need any evidence?"

"I am Muslim. Good enough evidence for Fafner and therefore good enough for Rob and Denny."

"But..."

"Plus, according to Rob Palmquist, the police have been here questioning the office staff about me and my family." Haroon stood to go. "It may even be true. They did question me and my dad at home."

As Haroon left, Xander sat stunned, staring across the room at the hostility on the face of Rob Palmquist.

"Wait," Xander climbed out of the tight bench space. Haroon turned back, frowning.

"Where?" Xander asked, "And when?"

Haroon glanced at the three boys. He spoke in a low voice. "Six to seven-thirty. Beverly Cleary Park, the north side, downhill from the Cleary fountain, kiddy slides and swings."

"I'll be there."

"Great." Haroon grinned and headed off toward the tray-return station. Just then, the bell rang for afternoon classes.

After Haroon left, Xander glanced back at Tekla's big brother, Denny Jones. The kid stood up and leaned over his cafeteria table.

"Watch out foreigner," Denny said. "Me and Rob and Buck, we're gonna find you alone."

Foreigner? Xander glanced at his buttoned-down shirt and chinos and understood. He'd grown too tan from years in the sun, and his clothes looked way different from these guys.

Xander looked into the eyes of the third kid. "Buck, huh? We've never met. What beef you got with me?"

The guy named Buck pulled on his most fake smile. In seconds, his smile became a grimace. "Don't like your face."

CHAPTER ELEVEN

Late that afternoon, Xander sat in the school library hunting the internet for any hint about what happened to the boys – the children he'd sent with Manzur and the teachers down into the cellar and the tunnels.

The community had carefully chosen to build on the site of an abandoned palace, destroyed during some invasion centuries before. Beneath it were tunnels and tombs where they could hide, so Xander still held on to hope. But after so many weeks, it seemed impossible ever to know what had happened to them; too much in Pakistan had fallen apart since that day.

He discovered one newspaper, *The National Courier,* which had some information about survivors from the attacks, but not about the kids and teachers from Friends School. *The National Courier,* it turned out, had big offices in Chicago and about five times as many news outlets as Grandpa's *Evans International.*

According to an editorial by Louis Lamb, *The National Courier* owner, a civil war threatened to break out in Pakistan. Some accused Musharraf's government of encouraging Taliban within the country. Others accused the People's Party and self-exiled Benazir Bhutto of fomenting trouble just to get back into power.

Lamb wrote, "If Pakistan's government can't control its own borders, the country should expect American air strikes and every bit of terror coming its way."

Xander thought, 'What if my friends survived the siege and then were killed by American air strikes?"

Mr. Lamb called them 'surgical strikes', as if the bombs merely took out Pakistan's infected gall bladder. Xander could hardly think beyond Edmund, Manzur and the little boys under the rubble of a collapsed building. His chest hurt. He stood and pushed back his chair, shutting the computer.

Leaving a big school library, heading toward sunshine, free and safe in America seemed wrong.

He'd nearly walked out the school's front door when he noticed the mural on the front wall. The thing covered the whole entry hall. On the west side – big men worked to guide a big ox pulling against its wooden yoke – the scene hinted at the struggle to create home in the wilderness. Pioneers.

The mural continued on the east side of the entry hall. A whole family of Northwest natives appeared to greet him. Women folded up a tent village while a young girl watched her tribesmen in ceremonial dress ride out on horseback. One man rode in front of the others, his right arm raised as if to say hello to Xander and to the farmers across the hall.

Xander raised his hand in greeting, too. *Where are you now?* he thought to the head tribesman and his fellows.

Both murals seemed to have been on these walls for a long time. Paint had chipped off of the green hills in a couple of places, but the colors still shone in the light from the afternoon sun He saw an artist's signature in one corner: *Edward Burns Quigley.*

Suddenly, a hand descended on his shoulder, heavy, harsh. For a moment, he thought the farmer pushed him out of the way of progress.

"Indian lover, hey?"

Xander wheeled. Rob Palmquist and his two friends grinned at him just before Rob's fist smashed into Xander's face. His cheek bone seemed to explode, but he raised his own fist. Rob pulled back for another try. Xander ducked the second blow. He rammed his head under Rob's swinging arm and brought his fist up into Rob's jaw. As Rob fell, another hand grabbed Xander's jacket.

An elbow to the gut from Xander sent Tekla's brother, Denny, reeling toward the native chief.

"Don't!" Xander feared for the mural. He grabbed Denny by the belt buckle just as someone else whacked into Xander's back. Even while the third attacker jabbed, Xander managed to pull Denny away from the wall mural, drop him to the floor, and then he whipped around.

The third boy, Buck, danced around Xander, fists in the air, jabbing at the wound on Xander's face. Xander saw Rob Palmquist start to rise. A smack to Xander's left ear turned his attention back to Buck.

Behind Buck, Haroon Qubadi ran into the hall. Haroon leaned down next to Rob and put a knee next to his chest. "Don't bother getting up, Rob," Haroon said to his prey. "You might get hurt. That Xander learned fighting methods in Pakistan."

Xander saw a frightened look come over Rob's face. Then Xander had to duck another jab from Buck. He stepped around Buck's dancing figure, putting his back to Rob and Haroon for a moment. He saw Denny Jones still sprawled on the floor, merely watching the proceedings. When their dance brought them back to face Rob, the big guy didn't seem to be putting up any fight either.

"Come on," Buck yelled at Rob and Denny. "This was your fight. Get up and help me out."

Xander used the moment to take Buck by the shirt collar and back him into the frame of the big front door. Buck's fists flailed, but Xander had moved in so close Buck couldn't get a good whack at anything but Xander's shoulders.

He could smell Buck's dead-rat breath. Xander stuffed his right fist hard into Buck's distended stomach. The guy let out a grunt and folded in half. Just before Buck's knees could buckle, Xander jumped back and let him fall.

Behind him, Rob hollered, "Terrorists! Terrorists!"

Denny rolled over and started to get up. Xander stood over Denny, who changed his mind about rising. At that moment, they all heard a door open around the corner in the main hall.

Rob surprised Xander by starting to cry.

The secretary strode around the corner. She took one look at the situation in the entry hall and shouted at Haroon, "You! Get away from Robby."

Haroon stood up. Rob slumped flat on the floor. "Gonna kill me," Rob shouted.

"These three attacked me," Xander explained, but the secretary's face became splotchy as she yelled at Haroon. Haroon backed up.

Xander stepped between Haroon and the lady. "See the cut on my face? Rob attacked me – Rob and his friends here."

"You liar," she said, hands up and ready to strike. "You are both known."

She started toward him, but when the office door opened again, her hands fell to her sides. She stepped in on Xander with a tight-eyed anger. Behind her, a man in a suit, a man that Xander had never before seen, hurried into the hall.

"Mrs. Palmquist," the man said. "I will deal with discipline."

Her face changed to white. She slumped, then straightened and faced the man. "These foreign boys have threatened my Robby."

"Haroon is not foreign," Xander said. "He's a citizen."

The mottled coloring started up her throat again. She took a step toward Xander, but the man touched her shoulder. That stopped her as if he'd switched off a power button.

"It's all right, Edith," the man said, his voice low and soothing as if he were talking to a frightened animal. "My phone is ringing. Go answer my phone calls, please. I'll take care of this situation."

Mrs. Palmquist nodded slowly, then slipped around the corner back toward the office. Xander figured the man must be her boss, the school principal, but he had more power over her than an ordinary boss.

Great way to end the second day of school, Xan, he thought.

The man turned toward Rob. "Mr. Robert Palmquist, don't you think your mother has enough on her mind?"

"But Mr. Klein, these guys attacked me." Rob pitched into a high whine. "You know Homeland Security is after Qubadi."

Mr. Klein said. "You need to be careful what trouble you bring to your mother, after all that's happened."

Xander glanced at Haroon.

"Sit up, Rob," Mr. Klein said.

Rob minded him, a sullen look on his face.

Mr. Klein turned to the rest of them. "Buck," he said, "why did you fellows corner Xander after school?"

Xander glanced at the man, surprised he knew his name – also surprised he had guessed exactly how this scene started.

Buck straightened from his stomach ache enough to point at Haroon. "He ate lunch with this one. You know he's illegal."

The man shook his head. "I know certain people want to believe that's true, but Haroon is as much a citizen as any of you."

From the floor, Rob said, "Mexicans and Muslims, and all them, they kill . . .."

"You are out of line."

"But they get false papers and then sneak into our country," Rob said.

Mr. Klein ignored Rob for the moment. Instead, he said to Haroon. "Next time, don't rescue. Come get me."

"Yes, sir," Haroon said.

Mr. Klein then raised an eyebrow toward Xander. "Welcome, Alexander Lloyd. I'm the school principal, Mr. Klein."

Welcome? Xander thought maybe the guy was into irony, so he merely nodded.

"You need to go into the nurse's room," Mr. Klein said, "Get some ice and a bandage for that cheek. Haroon, please help Alexander. Do not go through the office. That will only upset Rob's poor mother."

"Yes, sir," Haroon said again.

"And now, gentlemen," Mr. Klein said, "Denny, Rob, Buck into my office for a little chat."

"Why just us?" Denny Jones asked, still hunkered on the floor.

"Because I know how you operate."

"I never . . ." Denny started.

"Never stop to imagine getting caught?" Mr. Klein suggested.

The boys slowly rose, grumbling.

After they left with the principal, Haroon showed Xander into the nurse's office. The nurse seemed to have gone home, but Haroon gestured Xander to sit on the cot while he fished in a small freezer and came out with ice which he wrapped in a towel and handed to Xander.

"You seem to know where everything is," Xander said, packing the ice to his bruised face.

"Got to. Those guys usually attack when the nurse is nowhere in the building. She serves five schools."

Xander pondered that information while Haroon got out gauze, tape and scissors to fashion a bandage.

"Why would the police believe whatever Mrs. Palmquist said?"

"Well, it was actually one policeman named Bailey and one fellow from the FBI named Guy Saurus."

"I remember that name," Xander said. "He's the short man who hovered around Mom and Dad's funeral.

"Dark hair going white? Strong upper body, short legs, a look of barely civilized muscle?"

"Yeah. Menacing." Xander said. "Grandpa seemed to have known him before. Doesn't trust him."

Haroon nodded as if not surprised. "Mr. Guy Saurus has a little vendetta going, and Bailey is his stooge. Homeland Security, the FBI and the Justice Department need to fix up their lost reputations. They fouled up on the arrest of Mr. Mayfield last May."

Xander raised a questioning eyebrow.

Haroon explained. "They arrested this local lawyer, Mr. Brandon Mayfield. Said he was a terrorist. Claimed his fingerprint was found at the train bombing in Spain. All wrong. And it appeared they knew they were wrong way before they were forced to admit it."

"Why Mr. Mayfield?"

"Muslim. And represented another Muslim in a child custody hearing. Two counts against him in their eyes."

"But . . ."

"Don't get too naïve on me, Xander. It happens to all minorities. A lot."

Xander shut up and tried to fit the information into his picture of America the land of the brave and the free.

Minutes later, his cheek had stopped bleeding. A bandage covered his wound and the Ibuprofen had started zoning down the pain. Xander followed as Haroon opened the school's front door.

Once they were on the sidewalk, Xander asked, "What's with Rob's mother?"

"Her husband and Rob's big brother, both died in Iraq two years ago."

Xander suddenly understood Rob and his mother. Fear takes many forms. He still had to stop himself from cringing whenever he saw a black hat or a black shirt. To him, people wearing black were terrorists.

"So," he said, "Rob's always angry."

"And she's a little off-balance."

"And", Xander guessed, "any Muslim is automatically a terrorist?"

"Pretty much," Haroon said. "There are other people, lots of them, who think just like she does, and with less excuse. Just listen to talk radio sometime."

"Why is she working here, around kids that scare her?" Xander asked.

"Dad says she needs the job. He believes Mr. Klein hopes she'll get better by being here." Then Haroon asked, "Are you still coming to soccer practice tonight?"

Xander nodded. "Might be a little late. Gotta make sure my grandpa is okay first."

Haroon's face broke into a smile. "See you soon then."

CHAPTER TWELVE

At five forty-five that evening, Grandpa checked the bandage on Xander's cheek wound. Grandpa clucked about things not changing much in fifty years. Finally he left the house for his usual "constitutional". Xander didn't want Grandpa to know he was going to give soccer a try. He wanted to reserve the right to go once, quit, and hear no more about it.

He dropped the bandage in the garbage, swabbed his cheek with Neosporin, grabbed his house key and ran out the door. Grandpa wouldn't be back before seven-thirty. Xander wouldn't be missed.

He jogged down Sixteenth Avenue, saw Grandpa's back and changed his route to avoid him, then ran the mile to Beverly Cleary Park. Sure enough, at the bottom of the hill, near the kiddy slide, he found several boys dressed in sweats and doing warm-ups.

Haroon waved him over. "Coach wants us to do these stretches before he arrives. The Pauling Rats have gotten in the habit."

"Pauling Rats?"

"Linus Pauling? Scientist? Rat Mazes?" Haroon said.

"Nice!"

"Makes other teams not want to touch us."

Xander mimed a finger down the throat, then got to work.

Minutes later, as he stretched his back, palms on the ground, he glanced through his legs and saw his grandfather walking toward them. Xander kept his head down. Didn't want to have to explain his change of heart about exercise.

"Yo, Coach," one of the boys said. "New kid's here."

Around his leg, Xander could see Grandpa smile. "Glad to see it. Welcome to the team, Xander."

Xander stood up, his face hot. This, he never expected.

Grandpa smiled at Xander and said, "Okay, fellows. I see you got the stretches done, so twice around the park, and then we'll do some skill practice."

* *

Xander waited for Grandpa to ask how he came to join the team instead of hibernating in bed. Grandpa didn't ask during practice. He was too busy making them sweat, and teaching them how to steal the ball from each other.

Halfway through a scrimmage, Grandpa had to fill in to make the sides even. As he stole the ball from Xander, Grandpa whispered, "Too slow, Buddy."

Xander whipped a foot between Grandpa's legs and retook the ball. "Yeah. I shoulda stayed in bed."

As he ran down the field with the ball, he heard his Grandpa chuckle.

After practice, Haroon said, "My folks hope you and coach will come to the restaurant for dinner."

Suspicious, Xander squared off facing Grandpa. "Did you both know I was going to come?"

Grandpa said, "I hoped."

"You didn't tell me you coached," Xander said. "How come?"

"Didn't want to push you. Wanted you to do it for friends, not me."

"I still might want to spend whole days reading or sleeping."

"Up to you, my friend." Grandpa said.

"I'll bug you to come, though," Haroon said. "We need your foot and your strategy."

To get to the restaurant, Haroon, Xander and Grandpa trooped home together and retrieved Grandpa's car. While sitting in the car's back seat, Xander realized that Grandpa knew the way to Haroon's family restaurant. They turned south onto a bridge across a deep ditch called Sullivan's Gulch and then drove into the parking lot of a very old brick and ivy building.

"This once was the clubhouse for a golf course," Grandpa said.

Haroon said, "I found a whole set of golf clubs in the restaurant's attic – the leather on the golf bag was like parchment paper. And dusty . . . Whew!"

Grandpa chuckled. "Possibly as old as I am."

Haroon and Grandpa seemed to know each other lots better than Xander had guessed. Those two got out of the car and started for the restaurant, but Xander hung back. Grandpa as coach. Grandpa as Haroon's family friend. This was going to take some getting used to.

And this place, a clubhouse? Why play golf near a gulch? He glanced down into the gulch. Train tracks and a freeway ran the length of it, rails and concrete as far as he could see to the east and to the west. A few blocks east, even more rails heading east came into the gulch from the north side. Freight trains and local light rail plus six lanes of cars. A golf course? Not likely.

He heard Haroon coming back for him, so he turned around and for the first time, saw the sign at the front of the restaurant. In red letters, it spelled out *"Taziyan"* – a word so familiar to Xander that it hurt.

Haroon stood beside him, he glanced up, too. "*Taziyan* – we pronounce it Tah zee AHN," he explained. "Taziyan were hunting dogs – hounds – in old Persia. We're Americans, but we're from Northeastern Iraq, near old Persia, which you call Iran."

"I thought *Taziyan* was Persian for a special kind of religious play," Xander said.

Haroon looked at him a moment, then said. "That's Ta'ziyyah. Close. For us the meanings are close, too. I think inside you'll see why." Haroon smiled, "I'm glad you joined the team. I need somebody who understands my secret soccer moves."

At that, Xander realized that all of Haroon's shouted directions to pass and cover someone, had been in Gorani and Farsi. He hadn't entirely lost Pakistan and his friends. And now, he was afraid again – afraid to care so much.

*   *

As soon as they stepped into the restaurant, Xander ached with the feeling of home. Dark wood covered the walls in the entry. He and Grandpa followed Haroon into the dining room. The aroma of vegetables and warm Naan, lamb chops tashreeb, and Goste Miriske, bread with chicken, filled Xander's nostrils, and deepened the fearful thump in his heart.

There were no customers.

"We're closed on Monday nights," Haroon explained. "Mother wanted you here as our guests."

"We are honored, Haroon," Grandpa said.

They walked toward the dining room. Wood paneling covered the lower half of each wall. Above the wood, small lights focused on a mural painted on the plaster walls: Persian noblemen riding to hunt on slender, wide-nostrilled horses.

In the foreground of the painting were two Taziyan – greyhounds, or Persian hunting dogs chasing a frightened, wild goat.

Haroon waved an arm toward the tense hounds as he led the way toward the back and the kitchen. Xander stopped and stared at the goat. So small and weak. All the power of the hunt focused on one lonely victim.

Edmund, where are you?

The mural extended onto a second wall. In this portion, the hunt had cornered the goat near a cliff. A lone goatherd stood between the hunt and the goat, his arms and his herding crook extended to prevent the hounds from reaching their prey. The dogs, at a standstill, strained to find a way under his stick. The hunters nearby, sat on their horses and laughed at the goatherd's predicament.

Mohammed, this is what you did for us, holding the attackers at bay long enough for the boys to get to the tunnels.

To steady himself from the memory of that dark day, Xander reached out a hand and caressed the polished wood of a counter. At that moment, the kitchen door swung open. Out came an elegant lady, her dark hair streaked with silver – the Kurdish woman who had attended his parent's funeral. She dressed in western skirt and blouse, but her bright eyes and olive skin told Xander she had to be Haroon's mother – *strong like Mohammed's mother.* Xander took a deep breath and pushed down memory.

"Ah," she said. "Coach Evans. Welcome."

Grandpa made a slight bow to her. Xander had never seen him be so formal.

"And you, Alexander," she said, beaming a smile at him. "We are glad to meet you."

Xander ducked his head the way he remembered Mohammed bowing when he met adults. "I'm pleased to meet you, Mrs. Qubadi," he said.

The kitchen door swung open again letting out cooking noises, and also a short man, very strong looking, with a mustache as thick as his massive eyebrows. He carried a little girl of about four years old. She hid her face against the man's shoulder.

Haroon said, "That's my little sister, Gulbahar."

The rose. Gul is a rose, a spring flower.

She peaked at him. Her bright smile helped him breathe again.

"And my father," Haroon said.

"Mr. Qubadi," Xander bowed again.

When the man smiled, his mustache waved upwards, nearly meeting the smile lines at the sides of his eyes. Gulbahar wiggled down and ran to her mama.

"Gilbert," the man shouted above the din of bubbling pots and kitchen fans.

Grandpa grinned and then hugged him. "Nasdar. When are you ready to teach the boys to guard the goal?"

"I'll be there next Friday, for certain. I just flew in from home last night. Had to make sure my sister accepted the right man for her future husband."

"Home?" his wife said, lifting Gulbahar to settle on her hip. "Home better be right here, Nasdar, because I am not returning to Kurdistan, and never again to Persia as long as that man runs the country."

Mr. Qubadi laughed. "Of course, Nazneen. But where one's mother lives – that is also home."

"Bring Mama to us," she said, her sharp gaze focused on her husband. "That will make it right."

"Next year," Mr. Qubadi said. "Next year."

Mrs. Qubadi took Grandpa by the arm. "You must come, sit at the table, you and Alexander. Haroon …" she called over her shoulder. "Help me bring out the dolmades."

Xander's fear filled his throat. How could he make friends like this? Start life over and not have Mom or Dad, Manzur or . . . or Mohammed?

Grandpa put an arm around his shoulder, guiding him to the feast. "One step at a time, son."

*   *

After a warm and memory-stirring dinner, Xander leaned back to listen to the conversation and sip sweet juice. Gulbahar nestled in the lap of her brother. Xander's grandfather and Mr. Qubadi shared old soccer stories – Mr. Qubadi's stories were from northern Iraq, Grandpa's from the nineteen-fifties, before soccer grew in acceptance in the United States.

After a time, Mr. Qubadi took grandfather away, saying, "I need for you to see the last broadcast of the Fafner Show. The man is getting worse."

Xander glanced at Haroon. "Fafner Show?" he asked.

"One of those talk show guys. Ugly stuff."

Xander nodded. He'd heard talk show announcers on the radio in Pakistan. Always feeding fear to rake in listeners.

He helped clear the table, but afterward, Mrs. Qubadi told him to go out on the terrace and see the night. "The stars are out," she said. "In Oregon, stars are too often on the far side of a cloud, and the moon is covered with mildew."

Xander slid open the terrace door and stepped out. Right away, he noticed the stars hanging, brilliant and prophetic in the sky. Next, he saw the headlamp of a light-rail passenger train near the opposite ridge of the gulch. Last, he heard a sob and then saw his grandfather standing alone, leaning on the waist-high terrace wall, staring down into the gulch.

Xander stepped back. His running shoes squeaked on the terrace bricks. Grandpa turned around.

"Come here, Xan," he said softly. So, Xander moved next to him and cast about for some topic, some way to ignore his grandfather's sob. "Grandpa, um, do you know a man named Louis Lamb?"

Grandpa smiled, but his smile seemed tired. "Been reading the competition, eh?"

Xander nodded. "How come you didn't buy the *National Courier* chain?"

"Too big for me, son. We're just a northwest regional firm with some outlets in the Midwest and the East Coast."

"But you're called *Evans International*."

"Reporters in every hot spot in the world. News sales in the capitals of most countries. That doesn't make us big, it just makes us read. Besides," Grandpa added, "I only buy one newspaper in each town. Another team on the field keeps the players sharp, and honest."

"Well, explain this Louis Lamb. How can a guy who lived there think people in Pakistan deserve a war?"

Grandpa glanced down, as if looking for words. After a moment, he said, "When a person survives the kind of attack you had, it does things to his mind."

Xander wished he hadn't asked about Louis Lamb.

But Grandpa kept answering his question. "An attack like that can make a man angry at himself, like it did you," Grandpa said, "Or, it can make a man angry at the people who allowed it to happen."

"Mr. Lamb was there when the men came?"

"He was in Pakistan a couple of years ago, farther north. The same kind of situation. His wife died."

Xander didn't know what to say. Lamb lost his wife. Xander could understand him, but at the same time, he didn't understand him. "People don't deserve war," he said.

"No, they don't," Grandpa whispered.

Off in the distance, Xander could hear the horn of a Union Pacific train. It rolled toward the west, down in the gulch and into town on the heavier rails that followed by the freeway.

The big train's horn sound rose and fell, as if moaning. He and Grandpa stared down into the gulch in silence.

Grandpa took a deep breath and let it out. Then he said. "I used to fish down there."

"By the freeway and the tracks?" Xander asked.

"Before the freeway, there was a creek. Now the water runs under the freeway in a pipe. Back then, there was nothing but the creek, the Union Pacific rails and the brambles."

"Did Mother fish there, too?"

"No. The freeway was built while I was off playing basketball in college and before your mother was born. Wiped out all the quiet of the place, and the ugliness. For a while."

"Ugliness?"

"When I was your age, Xan, people were scared of communism. There was deep distrust of each other in our country."

"Yeah." Xander remembered his paralyzing alarm when the men with the guns came over the wall at Friends School. Now, sometimes he saw a black hat in a crowd and it made his stomach tighten, made his feet turn and run another direction.

"Suspicion," Grandpa said, "it makes people do things to each other, and the worst of it happened right down there."

Xander tried to read his grandfather's face, but it was dark, and the train whistle blew closer this time. Xander didn't ask again about the old ugliness. He'd had enough of ugliness.

CHAPTER THIRTEEN

On Saturday, Haroon and Xander played basketball in the parking lot outside the restaurant. Haroon stopped in mid lay-up, landed on both feet and held the ball as he stared down the block.

Xander turned in time to see a man come out of the nearest office building swinging a briefcase in his left hand and buttoning his suit coat with his right. Xander recognized him – the short, strong man who had hung around the trees at his parent's funeral – Mr. Saurus, the man Grandpa didn't trust.

Mr. Guy Saurus stopped next to a parked car, then he turned and looked toward the boys. He smiled his insincere mouth movement, waved his briefcase at them, and opened his car.

In a moment, he had his car in gear, pulled forward and stopped next to the driveway to the restaurant parking lot. He watched Haroon, who watched him. Agent Saurus gestured a noose around the neck and then pointed at Haroon.

Haroon's hands tightened on the basketball. His face lost all the redness that exertion had given it.

After thirty seconds, Saurus stepped on the gas and pulled up to Twelfth Avenue, where he turned right to cross the overpass.

"Breathe, Haroon," Xander said.

"What's Saurus doing there?" Haroon asked, his eyes still following the car.

Xander shivered. "I hope Evans' reporters can find out."

*   *

After that, to avoid having Haroon alone when the threatening Agent Saurus might be around, Haroon's dad picked him up at the end of a school day.

And, for the next few days, Xander made sure to avoid Rob, Butch and Denny after school by leaving with the mass of kids and not doing research in the library. He didn't go home the same way twice. He also watched to be certain Mr. Saurus wasn't following him.

Grandpa assigned his reporter, James Wray, to find out what Mr. Saurus had been up to in the neighborhood, but so far, nothing came out. No one wanted to talk about meeting with Saurus, but Mr. Wray got definite vibes from people. They knew who Saurus was, and they were scared.

On Friday, Xander wound his way home via a very circular route. As he came within a block of home, however, he spotted Rob and Denny waiting in front of Grandpa's house. Rob had a mitt and a baseball bat. Hardly the weapon Xander wanted to face, so he retraced his steps. He pulled out his phone and called *Evan's International Media.*

"Grandpa, the school goons are parked on our sidewalk, so I'm not going home for a while."

"You mean Denny Jones and Rob Palmquist?"

"Yeah."

"Please use their names from now on, and not just with me."

"Yes, sir." Heat rose in Xander's face. Dad would have said, *"Don't turn them into things, Xander."*

"So, I will pick you up after work," Grandpa said. "Where will you be?"

"At the Taziyan."

"See you there at six thirty. Help Nasdar and Nazneen."

"I will."

* *

As Xander swung through the door into the Taziyan kitchen, a man Xander didn't know stopped talking to the Qubadis. He glared at Xander. The man appeared to be Korean, or maybe Chinese.

Haroon holding Gulbahar on his hip, spoke to Xander. "Let's go.

"No," Nazneen said. "Xander can stay and hear this as well."

The man looked flustered. Nasdar said, "This is our good friend, Xander Evans Lloyd. We need our good friends to understand what you are telling us."

The man thought a moment, then nodded. "Yes, the known is better than the rumor."

Nasdar said, "Xander this is Mr. Liu, who owns the grocery store where we have traded for all the time we have lived here. His grocery is on the corner of 15th and Brazee, a few blocks from our house and two blocks from Linus Pauling School."

Xander shook hands, saying, "I'm pleased to meet you, Mr. Liu."

"So," Nazneen said to Mr. Liu, "the neighbors come into the store and you hear them talking?"

"Yes, and so I started asking the ones who came alone, in the quiet times. They all talk to this man, Mr. Saurus."

"Or he talked to them."

"Yes, to everyone on the blocks around your home. I met some farther away who asked me about you, and everything they asked was the kind of hint that Mr. Saurus made when he asked questions of my family and my store clerks."

Nasdar glanced at Gulbahar. She seemed to be playing with her dolly and not paying much attention to the conversation, so Nasdar asked Mr. Liu, "What hints?"

"Did we notice if you bought unusual items that might be used as poisons? Rat poisons? Insecticides? Did you buy charcoal? Fertilizer? Anything that can be made into an explosive?"

"Oh," Nazneen breathed. "What else did he say?"

"He asks the others did they notice when you left the country. Or when you took your guns out of the house . . .?"

"But we haven't any guns," Haroon said.

Xander's neck went cold. He stared at Mr. Liu. With rumors like that, it took a lot of courage for the grocer to come here – courage and deep friendship.

Mr. Liu turned to Xander and said, "My store window was broken by hooligans because I wouldn't pay them for safety. Nasdar Qubadi saw them come to my store. He knew who they were because they threatened all the businesses in the area. Nasdar wrote the car license. Police picked them up. Nasdar identified them at the police station. They are in jail now."

"Ah." Xander nodded. And then he asked, "How can we stop Saurus spreading rumors?"

Mr. Liu said, "Each man and woman must not buy the fear, and we must tell our neighbors that Saurus sells rotten fruit."

*   *

After school the next day, Xander grabbed his books and nearly ran from his last class toward the central hall. He wanted to meet up with Haroon so they could go together to Qubadi's restaurant. They hoped Grandpa's reporter, James Wray, had been able to discover how successfully Mr. Saurus sold his lies about Haroon's family.

Xander headed with the crowd of kids toward the school's front door. He flung his jacket over his shoulders to protect his books from the drizzle he could see outside. As he aimed his hip at the crash bar on the door, a hand came down on his shoulder – big, meaty and firm. At first Xander thought it was Denny, or Rob Palmquist, but when he turned around to face the guy, he realized it was actually a big lady.

"You're that young man from the Mission, aren't you?" she said.

"Ma'am?" he asked trying to see into her small eyes, hoping to see someone who knew, who understood.

She gazed at him with a sad and pouty mouth, and said, "Your parents, out there saving Islamic devils. I pray for them every day."

Xander stepped to one side. "No Islamic devils," he said. Sudden sweat prickled his hair.

She followed him, her voice softly earnest. "Pastor Lori says they were trying so hard to make a difference."

Pastor Lori? Lori Gotamere? The radio lady here in Portland? He shivered and glanced about, searching for somebody, anybody to help him get away. All around him, the other kids kept their eyes on their destination.

The woman kept on talking, leaning toward him. "Those heathens killing them like that," she said. "Crucifying Christ again."

He turned away, panicked by her sweet hatred. He pulled his shoulder from under her controlling hand and dashed down the hall.

"Boy, I pray for their souls," she called. "God loves your poor Mamma and Daddy."

He ran past other kids until he couldn't hear her. He scrambled upstairs through the mob that swarmed down. Gasping, he pushed his way free of the crowded steps and ran toward the second floor Boys' Room. Before he could barge into safety, he heard laughter echoing inside.

He pivoted and dashed down the hall, halting in a panting blindness in front of the bank of lockers near his homeroom.

I need my algebra book, he told himself. Flinging himself at the locker, he dialed the combination on his lock as if he had to have the book this minute. When he missed the last number on the dial for the third time, Xander reared back and punched the door.

"Ahh!" he screamed, and folded over, holding his hand to his chest while he sank to the cold floor. He saw the after-image of dark lockers, yellow against the inside of his lids. The pain in his hand jagged up his arm until the bullet wound in his triceps flamed red hot.

I need that book. I need that book. He knew it wasn't the book he needed. It was Mom, Dad, Manzur, Mohammed . . .

"Xander, I been looking for you." Haroon's voice seemed far away.

Xander opened his eyes. "I . . ." he could barely talk. "I think I . . . broke my hand."

"How did you . . .? Can you walk?"

"It's my . . . hand, dimbat."

Haroon laughed. "Shoulda broken your mouth. Let's go downstairs to the nurse's room."

Xander pushed up to a near standing position. He carried his hand in front of him, and hunched over to protect it. He stood still, unsteady and aware that the room was graying down like it did when he took Grandma's pills.

Haroon bent over, looking at the hand. "Swelling up, already. You get in another fight?"

Xander shook his head, but that made the hallway begin to whirl, so he reached out for the wall and used the wrong hand.

"Gahh!"

Haroon wrapped an arm around Xander's waist, put Xander's good arm over his shoulder and started toward the now-empty steps. "You got to stop hurting yourself," Haroon said, leading him down the stairs to the first floor. "You mad at somebody?"

"Mad at God. Mad at people who use God. Mad at . . ., I don't know."

"That list starts at the top, that one," Haroon said. "Next time, pick on somebody your own size. Me, for instance."

"You?" Xander asked, looking up from his pain to see they were hobbling toward the nurse's office. "Why you?"

Haroon opened the nurse's office door. "Because if you fight with me, you have a good chance of winning, or at least of going home with all your fingers."

"Don't hit me," Xander joked. His voice came out a feeble imitation of itself. Haroon raised a fist, pretending to pommel Xander on the head.

The secretary, Mrs. Palmquist, stood in the nurse's office, in the doorway to the main office next door. "Are you two fighting, again?" She stared at Haroon.

Haroon glanced at her, surprised. "No. Xander's broken his hand."

"You should know better," she said. "Sit over there." She poked her hand toward the chairs in the main office. "Mr. Klein will be right with you."

"Where's the nurse," Haroon asked, still hanging onto Xander's waist.

"Sit there. I'm calling for some help," Mrs. Palmquist said pointing at the plastic chairs in the room next door. "No more fighting," she said. "You, young Mr. Qubadi, sit two seats away from him."

"Hey," Xander said. "He helped me get here." He held his throbbing hand close to his chest and glanced toward the door to Mr. Klein's office, hoping the principal would come out.

"We were kidding about fighting," Haroon said. "If I meant to hurt him, I'd have left him on the Field of Gory."

Mrs. Palmquist didn't seem to recognize a joke. She pointed again at the chairs. "Sit." She said. "And don't move."

This lady lost people she loved. She acts nuts, just like me. He stumbled from the nurse's room into the main office and sat. Haroon sat two seats from him.

Mrs. Palmquist nodded, satisfied. She swung through a gate in the service counter between her desk and the visitors' area, and then she disappeared into Mr. Klein's office.

"Be careful," Haroon whispered. "She's not cool like she used to be."

"Used to be cool?"

"Well, more fair."

A moment later, she reappeared from the principal's office. "I'm sure Mr. Klein will be right back," she said and she returned to her desk, officiously stacking paper and watching them from behind the service counter.

Xander hunched over his hand. Face sweat dripped onto his knees.

"I think he's going into shock," Haroon said, standing up. "In health class, they said that sweat after a big injury, that was a sign of shock."

"You stay where you are, young man."

Xander's vision went dark around the edges.

Haroon hovered nearby. "If you put him on the floor, he'll be better." Haroon said. "Raise his feet above his heart. And cover him with that old gray blanket from the nurse's room."

Mrs. Palmquist glanced out the office window toward the street. "The ambulance will be here soon," Xander heard her speak, but he felt himself slide from the seat to the floor. Haroon lifted his feet up on the plastic chair.

Mrs. Palmquist shouted. "You get away from him."

Haroon flung his windbreaker over Xander's chest. He felt warmer.

"I'll get him that blanket," Haroon said.

"I warned you."

Off in the distance, Xander heard sirens coming toward the school. The other sound he heard was the spray of some kind of fizz under pressure. His nose stung, and his eyes. Haroon cried out and fell onto the floor beside him.

"Don't," Xander yelled. "Don't hurt him." His whole face burned. He tried to sit up, but his arm and shoulder were tangled with Haroon's feet, and his body wouldn't do what he told it.

Just then, the main office door swung open.

"Edith! What have you done?" Mr. Klein asked. He leaned over and touched Xander's face. While Mrs. Palmquist babbled about Haroon, Mr. Klein ran into the nurse's office and grabbed a blanket.

"So I had to use this . . ." Mrs. Palmquist said as Mr. Klein covered Xander. Xander blinked open one eye and could see Mr. Klein's worried face. His other eye wouldn't open at all.

"My God," Mr. Klein said. "You're not supposed to bring pepper spray to a school."

"I confiscated it from a student yesterday," she said.

"And didn't tell me?" Mr. Klein stood. He seemed to have gone again to the nurses' office next door. Xander heard him run water for a moment. He came back and covered Xander's and then Haroon's eyes with wet cloths. All the while, Mrs. Palmquist went on and on.

"Did you at least call an ambulance?" Mr. Klein asked, breaking into her plaintive monologue.

"And the police."

"Not the police again!"

"You weren't here. You didn't see them fighting," she cried.

"Not fighting . . ." Xander said, as Mr. Klein applied a cloth to his eyes and his burning nose skin.

"I know," Mr. Klein said to him. "Don't worry. Just keep this on your eyes and over your whole face."

"Broke his hand. . ." she said.

Mr. Klein spoke to Xander. "Tell me about the hand."

"I hit my locker. Angry at this . . . at death."

"And Haroon tried to help you?"

"Yes."

Mr. Klein leaned away from Xander toward Haroon. Haroon cried out "My face! My nose"

"I'm sorry, Haroon. The cloth should help a little, but we need a doctor to look at those eyes, and your throat and nose right away."

An ambulance and two police sirens screeched to a halt outside the office window. Through the wet cloth and his stinging tears, Xander could see the flashes of revolving red light.

Worse, he heard Haroon gasp with pain. Xander's own eyes burned, but Haroon had taken the biggest hit. Xander pulled at the cloth and squinted enough to see with his one eye that Haroon lay between two upset plastic chairs. Snot ran out of his nose. Mr. Klein tried to help Haroon wipe his nose and keep the wet cloth over his face.

Xander heard the shuffle of people coming into the room. Someone wheeled a bed into the room. When Xander glanced out his good eye, he saw legs for at least four men.

Mr. Klein stood. "I'm Mr. Klein, the principal here. These boys were pepper sprayed by my secretary – a terrible mistake."

"This one would not get away from that one," Mrs. Palmquist said. "Threats. And broke poor Alexander's hand."

"No," Xander opened his eyes long enough to see the bed was a stretcher. Two pairs of the standing legs wore blue wool pants.

"If this was a mistake, why were we called?" One pair of blue legs had a deep voice.

"You are Officer Bailey?" Mr. Klein asked.

"That's what the badge says."

"And is it your badge?" Mr. Klein insisted. Xander could hear tight anger in his voice

"Yes." Officer Bailey also sounded angry. "Why did you get us over here if you weren't going to cooperate?"

"The ambulance is here because I hurt my hand," Xander said. "Haroon helped me."

"He threaten you if you snitched?" Officer Bailey asked.

Mr. Klein said. "You're jumping to conclusions."

"Wrong conclusions," Xander shouted.

A fellow in a blue lab coat sat between Haroon and Xander. "Calm down, all of you. These boys' eyes are in bad shape."

A second paramedic began working on Haroon while talk whirled around them all. The fellow next to Xander replaced the washcloth with a cool pack for his eyes.

Mr. Klein said. "I'm afraid Mrs. Palmquist has not been herself for some time."

"You lie," she screeched. "My Robby knows these boys. They are illegals, foreigners and terrorist."

"She needs help," Mr. Klein said. "I should have insisted she get help weeks ago."

Mrs. Palmquist shrieked. "You don't want trouble in your precious school. You don't want to know what's going on here."

"Ma'am," said the voice of Officer Bailey. "Could I ask you to sit down and give me your statement?"

"Statement?" she cried out. "Arrest that Haroon Qubadi. Send him back to Iran, or Afghanistan, or where ever he came from. He's dangerous."

"Ma'am," the other policeman said, "I need you to tell me about what happened this afternoon."

"You may use my office," Mr. Klein said.

Officer Bailey said, "You go. I'm watching this Arab kid."

She must have gone with the second policemen, because the door opened, closed and there was a silence.

Mr. Klein sighed.

"Show me where else you're injured," the paramedic said to Xander.

Xander extended his arm. "My friend. How is my friend?"

The paramedic opened a blanket onto the floor next to Xander. "My buddy is helping him. It takes time to get that pepper stuff out of the eyes. We'll take both of you to the hospital, but I need to know what else is the matter before I move you."

"I punched my locker," Xander said, as loudly as he could. "I was mad at this woman who claims to pray for my mom and dad."

The paramedic chuckled. "Mad because she prays for them?" The man pushed Xander's sleeve up and let out a whistle. "Bullet wound," he said. "Not today's wound, but not too long ago."

"From when I was in Pakistan," Xander explained.

"Pakistan!" Officer Bailey said, and Xander knew he'd just made things worse.

"Mission School," he said. He had to get his eyes open so he could look at this man directly and convince him that Haroon had nothing to do with any of it. He managed a blinking stare at the paramedic.

"A Mission School in Pakistan," he said. "My parents were doctors there. The school was attacked."

"You've been through a lot, kid," the paramedic said. "This hand looks pretty bad. And look how you're sweating. We'll get you off to the hospital and stabilized."

"I want to call my Grandpa," Xander said, pushing upright.

The paramedic clasped him around the shoulder, gave him a little tug and he ended up on the blanket. The man wrapped it around him. "We'll call your Grandpa from the ambulance."

What happened to my muscles? Xander thought as the two paramedics lifted him onto a stretcher and belted him in.

Grandpa burst into the door. "Xan?"

"Pa!"

"I knew it was you: an ambulance *and* two police cars. Haroon! What's going on?"

"Mrs. Palmquist panicked," Xander said. "Thought Haroon was beating me." He could tell his voice was melting away. Grandpa leaned closer.

"You his guardian?" the paramedic asked.

Grandpa said, "I sure am."

"His hand is a mess. And both of them have pepper spray in the eyes and nose."

"She did that?" Grandpa asked. "These are good kids."

"Sir, Mrs. Palmquist has made some accusations," Officer Bailey said. "We have to investigate them."

Mr. Klein said, "First we need to get these kids to a hospital. Investigate while they get well."

The paramedic, said, "I want both on stretchers and out to the ambulance. This patient's clammy skin worries me."

"I tried to tell her," Haroon said, "Shock. His hand is bad."

Grandpa stooped down over both boys, and then leaned over toward Xander again. "I'm coming with you boys to the hospital, and Xan, I want you awake to tell me what happened."

"Grandpa," Xander whispered. "Do the Qubadis have a lawyer?"

"They will have one soon," Grandpa promised.

"Sir," the paramedic said, "let's go."

"I have to go with them," Officer Bailey said.

"Bailey, you can ride in the front seat with our driver," the paramedic said. "No room in the back, but there's communication between front and back through a sliding window."

"Good enough," Officer Bailey said. "The other officer will follow in his squad car."

Mr. Klein said, "I need to call for help for my secretary."

"Gerald," Grandpa said to Mr. Klein, "isn't the use of pepper spray on students a no-no for school personnel?"

"Gilbert, I have no comment at this time on that subject."

"You'd best give it some thought before too long," Grandpa said. "And so should she."

Xander felt Grandpa's hand grip his good hand. He opened one stinging eyelid and saw that his Grandfather had that frown, the one that meant worry and bad memories.

"Xan," Grandpa whispered, "close your eyes, we'll be there soon."

CHAPTER FOURTEEN

Xander told Grandpa about his hand, and about the woman who pretended to be Christian. Then he slept. It seemed a short minute before he felt his grandfather's hand on his own again. He grew aware of their ambulance siren, and of slowing down. In spite of his stinging lids, he saw that Grandpa also held Haroon's hand, and that compresses still lay over Haroon's face.

"Officer Bailey, you'll need to stand back as we get them out," the ambulance driver said.

"They are suspects."

"First, they are patients."

Xander cradled his busted hand against his chest and tried to figure how he could have been so stupid. He knew, with his history, that Grandpa must be imagining all kinds of bad reasons. The ambulance swung into the emergency drive at Emanuel Hospital, and came to a halt. Xander opened his one good eye.

The ambulance driver and Officer Bailey swung open the back door. The driver gave Grandpa a hand down. The crew pulled out Haroon's gurney with a jolt that made even Xander's hand stab.

And there on the driveway of the emergency room at Emmanuel Hospital, Grandpa called out, "Nelson, I'm glad you're here." A man wearing a brown suit and gold striped tie spoke to Grandpa. As he talked, he fiddled with his tie until Officer Bailey walked into the Emergency room following Haroon's gurney. Then the man, Mr. Nelson, spilled out information at a furious clip. "I've been on the phone while I waited. It didn't take long to find out that Mrs. Palmquist has gotten Homeland Security and the FBI looking at one particular family very closely," he said.

"What?"

"No kidding. Homeland, FBI, and the United States attorneys are very anxious to make up for the big noise that happened when they pointed the finger at Mr. Mayfield and ended up with egg on their pin stripes."

"So, they've decided to harass another citizen?" Grandpa asked.

"Looks like it. Just needed a Muslim that somebody didn't like – one who travels to the old country on occasion. The D.C. powers slobber over this like chained hounds."

Grandpa said, "I told Haroon's parents not to appear at the hospital because Bailey is here. Nazneen wanted to fly down, but Bailey is too dangerous. Their coming would make it worse for Haroon."

"You're right. Keep them informed about Haroon by cell phone."

The paramedics and Bailey returned through the Emergency door. Mr. Nelson stopped talking and loosened his tie a few more times. The ambulance driver signaled the other paramedic. They pulled out Xander's gurney and walked it through the sliding doors to the hospital. Walking near his gurney Xander heard Mr. Nelson say, "I could use a statement from your grandson and the Qubadi kid to back up our complaint."

"Soon," Grandpa said, "His name is Haroon."

He left Mr. Nelson behind as he followed Xander into a curtained cubicle. "Where's my other boy?" Grandpa asked the nurse.

"Right next door," she said. "Officer Bailey is with him."

"Damn," Grandpa said. He opened the curtain to the hall, and spoke to Nelson, "Get the chief of police. I bet she doesn't know Bailey is stooging for the FBI and Saurus."

"Done."

Next. Grandpa opened the curtain between himself and Haroon. Bailey moved to close it again, but Grandpa said, "I need to keep an eye on you, Bailey. You are suspect."

*   *

When Grandpa's Doctor Adam Whitney arrived, he asked Bailey. "Are you arresting someone?"

"No."

"Only family here," Adam said. "You can wait in the waiting room."

Bailey left in a huff, Grandpa turned to Doc Adam and said, "That guy should never be near either of these boys. He's not on police duty. He's at the beck and call of Agent Saurus."

"Saurus again?"

"The one."

Xander lay on the gurney wondering what both men knew about Saurus that he should know.

After Xander's hand had been bandaged and his nose, throat and eyes flushed of chemical, he and Grandpa waited for the emergency doctor to finish with Haroon's eyes. The doctor was concerned about permanent damage. He wanted to be certain Haroon's eyes would lubricate themselves again.

In the emergency waiting room, Officer Bailey paced for a few minutes, then took a call from someone. All Xander could hear of his call was Bailey saying: "The hell! She may not be all that crazy. I don't care what the doctors tell you."

After the call, Officer Bailey glared at Xander and then at Grandpa. "You and that kid haven't heard the last from me," he said.

"Has the FBI or Homeland Security been paying your wages?"

"I'm a Portland Police Officer," he said.

"I hope you remember what that really means," Grandpa said.

Officer Bailey put his hand on his gun butt and stared at Grandpa, but Grandpa stared at Bailey's bulging midriff. After a moment, Bailey huffed, turned away and walked out.

When he was gone, Grandpa asked Xan, "Did he do it?"

"Yep," Xander said. "He checked his shirt buttons and his pants zipper as he turned away."

Grandpa smiled. "The blustery ones are so predictable."

"Mom taught me that one," Xander said. "Stare where they feel most vulnerable. But Dad said it wasn't nice to make people feel self-conscious."

"Your dad was a better man than I am."

They lapsed into silence, while Xander remembered those last moments with his dad as they checked the gates and found Mr. Tallan's bottle and shoe prints.

"If he can't protect us," Dad said, "we need to know that."

Grandpa can protect. He knew right away to come to the school, to call the lawyer, and to get rid of Bailey.

The television in the waiting room was turned to a talk show. Grandpa glanced at the screen and scuffed his feet. "I don't know why Louis Lamb puts up with that guy," he said.

"What guy?" Xander asked.

"Lawrence Fafner," Grandpa said, gesturing at the television. "The truth is an unknown quantity on The Fafner Show. I thought Lamb had more integrity than this."

Xander folded his hurting hand toward his chest and listened to Fafner.

"Well," Fafner said, "down in Oregon they have encouraged so much love and acceptance that now they are reaping mosques, Muslims and terrorists. Socialist states and the Oregon Demo-Do-Gooder Party get what they ask for."

Xander glanced at Grandpa. "Where's this guy live?"

"Grew up right around here, but he lost his job at the local station for pulling dirty pranks and cruel jokes."

Xander watched, fascinated. The hefty blond Fafner leaned toward the microphone, his hair cow-licking over his forehead with the energy of his intensity.

"Does anyone believe that we are done finding terrorists who hide in the weak-sister state of Oregon? All they understand there is political correctness and knee-knocking niceness."

"That bully, Rob, Mrs. Palmquist's son – he needs to know this guy," Xander said. "They'd get along just fine."

Grandpa put a hand on Xander's arm. "Rob Palmquist is a grief-stricken kid with no one to listen to him."

Xander turned toward his grandfather and decided to test the waters by imitating Grandpa's voice. "Don't think about it, Rob. Just get out and do stuff and stop looking at the past."

Grandpa hung his head, shaking it. "Okay, Xan. You got me. You know how Rob Palmquist feels."

"Yeah, what I don't know is, can anybody help him? His mom? She's gone off the deep end, and just encourages his belief in foreign terrorists."

"One thing we have to hope is that he doesn't watch The Fafner Show."

"Too late," Xander said. "He practically quoted this guy in the hall-fight the other day. I just didn't know where he stole the line."

"Fafner would be pleased."

Xander took another look at the screen. Fafner slapped the desk in front of him and glared at the camera.

"Our federal government would be well-advised to put these people where no one can hear from them again, ever. Guantanamo is just a way-station to where these people should be."

Xander's neck hairs rose. Grandpa stood, strode to the television and changed the station. A man in one of the waiting-room chairs said, "Hey, man. You got something against the truth?"

"Against truth, nothing," Grandpa said, and sat in the chair nearest the control buttons.

Xander could see that the other man's tiredness and inertia worked on behalf of Grandpa's power play, but this was a waiting room for the injured. The rest of the world would not so easily give up Fafner's style of fog truth.

* *

Days later, Xander held the cast covering his broken hand in front of him as he stood on the sidelines. He wished to be on the soccer field with the Pauling Rats. At the midline, Haroon stole the ball from between the feet of one of Benson Tech's best players. The two opposing players ran down the field. Haroon passed the ball to a Pauling mid-fielder and then received it again. The Benson player surged ahead of him. Haroon turned his back on the Benson man and passed the ball to a Pauling defender just as the Benson player tried to steal the ball back.

The Pauling defender sent the ball forward. Haroon ran around his opponent, caught the ball and passed it to a Pauling forward named Dan Pine. Pine kicked it into the goal's upper corner and scored.

The game ended, Pauling winning by one goal. Coach Papa Qubadi celebrated by high fiving Grandpa and then he hugged Xander, shouting, "Next week, you will help the Rats beat Wilson High School. You'll be great."

Xander laughed. "I'll bash my opponent with my cast?"

Nasdar Qubadi turned serious. "Xander. You got to whack at something, I understand that. But whack stuff that can't whack back."

"All right," Xander said. "No more lockers."

* *

The next day, Xander sat down at a cafeteria table across from his friend. He carefully put his bandaged hand on his lap, safe from passing bumps. He glanced at Haroon, whose eyes were still bloodshot from the pepper spray.

Haroon said, "Now, One Arm, I'm getting a lunch tray for you and me. Want the steamed spinach?"

"You kidding?"

Haroon wiggled his eyebrows in a 'just you wait' gesture and swung his legs off the bench.

A few minutes later, Haroon maneuvered their plates through the lunch line. Across the cafeteria, both Denny Jones, Tekla's brother, and Rob Palmquist hulked their way toward Haroon. Xander stood up. Launching himself across the room, he stopped between Rob, Denny and their prey.

"You planning to do something with that fat hand?" Denny asked.

Haroon strolled around the knot of boys, carrying their lunch tray toward the table, but he glanced back at the conversation between Xander and Denny's crowd.

Xander gave Denny what he hoped was a benign smile. "Wanted to ask you about your football game with Jefferson this Friday," he said.

"Sure you did," Denny snarled. "I think the Pauling football team will be very hard on that hand, if you don't move it out of our way."

Just then, Denny's little sister, Tekla, pulled her brother's sleeve. "Denn, did Dad give you Chocolate Chip cookies? Can I trade you for Peanut Butter?"

"Get out of here, Tekla," Denny snapped.

"I don't much like Peanut Butter," she insisted.

Xander could tell this was news to Denny who reached out to push her away. Xander said, "I'll give you two raisin cookies for a Peanut Butter, Tekla."

"Deal," she said and let her brother's pushing hand fall from her shoulders as she strolled toward Haroon and the two lunch trays which were now safely on the table.

"You stay away from my sister," Denny growled.

Xander ignored him and walked back to Haroon who stood listening to Tekla's explanation about the cookie exchange.

After Tekla went off, Haroon said, "That one knows how to get what she wants."

Xander nodded. "Too bad about her brother."

"Don't underestimate him. He's the reason she's smart. She's had to learn to out-flank him."

"What do you mean?"

"She didn't give a fig about the cookies," Haroon said. "I saw her watch you get between me and her brother. She got the big-eye – afraid of what he would do. I'm certain that's why she appeared over there. Distract him, let you escape."

Xander turned around and stared at the girl. She talked to her seventh-grade friends, while stuffing the raisin cookies in her lunch bag, uneaten. "You think?" Xander asked.

"Plain as the bandage on your hand."

Xander returned his attention to Haroon. "Why?"

Haroon smiled. "I think she discovered on Day One that you are nuts and need protection."

"Seems to me," Xander said, "that protecting Alexander Evans-Lloyd can be a dangerous job. It put you in the hospital for hours."

Haroon shook his head. "It wasn't you. It was my name, my skin, whatever folks fear since the September 11th attacks. The police, Homeland Security, and especially FBI agent, Guy Saurus and his paid spies, got interested in my family long ago, even before Mrs. Palmquist's call."

"But why?"

"Because my father supports his mother and his village back in Iraq."

"Police? Grandpa told me the City Council voted not to let the police keep data for Homeland Security. Didn't want another Red Squad like Portland had back in the Communist-hunting days."

"The City Council doesn't control individual policeman," Haroon said. "And some of them, like Officer Bailey, don't believe in privacy. There's still a Red Squad in that department. Always has been."

"But, you said Saurus has paid spies."

"Yup. There's a sharp character who joined the mosque last year. He volunteers to do just about anything. He's always around. Last month, he was helping the members of the mosque work at the Oregon Food Bank. All the time they worked, this guy was hinting about how we should do something to strengthen the power of Muslim Americans. He's never specific, just talks, like he's trying to see who will go along with him. So, one day, different members of the mosque started following him when he left services or meetings. It turns out he meets a lot with the man we now know as Guy Saurus. They meet, shake hands and then talk for a long time. Then our spy puts his hand in his pocket and they part company." Haroon took a bite of his sandwich.

"How did you and Grandpa figure out Saurus was FBI?" Xander asked.

Haroon swallowed, then said, "It turns out that when Mrs. Palmquist called the police, Officer Bailey came to our house, and he brought what he said was a plain clothes policeman with him. It was the man, Guy Saurus. And we've got a friend in the police who said there is no such person in the police roster. So, crime boss? gangster? or FBI? We guessed . . ." Haroon shrugged.

Xander laughed.

And that was the moment he noticed a man coming down the stairs to the cafeteria, his barely-buttoned suit coat bulging in front of him. The vice-principal, Mr. Talon, glanced over the cafeteria until he spotted Xander and Haroon. Haroon glanced around to see what Xander watched.

"VeePee Talon," Haroon whispered.

"The hefty vice-principal actually climbs stairs?"

"Only when necessary."

"Where's Mr. Klein?"

"No idea," Haroon said. "But Vee Pee Talon doesn't trust boys or men. And the darker your skin, the less he likes you."

Haroon closed his eyes a moment, then lifted his sandwich to take a leisurely bite.

Talon stood behind Haroon and said, "Get up and come with me."

Xander stood up. "Sure," he said. "What do you need, Mr. Talon."

"Not you," Talon said. "This guy."

"Oh." Xander said. "You standing behind him and all that, looks like you're talking to me."

Talon glared at Xander, but said, "Qubadi, come with me."

Xander said, "What's this about?"

"This is not your business," Talon said.

"Maybe not," Xander said. "But your secretary jumped to conclusions and made a big mistake not long ago, so I'm wondering if you're doing the same today."

Haroon stood up. "Thanks, Xander. I'm done with my sandwich. You want to give Tekla my cookies?"

Xander realized that Tekla was right behind him at that moment, but so were a dozen other people. His stalling had drawn a crowd, and Haroon probably didn't want the attention.

Tekla reached out and let Haroon hand her the cookies. "Thanks, Haroon," she said. As Haroon followed Mr. Talon away from the table, she glanced up at Xander. "You want to call someone?"

He stared at her puzzled. Haroon started out of the cafeteria with Mr. Talon. The crowd moved on.

"Call?" he asked.

"My friend, Susan, says there's a police car out on the front street. A couple of policemen in the office with some guys in suits. The teachers' lounge has a phone."

Denny appeared next to her. "Tekla, bugger off," he said.

She glanced at Xander. "Thanks for the cookies."

Xander glimpsed what she'd been trying to tell him. He wished he had taken the time to bring his new cell phone to lunch. He'd never needed one in Pakistan and often left it in his locker.

He grabbed up his tray and Haroon's, and headed to the tray drop. Then he ran toward the steps to the main floor. Behind him he heard Denny shouting, "Tekla, stay away from these foreigners." Xander glanced back to make sure she was all right. She stood facing her big brother, but while she faced down Denny, her arm rose toward Xander. Her hand shooed him up the stairs. He took two stairs at a time, wondering, as he ran, how Denny and Tekla ended up in the same family.

When he arrived in the hall near the office, he saw Haroon surrounded by men in suits. Mrs. Palmquist's substitute secretary stood helplessly behind the counter. Mr. Klein was not there, only Mr. Talon. Several teachers and students stood between the suited men and the doors from the office to the hall and the exits. People shouted questions. The men in suits flashed badges in answer to the questions.

One teacher pushed his way to the front of the crowd. "Do you have a warrant?" he asked.

"Certainly," claimed a short man that Xander recognized.

"This is my student. Where are you taking him?"

"That's not your business," the man said, flexing his arms, as if getting ready to hit the teacher.

"I want to see your badge and your warrant slowly, so I can read it," the teacher said.

Students and teachers crowded around so tightly that the outsider looked beleaguered. He pulled out his badge again.

"You are Guy Saurus?" the teacher asked.

"That's what it says."

"I see what it says. Are you Guy Saurus?"

"What do you think?"

"I think you lie, or you would answer the question."

The man turned to his fellow suits. "Take this one, too, for obstructing the law."

The teacher whispered something to his neighbor, a woman teacher. The lady nodded, and they moved apart just before two men muscled the first teacher toward the front door.

There was so much chaos in the hall that no one noticed when Xander scooted past the nurse's room and two doors away into the teacher's room. The place was empty, since anyone not teaching was out yelling at or watching the action in the office.

He grabbed up the teachers' phone and dialed. Grandpa answered. "Grandpa," he said softly, "they're arresting Haroon in the school office. There are policemen, and Mr. Saurus, and several guys in suits. I think they must be FBI and Homeland Security."

"Damn! Where are you?"

"In the teachers' room."

"I'm calling Haroon's folks and Mr. Nelson. If you can get to Haroon, tell him not to talk without his lawyer."

"I will."

"I'll meet you at my downtown office after this is straightened out."

In the hall, Mrs. Wirkala, the art teacher, asked another teacher, "Why would Homeland Security arrest a seventeen-year-old?"

The other teacher, Xander thought he taught Economics, said, "You've read about these terrorist groups. To them, a seventeen-year-old is a soldier."

"But not Haroon Qubadi," a voice said.

"You can't tell about these people . . ." the Econ teacher said. "Look how they want to take over Europe. . ."

Xander registered cold fear for Haroon. He scooted back into the main office. When he caught Haroon's eye, he pretended to zip his mouth, then gestured a phone call and straightened his imaginary tie the way the lawyer, Mr. Nelson, frequently had done that night at the hospital.

Haroon nodded, then asked, "Mom, Dad?"

Xander nodded.

"What about your Mom and Dad?" asked one of the suits.

"I want to call them," Haroon said.

"Down at the office," said the suit, as he glanced at another colleague.

Uh-oh, Xander thought. Their FBI or Homeland friends are headed to Qubadi's restaurant this minute.

Xander nodded at Haroon. He backed out of the office, stepped down the hall to the school library and strolled back into the teachers' lounge. Xander walked in hoping to use the phone again. This time, however, he wasn't in there alone. This time, his math teacher, Mr. Findlay, was in there on his cell phone. Findlay hung up as soon as Xander walked in.

Xander went to the land phone as if he had permission. After he dialed, he said to Mr. Qubadi. "Did Grandpa get you? Good. But the same people are headed toward your house."

Just then, he heard Mrs. Qubadi in the distance. "See... warrant," she said. Then louder, "Warrant."

Xander said, "Demand your rights. Call your lawyer. Say nothing until he arrives."

He heard Mr. Qubadi say something – maybe to him, maybe to the police, "But Sir, I have done nothing. Why are you doing this?"

"Mr. Qubadi?" Xander called.

Then the phone at Qubadi's end was hung up.

Xander slumped against the table. Behind him, he heard his math teacher's voice. "Xander, is that Haroon's parents?"

He turned around. The math teacher was standing, now, holding the cell phone he'd been using, looking at Xander with concern.

"Yes. I . . . I don't know why. I don't know."

"Because he is Muslim," the man said, his voice strained.

Xander took a second look at Mr. Findlay, his blue eyes and curling brown hair, his resignation to prejudgment. Suddenly, something seemed clear.

"Mr. Findlay," Xander said. "Do you know their mosque?"

"I do."

"You'd better call their office." Xander pointed to the man's cell phone.

"I just did."

CHAPTER FIFTEEN

When the police, Guy Saurus and his men left with Haroon, Xander caught the first bus downtown. After showing his bus pass, he sat in the back, away from the few other mid-day passengers. He didn't want to talk to anyone. Within twenty minutes of Haroon's arrest, Xander jumped from the city bus and ran into Grandpa's newspaper office. He skidded to a halt at the lobby desk. Rick Johnson, the Head of Security at Evans' International Media, glanced up.

"Grandpa?" Xander asked.

Rick glanced down at his daybook. "Still upstairs in his office – with Mr. Nelson and some others."

"I'll wait in the news library," Xander promised Mr. Johnson, and ran to the elevator. He hoped the other visitors weren't FBI, Homeland Security or Immigration – *Geez not Immigration – Qubadi's are citizens.* Then he remembered what that TV guy, Fafner, said. "Guantanamo is just a way station to where these people should be."

Please, no. Please.

Xander glanced into Grandpa's office through the window in the door. Grandpa, surrounded by people, waved him away, then held up one finger. Xander read that as a promise to see him in a minute – or at least as soon as possible. He went down the hall.

The newspaper library had a long work table and hundreds of old-fashioned reference books arranged on rows of tall library shelves. Behind the shelves, on desks against the back wall, the library also had lots of computers hooked-up to the cyber-world. Xander grabbed a book and sat in one of the row of desks behind the shelves.

He glanced up at the security camera that scanned the room.

That moment brought him a revelation about the *Journal of the Americas*. Mr. Rick Johnson down at the security desk had to be the same Rick who knew his Grandpa back when they were in the eighth grade. He was the Johnson kid in Grandpa's stories about what happened in 1953.

Xander wondered how much he could trust such a guy after all these years. Grandpa hired him, but Grandpa seemed pretty naïve sometimes, and then other times, he seemed pretty sharp.

After about five minutes of sitting and worrying, the library door whooshed open. Xander nearly jumped out of the desk chair. Footsteps entered the news library. At least two men walked in on the other side of the rows of book shelves.

I ought to show myself and scoot out, but . . .

The heavy door clicked shut, and then Grandpa began talking. "They have family in Barzani, in the region of Harmota, near Iraq's border with Iran" Grandpa said. "And before her marriage, Haroon's grandmother used to live in northern Iran, near Lake Orumiyeh."

Xander decided to stay. Haroon was his concern, too.

"All that is true," Mr. Nelson said, "but the father sends her money through the Husayn Mosque. The U.S. Government has declared that a terrorist organization."

"Yeah? Did they inform the members?"

"Of course not," Nelson snorted. "They want to wiretap them. You can't wiretap people who know they are being spied on."

"What about the Oregon Survivalist Community Church? Eh?' Grandpa asked, sarcasm snarling his voice. "Anybody know what terrorists those people are? Anybody wiretapping them?"

"Community Churches are not on government radar, these days. Mosques, unfortunately, are."

"What's this about guns?" Grandpa asked.

"Haroon and his father have been spotted at the abandoned quarry on Mount Hood," Mr. Nelson said, "They were off of Highway Twenty-Six, target practicing."

"I've target practiced in that quarry," Grandpa said. "I introduced my whole soccer team to that quarry, and that includes the Qubadis. They going to arrest me for that?"

Xander straightened in his chair.

"You? Target practice?" Nelson asked. "I thought you were a Quaker."

"I can hit the center of a series of concentric circles without hurting anything or anyone. What's un-Quaker about that?"

Xander tried to put this new piece of information into his picture of Grandpa the pacifist. It didn't fit easily. He closed his eyes and saw his own acacia stick in a pile of hay on the dusty ground.

Grandpa said, "There is no proof that Qubadi, father or son intended anything other than to have fun. Hunting is an old part of Persian and Kurdish culture – like Dan'l Boone in Kentucky. Everyone in this country has a right to bear arms. Everyone."

"And so the court shall hear from us, but it's being painted up very bad." Mr. Nelson continued. "The Husayn Mosque is portrayed as providing financial support to Madrasa teaching in Iraq, Afghanistan and Iran."

"Madrasa means religious college . . ." Grandpa said.

The man said, "To the U.S. government, Madrasa means 'teaching violent insurrection' – you know that, too."

"U.S. government willful ignorance," Grandpa said.

"Fear, fed by fear, and some element of truth. Many Madrasas do teach violence."

Xander decided to cough or something, let them know he was back here. But the oak door opened again. The next voices Xander heard were Grandpa's friends, cartoonist, Mike Halverson and the writer, James Wray.

"Got this for the editorial page," Mike said.

"It's great," James Wray added, "Goes right over my editorial on house invasion without a warrant."

There was a moment of silence while the men seemed to study whatever Mr. Halverson had brought in. The lawyer laughed out loud, but said, "I don't think so . . .!"

"We've got to come out strong on this," Grandpa said. "But we have to keep that on the editorial page. And we have to say on day one that our Max Million Foundation for Justice is hiring legal assistance for the Qubadi family."

Mr. Nelson said, "Gilbert, you've gotta keep the newspaper neutral on this. You don't want the paper to lose advertising and readership."

Mr. Halverson snorted. "This isn't just about the Qubadi family. This cartoon lampoons the churches that hide behind pseudo-Christianity to create dread of non-Christians."

"Could you keep the paper out of this, and let my team handle it?" Nelson asked

"So, then Mike can sell this cartoon to *The Irvington Buzz*?" James Wray suggested.

"You wouldn't!" Nelson said.

"I would," Mike said. "*Irvington Buzz* is my own baby, and I'm going to skewer panic mongers in some form of print. *The Irvington Buzz* is news young people read."

Xander recognized *The Irvington Buzz,* a small, neighborhood newspaper and a really funny online blog. He hadn't known it belonged to one of Grandpa's friends.

"Nelson," James Wray said, "you want to put the news through a baby-food mill?"

"Your editorials are going to stir people. They'll make our legal job harder."

James Wray said, "Mr. Nelson, you make the news, we report it. And our editorial page tries to let citizens and the editors talk to each other. The exchange of views is a public forum. Without it, our newspapers get a pea-green pablum cast to them."

"I understand informing readers, but don't stir up the government any more than it's already stirred. They'll bring on the whole weight of Washington against us."

Grandpa said, "Washington wants us to beg to give up our rights. Who else besides good newspapers will warn against people who scheme to control how we think?"

"Gilbert, when you anger the public," Nelson said, "it makes finding a jury impossible. You saw what happened to public opinion when Washington used *The National Courier* to leak headline stories about Mr. Mayfield."

Xander stood, afraid for his friend, afraid for his old Grandpa, and worried that even the power of the newspaper couldn't help Mr. Qubadi tell the truth to the world.

"Un-biased news . . ." Mr. Nelson began.

"Having absolutely no bias means 'hiding from the tough truth'," Mike said. "It means we don't dig and do our homework."

"We don't feed a climate of hate," Grandpa said, "Not like the *Journal* back in the old days. We feed a climate of knowledge and understanding. That's what news is all about."

Xander pulled himself out of his silence. He walked out from behind the books. Mike, James and Grandpa stared at him. Mr. Nelson stiffened.

"Mr. Nelson?" Xander asked. "Aren't you going to find the truth?" He turned to Grandpa, "And aren't you going to report it?"

Mike Halverson and James Wray turned toward Nelson and Grandpa, and waited.

Grandpa's eyes flashed at Nelson. It seemed he'd grown very angry, and Nelson's eyelids crinkled into worried waiting, watching.

Xander wished he hadn't caused this zinging tension between the four men. "I'm sorry, Grandpa. I . . ."

James Wray put up his hand, telling Xander to hold his comment.

Grandpa started talking, to himself, it seemed. "Back then this old newspaper refused to be even-handed," He turned to tell Nelson with his next thought. "Radio and many newspapers stirred up alarm. In the end, it was the news and the men who used it to spread fear, that's what helped the final mob."

James turned to Mr. Nelson and said, "During the McCarthy era, *The Journal* and other papers ignored the truth because hate sells papers. The word Communist, and four inch headlines added oxygen to fires."

Mike added, "The opposite of selling alarm is not the illusion of balance. This seeming neutrality you want us to use, Nelson, that's spineless."

Grandpa grabbed the worn chair back near him. He took a deep breath, let it out in a whoosh and said, "Richard Nelson, we at Evans have a job to do – unbury the truth. You have a job to do – find the evidence the government thinks they have; and find the evidence that shows what Nasdar Qubadi really is. Use all your legal talent to free

Nasdar's family and allow them to be honored citizens again. Are you up for that job?"

"Yes, but, your editorials will get the anger of the Justice Department going and . . ."

"Then we expose the in-justice that department practices . . . and you know this from prosecutors you've talked to – the department has already gone after U.S. Justice Department attorneys who don't toe the party line – the ones who balk when the Justice Department asks them to accuse some congressman or senator who's up for election."

Mr. Nelson slumped into a library chair. "Gilbert, find the truth, but don't wave red handkerchiefs, for God's sake."

Xander drew up a chair at the same table as Mr. Nelson. He leaned toward him.

Nelson looked up and watched Xander's face.

"Sir," Xander said, "My friend, Mohammed had a poem he quoted whenever we read about bombs in the market place, suicide bombers at check points, attacks on other schools – whenever we were afraid."

Mr. Nelson gazed at him. So Xander told the poem, all the while picturing Mohammed's last act of courage. "Mohammed said:

> *'Fear is the cheapest room in the house,*
>
> *I would rather see you living*
>
> *in better conditions.' "*

The silence in the news library lay thick on Xander's shoulders. He couldn't tell what Grandpa or Mr. Nelson thought of his interference.

After a moment, James spoke. "Hafiz, Shams-ud-din Muhammad."

Xander looked quickly up at him. "Yes, that's what Mohammed called him, "the poet Hafiz."*

Mr. Nelson and Grandpa both stared at James. He shrugged. "Hey, I can read poetry."

They all laughed. Then Mr. Nelson looked at Xander. "Fear is the cheapest room in the house," he quoted, then studied his hands in his lap. His eyebrows tightened. He gripped his knees and seemed to be deep in thought. After a few moments, he said, "You had a good friend, Alexander. I will move out of the room of fear. I will work for your friend, Haroon and his father. And," he looked at Grandpa. "I'll not interfere with what the newspaper needs to do."

Grandpa let out a long-held breath. He spoke softly to his old friends. "Well, as Elizabeth used to say, let's roll up our pant-legs and get our feet wet. James, can you track down the reasons that the mosque, Husayn, is under a cloud?"

"Yes, indeed."

"Mike, I like your cartoon. That and James' editorial on warrantless invasion of privacy will be top of the editorial page tomorrow."

"Great," Mike said.

"But," Grandpa said, "I'll write an editorial for the top of the right-hand page revealing our connection with the soccer team, the Qubadi family, the involvement of our foundation in hiring the lawyer and all. Nobody is going to scoop us on that."

"And," Nelson stood, "the legal team will be at the court house requesting a hearing asking to allow Nasdar Qubadi out on bail." Mr. Nelson shook hands with Xander, and then with Mike and James before he left.

"What can I do?" Xander asked. "Can I organize the soccer families? Raise money to pay the lawyer?"

"Alexander, my boy, you do just that." Grandpa glanced toward Mike and James. "This kid has good ideas. Much better to get the community involved in supporting their cause. How about if the Max Million Foundation offers matching funding for community support. That will show the politicians, and those campaigning for election, that the whole community is paying attention."

Grandpa took Xander's hand, as if to hold him back from entering the race. "Xander, also please go to Mrs. Qubadi and find out what she needs to keep a roof over her head while we beat these crazy accusations of treason against her family."

Xander stood. He gave his grandfather a salute like the ones he'd seen during his recovery at the base hospital in Germany.

"Sir, yes, Sir."

From The Gift, Poems by Hafiz, the Great Sufi Master, translations by Daniel Ladinsky, Penguin Compass, 1999

CHAPTER SIXTEEN

Xander grew hopeful when Haroon came home from the jail. Jan Nelson said Haroon would not be charged with helping his father, since he never went to Iraq. But the judge refused to set bail for Mr. Qubadi. The government prosecutors claimed he would flee the country.

And although Xander followed the police reports every day at the newspaper offices, he never saw any mention of an arrest of someone from Masjid Maryam, the mosque near the cemetery in east Portland, or at Husayn, the mosque in west Portland that Qubadi's attended.

The first day back at school, the principal, Mr. Klein was absent at a national educators' meeting. Mr. Talon, the fat vice-principal, suspended both Xander and Haroon, supposedly because of the fight with Denny, Buck and Rob during the previous week. The seventh grader, Tekla, reminded Mr. Talon, that it was her brother and his friends who started the fracas, but that didn't seem to matter to Mr. Talon.

Xander worried about what would happen to Tekla at home when Denny found she'd tried to get him suspended, too. However, within two days, she brought her best friend Susan into Qubadi's restaurant while he and Haroon worked there. She seemed to be unhurt.

"Got any food we can afford, Haroon?" Tekla asked. "I've got a dollar-a-week allowance and Susie has fifty cents."

Mrs. Qubadi came out from the kitchen, wiping her hands on her apron and watching this exchange. Haroon smiled. He handed the two girls each two mints from the glass bowl at the check-out counter.

"Thanks," Tekla said, dropping a quarter in the tip jar. She nudged Susan, to do the same.

"You know, Mrs. Qubadi," Tekla said, "If you had something little, a snacky sort of thing that kids could eat on the way home from school, I could bring my whole class during the next weeks. We could raise a lot of quarters for the lawyers."

Mrs. Qubadi nodded, and then appeared to be thinking. "Tekla, could you come into the kitchen and look at something? You too, Susan. You tell me if this would work for your friends?"

Tekla and Susan followed her out of the dining room. Xander and Haroon glanced at each other. Haroon held up his hands to say, *No idea where this is going.*

Xander whispered, "Glad she's not my sister, that one."

Haroon nodded. "Nothing gets by her."

At that moment, the three came out of the kitchen. Tekla spoke in solemn tones. "What do you think, Susie?"

"I think the girls will like the dolmades," Susan said. "The boys will like the meat on a stick."

Mrs. Qubadi nodded. "We can have those for the after-school hour, then."

"Great," Tekla said. "See you tomorrow."

The two girls glanced at Xander and Haroon. "You're not missing much at school," Tekla said. "My brother, Denny, and his friend Buck, were suspended, too, but only for a week. That bully, Rob Palmquist, was expelled. The principal, Mr. Klein, discovered he was stealing lunch money and other stuff from Vice-Principal Talon's desk. Rob's mom, the school secretary, she's on leave for her health, but she says she didn't notice that Rob came in there often, or that he had extra money."

"Uh-huh," Xander said. He wanted to celebrate this news, but thought he ought to wait until she was out of earshot. Tekla puzzled him.

"Mrs. Palmquist, Rob's mom, says she is mortified," Susan added.

"Mortified?" Mrs. Qubadi asked.

Susan looked confused by her vocabulary question.

Tekla said, "I think it means she wants to die of embarrassment."

Mrs. Qubadi nodded her head, slowly. "That I understand," she said.

The girls swung out of the restaurant followed by the clang of the over-the-door bell. Silence remained behind them.

Then Mrs. Qubadi said, "That one is very smart." They both knew she meant Tekla. She turned to the boys and stared at them over her glasses. "In ten years, you'd better watch out. She'll have one of you wrapped around her little finger."

Xander guffawed. But Haroon jerked his thumb toward Xander and smiled at his mother.

* *

Even Xander grew amazed at the anger of soccer-team families because of the arrest of Mr. Qubadi. Within a week, the soccer parents had organized themselves to meet the matching grant challenge from the Max Million Foundation. The families not only raised three thousand dollars, they also bombarded all the regional and neighborhood newspapers with letters to the editor on behalf of Nasdar Qubadi, their team co-coach.

The continued jailing without bail of Mr. Qubadi made it to the Channel Eight news, announced by a good-looking red-haired lady. She also told about the community support for the Qubadi family and the matching grant challenge from the Max Million Foundation.

One afternoon, while visiting Grandpa's office, Xander found James Wray, the reporter, watching television. Glancing at the screen, Xander saw the talk-show host, Lawrence Fafner.

On the big screen, Fafner leaned back in his chair and shook his head as if in disbelief. "Max Million Foundation, indeed. Max Million was nothing but a bum – an outcast from society, a man in overalls and lice-ridden shirts who lived under a bridge. What kind of man names a philanthropic foundation after a loser? What is Gilbert Evan's game here?"

Now Fafner leaned toward the camera. He said, "The man who buys every newspaper in sight and makes friends with terrorists. Is this the kind of man we want serving up the so-called news in every large city in America? Is this the kind of man we want controlling over half the media in the United States of America and beyond?

"I tell you, something is very wrong with this picture. It wouldn't surprise me to see an uprising against Evans Publication. All over this nation people are not going to put up with the mockery of patriotism that a Max Million Foundation represents."

James Wray clicked off the television. "I guess we should have expected this pile of manure to work the boycott angle."

"Mr. Wray? Who is Max Million?" Xander asked.

James Wray turned his dark eyes toward Xander. "Boy, oh boy. You would have loved that guy. Independent old cuss. Dirty as anything before and after his twice yearly bath."

"Did he live under a bridge?"

"Yep. Bridge over Sullivan's Gulch. Right near where Qubadi's restaurant now stands. Back then your grandpa fished the creek in the gulch. Max Million loved your Grandpa something fierce, like the love of a wayward uncle, unpredictable and highly valued."

"He's not alive?"

"No. Died in your grandpa's bedroom while your grandpa played basketball in Ohio. Gilbert never forgave himself for not realizing how sick Max was when he left for college, but of course, Max would've hated any hovering and attention."

"So Fafner knows all this."

"Sure. Fafner lives up in Seattle now, but he used to be an announcer down here. He digs for information, and then he twists the truth to serve his need for attention. He loves to poke sticks at your grandpa. Gilbert wouldn't hire him when Fafner thought he deserved any job in Portland."

"Louis Lamb hired him."

"Louis Lamb needed an attention grabber for his morning show."

*   *

Soon, Xander began to see that other letters poured into both the *Journal of the Americas* and the *National Courier* – some for keeping Mr. Qubadi locked up, and others for sending him back where he came from, but many more were for treating him as any citizen would be treated – make an accusation, or let the man go was the general feeling of many of the letters. And they were letters from people who did not know Mr. Qubadi at all. Xander began to hope.

One morning, Xander noticed a headline about protesters outside the courthouse. In the accompanying photo was his Great Aunt Justine, sporting handcuffs on her gnarled and praying hands. Xander wondered if God's ears were burning at the moment of the photo.

The Qubadi arrest brought Lamb's *National Courier* reporters and lots of television cameras from other news companies to the town.

Many hung around the Federal courthouse, but a lot came to the Taziyan Restaurant. Each night, after working in the restaurant, Xander went home and watched the late news with Grandpa. Lawrence Fafner, talk-show host, had suddenly become a political commentator. Somehow, he got information about the Qubadi trips to the quarry for target practice. And he didn't mention that Nasdar was there with many non-Muslims, all doing target practice at the same time.

Xander and the soccer parents worked to keep the restaurant open for food, but the reporters just wanted the right to film, interview people and leave no money behind. Tekla kept bringing her friends after school, but reporters and cameras created an obstacle course. The kids had to push through the news crowd to buy their dolmades and shish kebab snacks.

Finally, one afternoon, Tekla shook the sleeve of Channel Eight's red-haired lady reporter. "I'm going to tell you a story about this place, The Taziyan," Tekla said, importantly.

She seemed to have picked her reporter carefully. Xander noticed that every other reporter outside the restaurant tuned in to their conversation. Cameras started rolling. Xander stood at the doorway and watched with apprehension.

"These are my friends," Tekla said. "They belong here. They are American citizens. They make great food, and you are ruining their restaurant. So, come on in and buy some dolmades – that's what my girlfriends like, or buy some shish kebab – that's what the boys like. If you're not going to buy food, please get out of the way and let the rest of us through. It would be better if you helped instead of running them out of business by just taking up space."

Loud laughter followed this announcement.

"Well?" Tekla said.

Several cameras ducked down as if in shame. The crowd mumbled and muttered.

"Want me to take orders?" Tekla asked. One cameraman started filming again.

"Sure," said the lady reporter whose sleeve she'd tugged. "I'll have dolmades."

"That'll be fifty cents," Tekla said, doubling the price and holding out her lunch sack for the reporter's change.

The reporter's camera man laughed, and then the lady said to her colleagues, "Ladies and gentlemen, our choices seem to be dolmades or shishkebabs. What'll it be?"

Xander shook his head in disbelief and stepped inside to warn Mrs. Qubadi that snacks were about to be a sellout item.

CHAPTER SEVENTEEN

There were two dads among the soccer families who never joined in the fund raising, Mr. Pine and Mr. Breiton. Xander noticed, and he wondered what those dads were going to do. Haroon's friend, Dan Pine came by the restaurant on Thursday afternoon after the snack crowd had gone home.

"Xan," he said, "Can you take this letter to your Grandpa?"

Xander took the letter and said, "See you at practice tonight."

Dan glanced over at Haroon and then bent over to retie his running shoes. When he straightened up, he said, "My dad thinks I should join the Classic team. I don't like that coach, but Dad thinks I'd have a chance at a soccer scholarship for college if I play classic."

Xander felt the heat rise in his face, but he said, "Yeah. A scholarship would be good. You ever miss the knock-it-around kind of game, you come on back to workouts with us."

"Yeah, sure," Dan said. Then he raised his hand in a half wave "See you around, Haroon."

Haroon nodded. "See you."

When the door closed behind Dan, Haroon said. "I knew that was coming. Now, I wonder when Mitch Breiton will become a Classic player."

Xander nodded. "At least their moms helped at the fund-raiser. We know somebody there believes in us."

"Us?" Haroon asked, leaning on the counter.

"Hey, Bro, I know this is scary for you and your dad. Lots scarier than for me. But I'm here for the duration."

Haroon stood up. "I know you are, Xander. I just hope Dad and I will be here. Iraq is a tough place. Grandma and her town need our money. How can we abandon her?"

Xander could only shake his head. He didn't want to think about the possibility of Haroon and Nasdar being whipped off to Guantanamo Bay with no access to a lawyer or justice.

Haroon started sweeping the floor.

* *

The next day, things were quiet in the morning, but early in Xander's afternoon shift, Mr. Breiton came in. "Your mother here, boys?" he asked.

The question jolted Xander into dumb silence. Does this man think we're brothers? Has he been to none of our games?

"My mother is here," Haroon said. "May I get her for you?"

Mr. Breiton glanced at Xander's paler face. His own face colored at his mistake, but he recovered and said to Haroon, "That would be very helpful."

While they waited for Mrs. Qubadi, Mr. Breiton looked around the room as if he were measuring it. He never glanced at Xander again, but paced off the front of the restaurant twice. When Mrs. Qubadi arrived, he offered to shake her hand, then when she didn't respond in the expected way, he pocketed his hand.

"Sorry," he laughed at himself. "I came to make you an offer, Mrs. Qubadi."

"Oh?"

"Yes, ma'am. I have a chain of five restaurants here in Portland, and three in Salem," he said. "I wanted you to know that if you ever need to sell your fine restaurant, Breiton's Halibut and Chips would make you a handsome offer."

She stood very still for an uncomfortable moment, then said. "I suppose it is good to have all kinds of options in mind."

Xander winced. He was sure Mrs. Qubadi's money options were growing fewer by the day.

Breiton added a chuckle to his heartiness. "It would be a good offer. Most of our restaurants are a bit larger than this one, but we can do our best, eh?"

She smiled slowly, "Yes. We do our best. Say 'hello' to Lydia. I'll see her at Saturday's soccer game."

"Oh, yes. Saturday. I'll be sure to tell her." He took his hand out of his pocket, left his card on the counter next to the register, then pushed open the door.

As he left, Mrs. Qubadi let air hiss between her teeth, and returned to the kitchen.

Haroon glanced at Xander. "Is he the scout for some pack of wolves?"

Xander's neck hairs rose. He had never mentioned the black sergeant, the helicopter medic, to Haroon. *"Nothing but a pack of wolves,"* the man had whispered.

*   *

That afternoon, Mrs. Qubadi showed Haroon and Xander a letter from the city denying their application to have tables on the sidewalk like other area restaurants.

"Mama," Haroon said. "Not everyone is against us."

"It doesn't take everyone," she said. "Just enough people in power, and the many will follow."

* *

The next morning, Xander brought his books to the restaurant. While they were suspended from school, he and Haroon got their assignments through the math teacher, Mr. Findlay, who collected them from the other teachers – the ones that agreed to cooperate. The boys hoped to keep up with their classes and graduate in spite of the suspension and whatever time Haroon had to spend in court.

Only the Economics teacher wouldn't send Haroon's homework. The English teacher who had questioned Haroon's arrest and had been arrested himself for a brief time, helped Mr. Findlay by getting the Economics assignments from one of the students. He turned copies of the assignments in for Haroon, but the teacher refused to grade them. Mr. Klein held onto the originals because he intended to make a case against this teacher for discriminating against Haroon.

After they finished their homework, Haroon cleaned tables without talking. Beside him, Xander swept the floor and then helped Haroon refill salt and pepper shakers.

After long minutes of heavy silence, Xander said, "What gives, Haroon? The sidewalk table license bugging you?"

Haroon threw down the last pepper shaker. "Your Grandpa's lawyer refuses to represent us."

Xander stared at him. "Mr. Nelson? Why?" He stooped to retrieve the shaker from the floor.

"He came over here this morning, before you arrived. Said he found we'd been lying to him. Says he can't represent clients who won't come clean."

"Lying? What's there to lie about? What's he mean?"

Haroon looked away, shaking his head. "Nothing to lie about. Mom told him that."

Xander pretended to go back to work, but his mind was scrambling for answers. What did the lawyer think they'd been lying about? And why wouldn't Haroon look at him when he asked?

As the time drew near for Mrs. Qubadi to make dinner, the boys began making ingredients for the afternoon snack crowd. Mrs. Qubadi asked Haroon to get a recipe from her file in their office.

Haroon held his hands up out of a deep bowl. They were covered with food-safety gloves and dolmades stuffing.

"I'll get the recipe," Xander said. He'd seen them pull recipes from the office drawer many times. So, he hurried in, pulled out the drawer, found the recipe box and saw a big envelope from United Air Lines.

When he turned to ask about it, he found Mrs. Qubadi already in the doorway.

"This is the secret the lawyer talked about, isn't it?" he asked.

She took a deep breath.

Haroon appeared behind her. "We never used them," he said. "My dad was already arrested. His sister had to get married without him. We didn't ask for our money back because it would have looked bad."

"Why didn't you tell the lawyer?"

Mrs. Qubadi said, "The man would use any excuse to get out of representing us. What difference could it make to tell him now?"

The doorbell rang out. Xander shoved the drawer closed. Haroon hurried back to his dolmades. Mrs. Qubadi gazed at Xander for a moment and then turned away to greet the next visitor.

Grandpa Gilbert's voice filled the front room. Xander relaxed until he heard what Grandpa said.

"Nazneen, why didn't you tell me about your brother?"

"Oh!"

Over the next minutes, Mrs. Qubadi cried as Haroon set her in a chair in the office and told her she had to trust someone. Grandpa waved Xander into the next room and asked Haroon to sit with his mother.

While finishing the dolmades wraps in the kitchen, Xander heard Grandpa say sternly, "Mr. Nelson can't help you without all the facts. Is your brother dead or captured?"

Xander heard Mrs. Qubadi crying.

Haroon said, "Mother, stop crying, now. You have to tell."

Her sobs slowed. "He is . . . in prison near Baghdad – that new prison of the United States. They torture men there. Who knows . . . what he has said about others when they . . . when they torture him. My poor Gamal."

*   *

Hours later, Mrs. Qubadi, Grandpa and the lawyer were in conference downtown. Haroon and a friend of his mother's from their Husayn mosque cooked dinners. Xander and Aunt Justine, who knew nothing about cooking, took orders from restaurant guests. Among those guests was the seventh grader, Tekla and her mother.

"Hi," Xander said to Tekla. "Denny coming?"

"Denny lives with Daddy," Tekla said. She stared at Xander, as if defying him to ask any more questions.

Xander nodded. He felt a moments' relief that Denny couldn't bust Tekla's jaw every night after school, and then he realized the sadness in Tekla's tight-lipped explanation.

"What would you like to eat?" he asked.

"Shishkebabs," she said without hesitation. "Beef shishkebabs."

Grinning at her, he remembered her friend Susie saying *Girls will like dolmades. Boys will like the meat on a stick.* Shishkebabs.

"Great choice," he announced.

*   *

Much later that night, when all the volunteer restaurant help had been excused. Xander trudged home where he sat on the side of his bed. Grandpa came in to help him take the shoes off his swollen feet.

"Gonna have to get you waiter's shoes," Grandpa said.

"Never waiting tables again after Qubadis are free."

Grandpa nodded. "Let's pray for that day."

"What will the newspaper do about this news – Mrs. Qubadi's brother and all that?"

"I acted today as her advocate with the lawyer, not as a newsman. But, in our paper, you will be seeing articles about torture and the statistics about truth and lack of truth, the result of tortured confessions."

"Why do U.S. prisons torture people?"

"Because we excuse it as necessary in times of crisis. Did you ever notice we always have some kind of crisis in this country?"

"Why?" Xander asked.

"Because it's easier to control people who are afraid."

"But people will see through that soon, won't they?"

"How long has it been so far?" Grandpa asked.

Xander saw the look of despair on his grandfather's face. He remembered the stories Grandpa told him about fifty years ago. "I know, Grandpa," he said, "It's been a long, long time."

CHAPTER EIGHTEEN

The next day, Xander walked into his grandfather's office. Xander leaned over Grandpa's sleeping form in the plush office chair. He whispered as quietly as he could. "Grandpa?"

His grandfather jerked awake. "Sign it! For God's sake, just sign it," he said.

Xander wondered who he dreamt about. He crouched down and looked up into his grandfather's face.

"I am Xander."

Grandpa's face cleared. "Oh. Xander. Boy, why are you in my office this time of day?"

"Your lawyer, Mr. Nelson, came to get us at the restaurant. There's bad news."

Sudden tears appeared in his grandpa's eyes. He leaned his head against the back of his chair. Xander couldn't tell if his sadness still rested in the dream of the past, or in what news he might hear today. Grandpa's tears streamed down his lined cheeks as if he couldn't feel them or control them.

"Nasdar is their scapegoat, and they circle the prey," Grandpa announced.

He is present at last, Xander thought. He pushed on. "Will you talk to Mr. Nelson?"

Grandpa nodded.

Xander said, "I'll get the lawyer and Mrs. Qubadi."

Mr. Nelson talked to those who gathered – Nasdar's family, Grandpa, Xander, Mike Halverson and James Wray. The court refused to set reasonable bail for Nasdar given the reports of his recent trips to Iraq, the airplane tickets for four which had never been used, and what they called 'other considerations of merit'. Mr. Nelson said those other considerations included the jailing of Mrs. Qubadi's brother in a U.S. prison at a military base in Iraq.

*   *

Two hours later, Mr. Nelson left for the Federal Courthouse to file papers. He hoped, without much hope, to force the FBI, Homeland Security and the United States Prosecutors to treat Nasdar Qubadi as a citizen of the United States with a right to a lawyer, a hearing and then, if necessary, to a trial.

An hour later, everybody in the office listened as Mr. Nelson reported by phone to Grandpa Gilbert, the Federal prosecutors stalled, wouldn't answer questions, said they didn't believe Mr. Qubadi had a right to insist on seeing a lawyer, but would have representation through a military hearing. Since he was an enemy combatant, he would be tried, they claimed, under some kind of Military Court set up by the recent Military Commissions Act.

Mr. Nelson cited court rulings against treating U.S. citizens as enemy combatants. But the prosecutors seemed certain the Supreme Court would soon reverse those rulings.

Nelson said, "The law and the constitution have frayed beyond recognition."

While the family and Evans Publishing news reporters hovered around Grandpa's office, Mrs. Qubadi did not cry. Instead, she grew angry. Grandfather asked James Wray to interview her for an article on the arrest, and about the evidence the FBI and Homeland Security Office claimed was so damning.

Then, Grandpa asked Haroon to get online in his big office computer and read the Military Commissions Act – all fifty-five pages of it. Next, Haroon started in on the recent amendments to the act. After he read it, Haroon started researching the court findings since that act had been passed – and President Bush's written statements that claimed the president didn't have to abide by the findings of the court.

This president could be in any dictatorship I've read about, Xander thought.

While Haroon did research at one desk, Grandpa urged Xander to type drafts of letters to the Oregon Senators and Representatives about the arrest of a U.S. citizen, and about his treatment as if he had no rights. James Wray helped suggest strong wording for the letters, asking the politicians to intervene.

"Remember," Mr. Wray said, "The Reverend Jesse Jackson senior said way back that Blacks weren't fighting for rights of Black People alone. We were fighting for the rights of all. And here we are … again."

So, Xander quoted Jesse Jackson and James Wray in his letters.

After he printed them, Xander showed the letters to Mr. Wray just to be sure they were professional looking and that he didn't say stuff wrong.

Mike Halverson also read them over, and he muttered. "One third of these elected officials are slick wafflers. Whatever is convenient today – that's what they do and say."

Mr. Wray said, "Let's hope after the next election, the new congress has some backbone."

"Hmph!" Mr. Halverson said, and he sat down to draw a cartoon.

While Xander printed some letters for the snail mail route, and emailed another set, Mr. Halverson drew a cartoon of a kid scribbling away at a desk. Around him, envelopes flew off into the air. In the upper right hand corner, a cloud of recognizable politicians played on harps and whistled, paying no attention to the mail clumped around their lounge chairs.

Xander hoped that cartoon image was one of Mr. Halverson's exaggerations. But a feeling of dread entered him as soon as he put his stamped letters into the office mail chute.

Mr. Nelson called to report. Xander's grandfather listened, grunted and nodded as if his gestures could be seen through the phone. Xander glanced across the room at Haroon and Mrs. Qubadi. They had gone to the floor, praying that Nasdar would be allowed a lawyer. Xander figured they had the right idea, so he bowed his head and tried to listen for a leading from God, as his mother and father would have done.

Grandpa saw the prayers going on. He took his cell phone out into another office and was gone for some ten minutes, then came quietly back into the room. Xander had no communication from God by the time his curiosity distracted him.

Off the phone, Grandfather waited for Mrs. Qubadi's and Haroon's prayers to end, then he said, "We've got a fight on our hands, Nazneen. I won't kid you. This is going to be tough. But here's what I think. Let me know if any of this doesn't sound right to you."

Mrs. Qubadi said, "Let us plan for Nasdar's freedom."

He nodded. "We put what we have for today in the edition that people get on their doorstep tomorrow. James has already alerted the rest of the editors for our newspapers in the Midwest and the east coast that we are going to hit this story and others like it very seriously."

She nodded.

Grandpa smiled. "Now for that hard part, Nazneen. I've asked my sister Justine to help out regularly at your restaurant. She has recruited two of her friends as substitute waitresses. If the women from your mosque can also help, I hope you can keep an income flow until we have Nasdar returned to you."

Through tears, she chuckled. "Justine did a fine job the other day. I thank her."

Xander smiled. He knew Aunt Justine – as undiplomatic a waitress as you could find.

"And," said Grandpa, "The mother of Tekla is recruiting soccer moms to help make the afternoon snacks. That seems to be a great community builder and should give you some cushion in your income."

Mrs. Qubadi nodded.

Xander stared at his grandfather. He'd really been busy in the last minutes. No old-man-thinking going on in his head right now.

"Also," Grandpa said, "since the boys are suspended from school, I would like to hire them to do a lot of research. Haroon has a good start with this afternoon's reading. And Xander has a list of necessary contacts."

"What will we research?" Xander burst in.

Grandpa said, "The government claims Nasdar Qubadi sent money to support terrorists. He sent it through his family mosque. We're going to chase that money down and find out who has it and why. We have a reporter headed for the hometown of Haroon's grandmother in the Kurdish area of Iran, and another reporter visiting the Barzani and Harmota area, the present family home in Iraq. We'll start with what they can find out, and go from there."

Haroon seemed perplexed. "How can we follow money in a place like Iraq?"

"Good question, Haroon. If this is okay with your mother . . ." Grandpa glanced at Mrs. Qubadi. "I need you to collect any letters you've had from your husband's mother, Grandma Qubadi. We especially need letters where she talks about receiving the money, and what was purchased with it."

Mrs. Qubadi thought about this a moment. Then she said, "Yes, I have such letters. But it is Nasdar's Uncle Bijar. He is the one who picks up the money and does the shopping for the whole family, even the whole community – he and my Gamal."

"Do you have letters from them? Maybe you can telephone Bijar. Does he give information about the uses of the money? Can you ask him more about the money system?"

She glanced at the floor then over toward Haroon. Finally she said, "Bijar does not like me because I encouraged Nasdar to come to this country. And there is very little phone service in that area. But Bijar will answer a letter from Haroon – Haroon is a man."

*   *

Two hours later, Mike and James had talked to the reporters for *Evans* publications who were located in Iraq. Haroon and Xander typed up the two men's notes from these phone calls. They pieced together the picture of whole communities without any kind of reliable postal service since the U.S. invasion began to fall apart back in May of 2003. Most of those communities used the local mosque, or the churches and synagogues for the delivery of goods and gifts from family in other parts of the world, or even from other parts of Iraq.

Meanwhile, one of the women reporters in Portland interviewed the Eisenhower School secretary, Mrs. Palmquist, about her involvement with Haroon's arrest.

James Wray began working his connections in the prosecutor's office. Mike Halverson took his football player body and his friendly good humor down to the police department to see what anybody could tell him about why Sergeant Bailey may have wanted to arrest Mr. Qubadi.

Haroon wrote to his Uncle Bijar.

When Haroon left to take his letter to the senior imam at the family mosque, Xander took a moment to stretch. From the office window, Xander saw Haroon walk toward the bus stop.

Across the street from the newspaper office, a man stood up from his seat on the park bench. He folded his newspaper, raised it like a flag and waved it toward a men's clothing store.

A second man came out of the store. Both of them followed Haroon to the corner bus stop. They boarded the bus behind Haroon.

Haroon didn't seem to be aware of either man.

"Grandpa, someone is following Haroon. Can you take me to the mosque in your car?"

"How do you . . .?"

"Two guys, actually. One from the park bench signaled the other in the suit store window. They both got on the bus."

Grandpa leaned over his desk phone and punched a button. "Rick, Haroon is being followed. Send someone to meet the bus at the Husayn Mosque in south west Portland. And please get George to pull one of the Subarus into the delivery tunnel. I want to make a trip after that bus and to the mosque on the quiet."

When Grandpa hung up, Xander said, "Subaru? I didn't know you had a Subaru."

Grandpa grabbed up his coat. "It's one of the cars that belong to any reporter who needs transportation. All green Outback Subarus, the most common color of the most common car in Portland, Oregon. Let's hustle."

CHAPTER NINETEEN

Grandpa drove the Green Subaru up the hill in western Portland toward the Husayn Mosque. They followed an old Chevrolet truck, spewing black fog. Through the fog, Xander saw the bus. He also saw Haroon's face in the bus's back window. Haroon looked at Xander and pointed toward the truck. Then, he turned around and stood up.

"He's figured out the truck is also following the bus," Grandpa said. "It hasn't tried to get around the bus, or pass it."

Xander pulled out his cell phone. "I'm calling him."

"Tell him to get out two blocks short of the mosque and run toward the front of the bus. We'll pick him up there, where the truck can't see him."

As he said that, Grandpa passed the truck and the bus.

At that moment, Haroon answered his cell phone. "'Sup?" he asked.

"Don't look around," Xander said. "Two men followed you onto the bus."

"I'm good at math. My homework is all done," Haroon said.

Xander stared at the phone, then decided Haroon was talking in code. "So you saw them? and the truck?"

"Yeah. My homework is right here with me."

"So, Math Man, we just passed your bus. Get out two blocks before the mosque and run toward the bus front so we can pick you up. We're in a green Subaru, license ORE 670, and we can see the bus right now in our rearview mirror."

"How am I going to turn my homework in?"

"We'll have to do it after we ditch your side-kicks."

"I'll be there," Haroon said.

Two minutes later, Grandpa drove across the street in front of the bus and parked as the bus pulled to the corner at Haroon's stop. Haroon jumped down from the front of the bus. He ran forward. Xander saw the two men push each other out the back door of the bus.

As Haroon climbed into the back seat of the Subaru, the blue Chevrolet truck tried to pass the bus, but the bus pulled away from the curb. The truck brakes screeched. Grandpa lurched way ahead of the bus through another block and through a yellow light, driving on down the street.

"The truck has license number GZZ 059," Haroon said.

Behind them, the two men flagged the truck over and climbed into the back of it.

Grandpa cruised a couple of blocks and then whipped around a corner. When the bus pulled again toward a corner for a passenger, they heard the truck gun its motor to pass the bus. Grandpa gunned the Subaru up into a very steep driveway. As soon as he reached the flat part of the driveway, he turned off the motor.

"Get down in the seat, boys," he said as he slumped below the steering wheel.

"What if the owners of this driveway are home?" Xander asked. He hunkered on the floor.

"I'll tell them the fog truth."

"Fog truth?" Haroon asked.

"Yeah, we made a mistake." Grandpa reached up to adjust his rearview mirror.

"That's pretty vague. You learn to tell that kind of truth working at a newspaper?" Xander asked.

Grandpa chuckled. "Nope. Learned it interviewing people who don't want to answer your questions. Fog facts and folksy stories divert attention from important facts." Grandpa stared upwards into his rear view mirror. "There goes the blue Chev truck."

"Okay," Haroon said. "I'll go into the mosque now."

"No," Grandpa said. "He won't give up that easily. Yes, sir! He's turned around, driving slower, studying the parked cars."

The truck driver seemed certain he had lost them in this block. Grandpa reported that the truck went by several times, but the driver never seemed to look up the steep driveway.

They waited until the truck hadn't returned in fifteen minutes. Next Xander, who might not be recognized by the men, plunked his grandfather's old Beaver Baseball hat on his head, got out and walked to the front yard. He saw no Chevy truck.

From there, he ambled clear around the block and found no Chevy. However, when he walked close to Masjid Husayn, the Husayn Mosque, hoping to deliver Haroon's letter, he saw the blue truck parked across the street. So, he wandered back into the neighborhood and Grandpa's car. They decided to go home and try to deliver the letter to the mosque another way.

Barely a moment after they backed out of the driveway, a tan sedan slowed behind them, then turned into the driveway where they had sat for twenty-five minutes.

"Phew," Haroon said. "Nearly had a very surprised guy, there."

Xander glanced at Grandpa and saw his jaw working overtime.

"Haroon," Grandpa said, "could you call the mosque? We'll have to work out another delivery method, and remember, their phone is probably tapped."

* *

As Xander set the tables for the Taziyan's evening crowd, Mr. Breiton walked into the dining room. Xander straightened from his job, glanced around and was glad to see that Haroon still worked with his mother in the kitchen.

"May I help you, sir?" he said to Mr. Breiton.

"Sure. You can tell your mother that I'm here, young man."

Mr. Breiton still didn't know what Haroon looked like. He saw Xander's tan skin and dark hair and made assumptions.

"Sir, she is preparing a large dinner menu and can't be disturbed at this time of day."

"Large? I doubt it. You'd better go get her. I've got an offer she needs to pay attention to."

"How about if you come back in the morning. That would be much more convenient."

Mr. Breiton moved toward the kitchen. "You're not helping her by this obstructive behavior, young man. I'll get her myself."

At that moment, Nazneen pushed through the swinging doorway, faced Mr. Breiton and said, "I have told you not to come here trying to do business."

"I have a new offer."

"Mr. Breiton, we are not in need of your offer. We are not selling, and I don't want to have to tell you that again."

"I hear your husband is not going to be here to help you out and protect you."

"You hear that? When?"

"A military tribunal? He's going to be deported anytime now, and probably you and the boy here with him. You might as well sell while you are here to make any money out of this old place."

"Who told you he might be deported?"

"That's what they do with enemy combatants. You can't sell from Guantanamo."

Xander strode to face Mr. Breiton. "Get out."

"Sonny boy, you got no leg to stand on. You don't own this place. Your mother may not even be able to sell it. That's a man's job, and God knows your daddy's in no . . .

Xander moved toward Mr. Breiton. "Get out or I'll call security." The man backed up.

"Security?" he said, "That's a laugh."

Xander moved closer. "Laugh in your car on the way out."

"We'll see what the judge has to say about you foreigners threatening me."

"For the record, I am not her son. You are dealing with white folks when you deal with me, so if I pop you in the gut, it will be hard to accuse me of treason."

Mr. Breiton glared. His eyes went from Nazneen to Xander to Nazneen. "But he's so . . ."

"Sun tan," Nazneen said. "It wears off in winter."

"You'll be hearing from my lawyer." Breiton said as he moved out the door.

Once his car left the parking lot, Haroon came out the kitchen door. "Dealing with white folks, eh?"

Nazneen laughed. "Call security? How did that one get in your head?"

"I think you'll need security around here," Xander said. "Let's talk to Rick Johnson about this guy."

"Security is expensive," Haroon said. "How about a big guy who gets paid to wait tables and bounce Breiton out the door?"

Nazneen said, "Did you notice that he already knows about the military tribunal? I wonder who gave him that information."

* *

That night, the Imam Faisal brought his family to dinner at the restaurant. After dinner, he stepped into the kitchen to talk to Nazneen Qubadi. He glanced at Xander and Haroon.

"They are my boys," she said.

He nodded and reached out to take the letter Haroon had written to Uncle Bijar.

"You're taking a big chance for Nasdar," Mrs. Qubadi said to Imam Faisal. "Homeland Security recently froze the assets of Al Haramain Foundation in Southern Oregon."

"I don't understand that," he said. "Al Haramain has always protected the poor."

Nazneen shrugged. "The idea the Justice Department people are selling is simple-minded. They claim that when the foundation sent money to help Muslim refugees in Chechnya, they freed up money for Chechnyan mujahedeen to spend on terrorism instead of philanthropy."

Nazneen gazed at the young man, as if she were his mother, leveling a shot of reality toward him. "We already know they are following your people, listening to your telephone calls."

He nodded as he tucked the letter into his jacket pocket. "We must help each other until the sellers of lies and fear, and their dog pack will no longer allow us that freedom."

"And after they use their logic on us and on you?" she asked.

"We have to pray that most U.S. citizens understand the difference between those of us who help the poor and those who are terrorists."

"Hmph!" she said, her angry eyes glittering with frustration. "It took the United States fifty years to apologize to the Japanese-Americans they put into concentration camps. And others, some accused of being Communists, they died in foreign lands – deported for nothing but American alarm."

"God is great and merciful," Imam Faisal said to her.

Nazneen Qubadi gazed up at the ceiling. "God is great," she said, "but sometimes very slow."

* *

One afternoon, as the boys filed papers in the news library stacks, the phone in the Max Million Foundation library rang. Mike Halverson lifted the receiver, listened to the caller for a moment and then said, "I need to put you on hold while I bring the phone to him."

Mr. Halverson said, "I think you boys will want to hear this conversation. Come on into your grandpa's office"

They glanced at each other – both afraid of what news might be coming. But they followed Mr. Halverson.

Once in the office, Mr. Halverson said, "Gib, that lady has called again."

"Aha!" Grandpa Gilbert glanced at Haroon and said, "Put her on speaker phone." He lifted a quieting finger to his mouth and then took the phone.

As soon he heard it, Xander knew the voice on the speaker, and he could see that Haroon knew it as well – Mrs. Palmquist, the school secretary who had called the police on Haroon. They'd nearly forgotten about her, her son Rob, and his bully crowd.

On the phone, she said, "Mr. Evans, Alexander can come back to the school on a probationary basis." Mrs. Palmquist seemed to be reading from a script. "He will need to check in with Mr. Talon early tomorrow morning and be willing to come to an after-school class in anger management."

Grandpa raised his eyebrows at the boys. He asked her, "And Haroon Qubadi?"

"He remains suspended until a review of his situation."

"And when will that review take place?"

"That is the business of that Qubadi family, Mr. Evans."

Mr. Halverson put his hand on Haroon's shoulder. The pressure seemed to help Haroon remain calm. Xander's grandpa glowered into space, where he appeared to imagine Mrs. Palmquist's face.

Grandpa asked her, "And what does Mr. Klein say about these suspensions?"

"Mr. Talon is handling all discipline cases at this school."

Grandpa's eyebrows raised toward Mike at that statement. Then he asked the secretary, "And what class will you be attending after school, Mrs. Palmquist?"

A moment of crackling silence in the phone line followed.

"Whatever do you mean, Mr. Evans?"

"A class in dramatic exaggeration, perhaps? A discussion of ethics? What do you think would most help you?"

After another silence, she spoke. "Mr. Evans, have your son here at eight in the morning."

"He will not be returning to school," Grandpa said. "He will be studying at a private school with his friend, Haroon Qubadi."

Grandpa hung up the phone.

"What private school?" Xander's voice cracked on the question. He didn't want to be sent away from his grandfather, away from his friends on the research team, or away from his bed in the room that used to be his mother's.

"You'll be attending the school of business, governmental relations and historical research called The Max Million Foundation for Justice. Mrs. Qubadi and I have worked that out with Principal Klein and the State Department of Education."

Xander let out a relieved sigh.

Haroon raised his fists. "Let's do this thing!" he said.

Mr. Halverson grinned and took the phone from Grandpa. "Okay, guys, let's get rolling." Then Mr. Halverson turned to Grandpa. "A conversation with Mr. Klein is coming, I think."

"Yes, it is. He needs to know what is going on behind his back, and the boys will want to graduate with their class next year. But while Nasdar is held, I still want the boys to go to school as we planned, right here"

*   *

Back at the library, Xander was about to plunk himself down at the table where he usually worked.

"Gentlemen," James Wray said.

Surprised, the boys turned to look at him. He stood in the library doorway. "Follow me".

"Another phone call?" Haroon's voice shook.

"Nope," Mr. Wray said, and started down the hall. So, they followed again.

Mr. Wray opened a door and showed them into his office. The whole room had been rearranged so that it held Mr. Wray's desk and computer on one side. On the other side of the room stood several filled book cases. Beside the book cases sat two oak desks, side-by side, with new computers on them.

"Your office," Mr. Wray said. "Mine and yours."

"Really?" Haroon managed.

"Gee!" Xander said.

"And, if anybody asks, I am your teacher at your private school."

Haroon's eyes were on those computers. "What are we going to learn?"

"Besides the homework Mr. Findlay brings you, we are going to learn to follow the money," Mr. Wray said. "Follow the money your dad sent to your grandmother and uncles. And we follow the money of the ones who want to get rid of him."

"Who?" Haroon asked.

"Who stands to benefit by having him in jail?"

The boys stared at each other.

"No ideas?" Mr. Wray said.

Xander felt as empty as the computer screen on his desk.

"How can we figure out who?" Haroon asked.

"We'll take one step at a time," Mr. Wray said.

CHAPTER TWENTY

The next day, the boys arrived by bike in the *Journal of the Americas* news delivery tunnel. In the tunnel sat two trucks. Xander and Haroon parked their bikes beside tall stacks of baled newspaper, locking them up, out of the way of the delivery trucks returning from the morning routes. Men in black t-shirts decorated with the *Journal of the Americas* logo, worked to get deliveries hustled in and out of the tunnel.

One big fellow hauled undelivered morning newspapers off the trucks. He cut their baling strings with a box cutter and tossed the papers in a recycle bin. Another man hoisted rope-tied bundles of freshly printed newspapers onto wooden pallets using a baling hook that looked like a scimitar. A third, very wiry fellow, drove the forklift up to the wooden pallets of the afternoon edition, lifted those pallets and whipped them over to the back of a newly emptied truck.

"Hey," Xander called. "Bike's okay over there?"

"Yup," said the guy with the box cutter.

Xander said. "That's a hefty afternoon edition, William."

Another of the guys waved his baling hook and nodded. "Adverts," he explained. "Lots of sales down at the old Meier and Franks."

Xander laughed and waved.

Inside the door, the boys passed the main security desk. Xander glanced at the screens beside Mr. Johnson. One camera showed William still driving the forklift back and forth.

Mr. Johnson said, "Boys, you oughta come in the front. The tunnel is dangerous when there's traffic."

"We parked our bikes in there, Mr. Johnson," Xander said.

Mr. Johnson frowned, then said, "How about next time you just bring the bikes on in here and park 'em behind my desk, or . . ." he glanced up with a mischievous look in his eye, "how about up in your grandpa's office?"

"Or Grandpa's private bathroom," Xander said.

"Geez," Johnson laughed. "Wouldn't want to slow an old man down when he's got business."

Upstairs, after researching the details about postal service in all of Iraq, and the use of mosques and churches as delivery systems, Xander and Haroon turned over their facts to James Wray.

Next, Xander and Haroon read a reporter's interviews with Mrs. Palmquist, the school secretary who had accused Haroon. Apparently Mrs. Palmquist didn't care who knew she hated Muslims in her 'Christian' country. She even said, "Evidence? What better evidence? The one kid has a broken hand and the other kid is an illegal foreigner."

The reporter made it very clear to Mrs. Palmquist that Haroon and his parents had been citizens for twelve years. In response, the secretary claimed, "I been here all my life. Now that's a citizen."

Xander could only shake his head. "What rock hatched her?"

Haroon shrugged, "She's like a lot of people, Xan. We look different, act different, so she's afraid of us. And remember her grief..."

A second news story by Mike Halverson told how making terrorism arrests earned rewards in locker-room betting among one cadre of about five policemen at the local police station. Facts and successful prosecution had nothing to do with winning or losing the bet. These same five policemen also bet on how many driving tickets they could hand out to Asians and Mexicans.

Other policemen were angry that those five were still in the force, but the quoted police had asked to remain anonymous. They were afraid their union would fight to keep the police on board even though they were an embarrassment – more power for the union.

"How did you get anybody at the police station to talk about that?" Xander asked Mr. Halverson.

"When thoughtful policemen discover the city council, their union and their bosses ignore these problems, they search for someone to talk to," Mr. Halverson said. "I make sure to be there and to listen."

"When are these stories going in the paper?" Haroon asked him.

"Tomorrow," Mr. Wray said. "Front of the *Around Portland* section. Right next to each other. And from our other newspapers, we're discovering that Nasdar is not alone in this problem. Neither is his mosque. Take a look at this article, boys."

Xander read out loud. "Washington Law Centre's Don Calley, a widely respected constitutional scholar, sees a correlation between the McCarthy witch-hunts of the 1950s and the government's current policies. Calley said, "In the 1950s, HUAC and the McCarthy committee decided certain organizations were Communist fronts – no proof needed. Today, it is a crime to support an individual or organization on a terror watch list. Our government can designate and freeze assets without proof of any actual ties to terrorism or, indeed, to any illegal acts."

James Wray said, "See, gentlemen, the U.S. Justice department seems to have decided that anyone who helps the poor in any Muslim country must be supporting terrorism."

"What if some of these people really are supporting terrorists?" Haroon asked.

"Then," Mr. Wray said, "the prosecutors should have to charge them and prove the case, as with any other kind of accusation."

*   *

At lunch time in the news cafeteria, Haroon put his sandwich down and leaned closer to Xander. He glanced around to make sure they weren't being listened to. "Xan, that spy I told you about in our mosque . . ."

"Yeah. The one who talks to Agent Saurus."

"I bet there is one in your Friends Meeting, too."

Xander backed up in surprise. "What makes you think that?"

We know from all kinds of reports that since nine-eleven the FBI is planting informants in other organizations all around the country, places where people just disagree with government policy"

"Like where?"

"Well, like at the mosque near the cemetery, Masjid Maryam, and other mosques – just like at ours. And there are spies in non-Muslim organizations, those organizations that argue against the war on terror."

Xander raised his eyebrows and signaled with a roll of his fingers for Haroon to reel out his evidence.

Haroon put his sandwich on his tray. "Recently, they planted someone pretty obvious to record who goes in and out of the Thomas Merton Center for Social Justice in Pittsburgh."

"Pittsburgh? How do you hear about this stuff?"

Haroon gestured phone and keyboarding. "By pony express . . . what do you think?"

"Okay, okay, the imam's share news."

"Not just the imams. There is a network of social justice and religious groups that protest the actions of the government since Nine-eleven."

"Okay, where else are there FBI informants that you know of?"

"In New York City, following around the family of a missing para-medic who happens to be Muslim."

"Missing since when?"

"Since the attacks on the World Trade Center."

"Wow. They think he had something to do with those attacks?"

"Homeland Security and the FBI are so messed up, they *hope* he had something to do with the attacks."

Xander's breathing slowed. He imagined how it would feel to have your father, your son, your friend go missing on such a day? He knew what that would be like – too well.

"Who else are they spying on?"

"In Greenpeace, in Catholic Workers, among you Quaker types – watch out for them at East Side Monthly Meeting, and for sure at Friends World Service meetings."

Xander thought of all the Quakes who'd come to his parent's funeral service – all long-time members, a complete Birkenstock and funky-shirt crowd of dedicated peaceables and their children. "Roon, you're imagining stuff."

"Hell, no. They show up in all kinds of peace rally planning meetings – they've got informants stuck even in PETA, People for the Ethical Treatment of Animals, for Pete's sake."

"Can you imagine how boring a detail that must be for a would-be spy?"

"Exactly. If they are spending money and time on animal rights groups, you've got to believe the FBI is pushing informants into mosques, and on Peacenik Quakers, too."

Xander took a deep breath. He didn't like the sound of this. Either his friend had gone bonkers, or the FBI had tipped over the edge.

* *

In the late afternoon, Xander and Haroon finished all the day's research and homework. They headed down the elevator toward the bikes, hoping to get to the Qubadi's restaurant to help sell snacks. As Xander passed the security desk, he glanced at the monitors. The tunnel monitor showed only the nose of a truck.

He said hello to Mr. Johnson and glanced at the man's name badge once more. "Mr. Johnson," he said. "You been friends with my Grandpa a long time, haven't you?"

Mr. Johnson nodded. "A long time. Since even before I became the goalie for the high school soccer team."

"Did you play football, too?"

Your grandpa telling you about the old days, eh?"

"Yeah."

"Well, I didn't play football so much. Not after eighth grade. But my little brother, he was front line, state high school champs."

"Kenny?"

Mr. Johnson glanced quickly at Xander. "Ol' Kenny," he said. "He died in 'Nam."

"I'm sorry. You must miss him a lot."

"I do, kid. I surely do."

As he left the news building, Xander thought again about Mohammed and Manzur. He missed them down deep. He was afraid all the boys and teachers had died in the basement of the school and no one would tell him what happened.

Well, he'd asked for that kind of treatment by taking Grandma's pills.

Exiting into the tunnel, Xander walked around the truck he'd seen on the monitor. It was parked at a funny angle. He looked around for any of the delivery guys that he might know. There were only three fellows now wearing the logo shirt of the *Journal of the Americas*. They weren't delivery people he'd met before. He and Haroon headed for the bikes.

As they turned the corner around the back of the truck, Haroon grabbed Xander's arm.

"Our bike wheels are gone," he said.

In the moment while he stared at the empty wheel spaces, Xander realized they were isolated from the rest of the tunnel by the truck – a blue Chevrolet truck. He glanced up and saw the three delivery guys coming toward them. In one man's hand was the scimitar-like baling hook. The other two held box cutters.

CHAPTER TWENTY-ONE

Xander glanced at Haroon. "Run to the news stacks," he whispered. They charged away from the three men, running down the tunnel toward bundles of evening news. The phalanx of three men reformed and strode toward them with menacing steps. Their slow wheeling around seemed eerily robotic.

"Might as well give up, boys," one of the men said. "Nobody coming down here for another hour."

So, thought Xander, they planted the truck in front of the camera and have time to close the trap.

Stepping behind a stack of news bundles in search of a protective wall, Xander nearly tripped over the unconscious and trussed body of this morning's forklift driver.

The man's *Journal of the Americas* shirt had been stripped off. Lying on the floor near the man's chest, Xander saw something shiny. A key. He glanced back at the three men, fast advancing. He lifted the key and pinched it between his first and second fingers, holding the jabbing end out.

"Give me that," Haroon whispered. Xander knew Haroon had an idea, so he handed the key over and groped for another weapon. Haroon ran farther down the tunnel between pallets of evening edition.

Xander turned to face the men – one guy must have weighed over three hundred pounds. Beyond the fellow's beer belly, Xander saw strong arms and mean eyes. That man stepped slowly toward Xander, hefting the curved baling hook. He said, "You gotta go, Baal worshiper. Hittite lover."

Xander's arm hairs prickled. The man spouted a familiar and deadly idea.

To the left of the fat fellow, a scrawny, blond man, narrowed his gaze. He raised a box cutter in one hand and a pocket knife in the other. The knife's long blade suddenly flicked out.

Xan had heard about that old kind of knife from Grandpa. Out of style or not, the thing looked deadly thin and sharp.

The third man, shifted his attention farther down the tunnel, seeming to follow Haroon's movements. The man tugged at the blue scarf that covered his head and glanced back at Xander.

Haroon still ran between news stacks and toward a silent machine. Out of the corner of his vision, Xander saw Haroon jump onto the forklift and poke the found key into the ignition. The motor sputtered. The forklift jerked forward and then stopped.

The flag-scarf man took off toward Haroon.

"Gear shift," Xander shouted.

The forklift motor came to life before the bald man reached it.

At that moment, Xander grabbed taut bale-wrapping rope, lifted the nearest bale of newspapers a half-inch off the stack and heaved it at the oncoming men. He might as well have been throwing a lead barbell. The paper bale thudded to the concrete in front of him. The thin, switchblade man laughed and rushed toward Xander. Xander lifted a second, smaller bale and swung it toward the man's face.

"Ooof!" The scrawny man went down in a collapse of rubbery legs and a flutter of dirty hair. Xander dropped the bale on the man's chest, grabbed up the man's box cutter, kicked away his switchblade, and turned to face the fat man, the one with the baling hook.

Nearby, Xander heard Haroon's forklift jerk forward.

The fat man faced Xander, but let his eyes shift right toward Haroon, then return to Xander's face, a glint of malicious joy in them.

"You gonna be gutted, Jew boy," the man whispered.

Jew boy?

"Wrong," Xander whispered back and circled to keep the hook aimed toward him, and the man's attention away from Haroon.

"Arab loving Devil," the man hissed.

Xander remembered the lady's voice – the hate spewing Pastor Gotamere.

"That military tribunal is going deport all of you anytime now. You and your brother."

Xander stared at the man. He made the same mistake Breiton made, and had the same message. No one outside the court and the defense team was supposed to know about the threat of the tribunal. Someone had talked beyond Judge Smith's courtroom.

Xander knew from the man's glazed eyes that, for this guy, things didn't have to make sense, they just had to be killed. Xander moved again. Over the man's ugly hook and beyond the guy's shoulder, Xander saw that Haroon had the front end of the forklift going up and down as he surged forward. The third man grabbed the forklift frame and reached for Haroon. His head scarf flew off, revealing a shaved head.

Xander jerked his attention to the eyes of the hook man. The hook swung from right to left, but the man's gaze never wavered, so Xander figured the man would come at him straight. Xander used both hands to hold the box cutter in front of him.

Power, he thought. Give me power.

Beyond Xander's big man, Haroon hung onto the right frame of the moving forklift and fought off the man who hung onto the left frame. The forklift moved wildly forward. Xander knew somebody's foot was on the power pedal. He just didn't know whose.

Directly in front of him, five feet away, fat man's hook stopped swinging. Xander braced for a rush.

The man's eyes shifted to Xander's shirtfront. At the moment of the hook's forward thrust, Xander tucked and rolled toward the man, slashing at his right leg with the box cutter. As the man screamed, his left boot kicked Xander in the head. The hook scraped through Xander's scalp, and back into the air above his head. Blood filled Xander's right eye as he finished his painful roll. He lost track of the hook and the man, but shoved to his feet and jump-turned toward where the man had been.

No one stood there.

In his quick, blind turn, Xander nearly tripped over his dropped bale of news and the inert body of the blond man. Xander whirled to the right and found the fat man standing beside the stacks, now holding the switchblade knife as well as the hook.

Behind his own back, Xander heard the forklift gun into high speed. The fat man stared beyond Xander at Haroon, and grinned. Xander jumped to the man's right. The fellow turned to follow him, and jabbed at him with the switchblade, just missing his forearm. The fellow pulled back his arm to deliver another stab, but Xander leaped onto the stacks of news bales. Scrambling upwards, he sprawled onto the top of the bales, but the man slashed into Xander's calf. At that moment, the forklift bashed the fat man into the bales just below where Xander lay.

Xander heard the hook clatter to the concrete floor. The mean eyes stared at Xander in disbelief. Xander brought his empty fist down on the top of the man's head. The eyes went slack and the man collapsed.

Haroon and the bald man hung onto the lift as it backed away from the man. Haroon jabbed a push broom into the face of his attacker while the two fought over the controls of the runaway lift.

Xander jumped down, ran around the fallen fat man, and toward the forklift. He dove at the legs of the bald man, pulling him off the machine. They tangled on the hard floor. Beyond them, the forklift came to a sudden halt, rammed into the blue truck. In a moment, Haroon was above Xander, whacking the bald man with the broom handle.

The man's legs went limp. Xander collapsed, drained, and blinded by blood.

"Any more of them?" he asked Haroon.

"Nope. But two of the guys that work down here are on the floor behind the bales. I'm dialing 9-1-1 for them, and for you."

"But you gotta disappear before they arrive. They'll arrest you, again."

"You're a bloody mess. I'm not leaving you."

Wiping his right eye, Xander realized the blood came from his head gash, not his eye.

"Just a graze." He failed to sound tough.

"More like a permanent part in your hair," Haroon said, holding his shirt tail against the wound to stop the bleeding.

Mr. Johnson's voice came from the doorway. "Good God!" He ran toward them, directing others. "Tie those three hooligans up with baling ropes. I don't care how out of it they seem, just tie them up – the police will bring handcuffs later."

"I found the boys," Mr. Wray shouted. "Xander, you lie still. Haroon sit down before you fall down." Mr. Wray took over checking out Xander's head wound.

"Cut his left leg, too," Haroon said. His voice faded, as if talking had suddenly drained him.

"Lord God A'mighty," Mr. Wray said as he lifted Xander's blood soaked pant leg. "That's a deep one."

"Where's Mr. Breiton?" Xander whispered.

"Why?"

"The big man talked like him, and Breiton's been in the Taziyan again."

"To buy the place?"

"To threaten with a Military Tribunal."

"Halverson," Mr. Wray called, "see what Everett Breiton might have had to do with this."

Mr. Wray used Haroon's shirt to tie off the flow of blood to Xander's leg.

Xander heard someone clicking what seemed to be a camera. "Got to get photos of this before the police come and call the place off limits," Mr. Johnson said. A moment later Mr. Johnson said, "Well, this one – sheez! Where's his pulse?"

Next, Xander heard his grandfather's voice "What the hell? Where's William and the guys?"

"Found 'em bound and drugged, but alive. Over here," Mr. Halverson said.

Then Mr. Johnson said, "I heard the forklift going nuts and nothing but the nose of their truck showed on my monitor. Xander and Haroon took these three gangsters out before I got out here."

"My God," Grandpa whispered. "Xander, blood . . ."

"I already called 9-1-1-," Haroon said.

As Grandpa sank to his knees next to him, Xander remembered the feeling of losing consciousness from that last day in Pakistan – the lethargy, the slow invasion of gray visions, the crescendo of sounds from things he couldn't see. As he lay on the cold floor, he thought he heard Mr. Din say, "So sorry."

And at last, he let go and cried about Mohammed, Manzur and all the little boys who were lost in Pakistan.

CHAPTER TWENTY-TWO

That late afternoon, for the second time in ten days, Xander watched Doc Adam Whitney work on his hand. First the break from hitting his locker, now the break from hitting a guy who wanted to kill him. He let himself remember better days, Mohammed's slight face, his smile of mischief.

Xander blinked hard. A few moments ago, he'd been drugged up so Doc could stitch the baling-hook cut on his scalp and the switchblade cut on his calf. In the mirror across from the exam table, fifteen spots of black thread showed in a shaved path down one side of his head.

Looking good, Xander thought through a haze of painkiller. Dye what's left of my hair black, and shove on a gold nose ring.

He glanced back at his hand, the one that hit the fat man's head. He found it hard to connect that swollen lump with his body. It didn't hurt. Yet.

But his leg had started throbbing minutes ago. He grew certain that when brain-fog cleared away there would be plenty of pain. He sat on the exam table mesmerized by his leg bandage, his good hand gripping the examination table.

"Now, young man," Doctor Whitney said, "Let's be done with fighting, eh?"

Xander glanced up to study Doc's face. "You think I like fighting?"

Doc Whitney raised his thick, dark eyebrows. "How about running away from a fight?"

"Doc, the tunnel doors were closed. We were trapped."

"Back inside the building?"

"Not an option. Are you thinking I started this?"

"Second time I've had to fix this hand. And that first break was a long way from healed."

"That first time, I hit my own locker, not somebody else's head."

"And this time?"

Xander sighed. "I don't look for fights against three middle-aged ex-football players carrying box cutters and baling hooks'

Doctor Whitney's eyebrows did their rising dance again. "Three adults? And weapons? That's not what it says here."

He grabbed a piece of yellow paper off of his desk and thrust it toward Xander.

In a scrawling hand, the police report said, "Youth fight in downtown parking area."

Lies, Xander thought. Next he thought, *They've arrested Haroon again.*

Xander jumped from the exam table, wrenched open the door and called out into the waiting room, "Grandpa, where's Haroon?"

Dizziness swamped him. Doc Whitney's arm grabbed him around his waist and saved him from collapse. As the doctor hoisted his butt back onto the exam table, Xander heard Grandpa's and Haroon's voices. He slumped with relief onto the table.

"What gives, Adam?" Grandpa's tense voice and body burst into the room.

"Look at this police report." Doc said.

Haroon appeared next to Xander, frowning down at him, and holding up his own bandaged hand. He whispered, "Blisters from the hot forklift engine."

"I'll be damned," Grandpa said, waving the yellow police report. "They better have those two in jail. Can I use my cell in here?"

"Yes, briefly," Doctor Whitney said. Grandpa flipped his phone open.

"James?" Grandpa said in his newspaperman's business voice, "I want you and Mike to make sure William, Phil and Josh are safe in the hospital, and that the two attackers who are still alive are in jail. This police report that came to the hospital claims that was a youth fight in a downtown parking area."

Silence followed, then Grandpa looked again at the yellow paper. "Yeah? It says it's preliminary. Find out what the final police report really says. We don't want these kids accused of murder."

At the word 'murder', Xander stiffened with fear.

"And James, what did Mike find from Everett Breiton?" Grandpa paused, listening, then said, "And the money to buy the Taz?" he nodded at the phone. "Yeah, but offered by whom?"

A moment later, Doctor Whitney spoke. "All right, fellows, I want both you young men into the hospital for observation."

"Hospital?" Grandpa asked, closing his phone. "They're fine to come home."

"Not until the Chief of Police can tell me their attackers are under lock and key."

"There's got to be a less expensive way to keep them safe."

"Maybe, but this is the way I've got to offer." Doc and Grandpa faced off like two dogs, then, after a moment, Grandpa nodded.

Grandpa's cell phone rang and he answered. "Yes? Oh, Chief, thanks. Which hospital? Okay, Chief, I want good officers outside all five of those rooms, and I mean good, not these guys that filed the form, or any of their buddies. Yes. Thank you, Ma'am."

Grandpa listened a moment. "Right, Officer Bailey and Sergeant Robb. The preliminary report copy is right here in Doctor Adam Whitney's office. You should have the original. I'm making several copies in case I need them."

Xander, flat on his back with his eyes closed, tried to imagine a 'ma'am' as chief of police, and he tried to imagine what she might be arguing with Grandpa about during the silences at this end.

Then Grandpa answered her. "I can't imagine that Officer Bailey thought he could get away with calling it a youth fight when the three attackers were clearly middle aged."

Grandpa finally answered, "I'll be glad to write what I saw. So will my Chief of Security, Rick Johnson."

The Chief's voice sounded like a buzz in the phone. Grandpa answered, "I'll have the victims dictate what happened as well. The 2006 Citizens' Review Board will also get copies."

She said something to that, but Grandpa said, "No, Ma'am, I insist on that. Plus, I want to see a copy of the final police report that this Officer Bailey comes up with."

She spoke, then Grandpa said, "You know where to send it? Good. I expect to see it within twenty-four hours."

Grandpa said goodbye to her, then clapped his cell phone closed.

Xander turned his head toward Grandpa's voice, but he found his energy nearly gone. "The delivery guys?" he asked.

Grandpa nodded. "They're being tested for internal injuries," he said. "Attackers and our delivery guys all in the same hospital, but guarded. Chief is checking on the guard detail. She says your attackers will be on their way to the city jail when they're released from the hospital."

Grandpa glanced at Haroon, "The worst case is the guy you rammed into the paper bales. He stabbed himself with that knife."

Haroon went pale. "He's dead?"

"You did not murder him," Xander said to Haroon. Even to himself, his whisper seemed full of dread.

But Grandpa's voice was firm. "And the state will know it was self-defense, if the Chief does her job right."

Xander said, "Besides, that fat guy cut my leg with that knife just before the forklift hit him. They were trying to kill both of us."

Grandpa nodded, then added, "Officer Bailey took the switchblade, so we hope the lab gets it intact – want DNA and fingerprint tests. But Officer Bailey clearly is not a man to trust. Mike promised he'll stand over all evidence of the fight that is still in the tunnel until the Chief comes to look at it personally and brings the proper crime investigation team."

Xander stared at his friend's freshly bandaged hand. "Isn't Officer Bailey the one who arrested you last week?"

Haroon nodded. "And he's the one who brought that FBI guy, Saurus, to our house last month."

Doc let out a whoosh of disgust. "What a botch."

"Boys," Grandpa's face grew more serious. "We have to be extremely careful now. It's no coincidence that Bailey was the first to come investigate the attack. Mike and James believe someone hired those three goons to get you because we're pursuing the evidence behind Nasdar's . . ." he looked at Haroon, "behind your dad's arrest."

"Let's be real public," Haroon suggested. "We write in the news about the attack and the things these guys said. Then people will see how crazy Dad's arrest is, too."

Xander sat up. His head swarmed with the buzz of bees. He leaned on his grandfather's shoulder and said. "The man with the hook called me a *Jew Boy*. Next, he called me an *Arab lover*."

Haroon said. "My dad's been railroaded, and now they want to get to him by killing us."

CHAPTER TWENTY-THREE

On Monday, both Grandpa and Xander were called to meet with the Chief of Portland Police for what was supposed to be one more interview. They waited together in a room at the city building. The Chief, a young blond lady walked in with a 'let's get this done' manner. Her lips were tight and her eyes angry. A man in a suit followed her.

Xander leaned over to Grandpa and whispered, "Saurus, the man who arrested Haroon."

"Yes," Grandpa said.

"Mr. Evans," the police chief said, "this is Mr. Guy Saurus, of the FBI."

"Oh really," Grandpa said, "I thought when you worked with Officer Bailey, that you were a plain clothes police officer."

The chief's eyebrows rose. "Bailey?" she asked.

But Grandpa went on, "That's how Officer Bailey introduced you. Was he lying? Or just misinformed?"

"He must have been misinformed," Saurus said.

"You didn't correct his impression that day you first invaded the Qubadi home," Grandpa said.

The police chief turned on Mr. Saurus. "When were you two at the Qubadi home?"

"Oh, that was some time ago. We were just interviewing them. An early investigation."

"And why?"

"Agency business," Mr. Saurus said.

"Agency business has nothing to do with an officer of the Portland Police force unless you …"

"Oh, I'm very sorry, Chief. At the time, I didn't understand that the Portland is the one police force in the country not allowed to assist the FBI in collecting security data."

She glared at him. "Not allowed unless the Portland city mayor approves the reasons for each instance of data collecting. You knew that. You know that. And you will stop ignoring that."

"Yes, ma'am," Saurus said, but Xander could see he meant to ignore the ruling again as soon as he wanted to. And Xander felt certain Officer Bailey would enjoy doing the same.

"I believe your welcome in this building just wore out, Mr. Saurus," the chief said to him. "You may exit now, and I will show you the door myself." She took the man's elbow and steered him out. As they left, Mr. Saurus glanced over his shoulder at Grandpa and smiled.

Grandpa watched them go. When the police chief returned, she said, to Gilbert, "I believe you will be visited by Mr. Saurus soon. Might as well go home and make tea for him. But understand that he is not working with the police. I will deal with Officer Bailey."

* *

Mr. Saurus didn't come for tea, but they knew, from Mr. Liu and other brave neighbors, that he visited more and more small businesses and homes near the Taziyan and around Xander and Haroon's homes.

"What did Mr. Halverson learn about Mr. Breiton?" Xander asked Grandpa.

"He's going bankrupt, but has what he calls a group of investors who want him to buy the Taz."

"And we can't find out who the investors are?"

"Not until they actually invest."

*   *

Xander and Haroon stumbled through pain and worry during the days after the fight in the newspaper delivery tunnel. The death of the man in the tunnel made both of them sick, and frightened. Mr. Beryl Plinder had meant to kill Xander, but that didn't make his death easy to think about.

Mr. Rick Johnson would not let any of the Evans or Qubadi family travel without security. Rick Johnson no longer trusted the police or anyone else. The families became his special responsibility. So the Taziyan now had a security force named Joe Krieger, who waited tables and waited to bounce Breiton.

In the Evans' Media building, the Max Million Foundation Library was the most comfortable place, so even though it was in the Foundation section of the building, reporters often used the big oak table to lay out their research and work. Several days after the tunnel fight, Haroon and Xander used one end of the table to straighten papers for the defense team. At the other end of the table, Mr. Wray worked on an editorial while Mr. Halverson drew a cartoon about the war on terror. Suddenly Grandpa Gilbert shoved open the door to the library.

"How can Louis Lamb be so blind?" Grandpa shouted as he slammed a copy of the *National Courier* onto the table across from Mr. Wray and Mr. Halverson. Xander and Haroon both stopped sorting defense notes.

"Listen to this," Grandpa said to Halverson. "Lamb writes, 'We're in a war with terrorists. American security shouldn't be jeopardized by the need to get warrants so we can move into a terrorist's house and capture evidence before it gets flushed down the toilet.'"

Mr. Wray frowned, "But Louis Lamb . . .."

Without hearing him, Grandpa continued to rave. "Flushed down the toilet? It's the damned United States Constitution they're flushing down the toilet."

For the first time, he seemed to realize that Xander and Haroon were in the room.

"You boys get back to filing those papers," he said. "And I don't want to hear you quoting me."

After he stalked out of the room, Haroon glanced at Mr. Halverson. That old friend of Grandpa's was smiling. Then he turned serious, and said, "Actually, boys, you can quote all but the *damned* part. What Lamb is suggesting we do – what President Bush and too many members of Congress are doing to the Constitution – is wrong. We will regret it, all of us."

Haroon asked, "Why does Louis Lamb make Mr. Evans so angry?"

"Well, they used to be friends. Lamb's a pretty good news man," Mr. Wray said, "but he is deathly afraid of another terrorist attack in this country. He's so afraid he'll endorse anything that looks like safety. His attitude frustrates your grandpa."

"Make no mistake," Mr. Halverson said, "the attacks of September eleventh were deadly, ugly, and deeply frightening. Lots of good people disagree about what we should learn from that day. Your grandpa believes the attacks happened partly because we weren't listening to the desperation of the poor in many parts of the world. Lamb, on the other hand, believes we just weren't paying close attention to suspicious characters."

"Suspicious? Like my dad?" Haroon asked.

Mr. Halverson studied Haroon and then nodded his head. "To Lamb, your father is suspect."

"Because he's a Muslim?"

"No, because he sends money to a border town and has flown there, planned to fly there again."

Xander said, "But that's where his family lives."

"I agree that it's all circumstantial evidence," Mr. Halverson said, "but suspicious to many."

"We have to prove that it is innocent," Mr. Wray said.

"Isn't that backwards?" Xander asked.

"Ka-shew," Mr. Halverson said, and he held up a big drawing of a toilet bowl. Its flushing water, sucked down a document. The flourish of penmanship at the top of the drowning document announced it as the "Bill of Rights."

*   *

Early November grew cold. The first November Saturday morning, Haroon blew into Grandpa's house followed by a noisy wind, and a flurry of red and yellow leaves. Grandpa motioned Haroon's guard inside as well. Haroon's security guard moved inside and closed the door. He stood, uncomfortable and silent.

"Just in time for breakfast," Grandpa said as he turned over his spinach, tomato and cheese omelet.

Haroon stared at the omelet pan, and then around the newly clean kitchen. He glanced at Xander, but Grandpa answered his unspoken question.

"Since Xander came, I've taken up cooking, and the more folks I get to cook for, the better."

"Thanks," Haroon said. Then he held up a large stack of papers. "Mr. Findlay handed me two copies of more homework.

Xander eyed the thick stack. "You know, Mr. Findlay was in the teachers' lounge when I called your dad the day they arrested him. Mr.

Findlay had already called the mosque, and warned them to brace for a raid."

Haroon frowned. "He did warn them, but nobody has raided the mosque, or accused them of passing on Dad's money."

Xander pulled a third plate out of the dish cupboard for Haroon and a fourth for the taciturn bodyguard. He said. "The really big newspapers like the *National Courier* have stories about your mosque and how radical it is."

"Well, we do have this one imam – kind of a junior leader. He's pretty out there about how a few U.S. companies are making money off of the war, and how the U.S. is going to end up with all the oil in a scorched desert."

Xander said. "I've been to some radical services at the Monthly Meeting of Friends. They say God tells them to resist the war, not pay war taxes, support candidates who call for an end to war."

Grandpa held up his spatula, waving it at the boys. "I think you're on to something there, Xander." He slid an omelet onto Haroon's plate, moved toward Xander's plate and said, "I think I'll ask for a meeting with the leaders of Ecumenical Ministries. There may be some support for our Nasdar in that bunch."

Haroon said, "Mr. Evans, most church people probably enjoy the idea that a Muslim mosque got into trouble."

"My young friend, I think you've been hearing from the wrong church people – the ones who grab an audience by encouraging hate."

Xander said, "You mean people who listen to that preacher, Lori Gotamere? She's a viper, not a Christian."

Haroon shrugged, "Other Christians aren't paying for radio time, far as I can hear. So, people like Lori Gotamere seem to represent all Christians."

"True," grandpa said. "Is she famous because she sells hate or because she sells Christ?"

"Her version of Christ," Xander said. "I don't think Jesus would recognize himself."

Haroon took his plate of omelet to his guard. "Here, Mr. Wright. You've got to eat to keep up with me."

For the first time since coming in, the guard smiled. He took the plate from Haroon and said, "You ought to be a track star, Buddy."

*   *

Thanks to Mr. Findlay, Xander and Haroon did regular school homework every morning before breakfast. At the newspaper office, Mr. Wray taught them calculus, then gave writing assignments and research assignments. He showed them how to use an accounting program to keep track of the money Nasdar had sent to Uncle Bijar and Uncle Gamal. Uncle Bijar wrote Haroon regularly, telling what he could remember about the use of the money, but he didn't have Uncle Gamal to help him remember the details.

One afternoon, the boys watched The Lawrence Fafner Show. Fafner started his story. "The murder of a man in the news tunnel at Gilbert Evan's *Journal of the Americas* building has been kept hush-hush for too long."

Fafner said, "We've discovered that the son of Nasdar Qubadi is known to have been in the building at the time and involved in the fight that killed this man. We have to wonder why this young man has not been arrested along with his Muslim father."

Haroon slumped in his chair. "I was there. I must be the murderer."

"Fafner needs viewers," Xander said. "He's in the big business of selling outrage. Not everybody thinks like Fafner."

"You want to bet on the percentage that does?"

After that program, Haroon began using an old video tape system to copy television news reports concerning his father's arrest. By the next Friday, the defense-research team watched Haroon's video collection. The tone of most of the television news assumed Nasdar's guilt, and every report mentioned that Nasdar was Muslim.

Haroon said to Xander, "This is like the family in New York City."

"You mean the paramedic that is missing?"

"Guilty of something, his neighbors are claiming. Guilty because missing and Muslim."

"All of his neighbors?" Xander asked, "Or only the loud ones?"

"Enough to make their life miserable while the family searches for him."

As the days went by, the defense team grew more and more angry about the number of times television and newspaper reporters, bloggers and news headlines mentioned that Nasdar Qubadi happened to be a Muslim, as if that made him guilty. Even interviews with the government people brought religion into the talk. Being Muslim seemed to be a big part of the evidence against him.

"Like being a Jew in the 1930s." Mr. Wray said. "Many assumed Jews were Communists, or child killers."

"And their proof?" Xander asked.

"Everybody else assumed it."

* *

A couple of days later, Grandpa Gilbert called the boys into his office. He said, "The Multnomah County Prosecutor's office has assigned someone to interview everyone involved in the death of Beryl Plinder."

Haroon's voice came out very quietly. "The guy who cut Xander in the tunnel? Are they accusing me?"

Grandpa shook his head.

Mr. Wray said, "Mr. Nelson tells us this is a legal expert who looks over all the evidence and then recommends that they have enough evidence to accuse someone, or maybe not take any action. Nelson will be there with you."

On November 11, 2006, Grandpa, Mr. Nelson, Mr. Johnson, Haroon and Xander waited to be interviewed. Haroon's mother waited with them.

The legal expert allowed Mr. Nelson to be present when Haroon was questioned. About forty-five minutes later, Haroon came out of the interview room looking tired and worried. He glanced at Xander and said, "I can't talk to Xander until he's done."

Mrs. Qubadi rose and took Haroon into her arms. "Oh my son, my son . . ." she crooned. Haroon leaned against her and closed his eyes.

Mr. Nelson appeared at the door and beckoned to Xander. Grandpa touched his arm and whispered, "The truth, as you know it."

Xander nodded, and stepped into the room.

The man doing the interview shook hands with Xander and said, "My name is Raymond Westwood. I'm here to get your account of what happened in the tunnel. Just have a seat here at the table and start where you think this all began."

Xander started with leaving their bikes in the tunnel. He ended with the forklift crashing into Beryl Plinder, and then Xander and Haroon subduing the man on the forklift. Mr. Westwood asked Xander to draw Haroon and the man on the forklift from his perspective at the moment when it hit Mr. Plinder. Xander answered questions about where the forks on the forklift were at the time.

"What was Mr. Plinder doing at the moment of impact?" Westwood asked.

Xander said, "He had just cut my leg with the knife and had pulled the knife back toward his chest. I turned to face him from on top of the stack of newspapers. The forklift had been going back and forth, making erratic changes in direction as Haroon and the other guy fought to stay on it. When I rolled around to face Plinder, the forklift already headed toward us."

"Did you see any of the three men before that day?"

"Not that I can remember, but that truck they had was used to follow Haroon one day."

"Tell me about that day."

After Xander finished that story, Mr. Westwood turned to Mr. Nelson and said, "That's all for now, but I may need to ask these boys more questions as my work continues."

"I want to be present when you do that," Mr. Nelson said.

"I will make sure you are informed."

Xander asked, "Can you tell me where the other two guys are right now? Are they in jail? Do we have to watch out for them? I don't want them coming ..."

"They are in jail," Mr. Westwood said. "Mr. Nelson will let you know if they are released."

Xander swallowed hard. He didn't want to admit how scared he was, so he just glanced at Mr. Nelson.

Mr. Nelson stood up and waited for Xander to walk to the door with him. At the door, he put his arm around Xander's shoulders and said, "You and Haroon have a right to be afraid of them. But Mr. Johnson will make sure you are kept safe."

Mr. Westwood, took statements from the two men in jail for the attack, Mr. Lexoff and Mr. Linea. The three delivery workers who had been drugged and tied also gave their stories.

One morning during the next week, Xander answered the office phone when Mr. Wray was out on a story. "James Wray's office," Xander said.

A man interrupted, "Wray, this is Sargeant Smith of the police. We need a report on the Lloyd boy."

Xander gestured at Haroon as he kept talking. "Uh, uh ... what do you need to know about Mr. Lloyd?"

Haroon came over and put his ear next to the phone.

"We need to know where he's going to school."

Xander's hand shook. "Oh, I see... Uhm, why do you need to know?"

"Routine information for our investigation."

Haroon shook his head at Xander. Xander said, "I'll have to find that information for you. Where can I call you?"

"I'll call you back in fifteen minutes." The man hung up.

Xander stood there holding the phone in mid-air. Haroon headed toward the door, saying, "We've gotta get Mr. Halverson or somebody."

Every day during the next week and a half, the man named Sergeant Smith, called the news office and the Foundation office, two or three times each day, asking for a report on the location of Haroon Qubadi and Alexander Evans Lloyd. After that first day, Mr. Wray took most of the calls. Each time, Mr. Wray asked Sergeant Smith what reason he had for asking. "Routine investigation," became Smith's inevitable answer. Mr. Wray then replied, "When you have a routine warrant, I'll give you a routine answer. Meanwhile, stop harassing those boys."

But the man kept calling. The police chief told Grandpa Gilbert that there was no such policeman on the force.

Haroon and Xander suspected everybody who crossed their path.

*   *

Two weeks after Mr. Westwood's investigation, Mr. Jan Nelson called everyone into the Foundation's meeting room. People filled the room, leaning on bookcases and sitting on window sills. Mr. Nelson glanced at Haroon and Xander and said, "Mr. Westwood recommended that the prosecutor's office continue investigating the assault and murder of Plinder. That means they are not charging Xander or Haroon, but they aren't in the clear either. The Prosecutor's office has accepted Westwood's recommendation."

Xander sat in paralyzed tension. Mr. Nelson continued.

"Mr. Westwood interviewed Officer Bailey and Officer Robb, the policemen who came to the tunnel. The crime staff took prints off the knife that killed Plinder. Many of the prints were so messed up that they couldn't tell if Haroon or Xander had ever had the knife during the fight. There were clear prints only for Beryl Plinder, the dead man, but they could have been on the knife because he tried to pull it out of his chest and was therefore the last person to touch it."

"But what about the forklift?" Mike Halverson asked.

Mr. Nelson nodded, then he raised his shoulders in a shrug. "That showed very little. The crime team took prints. These showed that Haroon Qubadi had used the ignition key. The other man, Caspar Linea had not touched the key. Prints established that Haroon hung onto the right side of the forklift and Caspar Linea, hung on the left side. Both of their prints were found on the steering. It was unclear which of them ever had complete control of the steering or the pedals."

"What about the coroner's report," Haroon asked.

"The body was examined by the state medical examiner. Here's what she wrote: 'The body of Beryl Plinder shows wounds commensurate with having been stabbed in the heart with a switchblade knife. It was not clear if this had happened before or during the time when the forklift hit him in the back.'

Xander closed his eyes against the memory of the mean face gone slack in death.

Grandpa Gilbert took in a long breath. "So," he said, "This will not be over for some time."

Aunt Justine sat upright and stiff. Haroon's eyes were closed. At his side, Mrs. Qubadi wept silently.

Mr. Johnson asked, "Are the police looking for whoever hired the men?"

Nelson shook his head. "As far as they are aware, Plinder, Linea and Lexoff were there on their own vendetta."

"What about Officer Bailey's false draft report?"

"He's back on desk duty," Mr. Halverson said. "The chief says she can't keep him off duty forever without a clear accusation of intentionally lying. I think she's trying to convince the union that he's a danger to them all. Too many vocal members are not buying her argument."

"And what about the phone calls every day?" Xander asked,

Mr. Wray said, "The guy never calls from the same phone twice. The chief has tried to check his calls against Bailey's phone records, and she's got nothing."

Mr. Johnson broke in. "You, all of you, have to continue to be wary of strangers."

*   *

On the next Saturday morning, the sun appeared between scudding clouds. Xander rose, stabbed his feet into a pair of slippers and trudged downstairs feeling heavy and sad. Empty echoes in the old house told him Grandpa was gone, but when Xander opened the front door to get the news, the security guard, Gary Patton, handed the paper to him and motioned him back inside.

"Morning, Gary. Who's with Grandpa?"

"Juan Muñoz," Gary said. "Off to the grocery."

A few minutes later, Grandpa came home carrying three small bouquets. Juan still sat in the car as if waiting. Xander glanced at the bouquets.

"Xan," Grandpa said, pulling the bouquets close to his chest. "I thought you'd still be asleep."

"I wish . . .. What are the posies for?"

"I'm . . . I'm going to the cemetery. I want to sit down with your grandma for a little while."

Xander closed his eyes and remembered the green hill and the sunshine on the day they buried his mom and dad. If he went there, all that stuff would come back and he was just now getting on top of it, no longer looking for Dad in the easy chair or Mom at the piano.

But his mind suddenly came alert. Grandpa hadn't asked him to go. Why?

On impulse, he said, "I'm coming, too."

"Umm . . . not this time," Grandpa said. "I need to be there by myself."

Grandpa glanced at Gary who looked at the floor. Gary rocked to the balls of his feet as if ready to get moving.

Something was up. If Grandpa didn't want him there, Xander figured he ought to be there. From Gary's tension and Grandpa's evasiveness, Xander believed neither of the two would let him go to the cemetery.

A plan came to his mind. He started sauntering up the stairs, and asked, "Who's going with you?"

"I am," Gary Patton said. "And Juan. Thomas is across the street watching the house and watching out for you."

Thomas – he was the newest recruit. Gary and Juan were the big guns in the security company. Now Xander knew what he needed to do. "I'm back to bed then," he said, and wandered toward the top of the stairs.

Below, Gary whispered, "I don't like this, Gib."

Grandpa whispered back, "Mike and James are already there."

"Why you?" Gary asked.

"My job," Grandpa whispered as he strode toward the front door and out to the Subaru that belonged to Evans International Media.

As the front door closed behind them, Xander hurried into Grandpa's bedroom, opened the top of his tall chest of drawers and reached under the shelf of wood designed to hold pocket change. He smelled incense cedar – an old-fashioned drawer in a chest at least as old as his grandfather, and the cedar still exuded its pungence. Amazing longevity. Like Grandpa.

His fingers felt the soft fold of leather that he sought. He drew out the leather key holder he'd seen grandpa use for his Buick LeSabre – the nineteen-eighty-one antique boat-of-a–car. Reaching into the other side of the drawer, Xander fished under the pocket handkerchiefs and pulled out the garage door opener.

In Pakistan he'd driven the tractor to help plow, plant and harvest. He could for sure drive a big old car.

Back in his own bedroom, Xander flicked into his laptop, chose Google maps, typed Masjid Maryam – the only place-name he could remember from the day at the cemetery – and printed off a map and directions to the area southeast of Portland near Happy Valley. He remembered that the cemetery sat behind the mosque and at the top of the mosque's hill.

He left the house by the side door. Standing in the driveway, hidden by Grandpa's overgrown cedar tree he checked that Thomas sat in a car across the street. But Thomas wasn't looking at the house. Instead, Thomas checked his mirrors for cars that might come up behind him, and then he fiddled with the dial on his dispatch radio.

Xander entered the side door of the garage, fumbled in the light of one small garage window until he found the keyhole of the driver's-side door. Once inside, he turned on the interior light and discovered that an '81 Buick didn't seem to come with a clutch. His tractor driving instincts were no use here. He'd never driven an automatic car, so he studied the levers and pedals.

When he thought he had it figured out, he put his foot on what he thought should be the brake pedal. The pedal gave a satisfying stiffness. He put the key into the ignition, turned the key, and felt a rough start and then engine clunk. The motor died.

He waited, thinking he might have flooded it the way the school tractor often flooded. After a minute, he braked and started again.

The motor came to life. He put the gear lever into the R position. Still leaning on the brake, he fished the garage door opener from the seat beside him, clicked at the ceiling controller and heard the noisy rise of an old metal wheel and track system. As daylight entered the garage, he put the gears in reverse, then let up on the brake. The car backed quietly until Xander realized he was headed for the side porch. He braked hard, then he turned the steering the opposite direction. When he let off the brake, he now aimed at the fence between Grandpa and the neighbor's yard. He braked and threw himself forward.

His forehead paid for it with a crack against the steering wheel. He buckled up and backed slowly, wavering between the side porch and the fence until the tail of the Buick was beyond the house. Xander checked Thomas in the rearview mirror. The guy still didn't look toward the house or the driveway. Thomas never expected trouble from the house itself.

Xander had to finish this maneuver as smoothly as he could, and that meant slow backing. He twisted in his seat belt, looked over his shoulder and let up on the brake. The big old car hardly needed any prodding to pick up speed. It felt like the steering wheel was all disconnected. Small adjustments made a big motion. Taking each foot of progress with care, he finally had the car well into the street before Thomas glanced up.

Xander barely remembered to punch the garage door gadget to close before he shifted into drive and started down the street. Thomas emerged from his car, shouting. The first corner to the north had a stop sign, but the side street had no traffic. He barreled through, then glanced in the mirror and saw Thomas rushing back into his car.

That was good, Xander thought. He'd hoped to make Thomas follow him to the cemetery so they'd have more help when they got there. He sure didn't want his grandpa there with just two body guards and two old-crony reporters. Whatever Grandpa expected to happen at the cemetery had to be dangerous, or he'd have taken Xander with him.

For the first two blocks, every move he made seemed to be exaggerated by the car. A small left turn made the car swoop left, over-correct and near take the paint off a parked car on the right. Within those two blocks, he learned that he had to barely touch the steering wheel to get action.

He turned right on Knott Street. After almost hitting the dip of the storm drain, he headed toward Thirty-Third Avenue, the street that ran next to their soccer-practice field. That gave him about sixteen blocks to figure out how to steer this battle ship.

Thanks to the map, he knew the way from the soccer field to the cemetery – down Thirty-Third, to Hassalo, left to Thirty-Ninth, left again and up to the Interstate 84 freeway entrance, east to Interstate 205 south. Take the exit to Willamette National Cemetery.

He had the steering figured out by the time he got on the freeway. Merging at the new speed scared the bejeezus out of him. These people drove way too fast, but he got into the flow of the right lane and stayed there. Somewhere down the road he'd have to get off and he didn't want to be in the wrong lane at the wrong time.

Behind him, he saw Thomas's car enter the freeway. So, Thomas probably had guessed where they were headed. Suddenly, his cell phone rang. He stared straight ahead, keeping track of the truck in front and the freeway wall to his right, but he managed to fish out his phone and flip it open.

"'Lo?" he said.

"Get off at the next exit, Xander," Thomas yelled.

"Can't."

"I'll get the police on your tail. You clearly haven't got a license."

Thought I was driving so smooth, he thought, but he said. "Police would be good. Wherever Grandpa is, he could probably use the help."

"Xander, you're headed into danger."

"You tell me what danger and I'll consider stopping."

"Shit, kid! Pull over."

"I'll see you there, Thomas."

Xander closed his phone and got back to reading the green overhead signs to various exits. The map had said to take I-205 south. The signs said the exit to I-205 came up in a quarter mile. He didn't signal, but Thomas followed him and kept ringing the phone that Xander ignored.

All the way down I-205, Xander thought about the cemetery. He hadn't been back since the memorial service. He didn't want to sit next to the place where his folks lay, dead, silent, unmoving. They once loved. Once hugged. Once . . .

He remembered his mother, glancing off at the Afghan hills with that worried pinch in her eyebrows. He remembered Dad looking at the acacia stick and saying nothing about it, except "We love you boys." Wasn't that what he'd said? Xander couldn't remember it as clearly as he used to. He thought he'd remember it forever, those last moments.

The one thing he knew for certain about that last morning was that he'd seen his dad hold his mother's hand as she jumped across the irrigation ditch, held her hand, and then kept it in his own as they strolled toward the hospital.

On the freeway south, after twenty minutes of eyeball-hurting attention to the zooming trucks and cars around him, Xander turned off and followed the signs to Willamette National Cemetery, which, from the symbol on the signs, he figured out was the U.S. military cemetery. He thought his folks were buried in the cemetery across from there, but he couldn't remember its name.

A military cemetery on the same hill as Mom and Dad – a little irony for you, Xander thought: Quakers and Vets and a mosque all on one hill.

As he approached Masjid Maryam which sat halfway up the long hill, he saw that his family must be in the place called Lincoln Memorial Park. The road to both cemeteries was now blocked. Cars and people milled around the Lincoln Memorial cemetery entrance and the side and front of the mosque.

He didn't want to get stuck in that crowd, so he turned off three blocks before the mosque. Driving into the neighborhood, he found himself on a steep downhill. He stopped the Buick and searched for a lower gear. Other than D for drive and R for reverse, the gear markers were all numbered and he couldn't tell for sure which was which. He thought probably the lowest gear was the furthest from D, so he shifted.

It worked, some, but he still needed to use the brakes until he found a parking space. He pulled Grandpa's big boat toward the curb. Turning off the ignition, he started to get out. Then he took a look at the car ahead of him. Its front end was aimed at the curb. Studying the other cars nearby, he realized that aiming at the curb was the local practice – maybe to keep the cars from rolling downhill. So he re-parked the same way.

This time, as he got out, he saw Thomas's car drive right past his side street. Thomas would get stopped at the cemetery gate by the crowd. It would take him a little time to figure out that Xander never got that far.

He started hiking uphill toward the crowd to find out where his grandfather might be. And why. He rounded the corner at the upper end of the residential block. The crowd at the mosque seemed like a gathering on the sidelines of a soccer match – maybe fifty people, some old, but also a lot of kids his age, all excited about what might happen next. At the edge of the crowd, he saw Thomas, out of his car, gesturing at the gate to the cemetery as if asking to enter. The men near him pointed that Thomas had to take his car somewhere off to the right – maybe a parking lot or another entry.

From this perspective, and because of the angle at which the building sat into the hill, Xander could see a lot of the mosque – all of the front, and most of the east side. The mosque's neat gardens appeared to end at its back fence – the fence marking the cemetery grounds.

Above the crowd and beyond the fence, about two thirds of the way up the cemetery road, the green Subaru sat parked. His grandfather stood next to graves. He'd already placed three vases of flowers on separate spaces.

Mom, Dad, Grandma.

Gary and Juan stood on the uphill side of the car. Gary trained what looked like small binoculars on the scene. Juan had a large lens on a camera. He swept it slowly across the crowd.

Closer to Xander, in front of the mosque, a broad entry walkway passed on either side of a fountain – a burble of ever-moving water coming from decorative spigots set in a marble wall. The water flowed into a drain. He remembered how Muslim worshippers and visitors would wash themselves symbolically in the fountain at Tiri before entering the mosque.

A car hurried past Xander, carrying six teenagers. The boy in the front passenger seat studied something in his palm – a large cell phone or a small computer. He seemed excited by what he saw there. The boys' car pulled over to park. As the kids piled out, the boy with the cell phone greeted Xander.

"Hey. Pretty good Flash Mob for only an hour warning." He waved the hand with his phone in it.

Flash mob? What's that?

The idea confused, but Xander wanted to learn more, so he said, "Took me only twenty minutes to get here."

"Yeah, I think more guys are getting the message. I just sent out an update to my buds, so this will grow huge."

"Which message did you get first?"

"Probably the same as yours, you know, "Meet at mosque. Abomination at war memorial cemetery. And then the address.""

The back of Xander's neck prickled with cold. He had to keep this conversation going to find out as much as he could. He fell in with the six boys. "But what are we going to do next?"

The kid grinned. "Get out the spray paint, man. That's what I bring to all these things."

Another kid waved a hammer, then hid it back under his winter coat. Two more showed short handled shovels beneath their jackets.

Ahead of them, some in the crowd were unfurling a banner. When they stretched it out, Xander read, "Pastor Lori". Other signs came out. He'd seen Pastor Lori Gotamere's rallies on television and knew what the other signs might say. He caught only a few letters because they faced in other directions, but he recognized "Unbelievers Out of U.S." and "This is a Godly Country".

These people are into irony.

Up ahead of them, someone turned on a radio and set it on the marble bench near the entry fountain. The voice on the radio echoed over the courtyard of the Masjid Maryam. The first voice was the man who always introduced Pastor Lori's events.

"In five minutes, Pastor Lori Gotamere will arrive at the podium of the Clark County Fair Grounds to address the crowd. Meanwhile, true Christians gather in many locations throughout northern Oregon and southern Washington to await her message."

CHAPTER TWENTY-FOUR

Xander looked ahead at the growing crowd. In most of Pastor Lori's television events, he had seen families – people with their little kids, not teenagers. But half this crowd was his age. The kid next to him had gotten messages on his cell phone – this Twitter-web stuff that American kids talked about in his classes. That would explain how fast the crowd came together. But it didn't explain how Grandpa knew to come here.

Grandpa and Twitter? No way!

Xander needed to leave the boys he was walking with to find Mike Halverson and James Wray. Searching for them would be difficult unless he were able to get above this crowd.

He waved to his new acquaintance, "I've got to meet my guys, and pick up my tools." The six boys gave a "See ya" to his leaving them and continued up the hill toward the mob. He dropped back and turned off at the last side street before the mosque.

Just as he turned, he saw Rob Palmquist and Denny near the mosque. Denny pulled a hatchet from beneath his coat and showed it to Rob. Rob laughed and pulled out a small chainsaw.

Xander dove into the next block so they wouldn't see him.

By skirting the block, Xander was able to come up on the west side of the mosque. Suddenly he could hear the radio more clearly. The man's voice continued as Xander studied his choices for moving forward. This side of the mosque lay at the edge of a hill and was surrounded by rhododendrons.

He heard the radio announcer. "The crowd at the Clark County Fair Grounds fills the main concourse and is lining up to enter an already teeming pavilion."

Gotamere is in Clark County. Isn't that the part of Washington State across the Columbia River?

He hadn't been in Portland, Oregon long enough to know for sure, but he thought it must be close because weather in Clark County was always part of the local news. He hiked past the west end of the mosque and entered the small forest of rhododendrons that edged the cemetery.

The radio announcer continued talking. "Twitter reports give us crowds of two hundred or more at each of various locations across the northwest."

So it was Twitter.

Hiking through the rhododendrons Xander discovered the corner of the chain-link fence. He looked around him to be sure the nearby neighbors didn't see him in this jungle of tall shrubbery. He climbed the fence and headed uphill through the trees and bushes of the cemetery, aiming toward the same elevation as his grandfather's car. A little above and west of his grandfather, he walked out of the rhodies and looked down on the crowd. A half soccer field off to his right, his grandfather stood by three graves, studying the ground. His mouth seemed to be moving. Maybe he talked to Grandma.

Juan and Gary studied the growing mob from the uphill side of the Subaru which provided them cover for the long-distance lense and the binoculars.

Below, the crowd had grown to at least one hundred people, about half of them Xander's age. More people parked their cars on lower neighborhood streets and climbed the hill.

Xander could not see any news camera men. Mike was big enough to stand out if he wasn't scrunched down in a hoodie or other disguise. And James, if he really were there, would be the only black man and easily spotted. But neither was anywhere Xander could see.

Xander glanced over at the graves. It amazed him to see that grass already grew over his mother and father. Then he remembered the stack of turf that had sat not quite far enough away during the funeral. *Unreal.* He thought. *Real grass, but unreal speed. People covered over and forgotten as soon as possible.* He turned his attention away from that sight.

From up here, because of the angle at which Maryam tucked into the hill, Xander could still see most of the entry courtyard and its fountain. He could see the east side of the mosque and all of the back. Over the east side stood a script that Xander translated as Ansaru Allah.

Ansaru, Xander thought, does that mean *helper? supporter?* Or *the path?*

It scared him that he suddenly couldn't remember the meaning of a word he had used many times at home. He remembered the imam in Tiri singing a Sura passage from the Quran that used the phrase *Ansaru Allah.* The clear, fluid voice of the imam came to him, but the meaning . . . the meaning was gone.

Ah! Those who helped Mohammed in Medina – those are the Ansar – a sacred phrase.

Far below, a man sat on the marble support for the entry fountain. He made a loud noise and then stood to spit into the fountain. Xander's throat tightened against bile. He watched the spitting man wipe his sleeve across his lips. Sickness rose in Xander's gut.

Suddenly, Grandpa stood at his side. "How did you get here, Xander?"

Xander stared, hardly believing he couldn't have heard him coming. "Gee, Grandpa, did you float over here?" he asked.

"I felt you and then saw you. You were deep in thought. Please answer my question."

"I drove your Buick." The sudden fear on his Grandfather's face shook Xander. "It was fine. Really. I drove in Pakistan, a lot."

Grandpa's gaze pierced Xander. "Was Thomas with you?"

Time to confess. "I left without telling him, but he saw and followed me."

His grandfather's jaw worked. "Drive the Buick without a license? I told you to stay at home. I expect you to . . . .."

"You expect me not to recognize when you're off into danger?"

Grandpa glared at Xander. "I want you safe."

Xander leaned over his grandfather. "Likewise, old man."

Grandpa jerked back as if hit. "Old man?"

"Well?" Xander said.

His grandfather took a deep breath, looked down at the growing crowd, and said, "Hot dang, I feel old today."

"Why feel old today, of all days?"

"I never believed that in Oregon there could be enough people who listened to Fafner or Gotamere to create a mob like this. Nobody I know has anything but contempt for their manipulation of others."

"Grandpa," Xander gestured at the crowd, "the problem is that, as a newspaper man, you should get outside Northeast Portland and meet more kinds of people. This crowd should not be a surprise to you."

"You haven't been in Oregon all that long."

"True, but as Dad said about radio in Pakistan, 'Wherever there are people who need someone to look down on, you have natural hate spewers and their listeners.'"

"I never wanted to believe that, but this," he gestured down the hill toward the growing numbers, "this shows me I've been naïve."

Xander put a hand on his grandfather's shoulder. "How'd you learn about this flash mob?" he asked. "Don't tell me you're on Twitter."

"Juan Munoz. Young enough to know we should follow Pastor Lori Gotamere's internet presence. Old enough to know she's a danger."

"This crowd doesn't just hate Muslims. They're probably willing to hate anyone who's different. So, where's James Wray?"

"James is in a car uphill from the crowd. Dark windows. He's using a camera mounted on the front of the car – a special crowd watching situation that Rick set up. Mike is in the crowd, tape recording interviews with crowd members."

"And you?"

"I have a microphone on right now, James and Mike can hear everything I say."

"So, you're directing news gathering?"

"Hummph," Grandpa's face grew grim. "Hardly directing. Barely keeping track. Depending on what Lori Gotamere has to say, this situation could become bad."

At that moment, Pastor Gotamere's voice crackled across the lawns and trees. The radio below amplified her voice. "Welcome, Christians."

Xander could not imagine why he ever thought her voice resembled Mom's.

She continued. "Like Daniel, you brave the lion's den. Like Daniel, you will walk through the fire and come out unscathed because you believe on Christ Jesus. Like Daniel, and like so many others since Daniel, you will prevail for the One True God. We live in a land over-run by the followers of the anti-Christ, the unbelievers, the defilers of the temple."

Never mind that everything she said was a mockery of the stories from the Old Testament. Never mind that everything she said mixed images from the three religions of the Great Book, including the fact that Daniel loved only Yahweh, also known as Allah or God – the one God of all true Muslims, Christians and Jews. And Daniel knew nothing about the future Jesus Christ.

The people in the crowd moved toward the radio, and therefore, toward the mosque. They waited on her word.

Pastor Gotamere continued to talk. And no one in the crowd paid attention to anything else. Grandpa pulled Xander toward the three graves. He touched the flowers he'd placed there and then said to Xander, "I believe your grandma and your parents are telling me it's time to get back to the newspaper business."

"So, what are we doing?" Xander asked.

"Lori Gotamere thinks she can rouse others to action without taking responsibility. These people are here because someone invited them to come at the time of her sermon."

"I bet we can follow her blog-traffic and find out who invited them and what they said."

Grandpa, nodded. "I think you're right. When we're back at the office." He reached inside his coat, pulled out his cell phone and punched a number.

Xander could hear Mike Halverson's voice, "Gib?"

"Now's the time to call the sheriff."

"He's waiting at Clackamas Town Center," Mike Halverson said, "and he's listening to the radio sermon, too."

"Washington County, Beaverton Police and Multnomah County Sheriff as well?"

"Yes," Mike said. "Each mosque has attracted a crowd. And one Sephardic synagogue, for some strange reason."

"Sephardic?" James Wray said, "That's the beehive shaped building in southwest Portland?"

Mr. Wray's voice came over the phone. "The Portland Police are watching that situation. And the chief is keeping Bailey and his buddies out of this roll call."

"That's one small favor," Grandpa mumbled.

Mike went on. "I've got a mobile camera unit coming from *Evans International*. Plus, that cameraman I told you about is on his way from Louis Lamb's local news outlets."

"Unmarked vans?" Grandpa asked.

"As you ordered boss."

Xander glanced down the front side of the hill toward Masjid Maryam. The crowd had swelled to about two hundred people. On the loud radio, Pastor Gotamere still preached. She harped again on Isaiah and the call to smite the Hittites.

Xander remembered Plinder quoting her as he swung his hook in the news tunnel.

Hurry, sheriff! Please!

A couple of men strayed toward the side of the mosque. If they wandered into the back, they would find only a small door between themselves and the inside of the mosque. Anybody inside would be trapped there.

I sent the boys to the basement, thinking they were safe.

Pastor Gotamere had been preaching for twenty minutes. Her voice rose in pitch. She grew louder and more insistent. The crowd began to move closer and closer toward the fountain.

A white van pulled slowly up the hill and parked a block from the mosque. A man stepped out of the white van's sliding side door. He pulled out a camera with a long lense. Xander had seen that tall man working in the Evans International building. Another man exited the van. He carried sound equipment.

"That our crew?" he asked Grandpa.

"Angus and George McCardle. Brothers. Angus on the camera. If that crowd knew who they worked for, they would be on them in a minute."

From beside the car, Gary watched the action through his binoculars. "Mr. Evans," he said, "that camera has the *Evans* logo all over it."

"Oh, hell! I'm going down there."

"You are not," Gary said, but Grandpa already strode across the lawn and straight down the hill.

Xander ran after him. "Grandpa, this is not going to help your crew."

Grandpa slipped on the grass as he turned around. He caught himself, but Xander saw the wince of pain. That knee. Xander knew it hurt all the time.

Grandpa straightened up as if nothing were the matter. "I can't let Angus and George stand alone in that bunch while she rants."

"But you'll bring more attention to them by barging out through the gate."

Grandpa looked down the hill at the situation. Pastor Gotamere's radio sermon seemed to be winding up. She reminded her audience "Indecision supports things as they now exist. Do we want to continue to harbor evil and the anti-Christ among us?"

The crowd yelled. "Never!" and "Jesus haters."

Angus' camera was trained on them. His mike man, George, held the equipment on a long boom. Xander thought the boom's purpose was to cut out crowd sound and get what Gotamere was saying on the radio.

Gary Patton caught up with Xander and now had Grandpa's sleeve. "You are a known face, Gilbert. You can't go down there and hope to make others safe. Your presence will create a riot."

Xander realized his own face would probably be known to the camera man, but not to the crowd. Even the news reports about the fight in the tunnel had not used his face. Everyone knew Haroon's face – a distinctive Kurdish face. His own face – not so interesting, not often used in news reports – and therefore, a lot easier to blend into a crowd.

*   *

Xander stepped back and back while Grandpa argued with Gary. Eventually, Xander stepped inside the forest of tall rhododendrons and ran toward the bottom of the hill. From his cover, he heard Pastor Gotamere ask for the crowd's prayers for her work. He heard the crowd cheer, heard the milling about and the noise of her microphone being handled before the radio was turned off.

As he stepped into the back of the mass of people, the only sign that Pastor Gotamere had ever been a presence here was the flush of anger he saw in the faces of the crowd members and the spray paint cans that came out of backpacks. The paint-can owners headed toward the marble exterior of the mosque.

And still there was no sound of police or sheriff.

* *

Angus, The Evans' TV station's cameraman, stood well over six feet with broad shoulders and a tree-trunk of a neck. He had begun filming from halfway down the block and, because the crowd faced the radio and the mosque, few had noticed his arrival. Where Xander stood, at the back of the crowd, women and old men milled about. People in the crowd talked to each other, and laughed at the paint and hammer destruction caused by the younger crowd members. Xander saw the six kids who had arrived with shovels and spray paint among the others. The boy with the shovel dug up the nearest rose bush and threw it in the fountain. He started after another rose.

Gulbahar, Xander thought. Haroon's little Rose.

By the front door, Denny hauled out his hatchet and whacked at the carved words on the building face – the supporters, the Ansar who loved Allah.

Rob and his small chainsaw tried to deface the oak door. The saw bucked back and nicked Rob in the leg. Xander started toward him, but saw he had on chaps – leg protectors. So Xander melted back into the crowd. Rob didn't need him.

Think, Xander. Don't just react.

Many in the mob shouted slogans left to them by Pastor Gotamere.

"Out, God-hating foreigners."

"U.S! Our Country for Christ!"

A hand landed on Xander's shoulder. He pulled away and turned to find Thomas, his bodyguard. Thomas reached for Xander's arm, but Xander leaned toward him and whispered. "Say nothing, but, look afraid."

"What?"

"You have to join me in this, or I will get beat up, but good."

Thomas's eyebrows rose in question. Xander approached an old man at the back of the crowd and spoke quietly. "I thought I heard a siren, out on I-205," Xander said.

The man turned. "An accident?"

"No. Police -- it makes an up and down wail. Maybe a couple of police cars. Where's the nearest freeway exit to this road?"

The old man's eyes flicked farther downhill toward Foster Road. "About half a mile," he said.

"'Spose the police had to come sometime," Thomas said. Xander threw him a grateful glance.

The old man barked out, "Mona, police coming. We gotta go now."

A few yards away, a woman in a cluster of others raised her head and said, "Way out here? Police never come. This is county sheriff's territory."

Xander moved into the crowd with Thomas right behind him, so when the man tried to point at them as his source, he jabbed his thumb toward another fellow. "He heard sirens. Police. Sheriff. Something."

Nearby groups grew heated in conversation, some urging others into the melee around the mosque, some trying to shush the crowd to listen for the sirens that didn't yet exist. The shushers created a short quiet space in the general hubbub.

To Xander's great relief, faint sirens wailed toward them, still about two miles south, maybe as far as the Sunnyside Road exit, but at least sirens.

"Uh-oh," Xander said loudly. "Here comes the sheriff."

"Thomas added, "Sheee-it." And he rattled the keys to his car. "I'm outta here."

Hearing Thomas's evident fear of arrest, the edges of the crowd stared around nervously. One or two reached for pocketed car keys and moved back from the crowd. Movement toward the parked cars grew.

Xander took the thinning of the crowd as a chance to push toward Angus and his camera. As he neared the man's elbow, he whispered, "Turn your camera on those behind us, Angus."

Angus glanced at him and then at Thomas. His eyebrow flicked up, but he turned and filmed, whispering, "How'd you get here?"

"Kid drove Gib Evans's old Buick," Thomas said.

"The sheriff and police are taking too long," Xander said.

"But where's Gib?" Angus asked.

Thomas said, "He is at the cemetery gate with Muñoz. Gib's basketball knee has gone bad on him, but to get him to stop coming down here, I had to promise I'd chase down his grandson."

A big man in the crowd jostled Angus's camera. The man shouted at Angus, "Leave off, filming." The man's fist cocked and aimed at Angus.

Angus turned his camera lens toward the man.

Xander stepped closer. "Sir," he said to the big man. "I'm with KOTV news. Were you lucky enough to hear the pastor's sermon?"

The big man's fist hovered in mid-air, but his eyes seemed to glow with the memory. "These people built this abomination in our community. She is damned right-on about that."

"You tell 'em, Chuck," shouted an older fellow. "Abomination."

Xander found his whole body shivering with tension. He wouldn't call it fear exactly . . . He pushed his voice lower, and asked, "So . . . umm. . . , Chuck, what does Pastor Gotamere want you to do?"

"We can't let these evildoers get a foothold in our land."

"Listen," a woman said nearby. At that moment, even the big man, Chuck, heard the sirens. The sound announced that the sheriff probably had exited onto Foster Road at the very bottom of the hill. Chuck glanced away toward the wail of sirens. He saw that the crowd behind him had thinned. Many were already driving toward the top of the road next to the cemetery.

Big Chuck glared at Angus and reached for the camera. "Gimme that."

Thomas stepped between them. "Chuck," he said, "you and I don't want to do jail time and pay camera damages. Let's just get out of here."

Chuck pushed Thomas out of his way and shouted at the crowd, "Stay, you coward bastards. Stay and finish what we started. Stay for Pastor Lori."

Xander shouted, "Where is Pastor Lori?"

"Yeah?" Thomas said, "Isn't she going to smite the Hittites, too?"

Chuck waved his arms at the people around him. "You know these Muslims can't be allowed to get away with invading. Terrorists. Jihadists. Unbelievers."

"You stay," a woman sneered. "Greet the sheriff for me, will ya?"

Chuck stopped shouting. Surprise and disgust twisted his face. All around him, people were leaving, but closer to the mosque, others sprayed or hacked with hammers and chisels at the Arabic script on the entry walls. Chuck glared once more at Angus. He pulled back his arm.

Angus pushed his camera into Thomas's arms. He raised one fist, looking huge and formidable. Chuck's eyes widened.

Recognizing strength and power, Chuck stepped out of Angus's way, but swung off to one side, instead. He punched the sound man in the face – Angus's smaller brother, George.

"You coward," Angus grunted. He took a swing at the man's belly. When Chuck doubled over, Angus gave him an upper cut that fist-lifted him up and then laid him out on the concrete sidewalk.

Next to Xander, George, the sound man, also crumpled. In slow motion, his microphone boom hit a nearby teenager. The boom's victim grunted and turned, ready to fight somebody. Xander put himself astride George's body. He raised his fist as if he had just clocked George himself. He shouted toward the crowd, "He's out of the action."

The victim of the mike boom raised an approving thumb at Xander and then ran off to join others, Denny, Rob and some twenty-five others, destroying the building and gardens.

On the ground, Big Chuck started to roll over. Angus pulled Chuck's arms back and tied him with a cord from his camera equipment bag. All around them, Xander sensed panic in hurried steps and darting eyes. He stared down at George, pale and reaching ineffectively for his clobbered head.

Xander also sensed the sudden presence of Grandpa. "Xan, I'll have your hide when this is over."

Angus gave a sharp bark. "Damn, I've got to hide you, Gib. Too recognizable." Angus grabbed the camera back from Thomas and shoved it at Gilbert, "Used to do your own news photos, I heard."

Gilbert took the thing. "Sure. Back when film was celluloid."

"Hide your face behind this camera." Angus said. "Stick with me. We're going in to the steps. Film faces and actions. This button here is 'On'."

Angus bent over his brother and put his hand on the man's chest. George moaned and tried to rise, but Angus pushed him back down. "Not this time, George. I want you to get that head checked out. Angus turned to Xander. "Make sure George here gets in that ambulance that's coming. That guy smashed him hard."

Xander nodded and knelt next to George. He reached for his neck pulse and found it.

CHAPTER TWENTY-FIVE

Angus said, "Up camera, Gilbert, before someone smashes you, too."
Grandpa pulled up the camera, fiddled with a dial that looked
like the zoom, and appeared to focus on faces.

Adults and kids ripped up the garden, sledge-hammered the
fountain and the building walls, defaced any part they could reach.
Xander wondered who started that first Tweet. Who warned them to
bring the paint?

George opened his eyes and looked beyond Xander to someone
else. "Go with Angus, Dell. News breaks."

Xander glanced behind him. There stood a man from the rival
news, the *National Courier* logo on his camera. "I'm Dell," he said
to Xander. "Angus and George's friend. Can I count on you to get
George into an ambulance?"

"I'll put a foot on his chest if he tries anything before the medics
arrive."

Dell raised his lens in answer. He followed in Grandpa's wake,
filming to the right as Grandpa filmed front and left.

From the bottom of the hill, police and sheriff's sirens howled up the cemetery road toward the mosque. Hurried feet scrambled to get away. Men and women shouted. No one stopped to help the fallen.

Xander leaned over George. He remembered his father's hands searching for damage on a patient. He looked down at George's blood covered face, and followed the lead of his memory. The bones under George's left eye appeared to be broken, and his neck probably needed a bracing board.

Next to them, Big Chuck began to moan and work against his arm and leg ties. Angus knew what he was doing, it seemed, because the more Chuck wiggled, the tighter the ties became.

Xander glanced behind him to see what Grandpa and Angus were doing. At the top of the entry steps. A man in the mob knocked Grandpa down. Others fell on him.

Xander stood, fearful for his grandfather. Angus and the photographer, Dell, tried to yank bodies off the attacking pack. Still, Xander couldn't see his grandfather, but he also couldn't leave George who needed help as soon as possible.

A sheriff's car screeched to a halt near the entry to the mosque. The sheriff and three of his deputies piled out. Two deputies brought out bull horns.

"Everyone stand still and put your hands in the air."

"You, with the paint can, hands in the air."

Help Grandpa, Xander thought.

Two more Clackamas County sheriff's cars arrived. Three Portland Police vehicles swooped in behind them. Each disgorged several men who helped set up a cordon around those who were destroying the garden and mosque walls. The men all wore riot gear, including a helmet with a face visor.

One policeman started toward Xander. Xander stared at the unreadable face behind the visor. To the policeman, it must look like he stood in the thick of the action. Two men lay at his feet, one of them trussed like a goose ready for cooking, the other, completely out.

The whoop of the ambulance forced Xander into action. He waved his arms at the paramedics. "Over here. Emergency. Over here."

The policeman said, "Back off, kid."

"This is my friend. He needs help."

The paramedics pulled up to George, the policeman watched, as if waiting to see what Xander really was up to. The paramedics climbed out of the ambulance and ran toward him.

Glancing back at the mosque steps, Xander saw his grandfather limp toward the porch of the building with the sheriff and Angus.

Over the crowd noises, the ambulance medic shouted to Xander, "Did you see what happened to this man?"

"Yes. This guy that's tied up, he punched this man. Broke his eye socket. And I'm afraid about his neck."

The policeman said, "Who tied this other fellow?"

"The camera man for one of the television stations. The victim is his sound man, George McCardell. This guy that punched George, Some lady in the crowd called him Chuck."

"I'm going to need your statement," the policeman said.

"I'll be here,"

The policeman flagged down a buddy. The two of them got Chuck up, and wrestled him into the police van. Chuck yelled at Xander. "You'll regret this, you and that camera man."

The look in his eye made Xander certain he hadn't seen the last of Chuck. The ambulance crew man, said, "Show me how he was hit. I want to know for the docs at the other end of this ride."

Xander demonstrated Chuck's fist and the jerking back of George's head. The medic nodded. "I'm immobilizing his neck and we'll x-ray it."

As the ambulance crew got George ready for transport, Xander noticed that Dell still filmed, closer and closer to the ambulance and the paramedics. Dell said, "Your grandfather is on his feet."

Xander glanced up at the steps and did see his grandfather standing, and looking pretty good from this distance. That sight gave Xander a moment's respite from worry. But then, the policemen returned and asked Xander to identify himself. Xander grew wary.

"I am Alexander Lloyd. Who are you?"

"Ah, the Evans grandson." The policeman raised his visor. "Sergeant Robertson. And, I assure you, I'm not with Officer Bailey. But I am curious about how you happened to be here at the center of this mess, again."

"Again?"

"I know about the tunnel attack."

"Ah. Well, that time I was attacked. This time, I came to keep my grandfather from danger, but he was knocked down on the mosque steps by the crowd. I see you've got people up there with him, now."

The man glanced at the crowd on the steps, then began asking questions again. He took notes as Xander told him how he came to this cemetery, and what had happened to George and to his grandfather.

The paramedics carried George and another injured man into the ambulance. Soon, the tail-lights of the first ambulance flickered, weaving around the people and cars left at the mosque. Another ambulance drove up. Behind it, a bus arrived. The sheriff's men and the police together began putting teenagers on the bus instead of with the adults in the vans. Sergeant Robertson excused himself to help with that process.

The *National Courier* photographer, Dell, approached Xander. "I hope you can get your grandfather to go to the doctor, Kid, but he's game and walking. Angus is having no luck with the doctor idea."

Xander registered the "and walking" part with relief. He said, "George went unconscious before the medics came."

"Yeah," Dell said. "I got that on film, too. Also the arrest of the big guy and his threat to you."

"I'm going to Grandpa."

"Naw. You'd best sit down here, kid."

"But, I want to see him."

"You'll see him soon enough, but if you leave here, you'll get arrested. Then, he won't be in good shape. Here, I can vouch for you. It's too chaotic up there."

Xander felt all the tension from watching the mob pile on Grandpa. He slumped on the broken bench of the ritual entry fountain and watched Dell film the sheriff's men filling a busload of arrested mob members.

And then he saw Rob and Denny pointing at him from the window of the bus. It surprised him that he hadn't thought to wonder what had happened to them in the mob. But at the side of the bus, he saw a pile of weapons of destruction. He assumed Rob's chainsaw and Denny's hatchet were in that pile.

Sergeant Robertson ordered three more teenagers toward the bus. One of them turned a shouted, "That kid was with us. He came at the same time." It was the boy Xander had talked to as he arrived.

One of the other boys shouted, "He got the same Tweet, too."

"Shut up," the first boy said. "You talk too much."

Sergeant Robertson said, "I'll talk to your friend there after you three are on the bus."

CHAPTER TWENTY-SIX

"So," Officer Robertson said a few moments after sending off the busload, "What's this about a Tweet?"

"I forgot about that."

"You want me to believe you just up and forgot?"

"I hardly know what a Tweet is. I've been out of the country since what? maybe second grade. But when I arrived at the hill here, those guys got out of a car and they mentioned that it was a pretty good crowd since the Tweet went out only an hour before."

"What Tweet? You came here because of a Tweet?"

"I don't know what a Tweet is, except it would probably be on that kid's cell phone records – he waved the cell phone at me when he talked about the tweet. I came like I told you – following my Grandpa."

"That kid said you got the same Tweet."

"I wanted to learn more from that boy. I let him think that's why I was here so he'd keep talking."

"May I look at your cell phone?"

Xander handed him the phone. Robertson flipped through text messages, other apps and then recent calls. He asked, "Who's this guy Thomas?"

"That's my body guard – because of the attack in the tunnel, *Evans International* put a body guard on each of us. Thomas kept calling my phone because I ducked him in order to use Grandpa's car and find out what was going on. I was pretty sure my Grandpa was leaving me at home because he knew there would be trouble here."

Sergeant Robertson looked around him at the mess. "Trouble is one way of putting it." His attention refocused on Xander. "Could I see your driver's license?"

"Sir, I don't have one. I drove tractors in Pakistan."

"Tractors? You kidding me?"

Xander looked at Robertson, who stared at him.

"You're not," Robertson said. He hauled a pad out of his back pocket and started writing. "You're ticketed for impersonating a driver."

"That's an offense?"

"That's a joke, kid. But the ticket is real." Robertson slapped the ticket in Xander's hand. "Don't lose this. I've got a copy. You have to appear in court and pay a fine. And no more driving that car until you get a license, which because of this ticket, will be some time."

"Yes, sir."

"Now get up there and find out if your grandfather is okay. I'm a busy man or you'd be in the back seat of my car and under arrest." Robertson strode off.

Xander watched him go. He was certain this ticket would be on his record for years, but he had to be here. He had to be sure Grandpa was okay.

Someone behind Xander cleared his throat. Xander turned and saw a man standing there.

"Aren't you Gilbert Evan's grandson?" The man wore a gray suit and tie. His sandy hair and blue eyes reminded Xander of someone he'd seen, but he couldn't place him.

"Who are you?" Xander asked.

"I saw you serving dinner at the Taziyan two weeks ago. I am Bruce Higgins, and I belong to Nasdar Qubadi's mosque west of Portland, Masjid Husayn. I was at the restaurant with Imam Faisal when he took the letter for the Qubadi family."

Xander remembered what Haroon had told him about a man who pretended to belong to the mosque, but reported to FBI Agent Saurus.

"Are you looking for Mr. Saurus?" Xander asked.

The man's eyebrows pulled together, as if he were puzzling out what to answer. Then he smiled. "Oh, Haroon must have told you about Jake Rochford – Saurus's pigeon in Husayn. I'm not connected to Saurus. I'm here because I know the old imam of Maryam, and I'm afraid he was inside the mosque and may still be hiding, fearful of showing himself."

The man knew Haroon's family. He was willing to talk about the spy in the Qubadi's mosque, and he seemed very concerned about the imam. Xander decided to test him. "My grandfather is inside with the sheriff's men. I'll take you to them."

The man nodded. "I can talk to the sheriff, but not to certain policemen."

"Which policemen?"

"There's an officer who would love to arrest any Muslim, name of Bailey."

Xander nodded, and said, "Bailey's not supposed to be here. Let's hope he's really stuck at headquarters." He led Mr. Higgins up the empty and broken steps to the door.

Once inside, Higgins gasped at the damage. The mob had hatcheted furnishings, torn curtains, smashed windows and spray-painted the walls. Xander hoped many of the destroyers had been captured on Dell's and Angus' film. Most had been arrested, but the work to repair the mosque would take great care and a long time.

Higgins and Xander found Grandpa and the Portland Chief of Police with the Multnomah County Sheriff. Xander gazed at his stoop-shouldered grandfather with worry.

As they approached, the police chief didn't notice, but talked to those around her. "Sheriff Zimmer, in a matter of hours, it isn't going to matter whose jurisdiction this is. The FBI will swoop in and we'll have no more opportunity to investigate."

The sheriff nodded. "Agent Saurus is going to requisition your film, Mr. Evans."

Grandpa said, "Dell and Angus are working fast to . . .."

All three stopped talking, aware of Xander and the new man. Xander studied the darkening bruises on his grandfather's face.

Higgins spoke up. "Mr. Evans, I'm Bruce Higgins. Your grandson brought me to you because I believe the oldest Imam who cares for Masjid Maryam has to be inside somewhere. He would not have left when the mosque was attacked."

"He could have escaped out the back door while Gotamere sermonized," the sheriff said.

"But he wouldn't do that. Maryam owns an ancient Quran copy, a copy in Kufic. He would not allow it to be destroyed. I'm certain he's hiding somewhere with that Quran."

"What's his name?" Xander asked.

"Moussa," Higgins said, "Imam Benjamin Moussa."

Sheriff Zimmer called to a nearby knot of uniformed men, "Bob, I want you to take a couple of the guys and comb this place for an old man hiding with his Quran copy."

One of the sheriff's men said, "We been all over this building, Zimmer,"

"Maybe, but this man will be afraid to come out," Grandpa said. "Take Mr. Higgins here with you."

"In fact," the sheriff said, pointing at Xander, "take the Evans kid with you. He may trust a kid when he wouldn't trust anybody else."

"Grandpa," Xander said, "you should be in the next ambulance."

"I'll be fine, Xander. Doc Adam will see me as soon as we're through here. Go ahead and look for Imam Moussa."

Forty-five minutes later, they had covered the tower and then the second and first floors of the mosque. The men followed Xander and Higgins to the basement – a large area sparsely furnished with a cot, now overturned, and a collection of books that had been thrown to the floor. It looked like someone slept here regularly, maybe Imam Moussa. Xander looked over the books and realized their owner mostly read in Farsi or Persian.

After searching the furnace area and the mess of a tool storage room, Xander opened a door at the back of the basement. Inside, he found a room filled with shelves, once painted white, but now broken, and with splintered wood fragments showing through the paint. Dented cans of food and smashed bottles of fruits and vegetables covered the floor of the storage room. Studying the scrapes and hackings, Xander figured the vandals had used hatchets on the shelves and walls as they destroyed the food.

Behind him, Higgins said, "Is he in there?"

Xander shook his head, "No."

He started to step out, but realized that something wasn't right in the room. Something unexpected seemed to be staring at him, hiding, but not hiding.

"Wait," Xander said. Higgins stopped backing out. Behind him, the sheriff's men peered over Higgins's shoulder.

Xander turned back into the room. He reached over the pile of cans and bottles to touch one shelf at the far end of the storage room. The white shelf had been dented instead of splintered. It felt smooth and cool – metal. He cleared away the glass and cans between him and the shelf so he could get closer, lean down, and study it.

Underneath the shelf, and at the back, he saw a small round bump. He reached back and pressed. A click released the shelf from the wall behind it. Xander pulled the shelf toward him. It swung, balanced and silent, on a small pair of hinges at the left end. Behind the shelf, Xander saw a small keyhole and another smaller hole. A thin wire emerged from the small hole and was attached to a screw-head at the back of the shelf – a way to pull the shelf closed and against the wall from the inside of the next room.

And then, only because he knew it must be there, he discovered the outline of a door. The join was smooth and hidden by the framing for the shelves. All the hinges and knobs had to be on the inside, within the next room. The door would swing into that farther space, away from the shelves in this room.

"What the . . ." one of the deputies said.

Xander glanced behind him and said, "Please, be quiet."

Higgins nodded and backed out of the storage room another step, signaling the men behind him to silence.

Xander knocked on the secret door. "Imam Moussa?"

Silence allowed his voice to echo around the concrete walls of the room. He knocked again, and spoke in Farsi. "I am Alexander Evans Lloyd. The mob is gone, arrested by the Sheriff's men. Mr. Bruce Higgins from Husayn told me you might be protecting your ancient Quran. He's afraid you won't know when it's safe to come out."

There was no sound on the other side of the door. Xander repeated what he had said and added a few details about his Grandfather's news team filming the mob. When still no sound came, the sheriff's men began to move about impatiently.

Xander blurted, "Mr. Moussa, I think you must be the one who takes care of the beautiful garden around Masjid Maryam. Some of your garden has been destroyed. My friend, Haroon Qubadi, and I want to help you replant it."

He heard a shuffling sound on the other side of the door. Xander signaled for Bruce Higgins and the other sheriff's men to stand still. He didn't want the old man to be frightened by all the people. As the lock turned in the door, he added, "I am out here with the sheriff's men. They've been helping us search for you."

The lock stopped turning.

"These men arrested the mob."

The lock turned. The door opened. A man wearing a long dishdashah tunic emerged, carrying a box.

Xander recognized it as a presentation box for a Quran. He said, "Imam Benjamin Moussa, you and your Quran are now safe."

CHAPTER TWENTY-SEVEN

Late in the day of the riot at Masjid Maryam, the FBI Agent Guy Saurus stepped in. When he came to the offices of Evans International, he cited racial and religious harassment as his reasons for pushing the FBI into the case.

"Irony on top of irony," Grandpa said.

Saurus glared at him, while Angus stood stiff and expectant.

"This is now a Federal matter, not a local matter." Saurus said, and then he put out his hand toward the camera that Angus carried. "I need the film of the mob that you fellows took."

Angus and Dell looked surprised by the request, but both handed over the memory cards from their cameras.

After that, Saurus and his associates interviewed Grandpa and his body guards, Juan Muñoz and Gary Patton.

By the next morning, Xander realized that the sheriff and the police chief weren't going to rely on Saurus and his team for a thorough investigation. During the week after the mosque attack,

Xander gave six, or maybe it was seven interviews to the Clackamas County sheriff's men and to city police detectives about what he knew concerning the mob at Maryam. Grandpa Gilbert was with the detectives a lot longer and more often. Grandpa Gilbert also limped more than usual, but by week two, his bruises had gone through the green phase and by week three were merely yellow.

Also during week one after the attack, Mr. Saurus knocked on the front door of the Evans' house and asked to interview Xander. Grandpa stepped onto the porch and closed the screen between Saurus and Xander.

"You have copies of Xander's statements to the police and the sheriff. You need to read those first, and then if you still need something, we'll let you talk to him with our lawyer present."

Saurus spoke toward the screen door, glaring at Xander. "I thought your grandson was seventeen. Isn't he old enough to talk for himself?"

"It's not him I don't trust," Grandpa said.

Xander watched the muscles on Mr. Saurus' jaw tighten. "I understand your kid speaks Arabic."

"He lived in Pakistan for a number of years. He speaks many Middle Eastern languages."

"He ever been trained in a military camp in Pakistan?"

Xander's back shivered. This man threatened him.

Grandpa snorted disgust. "Saurus, you clearly haven't read anything the sheriff gave you."

"Just wanting to check on some things," Saurus said, glancing through the screen toward Xander. His dark eyebrow rose and he fixed Xander with a stare that held promise for future encounters.

"Well," Grandpa said, "you come back when you've read those interviews."

"I can come back with a warrant. It seems mighty odd that your kid found that fellow hiding in the basement when nobody else could find him. Seems like he knew something . . ."

"That old man was hiding from a mob. You've decided to blame the victim, and anyone helping the victim. Get your warrant, if you think you can. Meanwhile, leave my grandson alone."

Inside the screen, Xander wondered if Saurus had been harassing the old man at the mosque the way he harassed Haroon's and Xander's families.

*   *

As soon as Grandpa came inside and closed the door, he said, "Xander bring me your computer." They copied all the data, documents, contact lists and emails to an external hard drive and then did the same with Gilbert's home computer.

"Agent Saurus will be after these next," Grandpa said, "and they have to be here or he will make something sinister out of their absence. But we'll make certain he doesn't take our contacts and our information completely away from us."

"Grandpa, I've been searching the internet for news about the kids at Friends' School. He'll see that, and say I've been contacting people in Pakistan."

"Yes, he will. There is nothing we can do about that."

Xander knew the deck was stacked against Haroon's family, and the imam, but he'd never realized it was stacked against him and Grandpa as well. He figured he should have known.

Two days after his visit to their door, a judge granted Agent Saurus a search warrant to look for what he claimed was evidence of anti-government activity in the Masjid Maryam and at the home of Alexander Evans Lloyd.

"Why does Saurus believe any of these accusations?" Xander asked.

Grandpa raised his left eyebrow. Xander knew it was a stupid question.

"Okay, why does the judge believe them?"

"Get ready for stuff, Xander."

"Yes, sir."

"And read your history books. Look up 'The history of dissent in the United States' and see what you find."

Okay, I deserved that assignment.

He saw that no one and no thing was safe from those who made a business of pitting ordinary people against each other. Over the next weeks on talk shows and interview shows about the day of the riots, the attacked became the suspects and the arrested aggressors became the victims.

At least Xander could be glad the beautiful Quran and its presentation box were safely at Bruce Higgin's home, a location that Saurus could not guess. He didn't want to imagine the damage Saurus's crew was inflicting on the mosque, tearing into walls and pulling up floor boards to find whatever Saurus claimed was there.

On the Friday after the mob attack of Maryam, Agents arrived at the Evans' porch with a warrant to take all computers in the house on the grounds that Xander may have used any one of them and that Xander was known to consort with terrorists.

"I consort with the same people," Grandpa said. "You can arrest me, too."

Saurus glared at Grandpa. He didn't arrest either Xander or Grandpa, but he and his men walked out the door with three computers.

The next Monday, Xander went to Aunt Justine's half of her duplex after Mr. Wray let him out of school. Grandpa didn't want him at home alone when Agent Saurus might show up again. He rested in her back den, watching cartoons and trying to chill when Aunt Justine answered a knock on the door.

"What the dickens are you doing here?" Aunt Justine's voice carried clearly through her home and over the beep-beep of a Road Runner cartoon. Xander pushed off the couch and hurried into the entry hall. There stood Agent Saurus and the same man who had taken their computers.

Aunt Justine stood between Xander and the door, edging him off to the side with her considerable shoulder and a sharp elbow. "I don't believe in computers," she told Saurus, "so you may as well take your little piece of paper back to that judge and tell him that."

"I have a warrant to search the house, Ma'am. I can do it nice, or I can do it quick, which isn't so nice ..."

Xander said. "You might as well let him in."

She glared at Xander. "I don't have to accept injustice and stupidity just because some judge is yellow to the gills."

Xander took hold of Aunt Justine's elbow and pulled her toward him. "This is not stupidity, it's harassment, so let him harass while we take notes. Notes make good story. Story gets around."

"Are you threatening me, young man?"

Aunt Justine stared at Xander, then at Saurus and his muscled backup man. She burst into laughter. "Threatened!" she cackled. "Tough Agent Saurus and his FBI goon feel threatened!"

Not a good idea, Xander thought. But he knew from history and experience that Aunt Justine never edited herself.

Saurus's muscleman pushed into the house and past Aunt Justine. "Where's your computers, boy?" he said.

"You have them," Xander said. "My aunt just told you she doesn't own one."

An hour later, Aunt Justine's house looked like a tornado victim. Saurus left with her collected carbon copies of handwritten letters to several congressmen, and to what appeared to be every newspaper in the nation, including Evans International. She had written about justice every day, all her life.

As she watched her collected letters go out the door, Aunt Justine said to Xander, "I don't write just to write. I write to encourage people to stand up for themselves. And look what happens when you do stand up."

"Yeah," Xander said, "Agent Saurus feels all threatened and shivery."

She glanced at him, anger pulling her lips tight. Then she realized he was pulling her leg and she let loose with one of her big guffaws — a laughter edged with tears.

* *

The next day, their lawyer, Nelson, issued a statement to Lamb's *National Courier* outlets across the United States, and the same statement to the *Evans' Media* outlets. He said, "Agent Saurus wants the freedom to harass the imam of Maryam and the Evans family without the need to present proof of a connection to terrorism."

On most channels, the evening news played Nelson's statement as background to an announcer's skewed synopsis of the events. Nobody listening could understand what Nelson said.

The editorial page of the Evans' editions of the *Journal of the Americas* said:

"Agent Saurus has film from two different news sources showing that the inspiration for the riots at several mosques and one synagogue was Pastor Gotamere's sermon. The Twitter invitations to create the mobs at those locations have been traced by computer forensics experts back to Gotamere's offices in California.

"The FBI and Agent Saurus have access to the same computer information and to the same film, but they choose not to listen, see, or share the contents with the judge. No one at the FBI or Homeland Security will discuss the film and computer information with reporters, or admit that they know about it."

Soon after this editorial went to print, someone leaked the information to national news that Alexander Evans Lloyd had been heard encouraging members of the mob to flee before the arrival of the sheriff's men.

Mike Halverson created a cartoon showing a clear likeness of Agent Saurus with four heads. One mouth shouted, "The Lloyd boy broke up the crowd." The other mouth shouted, "But the Lloyd boy started the riot." A third shouted, "The Lloyd boy rescued the victim." The last head shouted, "And the victim is guilty."

Mr. Lamb's photographer, Dell, published a few stills and an editorial denouncing harassment of the victim of a mob. That was the only helpful news from Lamb's media empire. Lamb's newspapers and television stations outweighed *Evans International* by five to one in every category. As the biggest news organization in the country, what Lamb's *National Courier* said got heard and read everywhere. What they didn't say left a very loud echo.

Gerald Fafner, Lamb's famous talk-show host, lived in a lime-lit fantasy world. Night after night, he claimed that "the presence at the cemetery of the Evans family with bodyguards and camera men is proof they incited the riot at this mosque. Isn't it obvious why they were there? What other purpose could Evans have to pick that day to visit the graves of his daughter and son-in-law who are buried in the garden behind the mosque? The Evans-Lloyd couple was killed in Pakistan during an altercation with other dissidents."

Xander seethed to Haroon, "Other dissidents? Fafner acts like Mom and Dad were revolutionaries killed by a fight between revolutionaries."

"He sounds desperate to me," Haroon said. "Only men who are afraid of something lie and stretch truth as much as Gerald Fafner."

"Scared, maybe," Xander said, "but look who buys everything he says."

*   *

Two weeks after the attack on the mosque, George, the sound man, returned from the hospital to work at *Evan's International* news offices. He wore a collar around his neck for support, but he was able to raise a hand in greeting as he passed Xander in the halls. He told Xander that his bandaged left eye had suffered broken bones, but he would see, and the bones would heal. However, Xander, remembered the crunch of fist on eye socket, and the courage George showed as he waited for an ambulance. He and Haroon liked George and sought him out at lunch time on many days. George told Xander and Haroon stories of working with big Angus on the frontlines of war and strife in Iraq and Afghanistan. He hoped to go back there again soon.

Xander asked him, "When you go back, will you try to find my .. . find my friends and my teachers?"

George studied his coffee cup and then glanced at Haroon before he looked Xander in the eye. "Pardon this question, Xan, but do you think they've found their bodies and aren't telling you because of . . ."

Xander's face felt hot. "Because I might commit suicide?"

George nodded.

"I . . . that's possible, but I've been reading everything, and it all agrees that they found nothing under the school. Even if my grandpa is trying to keep information from me, you'd think some hint about them would be in other people's reports."

"Yeah. Secrecy is a leaky boat – look at the leaks of information that are coming out of the Grand Jury while it's still in session."

Xander had read some of those just recently. Information that only the Grand Jury should have about Nasdar Qubadi's case had been filtered into Fafner's shows and other news outlets.

"Those have to be from Saurus," Haroon said. "Those leaks have a purpose."

George nodded, "Yeah, that man has a reputation for dirty dealings, and so does Fafner."

"So will you look for my friends?" Xander asked.

George drew circles in the rings of condensation left by his cup. He shifted in his chair and sat up straighter. "Okay, give me a list of their names," George said. "And I'll need to know where they came from. Their tribe and their families may have some word that they're afraid to share with anyone. And, I'll need a letter of introduction from you, with your photo."

*   *

The Grand Jury leaks did have a purpose. It seemed they fueled acid-driven speculation on Plinder's death in the news tunnel. The editorials about Xander and Haroon took on a new life as soon as Xander was mentioned as being at the mosque. A *Boise Times* writer said "One of Oregon's county coroners claimed Beryl Plinder stabbed himself".

Claimed? Xander thought.

A television commentator on what everyone now called *In the Hen House News* said, "The proof that *Evans International* owns the prosecutors of Portland, Oregon is the fact that Alexander Evans Lloyd and his accomplice, Haroon Qubadi, aren't being tried for the murder of Mr. Beryl Plinder."

"Damn!" Haroon said. "How come I'm just your accomplice?"

Xander glanced at him. "Isn't it obvious? I'm the white man, so I must be the brains of the outfit."

"Your brains? The brains that need Calculus help from my brains?"

Xander didn't laugh. He said, "How do news people get to lie like this?"

"Didn't you listen to radio in Pakistan?" Haroon said. "How is this different?"

"This is the United States. These stations don't belong to a dictator or a tribal leader who wants to control what people think."

Haroon shrugged, "Really? Maybe not an elected dictator, but they belong to somebody with power. Your Grandpa isn't like all newspaper owners. Some just want to pump out whatever story brings advertising. Others want to destroy any story that doesn't feed their ideas. You and me, free and not accused – that's not good PR for their attitude."

One afternoon, as Xander listened to a radio talk show, Haroon came to Xander's desk and listened to a caller. The man said, "Mr. Qubadi is clearly working with the Al Quaida-in-Iraq."

"That's Mr. Breiton's voice," Haroon said.

Xander turned the radio up, listening until the caller hung up. "Right," he said, "That soccer dad. The guy who offered to buy the Taziyan."

"He's been back to our place four times," Haroon said. "He offered Mom what he calls 'an easy fix for her financial troubles.'"

Mr. Wray glanced up. "Is he threatening her?"

"No. Well, maybe it's a threat. He says she might as well sell before she's arrested, too."

"I'd call that a threat. What has your security man done with him?"

"The one time he came after Joe started work there, Joe stood in Breiton's air space and told him not come back. I think he believed Joe might hurt him."

"Breiton's got a motive for pushing to keep Nasdar in jail," Mr. Wray said, "He'd get a good business location at a cheap price."

"Motive, maybe," Mr. Halverson said, "but not a big enough motive to have you attacked in the tunnel. But if that was him on the radio, he's sure egging others into believing the rumors."

"What station is this talk show?" Mr. Wray asked.

Haroon looked at the dial. "KKLP."

Mr. Wray seemed puzzled. "That one's hard to track. Belongs to some investment group called "Voice of Reason.""

"Reason?" Halverson snorted. "What a come down for the Great Enlightenment!"

"If we don't know who they are, what can we do?" Haroon asked.

"I've already got a detective on Breiton," Mr. Wray said. "Eventually, we'll see where Mr. Breiton thinks he might get money. Good listening, Haroon."

CHAPTER TWENTY-EIGHT

In mid-December, the Grand Jury finished its work in Portland, Oregon's Hatfield Federal Courthouse. The Grand Jury decided that the United States Government had presented enough evidence to charge Mr. Nasdar Qubadi with: "Conspiracy to levy war against the United States; Conspiracy to provide material support and resources to Al-Quaida-in-Iraq; Money laundering; Conspiracy to possess and discharge firearms in furtherance of crimes of violence."

When Mr. Nelson read the charges to the two families, Nazneen Qubadi closed her dark eyes and swayed in grief. Grandpa Gilbert hovered over her. Haroon put his arms around his mother's shoulders and she hugged him tightly.

In the days that followed, there were occasional reasons for hope in the darkness. The FBI found nothing at Maryam and failed in its bid to get an extension of its search warrant. Ecumenical Ministries of Portland arranged work parties of Christians, Jews and Muslims to clean up the mess at Maryam and the Sephardic Synagogue, which was the only other building severely damaged during the Gotamere riots. Several well-known builders offered labor and material to repair the damage done by the FBI and by the crowd. Xander and Haroon got the soccer team and their families to replant the gardens at Maryam and clean paint off the marble entry way. Imam Moussa directed their work, his strong arms digging holes for roses far faster than Xander or Haroon could manage.

At the Sephardic synagogue, Imam Moussa and Rabbi Hassan had a good time together, replanting the shrubbery that had been destroyed. Donations for the repairs came from many building and nursery supply companies around the city.

"You see," said Imam Moussa, "there is love as well as hate in the world. And some seek justice."

The biggest obstacle to finishing repair of the mosque was the Arabic script on the entry walls at Maryam. They had to await a skilled script artist to recarve the Quran passages. Rabbi Silver and his congregation at the Shalom Synagogue created a fund to pay for the carver when that artist was found.

Another hopeful sign began to appear. During the week leading up to Christmas, Xander discovered a letter to the editor in the *National Courier* from the father of a teammate.

"Fear rules this country again" wrote Mr. Takashi. "Fear rules just as it did in 1919, in 1942, in 1953. As in those earlier times, the accused is treated as guilty. For Nasdar Qubadi there has been no trial, no jury of peers, but most news outlets have convicted him. Fear refuses access to justice. Courage would allow the accused to present a defense. Our television and radio commentators stir up dread. They show no courage."

Haroon cut out, folded and carried this letter in his pocket. As the month wore on, a few more such letters showed up in the newspapers, including letters from the rabbis of the local synagogues. At least some people defended Mr. Qubadi's rights.

But there were also letters from members of a group calling itself "Sons of America" urging that Mr. Qubadi be sent to Guantanamo Bay as an enemy combatant with no rights to a trial.

At the restaurant, "Sons of America" picketers showed up, standing in the driveway and discouraging customers by waving signs whose message was "Don't buy food from terrorists!" The Sons of America kept the driveway blocked as often as they could, and traffic at the restaurant slowed to nearly nothing. Those who did come in the driveway were yelled at and their cars were whacked with signs.

Xander got the idea of taking photos of the picketers from across the street. Mr. Halverson took the photos of the most frequent picketers to the police station where an officer friend helped him identify one of the men as Officer Bailey in civilian clothes. It turned out that the police chief had suspended Officer Bailey for his multiple mistakes in the investigation of the attack in the news tunnel. The union had kicked up a half-hearted fuss about the suspension, but the Chief had stuck to her rights, so the fuss died.

The other person in the photos turned out to be Sandy Pollard, a small-time drug dealer and occasional informant for Bailey. Pollard and Bailey were registered members of The *Sons of America*. It turned out that no one could make them stop picketing as long as they were peaceful, or at least relatively so.

Jan Nelson got the police chief to tell her officers to haul away anyone who obstructed traffic, including the parking lot and driveway. But the police didn't come every time they were called.

The bouncer, Joe, from Rick Johnson's security force, could intimidate one or two picketers, but often many more demonstrators came. Mrs. Qubadi told Joe not to protect the driveway after dark, and never if there were more than two hecklers out there. She gave him a cell-phone camera to help prove what was going on.

Thus, December represented a big drop-off in the number of Muslim families willing to be seen at *The Taziyan*. That was when the seventh-grader, Tekla Jones, and her advertising campaign again showed its value. The soccer families began planning events there – weddings and birthdays. And Ecumenical Ministries urged its member churches to eat at the restaurant. More Christian and Jewish families came to dinner at *The Taziyan* during December than ever before. Nevertheless, business barely paid the cost of groceries, heat and light.

* *

"Look at this," Haroon said, one morning. "This has to have been leaked by Agent Saurus."

Xander read over his shoulder in the *Washington Courier* online. The headline said, "*Evans International* implicated in Qubadi support of Terrorists."

Xander felt his throat tighten and his body heat. "The *Washington Courier*? Isn't that a Lamb paper?"

"Yeah. Read."

"A forensic study of the computers taken from Editor Gilbert Evans' home shows that both he and his grandson, Alexander have been in close communication with members of the border town in Northeastern Iraq. Alexander Evans Lloyd has been a person of interest in the murder of activist Beryl Plinder. These communications raise the level of suspicion that Evans and his grandson provide support for persons of interest in an ongoing investigation of terrorism in that area."

Xander had read enough. He showed James Wray the online story. Soon they found similar articles in several other newspapers that were not related to Louis Lamb. Grandpa called Nelson. Nelson presented the evidence to the Judge Smith in the Qubadi Grand Jury hearing. The judge called Agent Saurus and told him to cease leaking information from the case to the public.

The next day, Nelson was with Xander and Grandpa in the Library at Max Million Foundation when the judge called him. Nelson put his call on speaker phone.

The judge said, "FBI agent Saurus claims he has no idea how that information got out. He promised to investigate and stop the leaks. But he also says that it is probably one of the members of the grand jury."

"Are you going to impound those computers?" Grandpa bellowed. "Are you ordering an investigation of the leaks?"

"I am, but the cat is out of the bag, and can't be put back in at this point."

"Agent Saurus and his methods can be halted if you call for a panel outside the FBI to investigate his methods."

"That's going a little far, don't you think?"

"Not far enough, Judge. Not anywhere near far enough. He's destroying me, but more, he's out to destroy my grandson who is the victim here along with the Qubadi family."

"Victim? That remains to be seen, and will be seen in the courtroom."

*   *

On the evening of December eighteenth, Xander and Haroon served dinner in the closed, private dining room of the Taziyan. The guests celebrated the wedding of a soccer team member's older brother. Afterward, while the families toasted and talked, Haroon and Xander left the private dining room and stood in the darkened main restaurant near the mural of the hounds of the hunt. The hunting dogs, the Taziyan, seemed, more than ever, to be slobbering after the goat.

The boys looked out the windows and whispered to each other. Three new men arrived on the sidewalk, carrying protest signs. After a moment, both boys stepped into the vestibule between the inner restaurant and the outer door. They wanted to get close enough to read the protest signs. Xander waited until each man stood in the street lamplight and tried to photograph without a flash.

One sign proclaimed, "Boycott Anti-American Restaurant."

Another had scrawled, "Terrorist Food Kills."

"And," Haroon said, pointing at the third man's sign, "Here comes the spelling winner."

"Qubadies! Terrists! Go Home!"

"That's the same big guy that's been picketing in the daytime outside Grandpa's *Journal of the Americas*?" Xander asked. "His name is Chuck, the guy at the riot at Maryam."

Haroon peered more closely at the guy. "He's the one who hit George McCardell?"

"Yep."

At that moment, Tekla came up beside them in the cool entry hall. Her coat bulged with her going-home sweater, but she also pulled something else from under her coat.

"My dad won this at darts down at his favorite tavern."

What she held up looked like a spherical spaceship with one foot and a knob on top. The metal body of the spaceship had been painted with bright primary colors. "It's a spinning top," she said.

"What would he want with that thing?" Xander asked.

"He didn't want it, so he gave it to me. Want to see what it does?"

"Uh-oh," Haroon said, pointing outside.

The three picketers had stashed their signs in the hedge. Now they strode toward the restaurant.

"They can't come here," Tekla said. "The police said 'sidewalk only'."

But the men were almost at the door. The biggest man, the one in front, reached inside his jacket.

"A gun," Haroon shouted, and grabbed at the door lock.

Xander pushed Tekla behind him toward the inner door. "Tekla, inside. Now!"

Haroon scrabbled at the lock of the outer door, but the front man pushed his way inside, flattening Haroon against the wall. Xander shoved Tekla inside the restaurant and slammed the door. He stood between the door and the man.

The big man, Chuck, brought his hand out of his pocket holding his wallet. He faced Xander and flipped it open. Xander breathed again, but he knew, gun or not, these men were dangerous. He recognized that wallet flipping gesture from the movies. A fleeting thought told him Chuck also learned it from film.

"My badge," the man said. "Officer Charles Streitheimer."

At that moment, Haroon slipped out the front door behind the men. Xander could see Haroon's shadow running for the back door of the restaurant. He had to keep the men's attention away from Haroon.

"What badge?" he asked Chuck. "Officer of What? Nobody can read that badge."

"The restaurant is closed," Tekla said from inside the second door, her voice small and high with fright.

"And we may have to take her with us to the authorities – child neglect."

"Her mother is right here, in the kitchen," Xander said.

"Keeping her out late at night – doesn't sound like a good mother to me," one of the men said.

At that moment, Joe, the Johnson Security man, stepped into the entry way. "You gentlemen need to get back to the sidewalk. I've called the city police."

Tekla squeezed out behind Joe. Xander moved to stand beside her, taking her arm to keep her from getting any closer to the men.

The men moved forward, leaning toward Joe. One held open the inner door while two of them surrounded Joe. The biggest man pushed his face toward Joe's. "You'd best stay out here then, little fellow, and wave the police off. Otherwise, this restaurant owner will be in deep shit with the Federal Government."

Xander hoped Haroon was in the kitchen by now, warning his mother.

All three men swept past Xander and shoved Joe inside, leaving Tekla behind. They seemed to forget their threat against her. Joe waved a 'get her out of here' gesture. As Joe fought to slow the men down, Xander yanked on Tekla's arm. She came quickly out the front door, and ran with him silently around the restaurant.

As they ran, Tekla gripped his hand. She seemed to know the danger she was in, but Xander hated leaving Joe to fight off three big guys. He glanced back. The men dragged Joe into the main dining room with them. Xander ran flat out down the path at the side of the restaurant. At the back deck, he came to a short brick wall surrounded by a pruned hedge. He swung his leg up, sat on the frozen bricks and reached to help Tekla over. They forced their way through the twiggy hedge and dropped down on the other side with scratches on their arms and hands.

The wall and hedge separated the back deck from the steep incline into Sullivan's Gulch and the Interstate freeway. As soon as they were on the gulch side of the hedge, Xander crouched with Tekla at the trunk of an old maple tree.

"Tekla," he whispered.

She nodded.

"You gotta stay here," he said. "Don't leave this tree or you might be seen, or worse, you might roll down to the freeway."

She wiped her sleeve over her nose, and said. "You're cold."

She was right about that, but mostly he shivered because of alarm for others. He had to find out what those men might be doing to Haroon, Mrs. Qubadi, to Tekla's mother, and to Joe.

"I'll be fine," he said. "I'll tell your mother where you are."

He wished he hadn't left his cell phone in his jacket pocket. At that moment, he heard two men step out on the deck of the restaurant.

"You know, Joe," the intruder said, "I think you been lying to us. Mrs. Qubadi has money stashed, and you know where. She's gonna send that money to Iraq and you'll be an accessory to a crime."

Joe's voice answered. "You've been warned. Get off of this property."

"I wouldn't be threatening a man with a gun, if I were you."

"You use that gun and you'll be in for the long stretch," Joe said, his voice amazingly calm.

Xander squatted down beside Tekla, pulling her where the tree completely hid her from any stray gunshot. He felt her hand go to her mouth as she muffled a whimper.

"Joe is smart," he whispered to her. "He brought the man outside away from your mom." He wanted to sound certain, but he knew there were two others in there, probably also armed.

The man on the deck said, "You can be arrested for obstructing an officer of the law."

"FBI don't like people impersonating them," Joe said.

Xander straightened to see if the two were alone. He thought Haroon might be hiding nearby.

And then he remembered the police sirens that had approached the mosque. He squatted near Tekla and said, "Do you still have that gadget, that spinning top?"

She nodded and pulled the metal toy from her coat. Xander could see the top's swirling colors even in the darkness.

"This makes a whining noise, right?"

She nodded.

"Can you make it do that noise, but stay behind this tree?"

Her face brightened as she understood. Tekla placed the foot of the top against the flare of the tree's root. Holding it firmly, she pulled up on the knob of the top and pushed down. The thing began to make a high wheezing sound. She pulled faster and faster on the knob. The sound rose and fell as she pumped.

"That's great," Xander mouthed.

Up on the deck, he heard Joe say, "Is that out on the freeway?"

"You bastard. You did call the police."

Tekla seemed to be tiring, so Xander held the top's foot against the root while she worked the knob. Its spin burnt his fingers, but he hung on.

On the deck, quick footsteps came out the kitchen door

A voice yelled, "Police! Let's go."

Tekla continued to pull and push on the knob. The sirens wheezed and whirled. Above them voices called, footsteps pounded. Xander's finger ripped against the twisting foot, but he kept it there, hoping.

When Xander glanced up to see what was happening, the intruder already was off the deck and running around to the parking lot. He said, "Okay stop." Tekla stopped, breathing hard.

Xander put his finger in his mouth and sucked hard on the torn blister.

Joe peered down at Xander. Off in the distance they could all hear real police sirens wailing toward the restaurant. The door from the kitchen opened.

"Joe," Haroon said. "You and the others gotta come in or the police will think you are the robbers we called about."

"What about the other two men?" Joe asked.

"They stole our cash," Haroon said, "and they were gonna take whatever they could get from the wedding guests, but they ran out the front as soon as they heard sirens."

Suddenly, Xander saw the blur of Tekla run past him up the hill, carrying her top. "Joe," she cried, "Xander and I, we're down here. Pull us up on the deck."

Xander climbed the hill after her, boosted her into Joe's grasp, and then let Haroon reach over to pull him up.

A few moments later, they were all in the kitchen, brushing dirt and tree grime out of Tekla's hair. They heard the police enter the parking lot. Mrs. Jones hugged Tekla to her, admiring the top and how much it did sound like police sirens.

Haroon said, "The wedding guests don't even know what happened out here. They're still upstairs presenting toasts."

"Joe," Mrs. Qubadi said, "could you meet the police while I warn the wedding party?"

Joe held up his cell phone. "I'll show the police my photos of the bast ... buzzards. They weren't FBI. For a while, I thought maybe they were that prosecutor, Jory's men."

Mrs. Qubadi shook her head. "No. Mr. Jory wouldn't send bullies and robbers. He'd lose his chance to win in court."

"Maybe they come from whatever crowd tried to kill the boys in the news tunnel," Joe said. "They scared the bejee ... the blisters out of me, threatening to take Tekla."

Xander moved to Mrs. Qubadi's kitchen computer. As he flipped through, looking for something, he said, "Joe, let me copy those photos onto the restaurant computer quick. The police might take your phone, and mine. Then we won't have photos for the defense lawyer."

Joe handed him the phone. "Right. Bailey might have gotten his job back and might intercept evidence."

Haroon fished the memory card out, and they began downloading the pictures. They were still working as the police banged on the front door.

Mrs. Jones hugged Tekla to her and said, "Let's all go talk to police while Mrs. Qubadi explains to the wedding party. Haroon can stay and get the photos downloaded."

Officer Bailey wasn't with the police cars. But Xander and Haroon figured he probably knew something was happening here. His group, The Sons of America, seemed to be around all the time.

An hour later, the police pulled out of the parking lot, taking Joe's phone and each of the adult's and the kid's statements with them. They promised to put the photos through the computer for identification.

Agent Saurus soon arrived. "I sent no FBI agents," he said. "You misunderstood what they said."

"We know what they said," Xander told him. "But we didn't believe you would send such clowns."

Saurus looked at Xander. "That's the first I knew that you understood me."

"I don't think you're stupid, Mr. Saurus," Xander said, "You just don't like to find out you're wrong."

Saurus studied Xander. "About your friend and his father, I'm not only right, but I have plenty of evidence. You risk doing time for aiding them – you and your high and mighty grandfather."

Saurus called the police and demanded they give him Joe's phone and its camera – evidence in a Federal case, he said.

"They broke in on us," Haroon reminded him.

Saurus just glared at Haroon. "So you say," he said.

* *

Soon after Saurus left, the wedding party prepared to leave. The groom's family offered to help Mrs. Qubadi clean up, but she sent them off with a blessing. "May this be the beginning of a long and happy life together – and not too eventful."

As the families said good bye on the front porch, Haroon whispered to Joe, "I downloaded your phone list, as well as your photos."

Joe let out a sigh of relief. "Thank you. Thank you. I really need that list to take care of all of you."

Haroon said, "I think when those guys decided to take our money, they were covering-up for trying to terrorize us."

Xander said, "The biggest of those guys is Chuck who clocked George. Charles Streitheimer is his real name. He's been hanging around the *Journal of the Americas* building. And I'm pretty sure another is one of the fellows who followed Haroon to his mosque that day, the guys in the blue truck."

"Yeah," Haroon said. "He drove that truck."

Joe said, "Maybe they were hired by the same person who hired Beryl Plinder. But who? And what would they gain?"

A moment passed in silence with no answers.

Beside Xander, Tekla started to head quietly back into the restaurant, but Xander caught her shoulder and said, "When I tell you to go inside, you don't come out and start arguing with strangers. Don't you ever do that again, Tekla."

"I was all right," she protested.

"If one of those guys had taken you – my heart . . ." Suddenly he realized what he had been about to say, and stopped with his mouth open.

Tekla glanced up at him. "I heard your heart. Thumps loud when you're scared."

"Uhm, yeah," he stammered. "Not good for it."

She seemed to stand taller as she turned to him. "I could have bitten one of them on the leg while you and Joe beat up on the other two."

Haroon said, "Tekla, do you know the difference between brave and foolhardy?"

She turned her back on them, and said. "You just think a girl who's brave *is* foolhardy."

Xander shuddered, and leaned against the nearest table.

Haroon and Joe studied the night, but Xander caught the smile that passed between them.

That danged Tekla.

*   *

The next morning, when Mr. Wray escorted Xander and Haroon inside Grandpa Gilbert's office, Mr. Nelson stood there with Mrs. Qubadi. Grandpa nodded at the boys and said, "The police arrested three men for the robbery at the Taziyan: Sandy Pollard, Charles Joseph Streitheimer and Martin Campbell. The men claim no one hired them to harass the Qubadi's, and their lawyer has gotten them out on bail."

Xander asked, "Couldn't they get any evidence off at least the big guy, Chuck – that Charles guy? He's the one that hangs around the Journal building. He had a billfold and a fake badge."

Mr. Nelson said, "Everything in the billfold was fake including the leather."

"But they got his real name," Xander said, "They wouldn't let him out on bail without a real ID."

"True," Nelson said. "His name is Charles Joseph Streitheimer. The badge says he's the new leader of the Aryan Nations. But there are several who claim that mantle, and none can get it together to lead anybody."

"They couldn't tie him into Pastor Gotamere's followers?" Xander asked.

"Pastor Gotamere wouldn't be caught touching someone like Streitheimer. And she wouldn't be giving him a written contract to do what he's already itching to do."

"What about the Sons of America. Is that Streitheimer, too?"

"We haven't found any real group with that name advertising for members or registering for non-profit status or doing any of the things most groups do. They are the puzzle."

"So what do we have?" Grandfather asked.

"We have a lot of people ready to believe whatever feeds their paranoia," Nelson said.

"So," Grandpa said, "we've got to step up security around the Qubadi residence and the restaurant."

Mrs. Qubadi said, "You're a target as well, Gilbert Evans. Saurus continues to leak misinformation about you and Xander to the newspapers."

Mr. Nelson said. "I want more security at your house and anywhere you and Xander go."

"Me, too," Haroon said, reaching out to touch Grandfather's arm. "We can't lose you and Xan. You are family for us."

CHAPTER TWENTY-NINE

For the Qubadi family November and early December had been a time of public alarm and harassment by television reporters and the national media. There seemed to be only one place the media didn't try to invade – the family mosque, Husayn, west of town.

Haroon said, "I heard that since the riot at Maryam, other reporters stay away from the mosques, because they don't want to be accused of feeding racial and religious prejudice."

Xander scoffed. "Not feed prejudice? Every time they report on us, they mention that people are Muslim, or supporters of Muslims."

"Well," Haroon said, "I'm willing to accept their stupid reasoning as long as they leave the mosques alone."

On the third Friday in December, Haroon and his mother and sister invited Xander to their mosque in west Portland, Masjid Husayn. Mrs. Qubadi wore her special worship clothes, a loose gray dress that covered her from neck to toe. She added a four-foot-square blue hijab, or scarf, to cover her shoulders and her hair. Haroon and Xander wore men's loose tunics and caps – Xander hadn't worn a tunic or kameez shirt since the day he was rescued from the garden shed in Pakistan.

Five-year-old Gulbahar came downstairs ready to go. She wore a little girl's long frilly dress over tights, but she had draped her mother's green hijab around and around her body, then she'd brought it up to cover her short curls.

As soon as she appeared on the stairs, Haroon said, "That's way too big for you, Gul. You'll trip on it."

Mrs. Qubadi said, "Leave her be, Haroon. She can wear hijab if she wishes. But here, darling …," she helped Gulbahar tuck the ends into the dress collar so they wouldn't fly away. "Now you are a real grown up lady. Have you got your prayer memorized?"

"Allahu Akbar," Gulbahar said.

"God is most great," her mother said. "You are ready."

When they arrived at Masjid Husayn, Xander stared at it. He'd been close only when the guys following Haroon, the guys in the blue truck had parked nearby, lying in wait. On that day, he hadn't paid attention to the building. He'd been too interested in avoiding the notice of the followers.

Today, as he looked at the mosque, the design seemed foreign to his eye. The entry court had the usual fountain for ritual cleansing, but instead of a mosque with a round dome and thin minarets, he saw a square building with a squat fat tower.

"It used to be a Baptist church," Haroon explained. The bell tower became our minaret. Inside we added a Qibla wall so we can pray toward Mecca."

"The only problem with this design," Mrs. Qubadi said, "is that the women's prayer space is in the balcony instead of to the side of the men's prayer space. One day, when the government gives us back our money, we'll make it more like a mosque."

The family dipped their hands into the fountain, and wet their faces, hands and arms. Then they climbed the steps to the door, removed their shoes and entered the worship space. Xander remembered the man spitting into the fountain at Masjid Maryam, but he said nothing. No one wanted to think about that day now.

Inside, Mrs. Qubadi and Gulbahar separated from Haroon and Xander and started up the inner stairs to the women's section. Xander waved at Gulbahar who turned back, wanting to be with the boys. She looked very forlorn in her funny wrap of a scarf and her party dress.

"We'll see you soon, Guli-booli," Haroon said, giving her a nod. She stuck out her tongue at him, but her mother took her hand and urged her upstairs.

"Mama," Gulbahar said, "It doesn't smell nice today."

"It's probably the cleaner the building committee used on the wooden wall, Honey."

Xander sniffed, but didn't smell the lemony scent his mother had used in their house, or the Clorox and lemon smell of the hospital. Probably old cleaning fluid.

A voice from inside the building called the worshippers to prayer. That meant the service would start in about ten minutes, so he followed Haroon into the men's section where they spread the prayer rugs Haroon had brought. Some were already inside, sitting in quiet contemplation, or already praying.

Xander knew the prayers from Mohammed and Manzur, but at Friends Welcome School, he had never been with so many adult worshippers. It made him think of his friends, and of the teachers they had lost that day.

Please, Allah, God, let them be safe, or take them to paradise with you forever —with Mom and Dad.

As Xander and the other worshippers sat or prayed, Xander thought about the ways in which his various friends contacted God for worship, or they contacted God for guidance about the small and the large things in their lives.

His Quaker family did the same thing, only they did it in silence, waiting and listening. He thought of his mother, holding the hand of a dying patient, talking quietly to her of God's love, Allah's love. He thought of his father, strong and gentle, operating to give someone new vision – that moment before the attack. That moment . . . .

Xander stopped thinking and just prayed with the others, or tried to.

A worshipper opened and closed the outer door. The leader, who waited to start the service, glanced toward the hall, and motioned the worshipper inside, and pointed upstairs, as if to help the new person know where to go.

Xander returned his mind to prayer. He let his mind think about all of the prayers he had learned. He whispered to himself those parts he knew he could say honestly. For Haroon, the whole prayer praising God and the Prophet Muhammad as God's Messenger had deep meaning. Xander didn't want their differences to intrude.

Xander heard footsteps on the stairs and figured it was the new worshipper. He tried to force himself to forget about outside distractions. He breathed in as he bowed, and then lowered himself to lean on his knees, and later to the floor in each raka'at. In Pakistan, he'd grown used to the ritual that aids prayer. He loved the smell of sandalwood, pine and cedar, the perfumes of wheat and acacia, orange blossoms and lemon. All these he associated with worship and the sacred in the Middle East where his parents had lived since they graduated from medical school.

But a new smell came to him as he prayed, a smell he didn't recognize. It stung his nostrils.

The imam began speaking. Worship had started. The imam read from the Quran. Xander and Haroon rose to their haunches. The imam spoke in English and then in Arabic, repeating a passage from the Quran about two of the five pillars of life with God.

"In Quran, Surah 2:177," he said, "we learn that Righteousness is not turning your faces towards the east or the west. Righteous are those who believe in God . . .; and they give cheerfully, to the relatives, the orphans, the needy, . . .; and they keep their word whenever they make a promise; and they steadfastly persevere in the face of persecution, hardship, and war. These are the truthful; these are the righteous."

Xander realized he was listening only to parts of the Surah. Something kept dragging his attention.

The imam said, "Today, we wish to emphasize charity, Zakat, "Remember Surah 2:272," he said. "Any charity you give shall be for the sake of God. Any charity you give will be repaid to you, without the least injustice."

Without the least injustice. Xander thought. Charity had brought Nasdar nothing but injustice. He glanced at Haroon. Haroon stared toward the balcony where his mother and Gulbahar worshipped.

"Is that smoke?" Haroon whispered.

Xander looked up as well. He sniffed the air again and said. "And kerosene."

The imam continued his homily. "We know injustice comes but -,"

Haroon stood in the middle of the worshippers and turned toward the balcony. The imam glanced at him, puzzled.

"Fire," Haroon cried, looking toward the Imam. "Fire in the entry, the stairs."

Upstairs, a woman screamed. "Fire. Fire on the stairs."

The imam and several men from the back row ran toward the doorway that led to the stairs. The imam pulled off his head scarf and beat at the fire, yelling. "Smother it."

Men yanked off parts of their clothing, long tunics and head scarves, revealing their everyday clothes. But as they tried to beat out the fire, it leapt up the stair wall.

Xander yanked out his cell phone and called 9-1-1. Haroon ran to the space under the balcony and yelled toward the women. "Let down your hijab. Mother pull off Gulbahar's scarf. Tie them together and sling Gul to me."

His mother leaned over the balcony. She held Gulbahar to her side. A whoosh of smoke billowed into the balcony. The women screamed and backed away from the smoke toward the balcony rail.

"Their scarves will burn," Xander yelled. "Take off your scarves."

"Mother, lower Gul to me on your scarf."

Nazneen talked calmly to Gulbahar. "Haroon and Xander will save you." To the other women she called, "Tie your head scarves to the rail and climb down them."

She unwound Gulbahar's green scarf, tied it quickly to her own and wrapped the doubled scarf under Gulbahar's arms. She tied it around her daughter's waist, and lifted the child who squirmed back toward Nazneen and cried, "Mama." Nazneen lifted her over the rail. All around her the women worked quickly to tie their scarves to the rail and around their daughters.

"Come to me, Gul," Haroon called. "I am here for you and for Mama."

Gulbahar screamed as she looked down. Nazneen lowered her quickly, but the doubled scarves only reached as far as ten feet above the floor. Haroon reached up. Xander stood behind him to back up his catch.

"Let go, Mother."

"Allaahu Akbar," Nazneen prayed. Then she let go. Gulbahar fell into Haroon. Haroon tottered backwards into Xander. All three fell to the floor. In a moment, Xander heard Gulbahar laugh.

"I flew."

Haroon stood quickly, lifting Gulbahar in the air. "Good work, Sisty. Now you, Mama."

In the hall and stairwell, a man called. "It climbs. It climbs."

Above, Xander could see flames on the back wall of the balcony. As Haroon held his sister, Xander untied Gulbahar's green scarf and said, "I don't hear any sirens outside."

One of the women climbed over the rail and started down her rope of scarf. At first, she slipped too quickly along the silken surface.

She grabbed tightly and righted herself and came down the rest of the way.

A second woman began her descent, but her scarf came untied. She screamed and fell the last sixteen feet. Xander ran to her. She pushed her knotted skirts down and turned her face from him. "I'm all right. All right."

All around them women screamed. They lowered their daughters to their husbands, they climbed up over the rail and hung there, unwilling to trust the scarves they had tied there, and unwilling to let go and fall.

Nazneen yelled to her son, "I must check the knots on the scarves. The grandmothers must not fall."

While Nazneen worked at the scarves, Xander ran toward the group of men working on the stairway. In Arabic and then in English, he said. "The stairs are lost, Come catch the women."

A man looked at him, his eyes startled at a European stranger who spoke Arabic.

The imam turned toward the men. His face had already suffered burns. But he shouted, "Go. All but three of you. Go save the women and girls."

Within moments, most of the men were helping the women. The rest continued to fight their way up the stairs, beating out flames.

Three little girls had been lowered toward Haroon. The last was a small baby. Xander ran to catch her. She came down safely into his arms. The baby looked at Xander and giggled. Xander smiled at her and then handed her to Gulbahar, who was hovering near him, clearly wanting to help.

"Stay behind the men, Guli. And you take care of the baby."

Smoke billowed out of the hall and the balcony. Soon the area would be filled with smoke, so Xander turned to Haroon. "We have to get people outside."

"We don't know who is waiting outside." Haroon shouted. He turned toward Gulbahar and the others who had come down. "Go stand near the door and the fresh air, but stay inside until we can go out with you."

Gulbahar and the other girls backed up closer to the back entry.

"Get down on the floor," Xander called to them. "The air is better close to the floor"

Most of the older women had tied their scarves together. Coughing deeply, Nazneen Qubadi pulled her collar over her nose. She tested each knot, then she helped lift a woman over the rail, telling her "Hold to the hijab with all your bread-making muscles."

Behind Nazneen, the flames leapt to the ceiling near the stair doorway. The ceiling paint blistered and crackled as the heat moved across the balcony. As Nazneen worked, her coughing grew shallower. Other women leaned over the balcony, gasping for fresh air. Some climbed without waiting for Nazneen's help. Others, much older, clearly could not climb and had to be lowered like Gulbahar. Another woman helped Nazneen with the older women.

One woman climbed the rail, worried that her skirts were hiked up and climbed back. Nazneen shook her. "Your family needs you. And no one cares about your legs. Just go." She was more afraid of Nazneen than of being exposed, so she climbed over the rail once more, held on and descended.

For some, the scarf fabrics were too slick. Descent came faster than anticipated. They landed in a heap on the floor. The men helped each one out of the way of the next woman. For most, the men were able to break the fall and keep the women from hurting themselves. One woman hobbled away from her fall as if she had sprained something, but ignoring her pain, she ran to greet her little daughter.

Nazneen had to coax the last woman to climb over the rail. She was a plump woman with such fear on her face that Xander thought she might hurt Mrs. Qubadi.

"You must for your children." Nazneen yelled at the woman. Above them, the ceiling crackled. Plaster fell all around them.

"I can't . . ." the woman cried.

Nazneen slapped the woman, hoisted her left leg over the rail and said, "You grab on the hijab. I'm pushing you off."

The woman grabbed at the scarf rope. Nazneen lifted the woman's right leg and then held tight to her hands to make sure she had a good grip on the scarf. She lowered the woman as far as she could lean over the rail, and then let go of her. The woman slid neatly down the fabric and landed on Xander. Once she untangled from her dress and Xander's battered legs, she fled toward the band of children. Xander sat in a daze until he saw what was happening upstairs.

Behind Nazneen, the flames bit into the wood supports of the ceiling.

"Get out of there," Xander yelled. "The fire surrounds you."

Behind him, Gulbahar screamed, and with her, the baby. Nazneen pulled up the fabric rope, wrapped the whole around one leg, across her back and over her shoulder. She climbed up onto the rail, leaned into the rope of scarves and took two steps down the wall below the rail. When the wall ended, Nazneen rappelled as if she had been a mountain climber all her life.

Xander and Haroon stared at her as she came smoothly down. When she landed, she ran toward Gulbahar. The men followed her toward the back door.

"Where'd you learn that trick?" Haroon asked.

"When I was a child, we lived in the mountains," she said, and calmly took Gulbahar and the baby in her arms, and marched the women out the back door.

Once in the fresh air, the men found no one waiting to attack. The relief of that moment lived briefly, but everyone coughed and spit up, trying to rid themselves of the smoke. They heard the far away wail of fire sirens and an ambulance. Women had found their husbands and children. They ran away from the burning church, leaving long ropes of colorful scarves tied to the balcony railing.

The last to come out of the building was the imam. His hands and face had been burned, but when his wife tried to touch him with a cream taken from her purse, Xander stepped between them.

"Please, ma'am, wait for the burn unit to treat him. Ointment makes it worse and carries germs."

"What do you know?" the woman asked. "My mother always . . ."

Xander said, "I know. Most people think of ointment first because for a long time that is all we had."

The imam said, "Marjan, my dear, we will wait. This boy's parents were doctors."

Xander asked, "Sir, who was the last worshipper that came in?"

"I thought it was one of the women – a long dress, the hijab . . . but the shoulders and the way she walked – a man, I'm sure now."

"Did you see him leave?"

"No."

Haroon held out a piece of paper. "This note was left under a stone at the edge of the entry fountain."

The imam studied the note. "Ah! It quotes St. Augustine, "A just war is fought to avenge or avert evil, to protect the innocent and restore moral social order." As he read on, he said, "And here is a quote from Isaiah urging Jews to stop the worship of false god."

"That's the same passage preached by Pastor Lori Gotamere," Xander said.

"Big surprise there," Haroon said.

Fire engines turned into the driveway, sirens whooping, engines roaring. The worshippers moved out of their way. While the men and equipment tackled the fire, the paramedics looked over the imam's burns. A woman on the paramedic team checked out the one woman who had suffered a sprained ankle in the descent from the balcony. Behind them all, flames shot from the roof of the mosque.

* *

A week later, the fire department declared what everyone knew – an arsonist had painted an oily cleaner on the balcony walls sometime before Friday prayers. The stairs were slicked with kerosene during worship, and then set on fire. The police said they could not find a clue to the identity of the arsonist except for the note which had only the fingerprints of Haroon and the imam.

On the same day as the fire at Husayn, fires burned parts of a Mormon stake house, the Shalom synagogue, the Beaverton Monthly Meeting of Friends, a Buddhist temple and another mosque in nearby Beaverton. The offices of Ecumenical Ministries also had a small fire that was soon put out. Only the Qubadi mosque, Husayn, was destroyed, and only Nazneen's strength and knowledge and the imam's leadership prevented many from dying.

CHAPTER THIRTY

Pastor Lori Gotamere worked her way down the California coastal cities. Each crowd she greeted got play in the news. No matter how small the numbers, she was in a prominent position in every daily news during December, and on television in short news clips each night.

Xander and Haroon realized the media created her fame. Two of her recent rallies were completely televised on Fafner's channel, and there were prime time advertisements for her *"Christ in Christmas Rally"* scheduled during Christmas week.

Little sister, Gulbahar, stormed about the Qubadi house on the afternoon she heard that Pastor Gotamere's rally was scheduled in place of *The Grinch Who Stole Christmas* and *A Charlie Brown's Christmas*. Other changes followed the success of that Gotamere rally.

"Gotamere Grinch," Gulbahar sulked.

Haroon glanced at Xander.

"Let the little children . . ." Xander whispered.

Haroon rolled his eyes.

On the television, Xander watched in awe as Pastor Gotamere's once medium-sized radio ministry was made into a news sensation within the few weeks after the attack on Maryam. On December 22nd, she preached to the crowds at the Staples Center in Los Angeles. The frenzy caused by that crowd brought about other schedule changes, and attacks on mosques and synagogues in Los Angeles.

"Mommy," Gulbahar wailed on December 23rd, "Zuzu won't play on Christmas Eve because of that lady."

"Who's Zuzu?" Xander asked.

"A little girl in a movie," Haroon explained.

It's a Wonderful Life thus slid off the schedule. The channel that usually showed it devoted Christmas afternoon to a Las Vegas Christmas extravaganza where Lori Gotamere was the headliner. During the show, Pastor Gotamere added, "The money-laden Evans family" and "his Quaker cohort" to her list of Hittites and Baal Worshippers. "Pacifist apologists for the anti-Christ," she called the Evans followers. "Evans moans about justice for a man who has been shown to support terrorism, while Evans lives in palatial splendor."

Hearing her speech, Xander glanced at the solid old home that his grandfather had inherited from his own parents. It was beautiful, especially the front window with its sunlight-splitting beveled glass, but it was pretty much like the house next door and the house across the street – all sitting on one hundred by fifty-foot lots in the heart of northeast Portland.

"Grandpa, are you money-laden?"

Grandpa shook his head, "I'm media-laden. And even that is shared property. Our newspapers, television and radio stations are owned cooperatively by the people who have worked for us for more than ten years."

Xander laughed, "Pastor Gotamere doesn't seem to know that."

"She doesn't want to know. It's public record."

"So, no hidden safe in the basement?"

Grandpa chuckled. "Just an old furnace and a great laundry chute."

During his Six O'clock News and Commentary, Lawrence Fafner stepped up the noise, claiming that Evans' money obviously controlled the investigations of the justice department and ought to be stopped.

On Christmas Eve, Xander, Justine and Grandpa attended services at East Side Monthly Meeting of the Society of Friends. After meeting for worship, they stayed in the fellowship dining room, arranging efforts to help with repair of the Beaverton Meeting House and other newly damaged worship buildings. All of these new attacks had happened after worship during the weeks of Pastor Gotamere's Christmas campaign.

Later that evening, all the members enjoyed dessert together. Close to ten o'clock in the evening, Xander and his grandfather left Aunt Justine still washing dishes with other Friends. Xander followed Rick and walked next to his grandfather toward Grandpa's old Buick. A second security man followed them.

"Long meeting," Rick said. "You're going to make a Quaker out of me, yet. You been trying that on me for fifty-sixty years."

"Too much silence for you, Buddy," Gilbert said. "I saw you nodding off."

"Nodding? I was conversing with the Big One. He, or She and I agree that . . ."

A shot rang out from above Xander. Rick Johnson fell on top of Gilbert, pulling Xander down to the sidewalk with him, and yelling at other Friends, "Get back inside and lock the door."

"Across the street, roof of the chocolate store," Aunt Justine called out from the meeting house.

Xander heard a second shot smack wood siding on the meeting house.

"Oh God," Grandpa said, "Is she . . .?"

Rick yelled. "Close the damn door, Justine. And get away from it."

The Friends Meeting door slammed.

Rick's man, whispered. "She's right. The shooter's on the roof of the Chocolate Kitchen, but he's lying behind the blinking sign and I can't get at him."

Rick shoved Xander and Gilbert next to the wheel of their parked car. "Stay there, Gib, or I'll shoot you myself," he hissed.

Grandpa threw an arm around Xander's shoulders and pulled Xander's head into his chest.

They could hear Rick stand. A shot blasted into something wooden. A scream came from above them. Something clattered to the walkway across the street. Glancing over Grandpa's shoulder, Xander saw a rifle hit the sidewalk, barrel end first.

"Got his gun hand," Rick said.

They heard the man on the roof swearing, and crying.

"Don't know if he has another gun," Rick said, "but my bet is he can't use it if he does."

"Get down, Rick." Grandpa's voice was harsh. "Call 911 and stay out of his sites."

Rick hunkered down near them and pulled out his cell phone.

After Rick's call, Grandpa yelled to the man across the street. "Ambulance and police are on the way, fellow. How are you holding up?"

"You blew off my fingers, you Fucker."

"Yes, I did," Rick shouted. "Tried to miss your heart and head."

"Damn you," the man yelled. "Shoulda killed me."

Grandpa stared at his friend. "Rick, you avoided killing him on purpose?"

"Well, I . . . the kid's here and all . . ."

"You're a Quaker, after all."

Rick frowned and suddenly had to clean the barrel of his gun. Grandpa glanced at Xander who noticed that a small smile wrinkled his grandfather's eyes for a fleeting moment.

Police arrived in five minutes, followed by an ambulance. Because of the injury to his hand, the police had to rig a sling and lower the sniper to street level. They arrested the man, who, it turned out, was Martin Campbell, one of the three who had pushed their way into the Taziyan.

Rick, as the shooter, had to go with the police. He sent Grandpa, Justine and Xander home with an escort. After being shot at, none of them felt like going to bed. Grandpa made some tea. They sat on the living room floor, below the level of the front window. Outside, Rick's man stood silently beside one of the porch pillars, watching for movement on the street.

Half an hour later, Rick called Grandpa from the hospital where he'd followed to make sure the guy was guarded by someone not related to Officer Bailey.

"Campbell's lawyer was at the hospital before Campbell arrived."

"Who's the lawyer?"

"Guy named Dean. Brian Dean. Campbell claimed he was innocent."

"Yeah? And I bet he threatened to sue you for damages."

"You got that right." Rick said.

"Who hired him a lawyer?" Justine asked.

"Beats me," Rick said. "And of course that information wasn't shared."

Justine raised her eyebrows and stared at Xander. "Okay. Okay. I get it," Xander said. "Follow the money. But what money?"

Grandpa just shook his head and raised his hands. "Beats me, too. Too many stand to benefit if we're not helping Nasdar Qubadi."

Rick said, "The list starts with the FBI agent Guy Saurus, who has something to prove."

Justine said, "Trouble is, he's only the most obvious member of the list. What about that Breiton fellow?"

"Or whoever is offering to fund his purchase of the restaurant," Grandpa said.

* *

On Christmas day, Haroon returned to their shared office after his weekly visit to his father's jail cell. He plopped into his chair, staring at the computer screen. Xander had noticed that each visit put Haroon in a near catatonic trance for hours.

"Haroon, is your Dad sick?"

"No."

Xander waited, but Haroon wasn't going to elaborate, so Xander asked, "Do they let him pray properly?"

"Mostly, except for finding Mecca. I took him a watch with a compass. Turns out the compass is messed up by the walls. So, I had to stand outside and figure where his cell is."

"Did that work?"

Haroon glanced up for the first time, a small smile on his face. "I took him some chalk the next time, and told him where Mecca is in relation to the jail. Dad drew the arch of a quibla wall on his cell. The prison psychiatrist thought he was fantasizing escaping through the arch to paradise. They put him on suicide watch."

"So, let me guess," Xander said, "The psychologist guy is really well-versed in the practices of Islam."

"He certainly knows more than he did. Mom let him have it between the ears."

Xander chuckled. "Remember your mom during the fire? Remember how she hoisted that screaming woman off the balcony and made her grab the scarves?"

They both laughed, but Haroon stopped suddenly and said, "Today Dad feels responsible for your Grandfather. The prison rumor mill told him about the shooting at the Quaker Meeting House."

"Dang," Xander said. "That's not his fault. That's ..."

"I know, Xan. And we told him that. Your Grandpa told him that. But he's feeling helpless in there."

"This is so ..."

"Shitty." Haroon said.

CHAPTER THIRTY-ONE

Verbal attacks against Gilbert Evans grew, especially on the Lawrence Fafner Show. James Wray called the crew into the Evans News Library. "You've got to see this. Fafner's Man-on-the-Street interviews are all about concern for the American Constitution, especially the Bill of Rights."

The first questioner asked, "What do you think of the recent gun attack on the Pacifist newspaper tycoon, Gilbert Evans?"

Xander said, "Tycoon? Pretty clear what answer they want using that word."

"Shh, just listen," Mr. Wray said.

After the crew had watched the segment, Mike Halverson said, "Yes, indeed. The Bill of Rights is safe among Fafner's followers. Some support a broad reading of the Second Amendment, ('*We can do anything with our guns, Baby.*"). Other folks support a narrow reading of the First Amendment (*Dearly Beloved, the government can't tell us how to worship. But all real Americans worship Jesus Christ.*').

Xander said, "That would be funny, if only . . .."

When Evan's publications reported on the lack of evidence against the mosques whose funds had been frozen without trial or proof of wrongdoing, Fafner loudly proclaimed that Evans' publications displayed "obvious bias". A few days later, Fafner bellowed that Gilbert Evans was "soft on terrorists" and urged Evans Media to stop interfering. He quoted the news about "Gilbert Evans and "that Pakistani-raised grandson of his, and their connection to terrorist suspects in Iraq". Then Fafner smacked his television desk and said, "Evans should let Homeland Security, the FBI, and the Justice Department do their job, unhindered."

On another evening, Fafner complained, "Gilbert Evans is trying to make us into a cringeing and weak country, apologizing for just wars and forgiving terrorists and their supporters."

Fafner then surprised everyone by quoting high-level Air Force trainers. "Even the United States Air Force teaches our officers that, as Saint Augustine says, it is just to bring war 'to avenge or avert evil, not to expand power and not for pride or revenge, but to protect the innocent and restore moral order'. Where is Gilbert Evans on Christian moral order?"

Xander waited for Grandpa to hit the roof about that question, but he seemed not even to hear it. All he said was, "Saint Augustine in the United States Air Force? What are they thinking?"

Fafner's next program again brought up Gilbert's Quaker pacifist beliefs. "The Air Force chaplain leading training of missile officers believes 'The American churches and their leadership say it's okay in their eyes to launch nukes.' If our military and our churches believe this, why does Evans think we need to crawl on our bellies and apologize to one terrorist? Does Evan's think he's the lone outpost of right thinking among all these Christians?"

"Fafner is desperate for press space," Grandpa commented.

"So, you're going to write an editorial about Fafner's stupid remarks?" Xander asked.

Grandpa shook his head. "Our job is to work for justice, not give Mr. Fafner more attention."

The next time Mr. Wray came into the news room, he handed Gilbert a *National Courier* said, "Look at what Louis Lamb is investigating."

The article showed that the Air Force had promised to study the program that Fafner referred to, but that Lamb's news team was researching why it ever had been the chaplain's place to teach classes for the Air Force about the ethics of bombing.

"Well," Gilbert said, "looks like Louis is back to real investigative journalism instead of selling safety instead of the Constitution.

Over the next several days, a letter to the editor of Lamb's *National Courier* asked, "What makes one chaplain in the Air Force believe he could speak for all Christian churches in the nation?" Another letter from a Presbyterian pastor asked "Why does the Air Force allow such skewed religious teaching in their leadership training?"

"Somebody besides us is listening and not buying either the Air Force chaplain's or Fafner's arguments," Grandpa said.

* *

The Max Million Foundation had hired an Iraqi and an American lawyer to represent Gamal Besaranî, Mrs. Qubadi's younger brother in the prison. The lawyers tried to get into the prison at "Camp Radamanthus" in Iraq, but the military ignored their requests, saying they were not recognized by the Iraqi courts and therefore could not represent anyone in Iraq.

Over the next weeks, these special lawyers petitioned both the military prison command and the Iraqi government for the opportunity to interview their client. Their petitions repeatedly were denied.

The lawyers discovered that the two men who informed against Gamal were given a bounty of $500 American dollars. The informers had driven away from the prison in Gamal's truck. So, Gamal's lawyers also petitioned the Iraqi courts for the right to represent Gamal. They asked for his release on the ground that those who informed against him benefitted from that act. This petition sat on the desk of a Shia judge who was related to the informants.

One day, as Xander and Haroon did their homework, Grandpa Gilbert came into the Evans News Library waving a paper. "Louis Lamb of the *National Courier*, wrote an editorial. He's urging the media to back off and let the court system play out the Qubadi drama with less vitriol."

Mike Halverson snorted as he took the page to read it. "He's the one who pays Fafner."

"Read on," Grandpa urged.

James Wray read aloud over Mr. Halverson's shoulder. "Lamb says, 'The Evans group should cease to publish stories connected to the situation when everyone knows their Max Million Foundation pays the defense lawyers, and their reporters are hunting for evidence to get Qubadi freed. But other media outlets should back off the incendiary editorializing as well.'"

Mr. Halverson laughed. "What others would that be?" he asked.

The next day, a coded message arrived from Gamal's lawyers in Iraq. As soon as the code had been translated, Gilbert called the team into his office.

"Listen to this." He held up the translation. "The lawyers write 'Someone in the prison at Camp Radamanthus sent us copies of the statements made by Gamal Besaranî during interrogation. We don't know who this is, helping us, but since the Arabic is cleanly translated, we assume it must be an Iraqi member of the prison staff. Someone in the prison doesn't like what is happening there. Attached are copies of these statements by Gamal."

The papers included things Gamal said while being 'questioned'. The transcriber even included a description of the type of torture at the time Gamal gave an answer. The description made Xander gag. He saw that Haroon doubled over with real physical pain for his uncle.

Gamal's answers under torture didn't make sense. His answers confirmed that a man might say anything he thinks will make the pain stop. The reports showed that sometimes Gamal wasn't even speaking Arabic coherently.

* *

Pastor Gotamere moved from Las Vegas to Sacramento and played to a crowd of 15,000. James, Xander, Mike Halverson and Haroon watched the broadcast on the television in the Foundation Library.

"The Lord is righteous," she shouted. "He abhors traitors and those who support traitors. Absalom was the son of David, but he was a traitor to David, the Lord's King of Israel. The Lord struck Absalom down. Even the citizens and the sons of citizens who are traitors, will become as the dust under your feet, oh ye mighty of the Lord."

Xander stared at the screen. Citizens and the sons of citizens . . . she wants Haroon dead.

James Wray watched her television broadcast, then switched it off. "She's moving back up California. I think she plans to be near Portland for the trial dates."

Haroon looked wide-eyed at Mr. Wray and asked, "Will she hold a rally downtown? Pioneer Courthouse Square?"

James looked at them both and said, "Gilbert has petitioned the city council not to allow her within eight miles of the Courthouse, but he's had no answer. Her lawyers are citing the free speech amendment."

"Well, let freedom ring," Mr. Wray whispered.

* *

Two days later, Haroon tuned into the Lawrence Fafner Show. A new face appeared at Fafner's desk. "Lawrence Fafner has the flu," the man said. "So, you get me in the interim."

Over the next several days, the same man, instead of Fafner, interviewed people and delivered the news instead of Fafner. He never again mentioned illness as a reason for Fafner's absence. Other news sources speculated on rumors about Fafner's absence. Some claimed that thousands of letters to Lamb's *National Courier* urged expanding the Fafner Show. His absence was due to the need to plan for such a big change.

In an interesting media twist, the substitute announcer on Fafner's show invited Gilbert Evans to a Portland studio to talk about why he took risks for an outsider. The invitation made Mike and James very nervous. Rick Johnson insisted he accompany Gilbert to the studio. He took his security men to stand outside the studio, watching any who came in.

At the hour of the interview, the whole Evans Media staff gathered around the television with their fingers crossed. Xander believed Mike Halverson and James Wray were hoping Gilbert would be able to say the right things and not stumble over his tongue. Xander and Haroon sat in the front row as the interview began. Haroon's hands gripped the side of his chair as if it might take off and fly.

The interviewer asked, "Mr. Evans, can you tell our audience why your Max Million Foundation supports a man who is accused of terrorism?"

Gilbert Evans said, "Yes, first of all, under our court system, all men are presumed innocent until proven guilty. Presumption of innocence should never be swept under the rug, by this present administration or any other."

"But war is a special case . . ." the interviewer said.

"War is an excuse to justify short cuts and injustice. Second, The Max Million Foundation was set up to be a resource for those in need of legal and investigative assistance. It was set up after the terror of anti-Communist accusations ruined many lives during an earlier generation ...."

The interviewer interrupted. "Communism is real, just as fanatical Islam is real. You can't duck the fact that these people intend to murder."

"Which people? Those who send missiles into border towns of Afghanistan and Pakistan? Those who declare war on the basis of falsified evidence? Which people intend murder? The Max Million Foundation supports those who are accused and tried in the media without benefit of trial. Is that support of the accused, who in this case is my friend, is that bias or loyalty?"

"But the Grand Jury found sufficient evidence to go to trial."

"A Grand Jury hears the prosecution's case only. A Grand Jury decides that the prosecution may have – may have – evidence worth looking at. It never hears the defense case until the trial. The accused is innocent until proven guilty. Is Mr. Fafner's assumption of Mr. Qubadi's guilt a bias? Or just sloppy reporting?"

For fifteen minutes, Gilbert gave as good as he got. Xander grew more and more proud of him. Haroon leaned forward and nodded at the answer to each question.

When the interview was over, the Evans staff sighed in relief. Gilbert had spoken clearly and to the point. James Wray slapped Xander on the back. "I guess your old man isn't as old as I feared."

Xander laughed, "He's as old as you are, Mr. Wray."

"Yup. And I'm decrepit compared to him."

Haroon pried his fingers off the sides of his own chair and had to straighten them out.

"Hey, Rune," Xander said, "He told it like it is, eh?"

"I wish I believed that one fifteen-minute interview would change anyone's mind."

Well," Mike Halverson said, "with any luck, your dad's judge was watching and understood it."

*   *

Later, Grandpa returned from the station. The team relaxed at Qubadi's for dinner. After dinner, Grandpa said, "Remember that TV station is owned by Lamb's *National Courier Media*. While I was there, I got the feeling everyone is uncertain. They clucked around me like a bunch of old hens. Also, they acted as if they wanted me to like them. Way too nice. Kept me off balance."

As they talked, Mr. Halverson drew a cartoon of hens wobbling around a prone rooster who sported Fafner's famous ski-jump nose and blond cowlick. Xander and Haroon moved near to watch over Mr. Halverson's shoulders as he continued adding details. Soon, the rooster had eyes surrounded by the circles that cartoonists use to mean sick, or drunk. Above the hen house door hung a sign with the call letters for the local *Courier* station. The caption read, "When the rooster is sick, the hens don't know their Right from their Left."

*   *

On the Friday after Christmas, Haroon hung the framed original of the now famous *In the Hen House* cartoon on the wall above their desks. Since the morning it had been published, it had gone viral on the web and brought many comments from people who were fed up with Fafner and his slanders.

Xander glanced up as Haroon straightened the frame on the wall. "That one hit a nerve, didn't it? Where were all those people before the cartoon hit the internet?"

"Seems they each believed they were the only ones disgusted with Fafner," Haroon said. "After it came out, they discovered they were part of a silent crowd."

"Wish that crowd wasn't so silent." Xander said.

Haroon came over to study Xander's news clippings where they lay on the desk. "Why are you reading that crapola again?" he asked.

"I'm making a list of the words news people use that make judgments."

"You mean this one?" Haroon pointed at an article in a Seattle newspaper. "The enigmatic prisoner, Nasdar Qubadi – enigmatic, as if Dad were hard to read, maybe hiding something." Or this one, 'The hapless victim of a stabbing' – as if those helpless guys in the tunnel just had the bad luck to beat up on people who fought back."

"And it's not just in the editorial page," Xander said. "These kinds of judging words are in the news reports. 'Muslim man arrested for sending money to support madrasa in northern Iraq.' Madrasa is American code for Evil indoctrination."

"You think the prosecutor, Mr. Jory will pay attention to your list?" Haroon asked. "Or maybe you think you can change the so-called reporters on "In the Hen House" news?"

Xander laughed. "You can't teach an old fox new tricks, but our lawyer might use the list to show how little substance there is in the government's case – and how much noise."

Haroon said, "The judge won't care."

Xander glanced at his friend. Defeat hunched his shoulders and lined his eyes with dark bruises.

Haroon said, "The judge never had an independent investigation of Saurus or the prosecutor's illegal leaks of Grand Jury information, or of Agent Saurus's leaks about the stuff from your computers. So, the judge is against us, too."

"But, we are not giving up," Xander said. "Giving up will break your father into pieces."

Haroon closed his eyes, as if he wanted to shut out those words.

"Did you and Gul and your mom visit him last night?" Xander asked.

"They let us in for ten minutes," He whispered as if telling his computer. But a moment later he sat up, pulled his laptop closer and rubbed his hand over his face. "I'm not giving up, Xan. I'm taking a rest from pumping out optimism."

Xander sighed. "I know, Rune. It's hard." They both turned back to their work.

*   *

During that week between a bleak Christmas and dark New Year, Lori Gotamere moved up the inner valleys of California, attracting a crowd at each stop. Xander watched her on the news each evening. By Wednesday of that week, her tight, righteous voice and thin prettiness made him shudder. She seemed to grow in the public's estimation with each stop on her campaign. By Thursday, *National Courier Media* attention gave five full minutes to her stop in the Sacramento Valley, plus the announcer used Gotamere news as a teaser for why listeners should stay up to see more on the eleven o'clock news. For Xander, the sound of her voice brought a feeling of impending danger. The sight of her pink suits and high heels tightened the dread in his stomach.

By Friday, he saw that other stations besides the *National Courier*, gave her more attention and air time. Her campaign built great momentum as it approached the Willamette Valley of Oregon.

*   *

On Saturday, the sun poked through the popcorn clouds. Xander did not want to turn on the television or hear any more about Lori Gotamere or the crowd that followed her. The very sound of her name on someone else's lips brought bile to his throat.

So, he and Haroon, their bodyguards and Mr. Wray went outside to take advantage of a day of wet sunshine. As the boys and Mr. Wray kicked around a soccer ball, Haroon asked, "Did you know Mr.

Breiton sent a letter to Mom, another offer to buy the Taziyan? This time, he offered two million dollars."

"Yep. I saw that letter – a contingency offer." Mr. Wray said.

Xander chased the ball out of the yard across the street and kicked it to Haroon. "Contingency? Does that mean he's offering, but only if something happens?"

"Contingent on her not allowing the reputation of the restaurant to fall any further," Mr. Wray said as he tried to block the pass Haroon sent to Xander. "That means that come time to buy, the buyers will claim she failed to keep the reputation high, so they will offer less."

Xander caught the pass and started toward the street corner, the traditional goal for a pick-up game. "Even if Breiton offers less, where's the money coming from?" Xander asked.

Mr. Wray took the ball from between Xander's feet and ran down the street with it. At the corner, he turned around with his arms triumphant in the air.

Haroon called, "Why aren't you on our soccer team?"

"Too classy," Mr. Wray said.

"What's too classy? You or us?" Xander asked.

Mr. Wray laughed. "Got a classic team for old guys?" He kicked the ball back to Xander. "As for the money, the guy has no money of his own. That purchase money either never will exist, or it is coming from some source we haven't discovered."

"What do you mean?"

Mr. Wray stopped running. "His restaurant in downtown Portland is close to going under. He let go two waiters just last month."

"So, how's he offering Mom a great bargain?" Haroon asked as he passed to Xander.

Xander captured the ball with his foot and stopped cold. An idea hit him so forcefully that he couldn't believe he hadn't thought of it sooner. "We've been looking for the potential Breiton financing, and we know deep pockets from somewhere are financing the lawyer of Campbell and the others."

Mr. Wray stared and then nodded. "Maybe the same deep pockets are dangling the offer of a loan, and encouraging Mr. Breiton to buy the Taziyan."

"If we could get an idea where the money comes from for any one of those people," Xander said, "we may have a chance to find out who is financing the rest."

"Right," Mr. Wray said, "and my bet is you're on to something about Mr. Breiton. So, while my man tails him, I get into his restaurant and wheedle more info from his disgruntled employees."

Haroon said, "Okay, ball hogs, let's not waste this sunshine. We can dig into Breiton's investors as soon as that cloud over there billows into our next rainstorm."

All of them looked up. Sure enough, an anvil cloud formed at the south end of town, over hills across the Willamette River. A storm prepared to roar into Portland.

*   *

In Iraq, with information from Uncle Bijar, the boys tracked down the names of people in the region of Harmota-Barzani that the reporters might want to interview. Those were the people who knew how Nasdar's money had helped set up a farmers' cooperative, buy seed, goats, and tools. At his computer, Xander read a report from Bill, an Evans reporter in Kirkuk, Iraq. Bill followed the trail of Uncle Gamal's purchases.

Xander realized something about the dates he saw. As far as he knew, Gamal Besaranî had been arrested in March of 2004, yet one reporter had found a record of vegetables, chickens and other things purchased in April that year.

Xander hit "reply" to the reporter, and began typing. "The chickens, veggies and the explosive TNT were bought after the arrest. What other purchases were made by after March 2004?"

A reply might take days. So, he moved on to a blog site he'd heard got a high number of hits. As he read, the hairs on his arms stood straight up. The blogger spewed.

"It doesn't matter that the coroner in Portland, Oregon claims Beryl Plinder stabbed himself with a switchblade knife, the world knows it had to be that Qubadi kid who did it. I mean, who uses switchblade knives anymore in the States? That's a Muslim weapon if I ever heard of one – right along with a scimitar and a shiv."

Staring at the screen, Xander shivered. He knew that bloggers didn't represent all people, just the people who liked to talk. Some had useful things to say. Some were heavy into conspiracy ideas. The trouble came when the talking wing-nuts attracted many followers, like this guy.

An answering blogger said, "You can bet the feds would have charged those two kids with murder. But in this country, Evans Publications is emperor."

Evans as emperor? With one tenth the media outlets of Lamb's *National Courier*? Not likely.

He glanced over at Haroon to make sure he wasn't into this same blog-site. Haroon seemed to be reading the *Washington Post* online, so Xander clicked on other replies to the accusing blog. After seven minutes of reading, he had found no one to refute the assumption that Haroon killed Plinder. Many believed he did it with Xander's help to cover up for Nasdar's and Evans' media treachery. He printed off everything, filed it under "Prejudicial atmosphere making a fair trial difficult" and took the file folder to James Wray's desk.

Mr. Wray glanced up from his own work, reached for Xander's file and flipped it open. His eyes scanned the all-caps print of the original blogger. His eyebrows rose. His forehead wrinkles became deeper.

"Oh, assigning weapons by religion are we?" he asked with an acid tone. "This guy's an idiot. Shivs are for us Black Baptists. Everybody knows that."

Xander had grown used to Mr. Wray's dark humor.

Mr. Wray glanced up again and whispered, "Xan, try to keep Haroon on the newspapers. At least newspapers disguise their prejudices as investigation."

CHAPTER THIRTY -TWO

That bleak December week slushed over into the newyear. In January, Xander decided to follow-up on a hunch about Louis Lamb and the weeks of absence of Lawrence Fafner from the air. He wondered if Fafner ever intended to come back on the air. Maybe the guy had found a better job – more money.

Xander pulled out a series of editorials in Lamb's *National Courier* newspaper. Mr. Louis Lamb had a reputation for his rock-hard stand against potential and suspected terrorists. His editorials were generally in support of 'wartime' suspension of the Fourth through Eighth Amendments in the Bill of Rights. He claimed suspension of rights would guarantee American Security.

"In a crisis, we have to treat suspects differently." He wrote. "The worst thing would be to allow an ordinary jury to find these scary people innocent."

In one recent editorial, Lamb even quoted Gilbert Evans.

"Soccer teammates know each other," Gilbert Evans told this reporter. "They know all the time where the teammate is on the field, and what that teammate can do for the team. As fellow soccer players, and as coaches, Nasdar Qubadi and I have learned to trust each other."

In Mr. Lamb's editorial, Gilbert Evans emphasized Mr. Qubadi's dedication to family, to the children on the team, and to community. The editorial quoted Gilbert, saying, "Nasdar Qubadi believes in the American ideals, including freedom of speech, and the separation of church and state. Do you believe in those ideals, yourself, Mr. Lamb?"

The rest of Mr. Lamb's editorial was his reply to Gilbert Evan's question. "Yes, I believe in those American ideals, but I also believe that Evans is a simple person who knows nothing of reality – an isolated and naïve old man who doesn't really know his friend as well as he thinks."

According to Louis Lamb, Nasdar Qubadi belonged to a radical mosque, and therefore must have bought into the radical ideas that the young imam of his mosque occasionally preached.

"After all," Lamb wrote, "the Portland Seven, were members of a similar mosque in nearby Beaverton, and their guilt has been clearly established. They were attempting to join jihad in Afghanistan."

"The Portland Seven? Did they really try to join jihad?" Xander asked.

Mr. Wray said, "They were found guilty of the attempt."

"How clearly established was their guilt?" Xander asked Mr. Wray.

It took a moment before Mr. Wray answered. Xander saw on his face a somber concern. It was as if he had asked the most ticklish question. Finally, Mr. Wray said, "At least some of them were found guilty as charged. The court showed that they corresponded with others about their hope that, by some fantastic method, they could get to Afghanistan and join in fighting against the U.S."

"But they never got there?"

Mr. Wray glanced at Xander and raised an eyebrow. "One did. He died there. Their plan was leaky, but it was a plan."

Xander saw the sad truth behind prosecuting such inept strategists. "Their poor plan gave people here someone to be afraid of."

"And it gave more power to others who want to use that fear."

Xander nodded, saddened that he couldn't feel a righteous anger on behalf of all who are accused. Some actually were guilty.

He went back to reading Mr. Lamb's editorials. Something about the way Mr. Lamb wrote told Xander that the man might really seek truth, but he made some nutty leaps in logic, such as the assumption that what an imam says is believed by all in his congregation. Plus, Mr. Lamb didn't seem to look for unbiased sources to help him find truth about Nasdar.

Then, as Xander flipped through Lamb's previous editorials, he saw something he'd missed earlier. "On one evening in December, the police reported a raid on Qubadi's restaurant by three men who at first claimed to be FBI, but moments before had been picketing with signs from the 'Sons of America' organization.

"The men threatened and pushed past children, broke a locked door and entered the Qubadi family restaurant during a wedding celebration. They took money and ran off as soon as they heard police sirens coming. The staff and family were terrified. When this reporter talked to the neighbor businesses, I was told these men had hovered daily around The Taziyan parking lot, harassing the Qubadi family and everyone who ate at the restaurant.

"As a city, we ought to be asking ourselves what protection we're giving this family. We owe it to this family to keep them safe from those who hide behind a badge, or the pretense of a badge to ruin lives. If we provide no protection for them, then we are just indulging in our own form of terrorism."

Reading this editorial gave Xander an idea. Could he contact Louis Lamb without getting Fafner mixed up in what he hoped to do?

"No," he whispered to himself. "Lamb's office is in Chicago. No way am I just going to pick up the phone and get through to him there. As soon as I give the operator my name, Fafner is going to be on it. His television rants show that he knows the connections between me and Haroon and Grandpa."

Nevertheless, Xander read many other past editorials by Lamb and became convinced there was something important they should explore. During their next snack break in the news cafeteria, he worked to convince Haroon that Louis Lamb might be their chance to get help from one respected newspaper outside the Evans news company.

"You read this guy's writing, Haroon. You'll see. I think he might really want to understand your Dad."

After Haroon read many Lamb editorials, he said, "Okay, I see this guy might want to know the real truth, but how do you explain Fafner? And besides, your Grandpa, Mr. Wray and Mr. Halverson would never see Mr. Lamb as someone we should trust."

"Well, let's ask. . ."

They made an appointment to talk to Xander's grandpa that afternoon.

As they trooped into his office, Grandpa asked. "What have you got, gentlemen?"

Haroon and Xander laid out the editorials they'd been reading. After Grandpa had skimmed the contents, he looked up. "Louis Lamb is a good man with some ideas I can't buy," he said.

Xander nodded. "Maybe all his information comes from people who want him to keep building a case against Haroon's dad."

"He hires his investigative team. He knows their biases," Grandpa said.

To Xander's ear, Grandpa seemed saddened by Lamb's biases. Xander wondered, at what point the man had disappointed Grandpa.

Xander countered Grandpa's pessimism. "But these editorials make it sound like if he got any other information he might want to know more."

Haroon interrupted, "If he heard from the outside, maybe he'd see that he's not getting all the evidence."

"And how would you propose to tell him?"

"We write him a letter," Xander said.

"Do you know who opens my mail?" Grandpa asked, pointing to the inbox on his desk, which had a stack of letters whose envelopes were long gone.

"Uhm," Xander said. "I'm guessing that neat stack wasn't made by you."

Grandpa smiled. "No way. Rick Johnson opens all my mail. And if he didn't want me to see something, he'd just toss it in the trash without me ever knowing."

"But he doesn't," Haroon said.

"No, he doesn't."

"But," Xander said, "Mr. Lamb might not have a Rick Johnson on his team."

"Right," Grandpa said. "However, you gentlemen have given me an idea. I need to contact Bill and the rest of the team on the ground in Iraq and see what they know about the way Lamb's team collects information. Following them might lead us to some interesting, and useful information."

In the hall, after their meeting, Xander said, "It's really neat that Grandpa got a new idea from us."

"Come on, Xan," Haroon said. "He just trying to make us feel better. You gotta know he's already got somebody spying on Lamb's people."

"Yeah, you're right," Xander said. "These reporter guys all sit in bars and lunch joints and just listen."

Haroon nodded. "Mr. Wray wanders into the Thirsty Lion Bar near the Central Police Station. Your grandpa pays him to listen to gossip."

"So, we contributed nothing, plus we struck out on getting to Lamb."

"Sure looks like it."

*   *

Two weeks later, the *National Courier Media Company,* owned by Louis Lamb, announced that Lawrence Fafner had been promoted to vice-director of national programming. He would be off the air, and his salary would be doubled. The team of people he worked with would be responsible for choosing programming throughout the country. Fafner, the announcement said, had moved from the Pacific Northwest back to Chicago to be in the home office of the company.

"Wow," Haroon said. "You are so bloody wrong. Lamb is promoting that guy. He'll be choosing programming for the whole company."

"This is the worst place he could have put him," Xander agreed.

But the next day, they learned that Louis Lamb had flown to Portland to interview replacements for the Lawrence Fafner Show.

"You wait," Mike Halverson said, "I hope this is Fafner's promotion to oblivion."

"What's that mean," Xander asked.

Halverson drew a cartoon showing Lawrence Fafner in an office with no windows. He seemed to be waving his arms and talking to a desk full of bobble-heads.

"We're not using that one, Mike," Grandpa said. "I hope you're right, but I don't want to wake the sleeping dog."

At that comment, Haroon glanced at Xander, a question in his raised eyebrows. Xander shrugged. Sometimes Grandpa and his old friends seemed to talk in code. Later in the hall, Xander said, "At least we know Lawrence Fafner won't be in town when Louis Lamb is here."

"What's that mean?"

"Well," Xander said, "here's our chance to test whether Lamb is who we think he is."

"We know who he is. He's the guy that put Fafner in charge of programming."

"Vice-director of – not director. So, Mr. Halverson could be right about promotion to the windowless office and the committee that does nothing."

"Even if that is true, we can't go visit Lamb with a troop of security guards." Haroon said.

"So ... we'll have to take a bathroom break and stretch it."

CHAPTER THIRTY-THREE

Two days later, Haroon waited inside while Xander hailed a cab for their appointment with Louis Lamb. When the cab stopped, Xander ducked inside the back seat. Haroon ran down the steps from the *Journal of the Americas* building, hopped in next to Xander and closed the cab door with a thud.

"That's it," the cab driver said. Pulling his keys from the ignition, he turned around. His face almost as hard as the club he pointed at Xander.

"You boys are clearly up to something, so get out of my cab."

"But . . .," Xander said.

"Out!" The man poked at Xander's face with the Billy club.

Haroon shoved open the door and yanked on Xander's jacket collar. Discussion with the cabby came to a choked halt. Xander rolled out after his friend, landing on his back on the sidewalk. They didn't even get a chance to shut the cab door. The fellow sped off and let momentum slam it.

"Rick Johnson's going to notice you rolling around on the sidewalk," Haroon whispered.

"Yeah?" Xander rasped out. "You're the one who choked me." He rolled to all fours and pushed up.

"Had to get you out. You were about to argue with a bat-carrying Mr. Hard-Nose," Haroon said. He started off, heading toward the bus stop.

Xander followed. "I was going to explain, not argue," he said.

Haroon shot him a look that would wither cabbage. "Look, we are not safe out here. There are people who believe I . . ." He glanced around. "We are going to do this trip below the radar. You got that?"

"I got that. You got bus tickets?"

"Always," Haroon said, handing one to Xander.

Five minutes later, they climbed aboard the bus and sat as far from the front as they could.

"I don't like this," Haroon said. "We shouldn't have left without telling Mr. Wray."

"Yesterday you agreed with the plan. Why get paranoid now?"

"I'm not so sure about this Louis Lamb guy," Haroon said.

"And you don't like being out here without protection."

Haroon frowned. "Well . . . that, too. But mainly, we're about to ask for help from a guy whose stuff we've read, but we really don't know him. Plus he put Fafner in charge of programming."

"Look. We've read what – maybe fifty of his editorials from way back to the September eleventh attack. He pretty consistently warned against judging all Muslims, right?"

Haroon nodded.

"And he urged the government to stop justifying torture."

"Yes, but he's also said the government probably has evidence against Dad that we won't know about until the trial."

"Yeah. I think that means Lamb doesn't think the evidence we've heard is sufficient."

Haroon glanced at Xander. "Do you think that prosecutor, Mr. Jory, has stuff he's not telling us?"

"He's probably got Gamal's statements, but those are worthless."

"Unless he uses them out of context, one at a time," Haroon said. "A couple of times, Uncle Gamal does seem to confess, and then back off."

"I think the main reason this happened is that FBI or Homeland Security went on a fishing expedition and came up with your dad's name – a traveling Muslim. Then they had to justify harassing your family."

"They can't be just doing this out of ego."

"Yes, they can," Xander said. "I read the news of the last time they accused. Ego drove them in the case of Mr. Mayfield. They knew early on, but refused to admit they had bad fingerprint identification."

"I think Dad's case got out of control as soon as it got in the hands of Fafner, Gotamere and the other blow-hards who love audiences."

"Here's our stop." Xander started to stand, then sat down fast. "Those guys up in front are getting off here, too."

Haroon glanced at the two men. "*Maybe,*" he whispered, "*are they the guys . . . ?*"

"From the restaurant?" Xander whispered, as the men stepped off.

"Don't think so, but how about we get off in two blocks and watch where they go," Haroon said.

"What if they go into *The National Courier?*"

"Then we bag this interview."

From the sidewalk at the next stop, Xander and Haroon watched the two men cross Second Avenue, away from the *National Courier* building. Eventually, they entered the Dekum Building.

"Probably work in there," Xander said.

"Could they be Agent Saurus's men?"

Xander frowned at that possibility. "What if they know about our visit and are spying from the building across the street. What if . . ."

"Are we being paranoid?" Haroon asked.

"We're being careful," Xander said. "Stuff has happened, and we can't ignore it."

Haroon took a deep breath. "Okay, then. Since I'm the one looking foreign, how about if you go into *The National Courier* first. If everything seems okay, come back to the door and wave at me."

"Deal."

* *

Ten minutes later, Mr. Louis Lamb welcomed Haroon and Xander into his office on the eighth floor of the *National Courier Building*, and then he offered them tea. While Xander studied the windows across the street, Haroon accepted the tea for them both. No drapes or curtains seemed to move, no shadows on the windows at the Dekum building.

Xander turned to gaze around the room and knew he'd made a big mistake. At the sight of a large oak desk, and plenty of leather on the chairs and sofa, Xander knew that Louis Lamb, owner of *The National Courier*, liked expensive stuff. He probably had big financial reasons to want Evans Publications discredited. Xander figured he'd gotten them into deep mud. Acting on his gut reaction to the man's editorials had been stupid. He glanced at Haroon.

His friend stared at the carpet then at Xander and gestured with a tilt of his head toward the floor.

The carpet was Khurdistani, hand-knotted, and a jolt to Xander's chest. He recognized the hook-shaped edges of the diamond patterns and the deep rose and blue colors. Manzur always prayed on a small version of this carpet. Xander's face grew hot. In his ears rang the sound of gunshots. His eyes focused only on the pattern.

"What do you see?" Mr. Lamb asked in a quiet voice.

"Your carpet," Haroon said. "Kurdish, no?"

"Yes, from my time in northern Iraq. You boys know this pattern?"

Xander nodded, then blurted, "I don't know what happened to my friend when the men attacked my school – the men who came down from the Afghan hills."

Louis Lamb stopped pouring tea. "Your friend – what was his name?"

The smiling face of Manzur moved in and out of a fog of memory. "Manzur David Zerbari," Xander said.

"That's a Kurdish name," Lamb said. "What was he doing in southwestern Pakistan?"

"His mother was a doctor, no longer allowed to practice in her town in Iran. She joined my folks in the mission hospital. She died there, too."

"Tell me about this attack," Mr. Lamb said, handing Haroon and Xander each a tea cup and gesturing for the boys to sit down.

Though Xander started slowly, trying to decide how much the man should know, Mr. Lamb asked good questions, questions that showed he understood the region, the tribes, the need for schools and hospitals. He really seemed to care about what happened to the boys that Xander missed. And that was why, eventually, Xander let it all come out, about the murder of the girls and their teachers, about the little boys, and the boy's teachers, and how Xander didn't know what happened after he sent them to the basement and the tunnels, about the doctors and the patients, about the deaths he did know, and the lives he feared were lost – about Edmund from Yorkshire, Mr. Bhatti, Mr. Din, Mohammed and Manzur.

After a long silence during which Mr. Lamb stared at his hands and then closed his eyes as if in pain, he asked Xander, "What do you think Mr. Din meant, saying Mohammed was a fool Quaker?"

Xander felt himself live that moment again – the ring of bullets on the wheelbarrow, the prayers of Mohammed in the chicken yard, Mr. Din's voice, "So sorry," and then the thud of the hatchet handle against Xander's head.

"I've thought and thought about Mr. Din and Mohammed," he spoke slowly. "I think Mohammed tried to delay the attack – the kind of action my Quaker grandfather would take. Mohammed did it by praying to Allah – maybe he hoped to make the attackers regret the violence they did. But when they killed Shazada – our hen, Mr. Din knew Mohammed was next, and he loved Mohammed like a grandson."

When Xander's story was out, Mr. Lamb glanced at Haroon.

And eventually, the boys told how Haroon and Xander both knew this carpet pattern – from Haroon's uncle's tribe – probably Manzur's tribe as well.

And that led to Haroon's story about his uncles and their efforts to keep a village fed and schooled during the chaos of the war in Iraq, about his grandmother, and the money, and the arrest of Uncle Gamal in the military prison.

When they finished telling the stories, Mr. Lamb asked, "Haven't Evans reporters searched for the boys from your school? And for your uncle?"

"Yes," Xander said, "but in Pakistan, so far, nobody knows what happened to the boys and teachers, except that the school building where they hid was demolished."

Haroon glanced at Xander who shook his head. They had discussed not telling about the $500 sale of Gamal, or about the statements the lawyers had sent from the prison.

So Haroon said, "In Iraq, the reporters can tell us where Uncle Gamal was up until he left the market in Kirkuk on March 8th, 2004. After that, we only know he's supposed to be near Al Kadhimiya, in a prison near Baghdad, but we don't know why."

Mr. Lamb said, "Isn't that town also called Kazimain?"

Haroon's eyes opened wide. "Yes, the shrine of Musa-al Kazim or Kadhim."

Mr. Lamb nodded and then shook his head as if in disgust, but Xander couldn't tell what exactly disgusted him. Then Mr. Lamb said,

"The U.S. calls it *Camp Radamanthus*, the prison and the military base there."

At that, Haroon suddenly looked tired. "Radamanthus, the judge of the dead."

"Yes, Haroon," Mr. Lamb said, "I can see that you have read the Greek myths, but remember, Radamanthus was a man of high reputation."

"Who chose that name?".

Mr. Lamb shrugged, then said, "Let me ask you gentlemen some more questions." He pulled over a pen and notepad from the side of his desk. So, they talked for another hour about what they knew, and what they could not find out, in Pakistan and in Iraq. When Mr. Lamb had asked all the questions he could think of, he sat back. He leaned his elbows on the arms of his desk chair, steepled his hands in front of his chest and studied the two of them.

After several uncomfortable moments, he said, "Gentlemen, I know you think the best of the people you love, but I have to warn you that sometimes adults do things, justify the violence they do because they can't see another way. Like Mr. Din. He couldn't see another way, so he hit you, Xander, to keep you safe. And then, he went out to hatchet anyone who threatened Mohammed."

"But . . .,"

"I know," Mr. Lamb said, "Mohammed needed protection. Or at least Mr. Din believed he needed it. I'm just saying that people we trust sometimes justify violence. We have to recognize that possibility from your uncles as well, Haroon."

Haroon shook his head. "Not Gamal or Bijar. Never."

"Ordinary good men do it all the time," Mr. Lamb said. "They get backed into a bad spot. They see no other way."

Haroon's head continued to move back and forth as he stared at Mr. Lamb.

Xander knew then that Mr. Lamb could not believe in hope the way his own mother and father had believed in it. He could not believe in the innate goodness of men and women. And who could blame him? After all, Mom and Dad were murdered because thirty men with rifles believed in the power of violence to change their world.

Where was the goodness of man on that day? Where was God, or Allah?

Getting Xander's eye, Mr. Lamb said, "I'll tell you what I am going to do, Alexander. I will work to find out what happened to your friends, and the other doctors and teachers. And then," he looked at Haroon, "And then, I'm going to try to find out what has happened to your Uncle Gamal."

Haroon's head came up, hope in his eyes, but Mr. Lamb raised a cautionary hand. "Things are tight over there. People are scared to talk. I don't know what I can find. But more than that, I'm afraid what I do find won't help your father."

Xander looked at Haroon. They both stood. Haroon said. "Mr. Lamb, the truth cannot hurt my father. He is a good man."

Mr. Lamb said, "I do know he is a man with a good son. And good friends. I will remember that as I search."

But Xander knew Mr. Lamb didn't really believe in Nasdar Qubadi, so his investigation would be stopped at the first blockade – probably at the prison gate.

CHAPTER THIRTY-FOUR

Haroon and Xander stood in the elevator of Lamb's building as the door opened on the main floor. There, they came face to face with the blond-haired, and forceful Lawrence Fafner. Before they could exit the elevator, several men with Fafner stood outside the elevator doors. Fafner stopped and stared at Haroon.

"What are you doing here?" he asked. One of the men with him raised a camera.

Haroon touched Xander's back as if to warn him to shut up. So, Xander waited to see what else Fafner would say.

"I asked you a question," Fafner said, still staring at Haroon. "You are that Qubadi kid aren't you?"

Xander finally spoke. "Mr. Fafner, did you want to interview Mr. Qubadi, too?"

Fafner stepped back in surprise. Xander stepped out of the small elevator box. Haroon followed him. The elevator door closed. In the silence of the hall, facing these men, they could hear the elevator leave the main floor.

Fafner looked at the man on his right. "So, that asshole replacement is even interviewing the kid?"

"Sir, you have an appointment with Louis," the man said.

Fafner pushed around Xander, saying, "I'll have a few words with Lamb about this ridiculous piece of ratings reduction. That new guy can't interview a flea and make it jump."

The men with Fafner stopped in their tracks. One of them raised a camera and began filming. Fafner smiled at the camera and then turned on Haroon.

"Kid, why aren't you in jail for the murder of that Plinder guy?"

"Do you mean the big man who tried to kill my friend in the news tunnel?"

"I mean the man you killed by driving the hand-truck into his back."

"You mean the forklift that his friend and I fought over? The accomplice who tried to kill me?"

"You're alive and Plinder is not. Hard to believe what you say he tried, when you're the one survived."

"You encouraged the thinking that I should have been arrested, and maybe the idea that I should be killed," Haroon said, "you with your pretend news."

Fafner waved the camera down, but for some reason it stayed up, trained on Haroon's face. Haroon said, "Somebody sent Plinder and his accomplice. Somebody hired them to drug and tie up the news crew in the tunnel. That left us alone with men who tried to kill us. Why don't you ever ask who that somebody was?"

At that moment, the elevator door opened again onto their lobby argument.

Louis Lamb stepped out. The camera man flicked the *off* button immediately. Lamb didn't even glance at Haroon or Xander.

"Mr. Fafner," Lamb said, "I was told you were in the building. Come on up to my office."

The other men filed into the elevator following Lamb and Fafner. One glanced out when he pushed the button. Xander and Haroon heard him say, "Who was the other kid?"

"Oh man! Take us back down" Fafner said. "That had to be . . ." The elevator door closed.

Haroon pulled Xander. "Out. We gotta get out."

Both of them rushed into the front hall and toward the revolving door. The man at the reception desk stood as they ran. "Stop."

Xander pulled Haroon toward the one push door. "Revolving doors are a trap," he said.

They pushed out the single door and ran down the steps of the National Courier Building.

Xander said, "Go right and walk. I'll go left and run to attract attention."

"Powell's Books, Kid Lit room. Meet you there."

Behind them the security man pushed the revolvers around in a rush to get outside.

Haroon walked into the crowd on the sidewalk and sank out of sight in a sea of adult shoppers.

Xander hesitated a moment until he had the man's attention, then he ran toward the next block, swerving around the near corner as the walk light changed. He stopped against the wall and took off his jacket so he would look different. He held it in front of him, freezing as he studied the display in a store window. Out of his peripheral vision, he saw the security man run across at the walk sign and sprint into the next block. Xander threw his coat back on and avoided the security guard by hustling west toward Tenth Avenue and Powell's Books.

Twenty minutes later, Xander dripped freezing sweat on the floor while he stood near the front of the kiddy lit room in Powell's City of Books. Haroon walked in, calm and smiling.

"Imagine that?" he said. "The great Lawrence Fafner would rather interview you than me."

"He probably wanted me to incriminate *Evans International*."

"Well, this day was a mistake," Haroon said. "Louis Lamb is going to hear about us from Fafner and everything we said will be tainted. Lamb is never going to do any searches for Gamal."

"I'm sorry," Xander shivered. "You were right. This trip was a lousy idea. And I'm in need of a hot drink."

"And a better coat."

*   *

One evening, a week later, Grandpa sat in their living room after supper with Aunt Justine and Xander. Xander could hear Rick Johnson prowling on Grandpa's front porch. Rick refused to come in. Aunt Justine took a plate out for him.

"Close the living room curtains, Justine," Rick said. "I don't want that fancy window to become a target."

Aunt Justine shook her head at Rick, but he merely stared at her.

"Jussy," Grandpa said softly. "Rick's got enough to worry about."

Justine did as Rick ordered. "Sunset's not going to be much tonight anyway," she said as she yanked the drape cord. Once the drapes were closed, she plopped into the rocking chair and put it in motion. Her rate-of-rocking told Xander that Aunt Justine was worried.

"That was a pretty good dessert, Justine," Grandpa said.

"You mean compared to the chocolate fudge I tried last time?" she asked.

"The fudge wasn't bad . . ."

". . . once you got the hack saw through it," Justine said.

Grandpa chuckled. "It was definitely chewy."

Her chair protested in both directions. "Okay, Gilbert," she said, "time to get to the reason for the dinner invitation."

Grandpa cleared his throat, glanced at the heavy drapes, and nodded his head. "I'm going to Iraq. I want Alexander to stay with you while I'm there, and I want you to finally accept Rick's help with security around your duplex."

Justine stood up with an abruptness that made Xander lean out of the way of her pacing shoes. "Iraq," she said. And then louder, "Iraq? You're an old coot."

"An old coot with friends in danger. Bill Sampson in Iraq says that something is going on at Camp Radamanthus, and he can't get permission to get in there to talk to anybody who might know anything about Gamal. One of the upper guys in the U.S. Army at Camp Radamanthus has been sent home with a cloud of questions around him. The guys who talk in the taverns don't even know why that officer is now under arrest in Fort Leavenworth Military Disciplinary Barracks."

"So, what makes you think you can get this information the U.S. Army doesn't want to let out?"

"I have an appointment to talk to the new commanding officer on the day I arrive. And I'm allowed to bring an aide – that would be Bill."

"So, you will fly in there, help Bill get his interview, and you will get right back on a plane and come out again."

"No, I need to follow up on some other rumors Bill has turned up, but can't get to the bottom of."

"Rumors about . . .?"

"I'm not throwing out rumors until they are shown to be facts."

"And you want to pass that excuse off to your sister?"

"It is the same excuse I gave Mike Halverson and James Wray – no rumor-mongering."

"How long do I get to have this security?" she asked, waving toward the sound of Rick's heavy footsteps on the darkened porch.

"As long as I am gone. Xander needs it. You need it, but you're too danged stubborn to admit it."

Aunt Justine stared at Grandpa long and hard. Then she turned on Xander. "You are thinking I don't want you living with me. That's far from the truth."

Xander laughed. "I know it, Aunt Justine. You just don't want Mr. Johnson and his guys to stop you from whatever political demonstration you're into."

"Humph!" she said, and then pointed her long fingers at Grandpa. "I've been asked to speak at the annual Earth Day celebration in Pioneer Courthouse Square. I'm not missing that because of Rick Johnson."

"Justine, I'm sure we can work something out with his team. Can Alexander live with you while I'm gone?"

She gazed at the ceiling and then at Xander. "Do you brush your teeth without reminders?"

He laughed, "Three times a day. And better than that, I've learned how to bake bread."

"How about fudge?"

"Yup. Cuts with a fork, too."

She straightened up, hands on her hips. "Well, boy, why didn't you say that before? Of course, you can stay with me. Bring all your security guards and their friends."

Xander glanced at Grandpa, who grinned as he shook his head.

Two days later, Mr. Gilbert Evans and two of his security guards took a flight to New York, and then on to Dublin and Baghdad.

* *

The week after that, Haroon showed Xander a column in *The National Courier*.

"Editor, owner Louis Lamb has returned to reporting in Iraq. Mr. Lamb lived in northern Iraq and in Afghanistan for several years before the present war. He wanted to see first-hand how things had changed since the fall of Saddam Hussein."

Haroon high-fived Xander. "Maybe Lamb really means to hunt down the truth." But Xander's hand stopped in mid air. "Dang! He's left Fafner in Chicago in charge of programming . . ."

"Oh . . . shit!"

* *

For a week, Xander and Aunt Justine talked to Gilbert every evening on the phone. Xander didn't mention the visit to Lamb's office, but, one night, using Skype, he told Grandpa the news that Lamb was also in Iraq.

"That right?" Grandpa said. "I'll have to look him up."

After they hung up, Xander asked Aunt Justine, "You ever been without Grandpa before?"

Justine took a deep breath and nodded. "He spent four years in Ohio at the university. He never came home for summers, just stayed there working through corn harvest and then took on the editorship of the university newspaper, and then the editorship of a small-town newspaper near the university. I thought he'd never come back to Oregon or even the Northwest."

"Why'd Grandpa go so far away for college?"

"He had a basketball scholarship, for one thing, but he had an offer from the University of Oregon as well, and they had just as great a team as Ohio in those years. There were things that happened here, things he wanted to get away from, and people couldn't let him forget."

"You mean the murder in 1953?"

Aunt Justine glanced toward the door, and then toward the front porch where one of Rick Johnson's men waited in the shadows. "We don't talk about that day, Xander. It still bothers your grandpa, but he won't talk about it much."

"I know," Xander said. "It comes out in little pieces, here and there. Seems like everything in Portland reminds him of that time." A memory of Mohammed and Mr. Din flashed across his mind.

"I was very young then," Aunt Justine said, "though that must be hard to imagine now. And even for me there are memories . . ., the easy accusations, the assumption of guilt, the dread of the unknown . . . so much hatred."

*   *

They watched for Lawrence Fafner, or any of his crooked ideas on Lamb's television station. Many of the announcers still spouted anti-Muslim talking points, but Fafner's face never appeared.

One morning, Lamb's Portland newspaper carried an editorial by Louis Lamb himself. Xander read it aloud to Haroon.

"Pastor Lori Gotamere wishes to hold a rally in downtown Portland. I recently visited Portland, myself. Lovely city. What the Gotamere planners don't seem to know is that Pioneer Courthouse Square is much too small for the kind of crowd that desperately wants to hear Pastor Gotamere. Plus, the square cannot be secured against those among her followers who are over-enthusiastic and may cause her harm. I can recommend two alternatives that would be safer for Pastor Gotamere and for those who wish to meet her: the county fairgrounds in Salem; and the beautiful fair grounds across the Columbia River in Vancouver, Washington. The latter are much more palatial and suited to Pastor Gotamere's expansive and critical presence."

When Haroon heard this, he said, "You thinking what I'm thinking?"

"I'm thinking Louis Lamb wants this Pastor Gotamere to have a huge rally near Portland during your dad's trial."

"What if he's sure she's coming, but he's trying to keep her away from the courthouse? Both fair grounds are about thirty miles from the city center."

"Before our visit to him, I'd never believe that. Now . . .? Not sure."

* *

Each time Grandpa phoned them from Iraq, Xander worried about the things Grandpa told them, but more, he worried about the questions Grandpa didn't answer.

"Does he think his phone is bugged?" he asked Haroon. "That Aunt Justine's phone is bugged?"

"How hard is it for the Department of Justice to bug a cell phone?" Haroon asked.

"Well, didn't Verizon, A Tand T, and Bell South turn over the call records of U.S. citizens to the FBI and the National Security Agency without a warrant?"

"I read that too. What else is Homeland Security using that stuff for?"

Xander also grew annoyed because when Grandpa called, no one could really know where he called from. Even when Grandpa used Skype, the background behind him always seemed to be an old sheet. For a time, he sent dispatches to the *Journal of the Americas* newspapers – deeply researched essays on life in Iraq during the mess that was war's aftermath – the lack of schools, hospitals, basic services, and the fights between Shia, Kurds, and Sunni over control of certain areas.

During the time of Grandpa's dispatches, James Wray and Mike Halverson had a good idea how Gilbert could be contacted. Later, however, even the dispatches stopped, and the phone calls went silent.

Aunt Justine fretted, and tried not to show it. Xander sweated, and had nightmares, but never told Aunt Justine about them. For days, the noisiest thing in Aunt Justine's duplex was the snoring of the little old neighbor – her next door renter. Neither Xander nor his great aunt laughed or talked about much.

One afternoon, visiting Aunt Justine and Xander, Haroon said, "You know, I've been reading the *National Courier*. Ever since your grandpa stopped sending reports to *the Journal of the Americas,* Louis Lamb has also stopped writing columns for his newspapers. There've been no editorials or other reporting from Lamb for two weeks – not since he suggested the fairgrounds for the Gotamere bunch."

One day, Xander pulled Haroon into the back of the Evans news library and whispered, "What if Lamb or Grandpa are prisoners of some faction – or held in some American detention?"

Haroon frowned. "Like Uncle Gamal?"

"Maybe held for ransom," Xander said.

"Or because they know too much."

"About what?"

"I don't know. Maybe your grandpa got too close to the truth about something."

"And Mr. Lamb?"

"I'm just saying . . ."

After a moment of thinking, debating, and finally deciding to say what was on his mind, Xander said, "Either one of them might have been in Kirkuk when that car-bomb went off in the park."

Haroon nodded. "Or last night in the market in downtown Baghdad."

"So," Xander said, "we've both been having the same nightmare. But all we know is that Grandpa is in a land of danger."

"On the other hand, what if Lamb is making problems for your grandpa?" Haroon said, "Lamb is in Iraq at least partly because of our visit."

"I wish we'd never gone to his office."

Haroon nodded.

The next day, as Xander worked in the news library, Mr. Wray came into the room to talk to Mike Halverson. He saw Xander at the table, so talked to him as well.

"Ed DiPlano, our reporter in Kirkuk, says Louis Lamb has returned to Portland," Mr. Wray said. "DiPlano says he and Lamb came from Baghdad on the same flight. Lamb got off the plane and got in a limousine, so DiPlano had his cab follow the limo. Lamb headed straight to the offices of the government prosecutors."

In that moment, Xander knew he'd been a big-time screw-up. He'd asked Lamb to find the truth, and whatever Lamb found, he thought it would help the prosecution and not Mr. Qubadi's defense. Xander got up and left to find Haroon.

After an hour of whispered worrying, he and Haroon searched for Mr. Halverson and Mr. Wray. They were together in the library.

Haroon said, "Umm . . . we need to talk to you . . ."

Both men turned.

Xander said, "We talked Mr. Lamb into going to Iraq to look for the truth."

"You what? On the phone?"

They confessed the whole thing. Mr. Wray sat in stunned silence, but not Mr. Halverson.

"You left this building without a bodyguard?" Mike Halverson loomed over them.

They nodded. Mr. Halverson spewed about danger. He cussed their impulsiveness, and he broke pencils on tablets.

Xander glanced at James Wray. After a while, even Mr. Halverson turned to him because Mr. Wray had said nothing for what seemed a long, gray moment. At last Mr. Wray spoke softly, "Why didn't you trust us?"

"Trust you?" Haroon said. "We trust you, but those readers out there, they only see Evans money helping my dad. I wanted to show them that it wasn't just Evans' money. My dad is innocent. If a *Security-First Man* like Louis Lamb could see that truth, then everyone will know the truth."

Mr. Wray shook his head, "I understand why you wanted to get Louis Lamb to believe, and write about his belief, but you didn't trust us with your idea, or with your safety."

Haroon glared at Mr. Wray.

Xander said, "You know you would have tried to talk us out of it."

"Lamb is at the prosecutors'," Mr. Halverson said, "not at the defense office of Jan Nelson. And yes, I would have talked you out of it."

Xander asked, "What if Mr. Lamb thinks he found something, and what he found makes him believe Mr. Qubadi is a terrorist?"

"No!" Haroon stood up.

"I'm just asking the obvious," Xander said. "Lamb may think he has real information. We've got to find out why he went to the prosecutor."

Haroon closed his eyes and grabbed for the table. "What have we done?"

Mr. Halverson pulled him into his arms. "You trusted a man to want truth. That is because you are honest men yourselves."

Xander looked from one stricken face to the other. "Where is my grandfather?"

A tense silence followed. Finally James Wray answered. "We don't know. He hasn't contacted us for a week. And Justine says he hasn't called you in longer than that."

Mr. Halverson took a deep breath, and then another. "We have Bill and several others hunting for him, Xander. They are hard on that trail."

"We have to function as if Gilbert Evans is coming back," Mr. Wray said. "We must get everything in order for Nasdar's defense."

Halverson glanced at Haroon and Xander. "These two pups went out on a limb, and it has backfired for all of us. It seems to me . . .," he said, while stacking half-pencils carefully on his drawing pad, ". . . their mistake is a done deal. Now, we've got to find out what rock Lamb turned over, and what scorpion he found under it."

"We'd better do it soon," Mr. Wray said, "because Nasdar's trial is coming up and I don't believe Nelson will get them to put it off."

CHAPTER THIRTY-FIVE

That evening, Xander and Aunt Justine served dinner at the Taziyan Restaurant. About 7:30 p.m., when the dining room was full of guests and Aunt Justine was at the hosting desk, Agent Saurus and one of his men strolled in. Saurus pulled out his badge and announced loudly to Justine, "FBI. We need to speak to Nazneen Qubadi."

"Mr. Saurus," Justine spoke equally loudly, "I am listening. What is it you wish to say?"

Saurus' frown menaced. "Look, Mizz Evans, we don't want any trouble."

"That's good." Justine continued speaking in a ringing voice. "Make an appointment. I'm sure Mrs. Qubadi and her lawyer will be glad to speak to you."

Saurus leaned over Aunt Justine. "Are you obstructing an investigation?"

"I'm telling you to mind your manners, young man. Make an appointment."

While she talked, Xander scooted into the kitchen. Mrs. Qubadi was in the thick of cooking dolmades and Haroon was arranging bowls on a tray.

"Saurus is here," Xander said. "Haroon, call Mr. Nelson. Mrs. Qubadi, I think you need to go for a can of spaghetti sauce at Fred Meyer."

"Can of spaghetti sauce – hmph!"

Though she looked disgusted at his suggested purchase, Mrs. Qubadi handed Xander the hot pad and the spatula. "Dolmades and mint sauce to table ten in three minutes. Stir the stew and stuff the tomatoes for table eight." She pulled her coat over her apron and left by the door to the back patio.

Haroon hung up his phone and said, "Canned spaghetti sauce?"

"Best I could think of."

"Nelson is on his way," Haroon said.

"You've got to leave, too. Go to somewhere for . . . for whatever." Xander said, shoving Haroon toward the door. "Tekla's mom will help me up here."

Haroon grabbed his coat and had just closed the outside door when Agent Saurus pushed into the kitchen followed by Tekla's mother, Mrs. Jones, and then by Saurus' tail of muscle. Xander had to force himself not to check that the door to the patio had completely closed.

"Where is she?" Saurus asked.

His man lifted the lid on the stew.

"Ah," Xander said, stirring the stew contents. "I think I've got this recipe mastered at last."

"Don't try to make me think you've cooked all this by yourself. Where is she and that kid of hers?" Saurus insisted.

Mrs. Jones said, "Xander, are the hors d'oeuvres for table ten ready?" Then she turned to Mr. Saurus and asked, "Sir, you should not be in the kitchen. Very dangerous. Customers are not allowed here by order of the Fire Marshall."

"Search the outside," Saurus pointed his muscle-man at the door.

Xander forced himself to act as if nothing worried him. He said, "Mrs. Jones, may I introduce you to Mr. Guy Saurus?"

Saurus nodded, but never glanced at Mrs. Jones. Instead, he stared at Xander and said, "Don't pretend you don't know who I'm looking for."

"Oh, I'm certain I do know," Xander said, "but you'll have to find her at Safeway. We ran out of mushrooms."

"And she took the kid with her? Not believable."

"The kid is with a sitter." Xander dished up the dolmades and dropped a mint leaf on top of the dish, trying to look as though 'chef' was his everyday job at the restaurant.

"I don't mean the baby," Saurus said. "I mean Haroon, and you know it."

"Haroon has homework tonight." Xander said, handing Mrs. Jones a plate of dolmades, mint sauce, and other small tidbits. "Table ten, and more on the way soon," he said.

"So, the kid is at home?"

"No," Xander said, as he created a second plate of dolmades. He listened for any sounds of Haroon and the muscle from outside the back door.

"Haroon said if I could take over here, he'd be hitting the books at a coffee house until whenever they close." There were no sounds out back, not even the footsteps of Saurus's man. Xander cut four tomatoes, reamed them with a small spoon, putting the contents into the food recycling bin.

"What coffee house?" Saurus had his notebook out.

Xander scraped his memory for coffee houses in Portland. He didn't drink coffee, but he had to come up with something. He stalled by pulling the tomato stuffing out of the refrigerator. "Probably at Pete's on Broadway, or a Starbucks," he said, waving a spoonful of stuffing toward the dining room, "but if you wait, I know that their lawyer and a couple of federal judges will soon be here for dinner. You could talk to them."

"Oh, I believe that. Lawyer and two federal judges!"

"They eat, too." Xander said. "Some eat too much. Those robes can cover a lot of sin and type-two diabetes."

Saurus snorted, "Think you're a doctor-do-gooder like your dad?"

Xander's face heated. He put his spoon down and faced Saurus. "Each of my parents had more value on this planet than you will ever understand."

"A little touchy, eh?"

The back door opened. Xander turned, expecting to see Haroon or Nazneen being pushed inside, Saurus's man came in alone. "There's nowhere to go out there. All cut off by the freeway and a wall."

"There's got to be a way to the front," Saurus hissed.

His man glared at Xander. "Yeah, there is a path," he said, turning his glare on Agent Saurus, "past the garbage bin, and I checked that, too. Nobody there, and nobody out front or in the parking lot."

Mrs. Jones entered from the dining room, "Nelson and his party are on their way," she said.

Xander's relief made him cold.

"I'll put them in table four," she said as she took a second plate of dolmades out to the dining room.

Xander wondered if Mrs. Jones had been listening outside the door. How else could she know to back up his story about Nelson and two judges coming for dinner? He crossed his fingers, praying the mention of a table for Nelson didn't seem a little too obvious to Mr. Saurus.

Saurus glanced at his man. He whispered to Xander, "You tell the Qubadis we've got new evidence, and they both might as well confess all they know. We've first-hand evidence of their collusion with the brothers in Iraq."

Xander whispered back, "What does first-hand evidence mean? That's a phrase I never learned in Pakistan."

Saurus straightened up and stared at Xander. "It means eyewitness, willing to come here and testify."

"For money?"

"For the truth," Saurus bellowed. "And the Qubadi's had best come clean or they will be in jail along with the father. A confession will make things lighter for Mom and son – you know, Dad's undue influence on them and all that."

Saurus pulled out his card and lay it on the counter. "Have them call me. And tell them that Nelson is not their lawyer. He is Nasdar's lawyer. As such, he's bound to give them bad advice so that things go better for his client."

Saurus waved at his man and they both exited the kitchen just as Mrs. Jones returned. "Table eight needs the stew," she said.

Xander turned back to the pot and began ladling the stew into the bowls that Haroon had arranged on a tray. "When they are truly out of the parking lot," he said, "let me know."

"I believe your aunt is watching their exit rather closely," Mrs. Jones said. "And she's composing a speech, or at least a letter to the editor about this visit."

Xander allowed his shoulders to slump. He leaned on the counter top with both hands. *How dare Saurus talk about Dad?*

Then he thought, an eyewitness, willing to come here and testify. Who has Lamb found? And what does Saurus mean about Mr. Nelson giving Mrs. Qubadi bad advice?

Where is Grandpa?

After the all-clear from Aunt Justine, Xander stepped outside to whisper for Haroon and Nazneen to return. Haroon stood up near the wall between the restaurant and the hill down to the freeway. Behind him, the moon had just risen over the east side of the city. "I need help getting Mom out of our hiding place," Haroon said. "Bring the step-ladder."

Running back inside, Xander grabbed up the two-step ladder that was used to reach pots from high shelves. He returned outside, following Haroon to the back yard. Near the hedge and wall, he saw Haroon disappear into a low bush whose leaves were edged with silver moonlight. The bush moved to the side as if it had no roots. And in its place Xander saw a rectangular hole with Haroon's head sticking out of it.

"What is this?"

"Give me the ladder," Haroon said.

Xander handed over the ladder and touched the bush – plastic leaves. And then he heard Nazneen's voice.

"This hole was a great idea, Rune, but we need to build in steps for your old mom."

* *

That night, after Nazneen finished dinner for the restaurant guests, Nelson and Haroon, Mr. Wray, Mr. Halverson and Xander held a whispered conference in the kitchen until the moon shown through the western restaurant window.

Because of Mr. Saurus' threat, Mr. Nelson offered to allow Mrs. Qubadi and Haroon to find a separate lawyer. They turned down his offer, and pledged to hold onto hope for a fair outcome. The biggest unknown elements in their discussion were the absence of Gilbert Evans and the unknown identity of the prosecution witness that Saurus claimed he had.

Xander assumed the witness was Mr. Lamb, but Mr. Wray shook his head. "Gilbert used to have deep admiration for Louis Lamb. I can't believe the man would change that much."

"Maybe he believes he found some evidence against Uncle Gamal and Bijar." Haroon said.

Mrs. Qubadi shook her head. "How could he, since there is no such evidence."

Mr. Nelson said, "Rumor and innuendo can be created to support whatever you want it to support."

"We wait for Gilbert, then," Mrs. Qubadi said. "Maybe he will know what, or who, the prosecution believes it has found."

* *

The next morning when Xander came to the Evans Media Building, Mr. Wray called him into his office. Cold ran down Xander's spine. He grew certain Grandpa had died, so he inched into the office, not wanting to be there. But he had to stay. Had to know.

"I received this letter from a good friend – a reporter in Pakistan," Mr. Wray said. "Your grandpa was well at the time he sent this. He still is well, so far as we know, but I want you to read this before we decide to use any of it."

Xander hesitated, then reached for the papers. The sweat that had formed on his neck cooled. He saw that the writer was Ted Oxnard – a reporter whose name he had heard whispered in the halls of the news offices, a man the other reporters thought was dead since the time of the attacks on the schools and hospitals.

Oxnard wrote:

"Dear James,

"After the attacks on the hospitals and schools of western Pakistan, our team was held captive by a combined group of Afghani Taliban and al Qaeda. All during our imprisonment, the two groups jockeyed for supremacy and power over us as pawns. This power fight resulted in alternate beatings and good care, the good and the bad in each of our captors came out when control over us threatened to transfer to the other group."

Xander remembered his grandfather telling about the film these men made on the night of the attacks. If this man still lived, maybe the boys also lived.

"Our release came because Gilbert Evans worked with local tribal members to negotiate with each group separately. Evans represented to each the dangers and the bad publicity and probable fallout among their countrymen that would follow further beatings and incarceration of prisoners. Finally, it was the Taliban group that prevailed and set us free in the town of Quetta. We were left near the hospital."

Xander glanced up at James. "Grandpa negotiated . . ."

Mr. Wray nodded. "Always been good at that. Learned it from his papa."

The letter continued:

"After our release, Gilbert Evans came to the hospital. The crew and I still were recovering from near starvation. A week later, I was able to take Gilbert to the site of the Friends School and Hospital at Tiri where his daughter, Dr. Rebecca Evans Lloyd and her husband, Dr. Daniel Lloyd, had been murdered. Thirty-five others also died during this attack, Muslim doctors and nurses as well as their Christian colleagues. Eighteen girls and their five women teachers died in the field near the school. One boy and an older man died in the boys' school yard. The rest of the boys and their teachers are still missing. The area was near total devastation. By the time we arrived at Tiri, the town had begun to rebuild the hospital, but the wheat field between the girls' and the boys' schools had become a graveyard for all who died during that battle. The new hospital is named "Love Survives".

Xander stared at the hospital name. One boy and an older man died. And doctors, girls, teachers, Mom, Dad . . .

He looked up at James Wray, who watched him with dark eyes filled with unshed tears. It hit Xander then that Mr. Wray and many others at the paper had known his mother as she grew up. They had loved her, and Dad, too.

Mr. Oxnard wrote one more line.

"James, I have to stop writing. Am still recovering. Will send real news story soon."

Ted

"There are photos," Mr. Wray said, holding out some printed pictures.

Xander took them and turned them over slowly. The first showed townspeople hauling building material and rebuilding walls where once there had been a complete hospital. Xander recognized most of the people, including Mohammed's mother. All of them had lost much weight. The wheat harvest had been destroyed, the fruit trees in the background were skeletons of their normal lushness. Some of the townspeople wore dirty bandages, wrapping wounds they probably received during the siege of the town and the school. It seemed so recent, but it had all happened months ago.

The last photo he looked at was of the graveyard between the ruins of the two schools.

Mohammed, Sophia, Mr. Din, Sophia's father Ali, Manzur's mother, the girls, the women teachers, all of them buried in what had been a ripening field of grain.

In his mind, a little girl in a blue and white dress floated above the field, never falling.

He dropped the photo on the table and let one sob escape. Mr. Wray stood and wrapped his arms around Xander's shoulders.

"Where is he now?" Xander asked, leaning against him. "Where are the boys? Where are they all – all gone?"

"Yes," Mr. Wray said, "so many lost, so many. It is bad, this destruction, this killing."

"Grandpa?"

"Ted Oxnard believes that after the day of their visit to Tiri, your grandpa moved up the gulf passed Iran and into Iraq. Ted thinks he went in search of evidence to free Gamal Besaranî – Mrs. Qubadi's brother. But we don't know where he is."

*   *

Two days later, as a wake-up call, Xander's bedside radio blared's voice: "Get ready Portland, Oregon. The rally of the century will be taking place in your Portland Convention Center. The biggest and most exciting religious event, coming to your east side. And not too soon, for the Godless nature-worshippers of the City of Roses. Brace yourselves, Portland."

Xander flipped off the radio and strode out of his bedroom, ready to butt heads. Fafner was back on the air. It seemed he could head the programming for the *National Courier* media and do radio advertising stints at the same time. Too bad.

Aunt Justine came out of her room wearing a robe and slippers. "Fafner and Gotamere . . ." she muttered. "They deserve each other."

*   *

Two days later, another reporter, Bill Sampson, wrote that Gilbert Evans had visited the prison at in Camp Radamanthus near Baghdad. He'd talked to all the same people Louis Lamb had talked to just two weeks before. At the end of the day, Gilbert had taken himself to the local hospital and checked in. But they didn't know what illness sent him there. Nor did they know why he went to a local hospital instead of the military hospital at Camp Radamanthus.

Two nights after they received this news, Aunt Justine answered a telephone call.

"Did Ted Oxnard send my message?" a voice asked. "And Bill?"

"You whompin' Buzzard!" Aunt Justine yelled into the phone. "Did you think those were messages? Did you think we weren't over here killing ourselves with worry?" By now, Aunt Justine was crying. "You get home. You hear me?"

Xander took the phone. "Grandpa?"

"Xander. I'm sorry. I . . ."

"Why were you in the hospital?"

"Just a little tired, son. Needed a check-up and a few nights of rest. And I'm booked on a flight back in the morning."

That didn't sound like the whole story to Xander. He thought Grandpa chose his words carefully – not lying, not telling the whole truth.

It came to him. Grandpa is certain the phones are tapped. Agent Saurus's men.

"But why not the military hospital?" Xander asked.

"Your dad thought the doctors in Iraq were quality people. He was correct."

Xander sat down hard. They never talked about Dad and Mom. Now Grandpa was quoting Dad. "Grandpa, did they find anything wrong?"

"A lot is wrong over here, Xan, but not with me, and not with this hospital."

"And Uncle Gamal?"

"We'll talk about all that when I return. I asked James Wray and Mike to pick me up at the airport because it's going to be in the middle of your night."

* *

Xander talked Mike Halverson into taking him and Aunt Justine to the airport when Grandpa came home. "I have to see him. I have to."

"And you won't sleep anyway," Mike commented, "so might as well be driving Gilbert nuts instead of poor Justine, eh?"

"Right on," Xander said.

At two in the morning, all the way to the airport, Justine mumbled to herself, "Hard-headed nincum-poop. I just know he's lost weight. Skin and bones – that's what he'll be. Skin and bones on a stoop-backed old man."

However, Grandpa, at sixty-seven years old, still stood a head taller than most passengers, so Xander saw him as he trudged with his security man up the hall to the waiting area. Aunt Justine was right, he had lost weight, but he looked strong and healthy, and he looked sad.

Xander tensed. When Grandpa's gaze fell on him, the old man actually smiled and walked faster. Xander ran the rest of the way and Grandpa pulled him into his arms. It wasn't until that moment that he realized how afraid he had been the whole time Grandpa searched in Iraq and Pakistan.

"You're here," Xander said, and knew he sounded like a kid. "You're home. You're all right."

"Yes, Xan." Grandpa hugged him tighter. "I'm home and I'm all right. I'm so glad to see you."

Rick Johnson and James Wray appeared beside Mike and Aunt Justine. Justine reached for her big brother, "B-Ball man," she said as she hugged him.

"Queen of the Night," he laughed, and held her close.

Xander watched Mike, Rick and James all laugh with his aunt and grandpa. He figured those nick names were part of an old joke. Maybe the names came out in public when Grandpa and Aunt Justine were really happy, or really pissed off.

Aunt Justine broke the hug and said, "You need some potatoes, and some good chicken soup."

"You offering to cook?" Grandpa asked.

"Xan is the cook," she said, waving her bony fingers in his direction. "And he makes twice baked potatoes with all the fixings." That made Grandpa laugh.

"Xan," Grandpa gazed at him, "How about if I try those potatoes tomorrow? No," he glanced at the airport wall clock, "we'll have them this evening. You need to sleep at Justine's the rest of this night. Then I'll help you move back to our house tomorrow afternoon. "

"Okay," Xander said, disappointed because he had so many questions. At least his grandfather was safe and well.

"And let's invite the Qubadi's over for dinner tomorrow, after prayers," Grandpa said.

Xander nodded. He felt certain he wouldn't hear the news about Gamal until the Qubadi's were present.

CHAPTER THIRTY-SIX

A blow to all of them came the next morning when a package arrived at Evans International Media from Gamal's lawyers in Iraq. In it lay a copy of a typed, clear confession. The confession said that Nasdar Qubadi was the source of funds Gamal used to support al Quaida in Iraq. The confession was dated August 8, 2005, over a year ago.

"How can this be?" Grandpa asked Mr. Nelson.

"It's a confession under torture, that's how it can be."

* *

The next evening, Xander cooked a supper he was certain no one would eat. Aunt Justine set the table in silence. Grandpa and Rick left to pick up the Qubadis from prayers at the temporary mosque. A nearby Presbyterian church had offered their sanctuary as a Friday home and weekday office space to the congregation from Husayn Mosque.

A half hour later, Xander heard footsteps on the front porch stairs. Aunt Justine opened the door. Xander glanced from the stove toward the front of the house. On the porch, he saw Mike Halverson and Haroon. James Wray held Gulbahar in his arms. Mrs. Qubadi stepped into the front hall with Grandpa. As the rest filed inside, Rick Johnson stopped outside to survey the neighborhood. He sent two more men around the back of the house.

Xander saw Haroon glance out toward Mr. Johnson, his eyes pinched together with worry. Grandpa called Xander and Justine into the living room. Xander turned off the stove. He carried dolmades cut into small slices as hors d'oeuvres, but Grandpa took the plate and set it on the fireplace mantel. He waited until all were seated.

"Nazneen, Haroon, Gulbahar," he said, looking last at Haroon's four-year-old sister.

Xander grew uneasy about what Grandpa would tell them, so he stood up, saying, "I'll take Gulbahar for a walk down the hall."

Haroon glanced up at him, then nodded. "It is best."

Mrs. Qubadi's eyes had grown large. "Please, yes, Alexander."

So Xander swung Gulbahar up into his arms and hugged her. "Come on, Honey. Let's look at what's for dinner. Gulbahar twisted to stare back at her mommy. But Xander walked quickly toward the kitchen. He didn't want Gulbahar to hear what might have happened before Mrs. Qubadi had a chance to take it in.

Moments later, he heard Mrs. Qubadi's wailing. In him, her cries awakened deep grief – the memory of Mohammed's mother wailing over her son's body. In his arms, Xander felt Gulbahar stiffen. Gulbahar's own cry rolled from her chest in a high keening.

As Xander turned toward the dining room to keep Gulbahar in motion and give Mrs. Qubadi more time, Haroon came down the hall, took his little sister in his arms and buried his face in her shoulder. "Uncle Gamal is dead," he whispered to Xander.

Xander stared at Haroon. Uncle Gamal was in an American prison. How could he have died?

Gulbahar cried because her mother cried. She didn't know her uncle, had never seen him, but she knew that her mother's pain should be her own pain.

Haroon and Xander knew Uncle Gamal by his acts. From all their phone calls, all their letters from Uncle Bijar Qubadi, all their reading of reports from Evans investigations in northern Iraq, they knew. Gamal drove the old truck. He bought the goats, the lambs, the vegetables. Gamal helped his brother-in-law. Gamal and Bijar fed a small town. Nasdar's money bought seed. His money repaired wells, bought machines to help dry olives and figs. The money ran a generator that kept goat milk cold . . . And Gamal had been the center of all this work until one day when someone from another town captured him, took his truck, and sold him as a terrorist to the Americans.

Sold for $500 American dollars. Now dead.

Gulbahar's wailing continued. Xander felt Haroon turn and run down the hall with Gulbahar in his arms.

Mike Halverson came into the dining room in time to see Xander's tears fall. Mike took Xander in a bear hug, "I'm sorry. . . I'm so sorry."

Xander nodded, wiping his face, but he felt his forehead grow hot and his face twist with renewed sorrow. "How?" he asked.

"We don't know."

CHAPTER THIRTY-SEVEN

On the opening day of Nasdar Qubadi's trial, Grandpa Gilbert recommended against taking little sister, Gulbahar, to the courthouse, but Mrs. Qubadi insisted.

"They need to see that this man has a whole family," she said. "They need to face the truth. We are not vicious beasts, but humans." Gilbert started to argue with her, but Mrs. Qubadi said, "Gib, I know you have Gulbahar's interests at heart, but right now, I have to do what is best for Nasdar."

So, Gilbert drove them all and parked the family car on the east side of the Willamette River, a block from the light rail stop. Rick's men, Aunt Justine, Gilbert and Xander joined Mrs. Qubadi, Haroon and Gulbahar. All of them climbed into the MAX light-rail train and headed toward downtown Portland. Grandpa figured they could avoid at least some of the news reporters by surprising them and using public transportation, appearing in an unexpected place downtown and arriving at the courthouse door without the usual drive-up, perp-photo opportunity.

Xander worried about the block they had to walk from the train to the court house. He was pretty sure there would be cameras, shouting reporters and hate signs as they approached the trial.

At eight in the morning, the Evans and Qubadi families arrived at the Mark O. Hatfield United States Courthouse. Xander's fears were fulfilled. Parked vans and dozens of television crews discovered that the families were among the pedestrians. The crowd moved in, leaving a grudging, narrow path through to the building – a path kept open by uniformed policemen.

Reporters called out questions to Mrs. Qubadi, to Haroon and even to Gulbahar, who hid her face against Mrs. Qubadi's shoulder.

"What does your daughter think about having her father in jail?"

"Your son is a murderer. Why is he free?"

And from the sign-waving fanatics. "Real Americans believe on the Lord Jesus Christ!"

Trudging through the hate became foot-slogging work. However, Jan Nelson had told them, "Don't react to reporters or the crowd. Walk across the street, into the building, and keep on walking. You can't hear anything but the birds in the trees."

Birds in the trees knew better than to be near, Xander thought. He walked between waving placards covered in blood-red paint, announcing "God loves those who follow Jesus", or "Muslim Terrorists are NOT Citizens" and "Islam teaches Hate".

Xander wanted to shout, "Who's doing the hating today?"

But he didn't shout. He kept his eyes on the back of Mr. Nelson. He guessed that behind him, Grandpa had a good grip on Aunt Justine, the person most likely to make a speech. Aunt Justine may have promised silence, but Grandpa didn't trust her not to give an angry sign bobber a nosebleed.

Haroon whispered to him, "I see the soccer families, too. They have signs for us."

Xander glanced around and saw one sign held by Mrs. Jones who was Tekla and Denny's mother. It said, "Innocent Until PROVEN

Guilty." One of the hate signs kept shoving in front of hers, but she worked her way to the front again, just as they crossed the street.

"We love you, Nazneen," she yelled.

At that moment, one of the reporters shouted, "Alexander Evans! These people killed your mother and father. How can you betray your parents?"

Xander felt his mind go numb.

Haroon touched Xander's arm to help him concentrate on strolling and bird-watching. Behind Xander, Grandpa Gilbert whispered, "That was the *U.S. National Daily* reporter. They're hemorrhaging money. A sound bite of your anger will bring advertising revenue."

* *

An hour later, at the courthouse, the families sat in a cordoned-off section of the hall on the second floor. Because of the long time, and the tension on this first day, Mr. Nelson had encouraged Mrs. Qubadi to stay in the hall until the jury was chosen.

"There are a lot of preliminaries to get out of the way first," Nelson had said. "I'll signal when it's time to appear. Your later entry into the courtroom with your friends will impress the jury."

The long hall where they sat contained many benches outside a series of courtrooms. Each courtroom had been assigned to a particular judge. Their judge would be a man named Dylan O'Flaherty. As they sat there, an elevator door opened at the end of the hall. At the same time, a man opened O'Flaherty's courtroom door and came out to greet the people from the elevator.

Xander saw Mr. Qubadi with Mr. Nelson coming from the elevator toward the courtroom. Mr. Qubadi spotted his family, and waved at them despite the handcuffs. Gulbahar leapt from her mother's lap and started to run toward him, calling, "Daddy. Daddy", but his guard ushered him quickly into the courtroom and closed the door.

Haroon ran and caught Gulbahar up in his arms. She cried and tried to wrench out of his arms. "Soon," Haroon said, "Soon, Daddy will be free."

Xander hoped Haroon was right, but Mr. Nelson had told them not to expect a quick decision. He'd said, "The government will win the first round. We'll have to appeal a conviction."

Haroon gave his sister to his mother and sat down again. Gulbahar cried. "Where is Daddy going?"

While Nazneen quieted her, Xander watched Haroon's hands tighten on the seat of the bench. He stared at the wood grain on the courtroom door as if his father's brief trip through that door might be the last time he ever saw him smile. Tears glistened at the edges of Haroon's eyes, but never fell. The end of his nose reddened.

Next, they heard the click of the prosecutor Mr. Jory's hard-soled shoes pacing inside the courtroom. Mr. Nelson had described this trick. Prosecutor Jory used his noisy shoes to distract people. From their discussions of strategy, Xander knew the prosecutor's reputation. Never surprised, never sweating, never beaten. In contrast, Jan Nelson seemed too calm, too unhurried, too easy to walk over.

Yet, this same, calm Jan Nelson had a trail of evidence for how Nasdar's money was spent in Iraq, including any bribe money that had to be paid to make transport of Barzani produce possible. Bribes were necessary on market roads where hijacking was a way of life. To Americans, the bribes seemed damning unless they understood the chaos of a country in civil upheaval.

Nelson had collected testimonials from citizens of Barzani about Uncle Bijar as a leader, about the Barzani School teaching children to read and do sums. He had statements showing that Gamal and Bijar helped farmers and small businesses, not terrorists. There was no one better prepared than Nelson to show that Nasdar's intentions were for his money to help his village.

But Xander knew the jury would have to overcome a lack of knowledge about how different life in the Harmota region was from ordinary life in the United States. The family had to hope that Jan Nelson was able to choose jurors willing to imagine those differences and willing to believe that evidence.

Xander sat next to Haroon remembering what Nelson said might be happening in that room when he had explained the process to them.

Nelson had said, "Judge O'Flaherty will look over questionnaires that potential jurors filled out. Then, he'll ask each of them two or three questions that might show why they should be excused from service. Are they able to serve the length of time? Do they have experiences that might make them partial to one side or another? Are they willing and able to sift through the evidence?"

The idea of a judge questioning the jury had surprised Xander. He'd never seen an American trial and only heard about those that happened in Pakistan.

Mr. Nelson said, "In the Ninth Circuit Court, the western circuit, the lawyers also get to question and excuse jurors they believe might be prejudiced for or against the accused."

As anguish and worry for Haroon's family mounted in Xander, he remembered how the indictment sounded when Mr. Nelson read it to the defense-research team: "Conspiracy to levy war against the United States; Conspiracy to provide material support and resources to Al-Qaida; Money laundering; Conspiracy to possess and discharge firearms in furtherance of crimes of violence."

The last charge was the one that most pissed Xander off. Wasn't the National Rifle Association all about the right to bear arms? Why did that belief in bearing arms break down if the citizen had a Kurdish last name?

Xander's anger only slightly masked his fear for his friend. If Nasdar Qubadi were convicted, what might happen to Haroon?

Haroon went target shooting at the quarry with his dad and the rest. Would Haroon be accused next?

Jan Nelson had everything anyone could find to defend Nasdar's actions, except that there seemed no way to refute the confession from Uncle Gamal of Nasdar's terrorist support. The prosecution would present the confession before Mr. Nelson had a chance to present evidence for the defense. And the confession would taint everything that followed it.

Xander did not know what to do, except pray for help. God, Allah, Yahweh, what he called him didn't matter as long as the Almighty cared.

As Xander breathed in, to calm himself, he smelled the wool and leather of his grandfather's suit coat. The warm smell reminded him that his grandfather had put everything on the line for his friend: the house on Sixteenth Avenue; the Max Million Foundation; the *Journal of the Americas of Portland*; the reputation of all his other newspapers. Grandpa had courage.

After several minutes, Haroon nudged Xander.

There came Louis Lamb. As they stared at him, Louis Lamb mounted the last of the stairs, crossed the hall and entered the courtroom. Xander was certain Lamb didn't come here as a reporter. He would present evidence for the prosecution.

Xander and Haroon had uncovered evidence that showed the struggle of the people of Barzani to live and to feed their families, but they didn't know what Lamb had uncovered

As Jan Nelson said, "The opposition has poor Gamal in Iraq, arrested and tortured and confessing that everything the government claims about Nasdar is true. That confession is very damning evidence."

Xander couldn't understand how the questioners got such a clear confession when, during the rest of the interviews with Gamal, it was pretty obvious he was too disoriented to make any sense.

Xander felt defeat looming. He glanced at Haroon and saw that he also felt the heavy hand of doom.

CHAPTER THIRTY-EIGHT

The day had been spent in the hall. Jury selection took the whole time. They saw Nasdar again as he was taken back to the jail, and for Haroon, giving his dad support had made the wait in the hall important. For Gulbahar, the wait had been excruciating and bewildering. Xander and Haroon had created a paper-towel soccer ball to kick around on the hall floor to keep Gulbahar entertained. Late in the afternoon, she had cried herself to sleep.

All during that evening after they left the court house, Grandpa and Xander sat in their living room. Xander sat near the fireplace, adding logs to keep the fire going. Grandpa Gilbert sat on the sofa and talked about when he was fourteen. He told Xander about the man whose photo was still in the family album, the man with the scarred face. The man was Brendan O'Connor, Grandpa's first coach, his eighth grade science teacher and eventually a good friend. Grandpa said that back in 1953, someone had accused Mr. O'Connor of being a Communist which was similar to accusing someone of supporting terrorism in this era. The accusation had changed everything for

Grandpa and for Mr. O'Connor. Everything Grandpa did with his life was because of that accusation and the ease with which people accepted it as true.

Xander worried about how an old man like Grandpa could go through having another friend in danger. This time around, Grandma Elizabeth wasn't here to help Grandpa keep his spirit. Since his trip to Iraq and Pakistan, Grandpa looked sad, thin and much older.

But Grandpa still had his friends, Mike and James. And somehow, he'd become friends with Rick Johnson, who'd evidently been a bully back in 1953. Xander didn't understand that friendship, but he was certain Rick Johnson would do anything to protect Grandpa.

At eleven o'clock, Xander brought Grandpa a hot chocolate, hoping it would help him sleep. They retired to their rooms, but during the night, he heard Grandpa pacing his bedroom floor.

The next morning, as the families met to go to the courthouse, Mr. Nelson appeared on the Qubadi doorstep. He spoke first to Aunt Justine, asking if she would take care of Gulbahar at her house. She agreed. Next he turned to Mrs. Qubadi.

"It's going to be a rough day, Nazneen. I don't think you want your little girl at the courthouse."

Rick Johnson added, "I've got people stationed at the front, the back, and inside of Justine's duplex, just in case."

*　*

So, they began the second day. As they approached the mob near the courthouse, Xander felt his body grow tight with fear. He saw the same tension in Haroon, and even in his grandfather, but Jan Nelson just kept walking in front of them, and Rick Johnson behind – a flock of goats circled by wolves.

They all pushed through the yelling crowd that had massed across the street from the courthouse. Fewer police were there than on the first day, but the crowd seemed even larger, and the anti-Muslim signs even more ugly. For a quick moment, Xander realized that Denny Jones and Rob Palmquist were in the crowd, yelling at Haroon.

Thank God Aunt Justine kept Gulbahar at home.

"Still," Grandpa said. "The hoard smells blood and circles."

However, Xander noticed one person waving a sign that said, "Trial by Jury, Not by Radio and Television." He tried to see the brave person behind the sign, but got swept into the Hatfield Courthouse with no idea who that person could be – someone on their side – or at least on the side of justice.

Once in the halls of the courthouse, Xander wiped sweat from his face and neck.

Rick Johnson called Xander and Haroon over to the long windows of the second floor. "Look down there," he said.

Below them, they could see the crowd of protesters.

"Count them," Rick said.

It was a little hard to keep track of a milling group, but after a time, Xander said, "I get fifty."

"Sixty," Haroon said, "but about twenty of those are holding signs for no trial by radio and other demands for justice."

"Look," Haroon said, "The Urban League has some signs down there."

Xander squinted until he could read, "Rights for Any are Rights for All".

"Yes," Xander said. "Jesse Jackson's famous speech."

"They understand," Rick said.

"There are Denny and Rob," Haroon said. "As we came, I saw that Rob had a tomato in his hand, but somebody grabbed his arm just as he started to throw."

"Did you see who?"

Haroon shook his head. "A woman. Couldn't tell."

"This morning, that felt like a huge mob. Where've the others gone?" Xander asked.

"That's pretty much the mob we walked through," Rick said. "My men have been tracking the numbers both days. There are more today than yesterday, but only fifteen more."

"But on the news last night . . ." Haroon said.

"I know." Rick said, "On the news, it's the same fifty or sixty from the side, the front, the back and soon, it seems like hundreds."

"Where is the groundswell? The public outcry that Fafner and Gotamere always claim?"

"At home," Rick said, "watching the news and letting others like Fafner and Gotamere tell them what it means."

"That will change when she gets to town for her rally," Xander said.

*   *

Mr. Nelson called them together in a far corner of the hall. "Today, it's important that you all sit in separate places toward the back of the courtroom. But Gilbert, I want you in the row directly behind me, next to the lady in the scarf. Nazneen, you sit by yourself in the third row from the back and near the windows. And you two boys, sit well away from Mrs. Qubadi in the next to the last row, not too close to each other. My assistant has put two dark brown coats where I want you two to sit."

"Why?" Haroon asked.

"We're going to confuse some people. Don't wave at your dad when you go in there. He'll seem to be looking for you, but he will wave at someone else."

Xander and Haroon separated from each other to enter Judge Dylan O'Flaherty's already crowded courtroom. They found the coats that Mr. Nelson's assistants had left to save places. Two other adults, their body guards sat between them, making it look like they weren't related at all.

Everyone in the courtroom seemed to have their attention on Haroon's father at the table near the jury. He looked well, even calm.

He turned to smile at a couple in the front row, a dark-haired woman about Nazneen's age who had covered her head with a colorful scarf – something Nazneen never did except at prayers. Next to the woman sat a teen-aged boy, much bigger than Haroon. Next, Mr. Qubadi nodded at Grandpa Gilbert who seemed to be with the other two.

Mr. Qubadi wore a brand new blue suit and sat up tall. After the family members were seated, Xander glanced across the room. Louis Lamb leaned over a book on the far side of the room. Lamb did not look at Haroon or Xander. That worried Xander even more than the crowd outside.

Xander looked around at the people who attended the trial. Some were friends of the family from the Quaker meeting. Moms and dads from the soccer team were seated together. There were some people he'd seen carrying signs in the mob yesterday, and also a whole row of men and women he knew, but couldn't place.

Haroon pointed toward those unknown people and sent Xander a thumbs up sign.

Xander then recognized the group -- the ministers from Ecumenical Ministerial Alliance. They had helped rebuild Maryam, Imam Moussa's mosque, and the Sephardic synagogue that had been attacked. These were the ministers who had taken out a half-page advertisement for this morning, and for every morning this week. Their huge ad would run in every newspaper of the region. It said, "We are Christians, Jews and Muslim leaders of Portland's places of worship. And we are radical – which means we work to solve a problem at its root source. The root source of our present problems is the fear that controls our decisions. We urge all who believe in the Almighty One, The God of Love, to protest the use of torture, protest the injustice of Guantanamo Bay, and the invasion of our homes with warrantless wiretapping. Protest all efforts to replace our Inalienable Rights with false security based on the Selling of Fear."

"We're not alone in this, after all," Xander whispered to himself.

And then he realized they never have been alone. He glanced at the soccer team families. He remembered the letters to the editor that questioned Mr. Qubadi's arrest. He thought about the signs outside – the ones that were against trial by radio and television, the ones that urged justice over prejudice.

Xander studied Haroon's face. He saw tension, worry, determination and one other thing he'd never noticed before. He saw understanding, maybe even tolerance of those who hate.

Haroon leaned over the bodyguards between them and sent Xander a note.

"People are good. Panic makes them back into a cave and strike out."

* *

The clerk opened the jury room door and the jurors filed in. Xander watched them, searching for signs of their attitudes. There were two tall men, one with a neck as thick as his head. Behind them came an older woman with dyed blue-white hair. The younger woman behind her had long red fingernails.

Three men in business suits and striped ties filed in, followed by three more ladies, one of whom was African American. A middle-aged lady followed them. She had long hair tied in a ribbon at the back of her head and seemed to think dressing up was wearing a vest over her wrinkled waistless dress. Behind her came an African-American fellow in a dashiki shirt of brown and tan geometric pattern.

Ordinary people, a cross section of Portland citizens. But not one of them glanced at Nasdar Qubadi. This fact gave Xander the gut wrenching feeling that all was lost. They already seemed to have decided he must be guilty of supporting terrorism, and they didn't want to make eye contact with such a man.

The clerk called out, "All rise for the Honorable Judge Dylan O'Flaherty." The judge entered from his chambers. After a few remarks from the judge about demeanor for the visitors and for the jury, the trial began.

Mr. Jory first called on the Homeland Security officers who had arrested Nasdar. They said that on that day they had found him talking on the phone with someone who was warning him of the imminent arrest. Xander knew they were talking about his own phone call from the school. A big mistake.

The arresting officers were followed on the stand by Agent Saurus who spoke about taking away the family computers and papers in order to study them. He said, they had found the planned return trip to Iraq – the tickets that were never used. And they found receipts for ammunition for a rifle, but, they said, the rifle had not been found.

Haroon glanced at Xander at that moment. Both of them knew the Qubadi's never owned a rifle. They had borrowed Grandpa's when they were target practicing.

Agent Saurus said they had discovered correspondence with a mosque and madrasa school in the Harmota area, northeastern Iraq. They also found a financial program in the computer that showed the Qubadi family regularly sent money to the Harmota mosque which was near Barzani. Later, Agent Saurus established that this money was funneled to Iraq through the local mosque, the one called *Husayn*, a mosque whose assets had been frozen by Homeland Security.

Xander felt sweat under his arms. Things did not sound good.

For the defense, Mr. Nelson asked the Agent Saurus for copies of the correspondence with the mosque and school in Barzani.

"Those are part of a classified report. Producing them would compromise U.S. security."

Mr. Nelson turned to the judge and said, "Your honor, as we prepared our case, we have asked to have these letters to Mr. Qubadi's family produced, but we have been stonewalled in this way all along."

"Mr. Nelson, we have ruled on this matter. You have seen these letters in my chambers, but for security reasons, you know they can't be brought into the court room. Nor can the content be quoted here." The judge then turned to the court stenographer and told her to strike the question and all following conversation.

Next, Mr. Nelson asked, "Mr. Saurus, I ask if you found any references to Al-Qaeda."

"All the references were in code."

"Code?" asked Mr. Nelson, "And you have broken the code?"

"Yes."

"And what is the code word for al-Qaeda?"

"I'm not at liberty to say."

"Might the word 'lettuce' be code for al-Qaeda? Perhaps 'rutabaga?'"

"Mr. Nelson!" the judge said. "No more on this subject."

Xander watched anger tighten the judge's eyes and mouth. If Mr. Nelson didn't quit pushing, they might lose him to jail for contempt.

"Yes, your honor." Mr. Nelson sounded calm, but Xander felt hot, and then suddenly cold. Nearby, Haroon closed his eyes and rocked as if in prayer. Mohammed's face flashed into Xander's mind.

And then Xander also prayed, "*Please, God/ Allah. Please, make Mr. Nelson stop.*" As he opened his eyes again, he noticed a short man in a very stiff, almost military brown suit. He sat quietly on the other side of the room, near the windows. Not far behind Mr. Brown Suit were the parents of several soccer families, including Tekla and her mother. A couple of the other soccer players sat with their families in other parts of the room. Mrs. Breiton sat in the middle row with her husband, the restaurant owner. Mr. Lamb sat close to the Breitons.

Xander stared at Mr. Lamb. He didn't understand how a man could seem to want to help them, and then have nothing to say to them when he returned. What bad thing could Lamb think he'd discovered about Uncle Gamal or Uncle Bijar?

Mr. Nelson next asked the FBI witness for more specific information about the type of rifle that would use the ammunition found in the Qubadi's home.

Xander relaxed, but Haroon still rocked slightly.

"The ammo was for some kind of twenty-two," the man answered. "Maybe a semi-automatic type . . . you can't tell without a used bullet."

"Maybe semi-automatic, but also maybe a single-shot rifle, is that true?"

"Well, yes."

"Did you find any spent bullets, any used cartridges?"

"None. The place was cleaned up."

Mr. Nelson turned away from the man and slightly toward the jury. "Mr. Smith, I'm not asking you to guess why you found no spent ammunition, I'm asking if you found any."

"No, we didn't."

"So, you have no way of identifying what type of hunting rifle the ammunition might be intended for."

"No."

"And did you find any other bookkeeping references to that rifle or any other rifle?"

"We found dates to go to the quarry on his calendar. Each time it said, 'With Haroon to quarry.' And this was in his handwriting, too."

Xander saw Haroon stiffen.

Mr. Nelson asked, "Are you a handwriting expert, Mr. Smith?"

"No. It just looked like . . ."

"Your honor. . ." Mr. Nelson started to say.

The judge raised his hand, leaned toward the court recorder and said, "Strike everything after the last word 'quarry'. The witness will refrain from speculating about things that are not in his area of expertise."

"Yes, sir."

At that moment, a new man in a rumpled gray suit came into the room and sat down near Mr. Jory's assistant. A place had been saved for him there. Xander glanced at Haroon and tilted his head toward the man. Haroon studied him and whispered, "Uh-oh!"

Mr. Nelson continued to talk to the FBI witness, "Please, tell us what the quarry dates on the calendar were."

The witness studied a card in his hand and said, "October twelve, two-thousand three, October twenty-six, two thousand three and October ten and twenty-four, two-thousand four."

"Four Saturdays during two years. That's it?"

"Yes."

"And why is the calendar not locked up for security reasons?"

"It reveals no sensitive material."

"No state secrets?"

"No."

"No code words?"

"It's not in code."

"Oh. So code might have been used sometimes, but not other times?"

"Evidently."

"Did you wonder why no code would be used for these notations that the FBI would like to believe are so damning?" Mr. Nelson asked.

"Objection," Mr. Jory said. "Asking the witness to speculate."

"Sustained." The judge said.

"Ah yes, beyond your expertise. No more questions."

Xander watched the judge's eyes follow Mr. Nelson back to the defense table. Warning daggers flashed from Judge O'Flaherty's glare, but Mr. Nelson had his back to the bench.

CHAPTER THIRTY-NINE

Next, Mr. Jory called a Mr. Derrick to the stand. Mr. Derrick dressed in slacks, a white shirt and a sport jacket.

Probably not Homeland Security, Xander thought.

After Mr. Derrick took the oath, Mr. Jory asked him to introduce himself. The man lived on a farm near the town of Rhododendron, Oregon, on the flanks of Mount Hood. He testified that he had seen Nasdar Qubadi and his son practice shooting at targets in the quarry a half-mile from his home. He identified Nasdar, saying "I 'specially remember him. He was a dead shot."

"Objection," Mr. Nelson said, without even looking at the witness.

"Sustained." Judge O'Flaherty glanced at the witness. "Answer the question without embellishing."

Mr. Derrick nodded.

"Did you hear me?" the judge asked.

"Yes, sir," Derrick said.

At his turn, Mr. Nelson rose and asked, "I'm glad you remember that Mr. Qubadi is accurate with a target. Were there others at the quarry on these days?"

"Oh, yes. It's a popular place for target practice."

"And you remember the others?"

"Well, not all of them."

"What took you to the quarry on those days?"

"I got a new rifle."

"And why do you need a rifle, Mr. Derrick?"

"My rifle is for hunting."

"And the other people who come to the quarry, why do they have rifles?"

"Objection," Mr. Jory said.

"Sustained," Judge O'Flaherty said.

Mr. Nelson turned toward the jury, then spoke to the witness. "All right, Mr. Derrick, I won't ask you to speculate on other people's purposes, but I will ask if you recognize any of the other people who practiced at the quarry – any who might be here in the courtroom."

"Well, the kid, of course."

"Oh? Which kid?"

The man pointed at the tall teenager near the front. "Qubadi's son, right there in the second row, the fourth person over."

"They introduced themselves to you on that day?"

"No, sir."

"Yet, you know his son?"

"Of course. Been in the news, you know."

"Certainly. I don't suppose you also know Mrs. Qubadi?"

"Sure, the one on the end of the row with the scarf."

"She was at the quarry, too?"

"No."

"Oh, I understand," Mr. Nelson said. "You recognize the Qubadi family from the news."

"Right," Mr. Derrick said.

"Objection," Mr. Jory shouted.

"Overruled."

"Mr. Derrick," Mr. Nelson said, "Are you sure you recognize Mr. Qubadi as the man you saw in the quarry?"

"Certainly."

"No more questions."

Xander breathed in. He glanced at the jury members. They seemed attentive, but he couldn't tell what they were thinking. He looked at Mr. Lamb. He seemed to be listening, but had a book open on his lap. A few feet away, the man in the stiff brown suit stared at the fingernails on his left hand.

Does anybody get what just happened? Xander wondered.

Within moments, Mr. Jory called the fellow in a wrinkled gray suit, a Mr. Jake Rochford. The man came forward from his place near Mr. Jory and took the oath. When Mr. Jory questioned Mr. Rochford, he said he had attended Husayn. He testified that the Qubadi family had also attended during the same time.

Mr. Rochford leaned a notebook on the witness stand. The lawyers and the judge held a whispered conversation. Afterward, the judge ordered, "Let the witness's notes be entered as evidence."

The court clerk marked the notes and returned them to the witness.

Using his notes, Mr. Rochford listed things he had heard at the mosque during meetings and during worship. "They made very anti-American speeches ..."

"Objection," Mr. Nelson said.

"Sustained," the judge said. "Mr. Rochford do not use vague words like 'they made speeches'. Tell us exactly who made speeches."

"Yes, sir. It was one of the imams. I don't know his name, sir, but he is the young imam at Husayn. He made speeches against the U.S. security systems put in place after September 2001, against the war with Afghanistan and then the war with Iraq. He spoke out against detainment of prisoners offshore, and against lots of stuff the government did to improve safety for U.S. citizens."

"And did others besides the speaker agree with these statements?" Mr. Jory asked.

"Sure. Everyone who was there. They talked about resisting an evil government in any way they could."

When defense took its turn, Mr. Nelson asked the witness, "You say they talked about resisting an evil government. And you said 'everyone'. Who exactly is 'They'? Who is everyone?"

"The other members."

"Can you name these members?"

Mr. Rochford glanced at Mr. Jory. "I didn't know their names."

"You took notes, but not names?"

"That's right."

"Is it? Are you a member of the Husayn Mosque?"

"No. I stopped going there."

"Is that when you joined the Portland Community Evangelical Church?"

Mr. Jory objected. The judge over-ruled the objection, so Nelson repeated the question.

Mr. Rochford glanced again at Mr. Jory who merely stared back at him, waiting. Then Rochford said, "I been a member at Evangelical off and on."

"Off and on since 1992?"

"I guess you could say that," Rochford answered. His glance darted around the courtroom, and then he added, "But they were at the mosque when that guy was foaming at the mouth, and they didn't do anything about him."

"Oh, and when you heard these speeches, what did you do about that one imam?"

"Well, at the time, nothing, but when they arrested Mr. Qubadi, I thought it best to tell what was going on at that mosque. There might be others, you know."

"So, you did nothing at the same time that you say Mr. Qubadi did nothing."

"Objection," Mr. Jory said.

"Overruled," the judge said.

"Please answer the question, Mr. Rochford. Did you do nothing at the same time that you say Mr. Qubadi did nothing?"

"It wasn't my place."

"You did nothing?"

"No, I didn't."

Nelson stood very still for a moment. Then he asked, "How long did you attend the services at the mosque?"

"Don't know. Maybe six months.

"So, during six months, you agreed that the United States headed down a wrong path, but at the seventh month, you changed your mind?"

"No, I never agreed with that guy," the man said.

"Yet, you were there," Mr. Nelson said. Nelson paused a moment, as if looking at his papers, but Xander heard his last words echo in the room. "You were there. You were there."

After that wait, Mr. Nelson said, "You knew the Qubadi family?"

"Oh yes, the father is that man at the table with you. I saw them there."

"And the others in the family?"

"The woman and the son are right behind you."

"Can you be more specific?"

"The second row, that big boy and the woman with the scarf."

"You are certain that the man at the table with me is the man you saw at the mosque during the services?"

"Sure. That's Nasdar Qubadi."

"I ask, sir, because you have also identified his son and wife, but you have pointed to people who are not his son and wife. You have mis-identified the same people that the previous witness, Mr. Derrick, mistakenly took for the Qubadi family."

"But I . . ."

"You have pointed to two people who may have some features of a Middle Eastern nature, but they look nothing like the son and wife. Even though you claim to have seen them at church, and Derrick claims to have seen them on television news, your identifications are not accurate."

"I know him. I know him."

"No more questions."

The people in the courtroom whispered to each other. The jurors glanced at the woman and boy near Grandpa Gilbert, and then looked around the room as if to find the real Haroon and Nazneen Qubadi. They seemed as puzzled as the witness.

The judge brought down his gavel. "Order."

Mr. Jory stood quickly, rustling papers and walking toward Mr. Qubadi, then back toward the jury as the witness left the stand. His noisy shoes clicked – *a distracting method*, Xander thought.

That afternoon, Mr. Nelson told the Evans and Qubadi families they could sit together. Their separation in the morning had served the purpose.

During the rest of that day, Mr. Jory used testimony from Agent Saurus and other witnesses from the CIA and Homeland Security to establish that the family had sent money from Husayn Mosque to the mosque in Harmota, northeastern Iraq. He established that the village of Barzani sat near the border with Iran, that Mr. Qubadi's brother ran a school, and that Mrs. Qubadi's brother Gamal Besaranî, helped to purchase material for the school. Mr. Jory and Agent Saurus constantly referred to the school as a madrasa.

In his turn, Mr. Nelson asked Agent Saurus, "Are you aware that the word *madrasa* simply means school or academy?"

"Many madrasas teach a form of Islam that encourages terrorism against non-Muslims."

"And what was taught at the madrasa, or school in Barzani?"

"Of course they wouldn't be teaching that stuff if one of our people was around."

"And when were your people visiting there?"

"After Mr. Qubadi was arrested."

"And what were they teaching then?"

"Well, at that time, they were teaching reading, writing and mathematics."

"So an ordinary school curriculum."

Xander saw many jurors frown, or shake their heads. He thought the jury didn't quite believe the interpretation of *madrasa* as a school.

*   *

That afternoon after the trial, Xander arrived to help out at the Taz. Out the entry window of the restaurant, Xander saw Mr. Breiton walking up the street toward the *Taziyan*.

"Juan, I'm headed to the john," Xander said.

Juan Munoz nodded. "Go," he said – a little bathroom humor between them.

Instead, Xander stepped into the bathroom, noticed how much his tan had faded and slicked back his hair with water to look as if he'd been sweating from a run. He went to the side door and slipped out before Juan caught on. Once outside, he acted as if he were out for a jog, trotted three houses down the street then stopped as he past Mr. Breiton.

Mr. Breiton looked up. He had no idea who Xander was. The guy never came to soccer games and had only seen him that one time in the restaurant – the time he thought Haroon and Xander were brothers. In the courtroom, he hadn't even looked at Xander.

"Hello, Mr. Breiton."

Mr. Breiton frown deepened. "Do I know you?"

"I know some fellows who worked at Breiton's Fish House in Lake Grove, before it closed. I wanted to work there, too. Nice place."

Mr. Breiton's round face came as close to a smile as sour could manage, "Well, you be sure to apply when we get up and running again. Won't be long now."

"Geez, that's great. I hear you're expanding into this place?" he waved at the *Taz*.

"Sure am."

"My dad's a real fish eater. Been looking for a place to put his investment money."

"Really? What's your dad do for a living?"

Xander had to look away, he hadn't thought how lying about Dad would make him feel. He took a deep breath. This man held a key to the money. Or at least that's what James Wray believed.

"My dad is ... he's a doctor."

Mr. Breiton brightened. Xander could see he equated the word *doctor* with *rich*.

"Let me give you my business card," he said, fumbling in his jacket pocket. "You can take it to your dad."

Xander took the card and glanced at it. It said something more than "Breiton's Fish House" but he didn't want to seem too interested in the info there.

"Dad'll want to know about the other investors," he said.

"Sure," Breiton said. "Just tell him the *National Courier Investment Group* is very interested."

Xander felt cold run down his back. Lamb's news organization. He'd made a huge mistake talking to that guy, Lamb.

Mr. Breiton said, "You okay, Kid? Looking kind of peak-ed there."

Through his fog of self-loathing, Xander jerked with surprise. Mr. Breiton actually seemed to notice something about another human being.

"I'm ... I'm fine, really. Just haven't had any lunch."

"Well, tell your dad to get me at that number. Be sure to apply for a job when we're ready."

"I'll do that."

"And one hint, Kid." He waved at the Taziyan. "Don't eat there. They don't have anything near as good as Breiton's."

"Yes, sir. I will." Breiton didn't seem to hear the ambiguity of the sentence or the awkward defiance in his tone. Just as well. Didn't want the guy to think much about it.

Xander started to jog away from the Taziyan, while Breiton went toward it, probably intent on checking the space out to harass Nazneen one more time.

Juan Munoz appeared on the porch of the Taziyan. He hadn't seen Xander yet, and Xander hated to do it, but he pocketed Breiton's card and walked up the neighbor's driveway to pretend he was going home. He'd give Juan a huge apology when he got back to the restaurant.

After his safe return, only James Wray took the comment about *National Courier Investment Group* seriously. The information on the card wasn't conclusive. It just mentioned investment opportunities in Oregon, and had a telephone number answered by a machine.

James Wray took the card and promised Xander he'd track down the group behind the investments. If it included Mr. Lamb, James Wray would find that out.

The rest of the fellows on the defense team spent way too much energy blasting Xander for skipping out on Juan's protection. And Juan no longer joked around. He went to the bathroom with Xander.

* *

Over the next several days, after enduring the walk through crowds to get to the courthouse, the Qubadis and the Evans families got used to the heckling – mostly. Also, Xander noticed more and more placards held by friends. These signs said, "Fafner Shouts but Never Proves!" or "Entertainment is Not Real Journalism." "Entertainment is Not Proof."

The Qubadi and Evans families sat in the courtroom together. They were a comfort for each other as Mr. Jory worked on the jury. One morning, Mr. Jory recalled Agent Saurus to the stand and took his testimony concerning information contained in many notebooks full of evidence about the amounts of money Nasdar sent.

"He not only sent money, he also flew to Iraq twice a year," Saurus said.

"What was this money used for," Mr. Jory asked.

"It was sure to buy more than food – they paid bribes to local tribal leaders with it, they purchased iron and a forge. And later," Saurus said, "Gamal Besaranî and Bijar Qubadi purchased five rifles, ammunition, two rocket launchers, and explosives."

Next, Mr. Jory asked, "Why was Gamal Besaranî arrested and taken to Camp Radamanthus near Baghdad?"

"His neighbors turned him in. I guess they were afraid of his actions."

"Objection," Mr. Nelson said,

"Mr. Saurus," the judge said, "please refrain from guessing what others may have thought or feared."

On cross examination, Mr. Nelson walked slowly toward Mr. Saurus. "What was the payment from the United States at that time for turning in your neighbor?" he asked.

"This was a reward," Saurus said.

"How much?"

"These men were rewarded $500 for turning him in."

"And the truck they brought him in, who drove away with the truck?"

"They drove him in and they drove away," Saurus said.

"Even though the truck was registered to Gamal? They got five hundred dollars plus his truck?"

"At the camp, they didn't know whose truck it was."

"And they didn't bother to find out." Mr. Nelson said.

"Objection," Mr. Jory roared.

"Sustained," the judge said. "Strike that statement from the record," he ordered the court stenographer.

"And was this truck later seen by your people?"

"Yes. We saw it in a village in the region of Harmota."

"When were you in that village?"

"The people in that village showed us a cave near Barzani where Gamal had hidden five rifles and two rocket launchers."

"So, you visited a village near Harmota. When was that?"

"In June of that year."

"After Gamal Besaranî was incarcerated at Camp Radamanthus?"

"Yes. A couple of months after."

Mr. Nelson's finally asked, "When were the guns and explosives purchased?"

"We don't know exactly."

"When did you discover there was such a purchase?"

"When the leaders of the village near the cave showed us the material and told us who bought the guns."

Xander swallowed hard. This was bad. Very Bad.

"Ah, the village near the cave," Mr. Nelson said. "Was that the same village where you found the truck that once belonged to Gamal Besaranî?"

Mr. Saurus's eyes widened. He sat in silence for a moment. Mr. Nelson said, "Was this the same village where you found the truck?"

"Yes," Saurus answered slowly. "Yes, it was."

"Do you have proof other than the word of these village men that the guns and rockets were purchased and stashed there by Gamal Besaranî?"

"That's what they told us."

"And you decided to believe them?"

"Yes."

"So," Mr. Nelson said, "The guns could have been purchased after Gamal Besaranî was sold to the prison."

"He was turned in," Mr. Jory said from his seat.

"Mr. Jory," Judge O'Flaherty said, "If you have an objection, you must state it."

At that moment, Xander felt great pride. Mr. Jory was on the defensive for a moment. Xander's early question about purchases made after Gamal's arrest might now begin to pay off.

"Follow the money," James Wray always said. This memory made Xander think, I've never found out who hired the lawyer for the guy who shot at Grandpa after Friends' Meeting.

The lawyer had claimed to work pro-bono, but James Wray had said, "That man wouldn't represent his mother for free." Following that money was like trying to prove whose money bought the rockets in the cave.

Later in the afternoon, Prosecutor Jory asked Mr. Saurus, "What would have happened to any man who lived in Barzani who took you to that cave?"

"They would most likely have been killed by their own people," Mr. Saurus said.

"Objection," Mr. Nelson said.

The judge started to speak, but Mr. Jory had turned away from him, and said loudly, "So, it had to be someone from another village who could safely inform on the Qubadi brothers."

"Objection," Mr. Nelson said. "Asking the witness to guess . . ."

Judge O'Flaherty said, "Mr. Jory, ask your question. Don't lecture, and don't write fiction."

"My apologies, Your Honor."

Xander felt heat rise in his chest. He watched the jury for any sign of disgust with Mr. Jory for putting words in the mouth of the witness, or for calling Haroon's uncles 'The Qubadi Brothers' as if they were gangsters.

He saw no flicker of emotion on any face in that box.

Then, the door opened and someone wheeled a device into the courtroom. It was a tape machine, probably the biggest and noisiest machine Mr. Jory could have found.

He doesn't just use his shoes to distract people, Xander thought.

Mr. Jory called a witness who turned out to be the person who listened to Qubadi telephone calls. In questioning the witness, Mr. Jory established that a judge in Washington, D.C. had signed a warrant for a wire-tapping of the Qubadi home.

Xander watched Mr. Nelson and couldn't tell if this were a surprise to him. It sure was a surprise to Haroon and Mrs. Qubadi. He knew that from the sudden red in both their faces. Xander knew Nasdar Qubadi must mentally be playing over every telephone conversation in the last few months, wondering what family arguments, or love-talk might be on those tapes.

The witness testified that the tape the court was about to hear had been made during the legal wire-tap of the Qubadi home.

The first voice was Mrs. Qubadi's. She spoke in English. "Nasdar, you cannot keep sending this money to Barzani."

"But we have every right to help our family. They cannot prove we used the money to buy explosives, or anything like that."

"What if they find a way? What if they find proof?"

"The only thing they can prove is that Gamal had to use some of the money to bribe the highwaymen between the Harmota region and Baghdad, and he did that so he could use the road to deliver farm goods."

"Nasdar," Nazneen said, "they can find proof of anything – of anything – if they decide they want to find it."

The technician turned off the tape. The courtroom sat in stunned silence. Next to Xander, Haroon's face was wet with sweat. On the other side of Grandpa, Nazneen covered her face with her right hand, but Grandpa pulled her sleeve so her hand came down.

After a moment, Mr. Jory asked the witness to verify that this was exactly the conversation he had overheard. The man said it was.

Mr. Nelson rose. "I would like to hear both interpretations of what you think you heard."

"Both?" the witness asked.

"Yes," Mr. Nelson said, and then he waited patiently.

"Well, it's obvious that Mr. Qubadi knows his brother-in-law had to bribe some people in order to use the highway."

"And . . .?" Mr. Nelson encouraged.

"And that there is other stuff that the government could prove – that 'anything' that Mrs. Qubadi talks about."

"And what is the other interpretation of that line? I believe she said, 'They can find proof of anything – if they decide they want it.' What else does that mean?"

"Objection," Mr. Jory said.

"Sustained," the judge said, "asking the witness to speculate on the meaning."

Your honor," Mr. Nelson said, "I'm trying to find out if the witness thought of the possibility that Mrs. Qubadi believes evidence can be manufactured by anyone who wants it to be there."

The judge glared at Nasdar's defense lawyer. "Mr. Nelson, the objection has been sustained. If you want to establish what Mrs. Qubadi thought, you must wait until you present the case for the defense."

"Yes, sir," Mr. Nelson said. But now Xander understood that the jury had the chance to think of many interpretations for what Mrs. Qubadi said.

Judge O'Flaherty turned to the court reporter and told him to strike that line of questioning. Xander watched the jurors' faces. He couldn't tell if they were angry at Mr. Nelson because he fished for two explanations, or if they were working their minds around how many interpretations there might be for a statement like Mrs.

Qubadi's. They sure were a straight-faced bunch. He saw no wheels turning in there.

Next, Mr. Jory held up a piece of paper. "Your Honor, we wish now to introduce the confession of Gamal Besaranî, Mr. Qubadi's brother-in-law. The confession was sent to us by U.S. military officers in Camp Radamanthus."

Xander waited for Mr. Nelson to object. He'd read that confessions that incriminate anybody other than the confessor shouldn't be allowed as evidence. Mr. Nelson leaned back in his chair and said nothing. Xander glanced at Haroon whose gaze could have drilled holes in Mr. Nelson's back. Why did Nelson not object?

Even the judge seemed to wonder, leaning forward and waiting. Still, Jan Nelson did nothing more than write on his note pad as if he hadn't heard about the confession.

"Mr. Nelson, Mr. Jory just offered the confession of Gamal Besaranî. Why are you not objecting to this?" Judge O'Flaherty said.

Mr. Nelson appeared to awaken from a thought. "Oh, your Honor," he said, "I have no reason to object at this time."

"Mr. Nelson, I want you to confer with your client in the presence of this court."

Xander relaxed. Now Nelson would realize his error.

Mr. Nelson turned to Nasdar Qubadi. Both of them spoke in low tones. As they whispered, Jan Nelson once tapped his yellow writing pad with his pencil. Mr. Qubadi studied what it said there, then nodded at Mr. Nelson who gestured at the judge.

Nasdar Qubadi glanced up and said to the judge. "We have no objection, sir."

The judge leaned his chin on his hand, studied Mr. Nelson and Mr. Qubadi a moment, and then leaned back. "You may proceed, Mr. Jory."

Xander's head felt heavy and painful. He let it lower to his knees. The confession and the wiretap were the heart of the prosecution's claim that Nasdar Qubadi knew his money would be used by terrorists.

Mr. Jory wasted no time. "Your Honor, for the record, we will show that this confession was signed at Camp Radamanthus, brought to us in a military dispatch. And we have a witness to the questioning of the defendant's brother-in-law, and to the later death from disease of the prisoner. We have brought this witness out to Oregon from his family farm in North Carolina."

The confession was taken in as an exhibit. Xander's chest felt tight. Next to him, Haroon slumped in his chair.

Mr. Jory called the next witness for the government. It was the man in the stiff brown suit who had been sitting in the same place during the previous days of the trial.

After swearing him in, Mr. Jory said to him. "Please identify yourself and your job with the United States Army."

"My name is George Jakes. I retired from the Army as a Lieutenant Colonel. I worked in the Army in my capacity as a doctor and a psychiatrist."

"And what do you do now that you've retired?" Jory asked.

"I now work as a civilian with a non-governmental aide organization; I work at the hospital in al Kadhimiya, Iraq. I am on leave from that job, and in the States, visiting my parents."

"Lieutenant-Colonel Jakes, will you tell the court where you were assigned while in the Army, just before you retired?"

"Before I retired from the Army, I was assigned to the military base near al Kadhimiya, which the United States Army calls *Camp Radamanthus*."

"And your responsibilities while at Camp Radamanthus?"

"Because I speak Arabic and several languages of the area, I interviewed the Iraqi prisoners as they arrived at the prison. I kept track of them, watching for signs of suicide attempts or illness. I attended to both the soldiers and the prisoners who were in the hospital."

"And did you sign the death certificates when prisoners died?"

"Yes, I did."

Xander saw Mrs. Qubadi's hands tremble. On the other side of Grandpa, Haroon leaned into the tweed of Grandpa's suit. Xander stuffed his own fists into his jacket pockets. They all knew what was coming, but Xander's ears rang with the sound of remembered gunfire, of a chicken squawking, a woman wailing ... he barely heard Mr. Jory's questions.

"Yes," the Lieutenant-Colonel answered, "that is the type of death certificate we used at Camp Radamanthus."

"Would you read the name on the death certificate?" Mr. Jory asked.

"It is for Gamal Besaranî," the man glanced at Mrs. Qubadi.

"Do you remember signing this certificate?"

"Yes. Yes, I do." He stared now at Mrs. Qubadi. "I remember Gamal Besaranî."

"And what is the cause of death?"

Lieutenant-Colonel Jakes sat for a long moment staring at the certificate before he answered, "This is difficult to read."

Mr. Jory pointed at the paper. His voice lowered with hard-won patience. "Doesn't it say *diphtheria*, Doctor?"

"No. It might. But it could also be *diarrhea*. Perhaps, I could give a more accurate answer if I refer to my diary of that time." He pulled a small notebook from his suit jacket pocket.

The judge interrupted. "Has this diary been put into the evidence list?"

The doctor looked startled, as if referring to the diary were not significant.

Mr. Jory shrugged. "I didn't know about the diary." He turned to the doctor and said, "The certificate says he died of *diphtheria*."

"That might be what it says," Mr. Jakes said. "I can be more certain if I just look it up here." He began to thumb through the notebook."

The judge interrupted, saying, "We're not introducing new evidence willy-nilly. Please take the jury to the jury room while we discuss this."

As the jurors filed out, Xander glanced at Grandpa for an explanation. Grandpa spoke to Haroon as well. "The judge sends the jury out so he can have a discussion of this new evidence without influencing their decision about Nasdar's innocence or guilt."

"But all these other people stay here?" Haroon asked, gesturing at the crowded courtroom.

"We are not jury, not able to decide the case, so we stay."

At that moment, the judged asked the witness for the diary. "Mr. Jakes, why this diary?"

"Well, sir, early on in my time at Camp Radamanthus, the papers my commanding officer asked me to sign were exactly what I saw, my diagnosis, my observations of patient health and so forth. I began keeping a diary of all these things because I became concerned with the turnover in the ranks, the people entering data and filing death certificates and so forth. If anything went missing, or was mis-entered, I thought the diary would help correct mistakes or relocate missing information."

Mr. Jory said, "So, this diary will help you decipher what it says on the death certificate?"

"It will tell exactly what my diagnosis was at the time. The diary is my memory of the men and the events."

The judge turned to Mr. Jory and Mr. Nelson. "Would either of you gentlemen care to look over this diary?"

Mr. Jory nodded, and Mr. Nelson said, "I would, your Honor."

The judge handed the book to Mr. Jory. He turned to one date, and then forward to another, read what was there, and then, looking satisfied with what he found, he handed the diary to Mr. Nelson. As Mr. Nelson read, he flipped through more pages. It seemed like he hunted up almost four dates before handing the book back to the judge. Mr. Nelson's face showed worry; Mr. Jory's, impatience.

"Well, gentlemen?" The judge waited.

Mr. Jory smiled and said, "It seems to be what Mr. Jakes claims, a diary of events as he witnessed them. I've no objection to him using it."

Xander felt Haroon tense next to him. He knew both of them were hoping Mr. Nelson would finally object. This Mr. Jakes and his the diary would tell the court that Gamal had signed the confession while in his right mind, and then a month later died of some stomach disease, diphtheria or diarrhea, or whatever his book said.

"I have no objection to it being entered as evidence," Mr. Nelson.

The judge frowned at Mr. Nelson, who seemed to be studying the man in the witness chair. After a moment, Judge O'Flaherty held the diary out to his clerk, who tagged it the same way all the trial papers, receipts-for-purchase, and even Mr. Rochford's notes had been tagged as evidence.

Then, the judge announced a fifteen-minute break in the proceedings.

CHAPTER FORTY

During the break, Xander walked with Haroon up and down the hall. They both knew that whatever lay in the lieutenant-colonel's notebook could spell the end of hope for Haroon's father. Gamal's confession and death lay at the heart of Mr. Jory's case against Mr. Qubadi.

"I'm afraid," Haroon said. "He will read about my uncle's death and it will cut my mother to the heart – her little brother dead because of money we sent to Barzani."

They glanced toward the wooden benches of the court hallway. Grandpa sat with Mrs. Qubadi, listening. Near them, Mr. Wray talked quietly on his cell phone, dictating a story for tomorrow's *Journal of the Americas*. Mr. Halverson had his drawing pencil out as usual, but he seemed merely to be staring at his blank page.

Xander and Haroon stopped by the window and stared at the placards and shuffling of the crowd below. The protesters wandered aimlessly, as if they were a pack with no leader. And then a car pulled up to the nearby stop sign. Many rushed toward the car as if hoping for a celebrity sighting.

After a moment, Xander said, "It seemed like the whole city was yelling at us when we came."

"They wanted us to feel that way." Haroon said.

*   *

Xander noticed that Mr. Lamb kept his distance, but he didn't seem to be calling in a story to the *National Courier*.

So much evidence already . . . why isn't Lamb filing an update?

Thinking of the evidence presented that morning, Xander realized how many seemingly minor details add up to an ugly picture: a wire-tapped telephone call that everyone heard as revealing Nasdar knew Gamal bought guns and explosives; the Qubadi family attended a mosque where an angry religious leader seemed to advocate using violent means to help his people; a father used his mosque to wire money to his family and town; a brother of the family was turned into the U.S. troops as a terrorist; another brother ran a school and a mosque in a country where some schools teach hatred; target practice – two cultures that love hunting, but that don't trust the hunter who looks different; and worst of all, the captured brother confessed that the Qubadi family planned attacks on U.S. troops.

Xander grew terrified for his friend. Nothing about this situation seemed solvable. He couldn't see a way to the truth in this trial, not as long as even a modern and supposedly superstition-free nation like the United States still clung to the medieval belief that torture wrings the truth out of people.

Xander knew Gamal Besaranî from his deeds, a good man working hard to keep his village fed. For him, the image of Gamal being tortured until he confessed loomed at the back of his mind every moment – an image difficult for Xander to accept, how much more excruciating for Haroon and for Mrs. Qubadi, Gamal's sister.

The boys walked in silence. After they passed the elevators and the stairs a second time, Xander asked Haroon about the imam at the family's mosque.

"Well," Haroon said, "there is this one imam, younger than the others – he's real angry over attacks against Muslims."

"Why him, more than anyone else?"

"My dad says on September eleventh, 2001, that imam, his mother and sister were leaving their mosque in Arlington Heights, this suburb of Chicago. A crowd of local high school kids yelled at them, threw stuff at them. And then the crowd threw stones at the mosque windows. It got real ugly. The police had to come protect the building and the members of the mosque."

Xander nodded at Haroon, but at that moment, there was nothing he could say. He understood that anger – the anger you carried with you against the people who attacked your family.

Haroon must have been thinking the same thoughts, because he suddenly walked back and sat next to his mother, putting an arm around her. Xander had to stride down the hall to keep his thoughts of the death of his own mom and dad from pushing into his head and taking over. He had made two tours of the hall when he found Mr. Johnson walking next to him.

Xander confronted him. "Mr. Johnson, who told Grandpa about Uncle Gamal?"

"Until the trial is over, I can't say."

"Gamal's death is going to hurt Mr. Qubadi's chances. And his confession."

"Mr. Nelson says all depends on if we get to bring in certain facts, and how the jury interprets those facts."

"You mean, will the jury think Gamal deserved to die?"

Mr. Johnson blinked at that. He stared up at the ceiling for a second, still blinking. Xander thought the big man might be trying not to cry. That image made Xander very afraid.

At last Mr. Johnson said, "Some might think he deserved it."

"Yeah," Xander said. "He was in an American prison." Xander's throat hardened around his spew of words. "They'll think, 'Our guys caught him, so he must have done something. If he did something, maybe he deserved whatever he got.'"

Mr. Johnson laid his hand on Xander's arm. "Your grandpa tells me you know most of our story from back when we were kids – back in 1953."

Xander glanced at Mr. Johnson, surprised he would bring it up. That whole time from back then had to be a sore topic for this man.

"Yes, I know what happened."

Mr. Johnson nodded. "But your grandpa says he didn't tell you what happened to the killers."

"No," Xander said, thinking he hadn't even asked that question. "No, he didn't."

Mr. Johnson turned to face Xander. "He figures that part is my story to tell. And, in case Mr. Qubadi goes to jail after all this, I think you and Haroon need to know what happened back then."

"Go to jail?" Xander's voice came out with blasting anger.

Mr. Johnson looked Xander in the eye and said, "You know that Mr. Nelson told us to expect to have to appeal the verdict we get in this court."

Xander nodded, but fear slithered into his gut.

Mr. Johnson said, "My dad went to jail for murder. He was guilty. He killed on that day. Your grandpa saw some of what Dad did – what he did to me. Gilbert had to testify against him, but Gib was my friend, and he got real sick about testifying. He didn't want to do that to me, but it had to be done."

They walked down the hall together while Mr. Johnson continued. "Kenny and I, we visited Dad in jail for the first few months. We had to talk across a wire enclosure. Never got close. Dad, he talked to me way different from what he said to Kenny. To Kenny, he was all innocent and put-upon.

"Me . . . Dad just called me a traitor and a no-good. I guess he figured he'd already lost me when he beat my mother. She was a good mother, petrified most of the time, but she stood between him and us at the end. I knew he would have done worse to Kenny and me, given time."

"Did your dad mean to do it?" Xander asked, then wished he hadn't.

Mr. Johnson said, "You take an uncontrollable temper and heavy stick to someone, it doesn't matter if you meant to. You carried a deadly weapon and you used it. Same as a gun."

They now faced the family huddled on the bench in the hall. Xander thought about how frightened he would have been to have a father who lashed out at you, to have a father so controlled by his hatred that he murdered someone you loved and urged the killing of others.

He saw Haroon glance up at them. Xander motioned to his friend who pushed himself up and joined them.

"That reporter," Haroon said to Mr. Johnson, "That Mr. Lamb . . . he's going to testify about my Uncle Gamal's death, isn't he?

Mr. Johnson turned to both of them. "Fellows, I think it would be safest to keep your guesses about things to yourselves. Let's allow Mr. Nelson to decide what evidence to use, and when to use it."

"Yes, sir," Xander said.

"Was he there?" Haroon asked. "Did he meet my uncle before he died?"

Mr. Johnson shook his head. "Haroon, I only know that Mr. Nelson wanted your family to know about Gamal before anyone else learned of his death. The rest we will find out when Mr. Nelson tells the court."

At that moment, the courtroom door opened. Mr. Nelson came out and told the family that something had come up, so the court would have to convene again in the morning.

"Nasdar?" Mrs. Qubadi asked, her face blotchy with worry.

Mr. Nelson glanced at all of them. "Nasdar is in a cell by himself. He's healthy. He sends you his love."

Now Mr. Nelson put his hand on Haroon's shoulder. "Your father says you and your mother should keep setting aside the money he normally sends to Grandma Qubadi. She and the town will need it when he is free again."

Xander let out his breath, relieved that Mr. Qubadi spoke with hope about a future.

Mr. Johnson spoke to Mr. Nelson, "I'll bring up the rear as we exit the court."

Mr. Nelson frowned, then nodded. "Yes, thank you, Rick."

Xander knew Mr. Nelson must be as tired as everyone else. They all were forced to trudge through the news cameras again and again, every day of the trial, twice a day. Was Nelson so tired he just let the confession be entered in order to get it all over with?

CHAPTER FORTY-ONE

The next morning, the Gotamere prayer meeting whirled into town and began setting up in the Oregon Convention Center which was about half a mile from Pauling High School and right on the MAX line. The families boarded the MAX a mile east of their usual stop and ground their way past the hullaballoo that pretended to be spiritual enlightenment.

It was clear from the banners and signs surrounding the area that Pastor Lori Gotamere intended to use the Qubadi trial as a theme in her "tent" revival meetings.

Xander and Haroon stared at their books when they passed Gotamere's signs. The train slowed just west of the convention center. Rick and his men stood to fill the aisles and doorway into the car where the families sat. The milling crowd moved on to the next doors and entered the car behind. Each of the crowd members carried rolled up banners.

The young men laughed loudly and talked among themselves as if no one else might object.

"That raghead will hear us from clear inside the jail," one boy said.

"Bet they have to transport him to Fed Security in an armored van just to keep him all safe."

A dark-haired girl smiled up at one of the boys. She waggled her rolled up banner and added, "When they duck his head into the van, he'll for sure see our signs. Then, he'll know what people think of him and his murdering kid."

The crowd in the next car seemed to have no idea how close they were to the cause of their manufactured righteousness.

As they rode across the Steel Bridge and toward the court, Xander heard Mrs. Qubadi whisper to Haroon. "They discovered the body of the Hamdami boy in New York."

"The one they accused of being one of the airplane hi-jackers?" Haroon asked.

Xander remembered the story. Salman Hamdami had been missing since the September eleventh attacks, back in 2001. The media had guessed that he probably was one of the terrorists. Hundreds of people were missing since that day, but he was Muslim.

"Where did they find his body?" Haroon asked his mother.

"He was a paramedic," she answered. "He died working on someone who was hurt in the World Trade Center."

Haroon let out a sigh of sadness.

The crowd of banner carriers alighted from the train at the courthouse stop. The Qubadi, Evans families sat still for two more stops.

As they all descended from the MAX train about four blocks from the courthouse, Mr. Nelson met them. "Mrs. Qubadi," he said, "More protesters have shown up from out of town. The judge has ordered more security and more policemen. You walk with me. Gilbert, you stick very close to us."

Then Mr. Nelson pointed at Xander and Haroon. "And you boys follow right on Gilbert Evans' heels. Mr. Johnson and his men will be right behind you, and some of them in front of us."

Mr. Nelson studied us as we lined up, then he spoke to Mr. Johnson. "Rick, let's do this at top speed all the way."

"Yes, sir."

There were a lot more policemen, but there were also more signs and more yelling people.

"Look," Haroon said pointing toward a sign.

In bright purple print, the sign said, "Justice Doesn't Yell. Justice Weighs Evidence."

Another said, "Torture distorts Truth" and a third said "We're with you, Nasdar Qubadi".

Xander's spirits rose. Some people thought about justice, and cared enough to come down here in this dangerous crowd. But, he wondered, where did the others come from – those out of town folks the Gotamere message had sent?

Mr. Johnson's security men hurried so fast that Xander didn't have a chance to see if any others in the crowds were protesting for them. Still the loudest sounds were boos, and jeers, and the shriek of one irate woman

"Murderers. My son died in Iraq because of you."

Xander saw Haroon glance up. Both of them recognized Rob and his mother, Mrs. Palmquist. If Haroon intended to say something to her, he never got a chance because Mr. Johnson pushed them from behind. They crossed the street – the spectator-empty no-man's land that the judge had ordered around the courthouse block. They ducked inside to the now-familiar metal-detector and bag-inspection routines of the Hatfield United States Courthouse.

* *

First thing that morning, Judge O'Flaherty told the jury he had decided to admit as evidence the diary of Mr. Jakes, Lieutenant-Colonel, Retired. His notes could be referred to during the man's testimony. Haroon glanced at Xander, a look of despair darkened his eyes.

Nearby, a reporter for the *Columbia Weekly* whispered to his seat partner, "This diary and this witness are as close as we are going to get to firsthand testimony about that prisoner, Gamal Besaranî."

Xander was sure everyone in the courtroom heard that whisper, but Haroon's gaze didn't waver from the face of his father. However, he held his mother's arm.

Mr. Jory again called Mr. Jakes, Lieutenant Colonel, Retired, to the stand. After he was reminded of his swearing in, Mr. Jory asked him, "Were you present when the prisoner confessed?"

"I was the attendant doctor during his interrogation. I never heard him confess."

"But you read his confession?"

"I read such a document. It was in August that it came to my attention."

"I show you a confession, dated August 8, 2005. Is this the confession you were shown at Camp Radamanthus?"

The lieutenant colonel studied the paper Mr. Jory handed him. "Yes," he said. "This is the paper I was given to file on August . . . oh, let me see exactly." He leaned his arms on the wooden railing in front of the witness chair and opened his diary. He thumbed back to the middle of it. "Yes, the paper was brought to the office for filing on August 12, 2005."

"And now, "Mr. Jory said, "I ask you to read his confession to the court."

Mr. Jakes glanced up at the judge and said, "It is in English."

"Yes," Mr. Jory said. "Please read it to the court."

"But, I have always wondered where the original went," Mr. Jakes said to the judge. "Mr. Besaranî didn't speak much English. When I took care of him, I had to talk to him in Farsi because it was a language we both knew."

Judge O'Flaherty merely looked at the witness, and blinked slowly. But next to Xander, Haroon leaned forward, staring at Mr. Jory.

Xander remembered the reports given to Gamal's visiting lawyers, always a mix of languages, little English, and often talk that made no sense even to Mrs. Qubadi or to Haroon.

Mr. Jory's curt voice showed impatience. "Of course this is in English. This is a translation, sent by your superiors for use in the courtroom."

"Ah," Mr. Jakes said. "I will read it."

I, Gamal Besaranî, do confess that I have trafficked in guns, ammunition and explosive materials. I have aided Al Qaeda-in-Iraq in their attacks on American bases and at key sites in northeastern Iraq where the elected government of Iraq is attempting to rebuild hospitals and roadways.

My brother-in-law, Bijar Qubadi, knew that I used money sent to our mosque from America for this purpose. The money was mailed to us through a mosque in America, by my sister's husband, Nasdar Qubadi. My sister's husband also visited us in Barzani last year to plan attacks against American bases. In the United States, Nasdar Qubadi trained in sharp shooting because he intended to come back soon to help us carry out planned attacks on Camp Radamanthus, the Green Zone and other targets.

The Lieutenant-Colonel glanced at the bottom of the page and read, "This confession is signed Gamal Besaranî, August 8, 2005."

"Thank you, Lieutenant-Colonel," Mr. Jory said. "Now, I ask that you look in your diary and read the cause of death for Mr. Gamal Besaranî."

The retired Lieutenant-Colonel again leaned his diary on the rail. The court, judge, jury and listeners all watched him turn back through his diary until he seemed to find the correct page.

"Yes, here it is. I will read it.

"Today I was called to attend the victim, Gamal Besaranî. He lay dying of blunt force trauma to the chest, choking on his own blood and unable to breathe. Within minutes, he died. Today is July 14th, 2005, Bastille Day."

"No," Mr. Jory shouted. "That is not the date on the death certificate."

The witness continued to read his diary in a louder voice. "My commanding officer wrote the word diphtheria as the cause. A lie. I can no longer stomach this. I am amazed they let me examine the body. If I talk, or if they discover my diary of the torture, the maiming, the deaths, I will be a dead man."

"Your honor," Mr. Jory shouted.

The Lieutenant-Colonel said again, "July 14ᵗʰ is when he died, and the cause – blunt force trauma . . ."

"The death certificate says 'diphtheria'. It has your signature on it."

"It says *diphtheria* in the scrawl of my superior officer, and the date on the certificate has been changed. I signed that certificate on July 14ᵗʰ. My commander insisted I let the *diphtheria* stand. This is one reason I was using my diary to tell the truth. Death happened – violent death for prisoners. The reasons were changed on the papers. I was ordered to sign lies."

"But the confession was August 8. And the death certificate says August 10, 2005," Mr. Jory said.

Lieutenant-Colonel Jakes didn't wait for a question. Instead, he said, "In writing dates, I use numbers and slashes: 07 slash, 14 slash, 2005. You can see that the person who changed the date used words, August with a very long skinny letter "G" where my original slash existed. See? Long letters to cover the slashes. I never do that. You can look at my work for several tours of duty. I . . ."

"Your honor," Mr. Jory said, "I object . . ."

"Overruled," Judge O'Flaherty said.

Mr. Jory stopped talking, his right hand an incomplete gesture in the air.

Several people in the courtroom stood, and hustled toward the exits. Xander recognized one of them as a television announcer – one of the ones who worked for a station that always slammed Mr. Qubadi.

Next to Xander, Haroon seemed transfixed by Mr. Jory. Prosecutor Jory glared, but not at the witness, Jakes. Instead, he glared at Louis Lamb, who held his stare with unblinking eyes.

"Your honor," Mr. Jory said, still staring at Louis Lamb, "this is a travesty."

"I believe it is time to recess," Judge O'Flaherty said. "Will you and Mr. Nelson please meet me in my chambers?"

* *

After the conference in the Judge's chambers, Mr. Nelson came out to talk to the family.

"Mr. Jory attempted to convince the FBI agents that there was no case. The confession was shown to be a forgery. The death certificate date had been changed."

Grandpa said, "All other claims turn to ash without the confession."

"You'd think so," Mr. Nelson said, "but the FBI and the Justice Department insisted Jory surge forward."

"They hope the jury still will find Dad guilty," Haroon said.

"I think that's what they count on," Mr. Nelson said, "a jury who sees only a Muslim. So we proceed."

That afternoon, during Mr. Nelson's defense, a most important moment came when Mrs. Qubadi interpreted her meaning during the wire-tapped discussion.

"I meant that if the government wanted to convict my husband, my brother and my brother-in-law, they could create evidence and see that it would be discovered."

Prosecutor Jory asked her many convoluted questions, but he was unable to shake her explanation of her statement on the phone. On redirect, Mr. Nelson allowed her to have her say.

"I believed the government could and would create evidence to win their case. You saw this morning, how they lied about my brother's death and faked his confession."

Mr. Jory objected. Judge O'Flaherty sustained.

Mrs. Qubadi sat up and said, "Even in the United States, police can plant evidence. How much easier to do it in the chaos of Iraq."

Mr. Jory objected again. Judge O'Flaherty said, "Sustained."

Mr. Nelson excused Mrs. Qubadi.

Objection sustained or not, Xander knew everyone in the room must now be questioning the government evidence. The lies about Gamal tainted every accusation aimed at Mr. Qubadi.

The trial ground on, with Mr. Nelson presenting the receipts for purchases of food, school supplies, goats, milk storage cans, farm hand tools, irrigation pipe. He presented a time-line on a chart of the money sent, purchases made.

And finally, Mr. Nelson called Mr. Louis Lamb to the stand. As Mr. Lamb rose, he did not look at Xander or Haroon. Xander couldn't understand why Mr. Nelson called the man. As far as Xander knew, Lamb had never talked to Mr. Nelson since his return from Iraq. Lamb might say anything. Why would Nelson want to risk asking him questions when he might give damning answers?

"You visited the town of Barzani during the weeks following Christmas, is that correct?" Mr. Nelson asked.

"Yes, I stayed with an old friend of mine in that town," Mr. Lamb said. "I visited a new goat-milk processing plant, I saw the irrigation system for the community vegetable gardens, I visited the school and found girls studying as well as boys. I read the books my friend's sons and daughters studied in the school – all of the books. There was no propaganda against Americans, no urging of attacks on others. The children studied music, mathematics, physics, dry-land farming practices, English, Kurdish, Arabic and the ancient poetry of all the people of Iraq and Iran. The eldest son studied the Quran, but there was no emphasis on destruction of non-believers, as I have heard from some religious leaders – even some in the United States."

As Mr. Jory came forward to question Mr. Lamb, Xander could see anger in his jutting jaw. Xander wondered why.

Mr. Jory smiled tightly as he began cross examination. "Mr. Lamb," Jory said. "In the United States, you have heard some religious leaders urging destruction of non-believers?"

"Yes, I have," Mr. Lamb said.

"And would you care to name these imams for us?"

"Pastor Lori Gotamere and . . ."

"Mr. Lamb . . ." Mr. Jory said.

"Lawrence Fafner quotes bile that pretends to be religious on my company's television station." Lamb added.

The judge whacked his gavel. "Mr. Jory and Mr. Lamb, this trial is not a deposition."

"Yes, sir, Your Honor," Mr. Jory said.

The silence in the courtroom lasted almost a minute. The judge waited, as if hoping Mr. Jory could take a new tack. Finally, Mr. Jory said, "I have no further questions for this witness."

Soon after that moment with Lamb, Mr. Nelson summed up the defense. Mr. Jory summed up the prosecution's case. Judge O'Flaherty charged the jury, explaining the laws pertaining to the several charges.

The jury retired to their ante-room for deliberation.

*　*

In the hallway, Haroon and Mrs. Qubadi sat with Grandpa, who talked to Mrs. Qubadi about her brother, her memories, her regrets, and her sorrow at how he had died. Xander walked away from them so they could talk alone.

At the end of the hall, Mr. Wray whispered with Mr. Breiton. Breiton's head pushed forward, but his arms hung slack. Wray said one more thing, then Mr. Breiton hissed, "Winning this has nothing to do with a good investment." He strode away from Mr. Wray and past Xander without even seeming to recognize him.

Grandpa walked up next to Xander. "Wonder what James Wray knows about Breiton."

Mr. Wray waited a moment and then sought out Grandpa. "Gilbert, Everett Breiton isn't talking to Lamb. He doesn't even seem to know him by sight."

"So, the *National Courier Investment Group* Mr. Breiton mentioned to Xander is a fiction."

"Or it's somebody other than Lamb. Anybody over there capable of pulling the company out from under Lamb?"

"I don't know," Grandpa said, "Worth investigating."

"Grandpa, is that Fafner guy making a move to take the company over?" Xander asked.

"Well, he may hope to."

"He's a VP there. He's got more power now."

"Maybe. We'll have to see."

Xander said, "I wonder why Lamb hasn't been sending in reports."

Mr. Wray spoke up. "He can't both report and be a witness."

"Yeah," Xander said, "But he also might not report if his company is out of his hands. He's been gone a long while. Maybe he's lost control."

"Possibly," Mr. Wray said.

Grandpa's head came up. He looked straight at Mr. Wray, "When men lose control . . ."

"You're right," Wray said, and strode away.

"Grandpa, what's that about?"

"I think we should wait and see what James Wray comes up with. Right now, I'm doing a lot more praying than I remember doing for months." Grandpa sat on a bench, folded his hands and leaned his forehead against them.

Xander felt too nervous to sit, but he realized he, too, was praying for Mr. Qubadi, and for Haroon.

Mr. Halverson sat at the end of the hall, drawing a series of cartoons. Some, he crumpled and stuffed into his pocket. Xander walked past him as he drew. Around the corner Xander came to a rail of the balcony hall that over-looked the floor below. Down there, Mr. Jory paced back and forth. Louis Lamb stepped down the stairs toward Mr. Jory.

"The bathroom's that way," Jory said, his voice as harsh as frozen concrete.

"I'm looking for you," Mr. Lamb said.

"To introduce me to another turn-coat witness?"

"Turn-coat? Who turned away from the truth?"

"Were you truthful when you said you had an interesting witness for me?"

"I urged you to look at what evidence you had. I hoped you'd decide if any of it would stand without the confession." Mr. Lamb said.

"Why did you tell me about Lieutenant-Colonel Jakes?"

"I hoped you would learn from him about the shaky ground on which you stood."

"No. You wanted me to use him."

"Yes, if you persisted even after what he had to say about the camp, and the commander who ran it."

"The government assured me . . ."

"Who had the most to lose here?" Mr. Lamb asked.

"The safety of the country was at stake."

"You have seen what truly was at stake," Mr. Lamb said.

"Your reputation as an honest journalist."

"Not close," Lamb said. "What is at stake is the reputation of the United States. Are we an honest people?"

Jory walked away.

CHAPTER FORTY-TWO

Five hours later, all were called back into the courtroom. Xander sat down next to Mrs. Qubadi. Haroon sat on her other side. Haroon's right hand gripped the end of her scarf.

Xander felt certain that if Haroon had been Gulbahar's age, he would have been holding his mother's hand. The scarf fringe was as close as a seventeen-year-old, a boy who is supposed to be a man, could come to admitting he is afraid.

Xander closed his eyes. His mother's face formed in his mind, that last anxious glance she took at the Afghan hills, as if she knew. He wished for the feel of her next to him, even her scarf, or her hair. And Dad . . . holding Mom's hand as she jumped the ditch.

As Nasdar Qubadi was brought into the courtroom, he looked at his wife and then at Haroon. Xander saw longing in Mr. Qubadi's eyes. Haroon and Nazneen returned that deep gaze.

Nasdar had grown thin over the weeks in jail. But he still seemed strong, his shoulders straight, his head unbowed. He winked at his son and then sat down next to Mr. Jan Nelson and one of Nelson's partners.

The jury filed in and took their seats. Xander had heard people say the accused would know his fate if the jury refused to look at him, so he watched what they did. It seemed to him that some of them glanced at Nasdar, but then looked away quickly.

The judge asked if they had come to a conclusion on all counts. The jury foreman stood and said, "We have, Your Honor."

"Would you read your findings?"

"Yes, Your Honor."

The foreman opened a folded piece of paper. He stood very still, but Xander saw his Adam's apple go up and down several times before he took a deep breath and began to read. Next to Xander, Mrs. Qubadi's twisting hands went very rigid in her lap.

The man said, "On the charge of conspiracy to possess and discharge firearms in furtherance of crimes of violence, we find the defendant Not Guilty."

The people in the courtroom stirred. The judge smacked his gavel and glared at the gallery. At Mr. Jory's bench, the assistant's shoulders slumped, but Mr. Jory sat tall and quiet.

The foreman read again. "On the charge of money laundering, we find the defendant Not Guilty."

Mrs. Qubadi gripped Xander's hand and Haroon's on her other side. She stared at the Jury Foreman, her eyes penetrating.

"On the further charge of conspiracy to provide material support and resources to Al-Quaida in Iraq, we find the defendant Not Guilty. On the last charge of Conspiracy to levy war against the United States, we find the defendant Not Guilty."

Haroon leaned against his mother. When she touched his face, he seemed to let go of all tension. He cried openly. Nasdar glanced back at his family, tears running down his cheeks.

Cheers rose from the friends sitting all around the room. But along with the cheers, Xander heard one man yell, "Traitors. Weaklings." The man rose and shook his fist at the jury members. The judge gaveled for silence, but others joined the angry man. The bailiff and other court security circled the room.

The judge said, "Bailiff, arrest that man for contempt of court."

Another man yelled "Bought Judge. Bought Jury."

A third man called out, "Sell-out to Evan's money." The security men grabbed all three and hustled them out the door on the far side of the room.

*   *

After order had been restored, the judge thanked the jurors for their service. He ordered a police escort home for the whole family and released Nasdar Qubadi. The jurors were taken out a side door. Grandpa whispered to everyone, "The judge has a plan to keep the jury safe."

"I pray they are safe," Mrs. Qubadi said. "Many people will feel the same as those three men."

"They'll be on the hunt for a new scapegoat." Grandpa whispered.

As the families left the courthouse, television cameramen jockeyed for position. Interviewers pushed toward the family. Someone thrust a microphone in front of Mr. Qubadi. He recovered quickly and stopped to thank those friends and neighbors who had always believed in him. "I honor the system of justice in our free and democratic country. There are times when we are tempted to forget that a jury of citizens decides innocence or guilt. Each time we judge from rumors, or guesses, we attack the greatest strength of our country."

Some on the stairs jeered, but Nasdar ignored them, speaking to the larger audience of the radio, the newspapers and the television.

"When we allow true justice for all, then the light of America shines for the rest of the world. In protecting citizens from arbitrary and capricious accusations, America gives hope to those who live in fear of the knock on the door, the Military-run government, the KGB, the SAVAK or any organization designed to make people afraid.

"I thank my defense team who all worked very hard to find the truth and present it to the jury."

Then, he hugged his wife and son, and stepped away from the microphone.

Next, Mr. Nelson answered questions for thirty seconds and then said, "You, members of the press, now know that a brave, retired Army officer came all the way from Iraq to bring proof that unraveled the case. His evidence showed that Mr. Qubadi had been framed by people more interested in conviction than in justice. We urge all the Armed Services to protect this witness and also to protect Mr. Qubadi's remaining family in Iraq. We urge the Army not to make this brave Lieutenant-Colonel into a victim, someone they use to distract the spotlight from their failure to control rabid outliers in their ranks."

Mr. Nelson walked away from the microphone and gestured to the police escort that the family meant to leave. As the family and friends walked down the stairs, Xander glanced up to the Courthouse door. He saw Louis Lamb standing there. For the first time since the trial started, Mr. Lamb looked Xander in the eye.

CHAPTER FORTY- THREE

At the bottom of the stairs, several cars had lined up next to the curb. Mr. Johnson arranged a quick departure for all in the defense party. He opened the door to the first car and said, "Mr. and Mrs. Qubadi, Haroon, get in quickly."

Xander and Grandpa Gilbert were hustled into the second car with Mr. Nelson. Xander turned around in the seat to see television cameras focused on Louis Lamb and Lieutenant-Colonel Jakes at the top of the stairs. Mr. Jakes seemed to be making a statement. There was no police escort arranged for them, but Rick Johnson and his men were walking up the stairs to act as safety net for Lamb and Jakes. To their left, Xander saw someone he knew very well.

"Grandpa, that guy from the tunnel fight, the one who fought with Haroon on the fork-lift – he's in the crowd, and up near Mr. Lamb."

Grandpa pulled out his cell phone. He punched a number. Xander saw Rick seem to start talking to the Bluetooth on his ear. "Xan, describe the man to Rick," Grandpa said.

Xander took the cellphone. "Man with a head scarf and big blond mustache, near Mr. Lamb. He's from the tunnel fight."

"Got him," Rick said and hung up.

Xander twisted further around. Rick moved between the head-scarf fellow and Mr. Lamb. A policeman moved in beside them and pulled out hand cuffs. In a moment, the man did an about face and slouched away with his hands cuffed behind his back. Xander scanned the crowd for any other threatening people, but he saw that Rick and his men were also scanning the crowd.

At the moment, when Mr. Jakes stepped away from the microphone, the car Xander rode in started up and turned the corner toward the Willamette River bridges and toward home.

Grandpa leaned back. "Rick will make sure Jakes and Lamb come to us safely. We will all meet at the Taziyan, now," Grandpa said. "We need to be together and not spread out our security."

"If I know anything about Mr. and Mrs. Qubadi, they'll need help with the feast they'll prepare," Xander said.

Grandpa chuckled and nodded.

However, Grandpa was alert all afternoon and so was Rick, expecting something – a mob, a torching, something . . ..

Late in the afternoon, Mr. Wray came with one of Rick's men. He took Grandpa and Mr. Lamb to one side saying, "Lawrence Fafner's not in Chicago."

Xander followed them. Grandpa waved him into the huddle.

Mr. Lamb said, "Fafner told the programming staff he was on to something, a good story in Iraq, and he took off."

"Does Bijar Qubadi know?" Xander asked.

"Yes," Mr. Lamb said. "I sent a message yesterday. He's aware of who Fafner is and what might happen."

"And what is that?" Xander asked.

Mr. Lamb put his hand on Xander's shoulder. "Right now, Lawrence Fafner is a missile with no guidance system. He senses that I'm about to fire him."

Just then, Nasdar came in from the kitchen. Everyone not involved in security became involved in the cooking, celebrating and laughing. Xander, however, was aware that Fafner was out there. Grandpa glanced at him and shook his head. Tonight was for celebration. Afterward, they would deal with Fafner.

The kitchen was a beehive and Mrs. Qubadi, the queen bee. Mr. Qubadi worked the pastries while she and her crew created stews and salads. After much chopping of vegetables, they stuffed leaves and created many foods. Braising, grilling, baking and broiling, filled the air with sharp spice odors, the freshness of chopped herbs, and the warmth of oven air and love.

But in the back of Xander's mind was worry that Bijar Qubadi might be running into Fafner. As Grandpa had said, "Men who lose control are the most dangerous." That was, after all, why the murderers came to the Friend's Welcome Hospital and School. They were losing power.

That evening, in the face of worry for Bijar and the village of Barzani, the family and friends celebrated freedom at the Taziyan. Nasdar put together all the tables from the big dining room and set out the best plates and silver for everyone. Then he disappeared into the kitchen, to reappear frequently with a new dish. "Yaprak!" he announced. "Like dolma. This time, we stuffed the tomatoes."

As he made these announcements, he handed each dish to Haroon and returned to the kitchen to help Nazneen bring on another wonder of flavor and spicy aroma. Haroon and Xander took the dishes around the table, serving everyone.

Gulbahar sat on Aunt Justine's lap, but often she jumped down, running to the kitchen to be swung in the air by her father. Back to Justine's lap she came, to play drawing games on the paper tablet that Justine kept in a bag of toys for Gulbahar.

The Qubadis had invited everyone involved in their freedom – all of the security men who had worked with Mr. Johnson, Mr. Nelson and the defense team, Mike Halverson, James Wray and the newspaper team, Grandpa Gilbert, Mr. Lamb and Doctor George Jakes.

* *

To see the next smile on Nasdar's face everyone ate well past full. When the main meal finished, and all had eaten more than they ever thought possible, Nasdar and Nazneen left the kitchen to join them for dessert of baklava and sorbet. The friends settled into juice or coffee while Gilbert, Louis Lamb and George Jakes told their story of what followed Haroon and Xander's visit to Lamb's office.

The three men stood with their backs to the kitchen door calling up their memories. Doctor Jakes first talked to Nazneen and Nasdar about Gamal's courage during torture, and about how the Foundation lawyers and researchers worked to expose the truth of Gamal's death and his faked confession. Mrs. Qubadi seemed stunned by all Dr. Jakes told her, even though he was careful in his language not to frighten Gulbahar.

"Your brother was a brave and honest man. All in the Harmota-Barzani region, and many others in Camp Radamanthus recognized his courage and his deep commitment to his village," Jakes said.

Xander noticed that Mr. Johnson got up and paced the room. Xander smiled at that, because he knew Mr. Johnson wasn't going to lay down his protection instincts very easily.

Mr. Lamb and Dr. Jakes explained how they found each other. Mr. Lamb said, "I saw Doctor Jake's name on the death certificate for Gamal Besaranî, and I thought Jakes might know more about what happened to Gamal in prison. But I couldn't get him to be open with me."

"I didn't trust you, at that time," Dr. Jakes said. "I knew you owned the stations that hired commentators like Louis Fafner."

"I let that man have his head for far too long," Lamb said. "I didn't take the time to learn how toxic he was on air."

"Subsequently," Dr. Jakes said, "Gilbert Evans arrived in my hospital. He told the hospital staff that he thought he needed to have his heart checked. Gilbert used that cover to find me. I knew Evans of Evans International and the *Journal of the Americas*, so I confided in him about everything."

Gilbert said, "As soon as George Jakes showed me the diary, I knew we had to bring Louis Lamb in on the situation."

"After all," Jakes said, "you boys convinced Louis Lamb to follow the truth and he sacrificed a lot to see where it led him. Your Grandpa told me of your visit to Mr. Lamb. Gilbert thought we'd get the truth out better if all three of us worked together."

Grandpa said, "Louis and I met at Camp Radamanthus. We decided to keep any hint of the diary out of the news until Lamb succeeded in getting the FBI and Jory's prosecution team to back off. But they would only back off if they believed the truth about the abuses at Camp Radamanthus."

Jakes nodded, and said, "We agreed not to mention my diary until Jory decided to use Lieutenant-Colonel Jakes' first-hand testimony to back up the story of the confession."

Grandpa continued his story, "Mr. Lamb came home first as we planned. He convinced Agent Saurus and Prosecutor Jory to call on Dr. Jakes and fly him to Portland. From then on, only Lamb could have contact with Dr. Jakes.'

"But now that Nasdar has been freed," Lamb said, "both newspapers can be relentless in following stories of torture. We know the commanding officer of the time has been held incommunicado ever since he arrived back at the states, and we want the right to find out why."

"Follow his connection to the money," James Wray said. "And don't forget the money for unbuilt and badly built barracks, electrical power, phone lines, hospitals, lost armaments and the money they generate. Follow every dime. This may lead to that camp commander, and to many others who need to be brought to justice."

Lamb said. "On it. Every dime."

Mr. Lamb turned to Haroon and Xander. "You boys set me on a path," he said. "You opened my eyes to what happens when I desperately want security instead of truth. It took courage for you to ask for my help." He glanced at Grandpa Gilbert, Mike Halverson, and James Wray. "And it took courage to go against these old codgers when you came to my building."

Grandpa laughed, "Never again, Lamb."

Lamb smiled, "We'll see. I think these boys would make good investigative reporters. They may have a future at *The National Courier.*"

Then he grew quiet and sobered. He studied Haroon and Xander. "You trusted me with the people you love. I can't tell you what that meant to me." His eyelids reddened. He paused.

Nasdar Qubadi put his arms around his son's shoulders and kissed his forehead. "No words," he said, his voice choked. "No words good enough for my son, my wife, and my friends. So very happy."

There seemed to be nothing more to say. The team had won Nasdar's freedom. Grandpa's use of the Max Million Foundation for his friend's defense had been justified. The government had lost its attempt to railroad Nasdar Qubadi.

But Xander sensed something wrong. Johnson still paced.

Gulbahar turned in her booster chair. "Bad smell?"

Dr. Jakes turned his head toward the kitchen door. At that moment, Mr. Johnson dove at Jakes and Lamb, taking them both to the floor. The kitchen door exploded. A ball of fire whooshed into the dining room. Aunt Justine hauled Gulbahar into her arms and ran. In moments, Xander could no longer see, but he heard Nasdar yelling at Nazneen and Haroon to run to the front. Xander grabbed Grandpa's arm and spun him in the right direction.

"Lamb and Jakes!" Xander hollered. "Mr. Johnson!"

Mr. Halverson's voice came through the smoke and flame. "We've got them."

"Get out," Mr. Wray called. "All of you. Just go."

They ran through the growing smoke. Xander saw Haroon take a last look at the murals on the wall. Xander also glanced at them. Heat blistered the paint near the kitchen. Then they all dove outside where Rick Johnson's men opened a way through an unexpected crowd of spectators who seemed to just be arriving.

Xander thought, someone told this mob to come.

The signs Xander had seen on the way to the courthouse were here. Rick and his men became the only thing between the family and a mob of thirty yelling people.

The crowd circled like a pack of dogs, then surged forward. Rick and ten security men locked arms. Xander moved into the line next to Rick. Behind him he heard Haroon's tense voice. "Gulbahar, up you go. Come with me to find Mama."

The heat on their backs grew intense. Xander hoped everyone escaped the building, but he couldn't see them all for the crowd.

At that moment, Tekla Jones and her mother ran around the corner from the Twelfth Avenue Bridge. Tekla's mother tried to grab her daughter's arm, but Tekla moved fast and put herself in front of the biggest man with the ugliest sign. The sign said, "Fanatics go home."

"Hi," she said. "I'm Tekla Jones. Did you set that explosion?"

"Get out of the way, little girl," the man said.

Xander moved up near Tekla. On her other side, Tekla's mother stopped, fear widening her eyes, her hand hovering close to Tekla's shoulder.

Tekla spoke again to the man. "I got a message to come here, too. But I didn't know there would be a fire. Did you know about the fire?"

The big man glanced down at her and then across the parking lot to the burning restaurant. "Nobody said anything about a fire." His sign drooped.

Xander said loudly, "Started with that huge explosion."

"Who are you?" The man asked, straightening his sign.

"I'm Xander Lloyd." His name seemed to make no difference to the man. Xander added, "Maybe they set other bombs near here."

The big man set the staff of his sign on the sidewalk. "Nobody said anything about this explosion and fire." He turned toward the people behind him. "Did you hear there would be an explosion?"

"Naw," a man said. "Serves 'em right."

The big man said, "Nobody can pin a bomb on us."

The man said, "They said come here to picket. That's it."

Tekla's mom said, "Let's go before something else blows."

Xander said, "The police will think we set it, because we were here when it went off."

"No." The big man shook his head as if clearing his thoughts. "Everybody to the sidewalks."

The crowd started to move out of the parking lot, slowly, at first. Then when the sound of the sirens grew, they moved faster. The big man moved to the back of the mob. Xander watched him lower his sign, and then silently drop it into the bushes surrounding the parking lot. He started to slink away like a guilty dog.

But at that moment, fire engines and police cars wailed across the Twelfth Avenue Bridge. Police arrived and surrounded the crowd, including cutting the big man off as he tried to jump the boxwood hedge.

Xander recognized the Chief of Police as she directed her team to arrest all. "We'll sort out culpability at the station," she said.

She recognized Rick Johnson and his men. "These men are security for the Qubadis," she told the police sergeant. "Let them get their people out of here."

So, Johnson hustled Tekla and her mom into a car with Grandpa, Justine and Xander. Then Xander glanced up and saw someone run toward the back of the restaurant.

"Xan, who'd you see?" Johnson asked.

"The forklift guy again, behind the restaurant into the trees."

"The guy we got this morning?"

"Yes, but this time in a leather jacket. No head scarf. He's bald, but he still has that mustache."

"We're on him." Johnson stalked away, pointing and yelling toward the police chief. She directed three of her men to give chase. They took off around the restaurant, and then Johnson motioned his driver to get them all out of the crowd, as he plopped into the front car.

*   *

Glancing at Johnson as he moved away, Xander grabbed Grandpa's sleeve. "Rick Johnson's shirt's completely gone in the back and he's burned bad."

Before Grandpa could do anything about it, the driver of their car sped off. Their caravan included Mike Halverson and James Wray with the Qubadi family in one car, Mr. Jakes and Mr. Lamb were in another security car. Johnson's car led them all out of the parking lot, onto Twelfth Avenue and north toward the Lloyd Center Mall. Near the mall, Johnson's driver parked. His men piled out and surrounded all the vehicles in their charge.

Johnson strode back to the car that held Xander. Xander rolled down the window watching how Johnson winced as he leaned over.

"Police chief already had seen him," he said to Xander. "Some of her guys and ours are chasing him down."

"Mr. Johnson, you should be in the hospital," Xander said.

Johnson slapped the car, as if business was done here. "I'll be right back. You're covered." He waved at his men and strode back to his car.

Grandpa hauled out his cell phone and called the driver of Johnson's car. "Take all of us to the hospital. Your boss is burned and won't quit until you force him to."

After Grandpa hung up, he turned to Tekla. "How'd you know to come?"

"I figured it wasn't all over," she said. "I remembered what Xander told me about mobs getting together by texting. I thought somebody would send a crowd to the restaurant because everybody knows it's theirs."

"You scared your mom." Xander said. He didn't want to mention how scared he'd been.

"Scared me, too," Tekla said. "But I run faster than I think, so I was already here before I could really be afraid."

* *

Back at the restaurant, three policemen, Juan Munoz and Gary Patton cornered the forklift fighter in the trees below the Taziyan and above the freeway, the area where Tekla and Xander once hid. The police arrested the man for the second time that day. While Juan kept track of police at the Taziyan restaurant, Gary went to the police station to find out why the guy was let go the first time.

* *

Later, in the hospital waiting room, Grandpa and Xander sat next to each other among the families. All of them had been checked for smoke inhalation and burns. Rick, Mr. Lamb and Mr. Jakes were the most affected, especially Rick's back. Grandpa seemed like a tightly wound ball of rubber bands. He kept whispering, "Not again. Not again."

A couple of hours into their wait, Gary Patton reported to Gilbert.

"Sir," Gary said, as he fell into the chair next to Grandpa, "It turns out that Officer Bailey put himself on desk duty just before that fellow was brought to the station this morning after the trial. No surprise that Bailey "lost" him in the crowded station house."

Grandpa slumped, "When will this stop?"

"Well, the chief finally fired Bailey."

"That took backbone," Xander said.

Gary shrugged. "Not as much backbone as you might think. Only five of his union comrades are protesting the firing. The rest have had enough of Bailey's antics."

"So he's free, on the streets to harass the Qubadi family." Grandpa said.

Gary shook his head. "Nope. As soon as he was fired, Bailey was arrested for impeding an investigation."

"Thank, God."

"Qubadis are safe and guarded. How's our boss?" Gary asked.

Grandpa sighed. "We won't know about any of them for a while. Have a seat."

As night turned to dawn, the doctors told them. "Doctor Jakes rests. We treated him for burns on his back and one arm. Louis Lamb's broken leg is set, and we're continuing to check him for possible internal injuries. Your Rick Johnson landed on him."

"And Rick?" Grandpa asked.

"Broken arm. Burned patches on his head and an extensive burn on his back."

Xander said, "He got between Lamb and the explosion."

The doctor nodded. "Saved Lamb's life. Certainly saved his face. We've started work on Mr. Johnson's back, but the break in the arm is compound and difficult, especially since that arm was so damaged when he was a teenager."

Xander glanced at Grandpa. No wonder he worried about Rick, Xander realized. His grandpa and Rick had been through this before.

Right before they wheeled Rick Johnson into the operating room, he grabbed at Grandpa Gilbert's torn shirt front. "There's a connection here," he said in his smoke roughened voice. "Remember Campbell?"

"The guy who shot at me near the Friends' Meeting House?"

Rick nodded. "This morning, when Juan and Gary brought the forklift fighter into the station, Campbell's lawyer arrived to represent him."

Grandpa said. "We've been trying to find who pays Campbell's lawyer. The same person probably pays Campbell, Bailey, and Streitheimer. These guys are not just dedicated kooks."

"Somebody pays that lawyer, buys those guns. Somebody sends protesters from out of town to the courthouse and to the restaurant. There could be others still out there, and still willing to get at you. There's money in this."

"You get well, Rick. Your men have got our backs, and you trained them all."

"There's always someone . . . someone like my dad."

"Rick," Grandpa said, "*You* are important to me. Stop thinking about your dad. Stop trying to make up for him. You are my trusted friend."

Mr. Johnson blinked. He waved the orderly to haul him into the operating room.

Rick Johnson is right, Xander thought. There is always someone.

* *

Juan Munoz came to the hospital to report.

"Mr. Evans, the firemen have found something at the Taziyan." Juan glanced at Xander.

Grandpa said, "It's okay, Juan. Xander is okay."

Xander felt his chest tighten. Grandpa trusted that he would be all right. He knew that trust was well-placed. He hadn't forgotten anything about Mom and Dad, Mohammed or the boys, but he could face life again.

"Okay," Juan said, "They found a burned body. Forensics determined the man was Charles Streitheimer – that guy 'Chuck' who smashed George McCardell out at the mosque. He was also one of the men arrested for the invasion of the restaurant."

"He wasn't doing this on his own," Louis Lamb said.

"No. Detectives swarmed Streitheimer's one-room apartment. They found cash – a lot of cash in an envelope hidden behind a desk drawer. In the envelope was a note. They're coming here to show the note to us all, see if we recognize anything about it."

An hour later, the Chief of Police arrived at the hospital. She showed the note to each of the fire survivors.

The type font was bolded and blocky.

"MAKE IT COUNT THIS TIME!"

"My God," Lamb said, "Arial Black. That's the font Lawrence Fafner uses – thinks it makes him look strong."

*   *

Within the hour, the police received a warrant and moved in on Fafner's Portland and Chicago computers. It turned out that Lawrence Fafner had not left the country after all. He had sent someone else to harass Bijar in Barzani. Grandpa and Louis Lamb contacted their reporters and warned Bijar.

Police had the famous Lawrence Fafner in a Chicago jail by six in the morning on a charge of "Conspiring with at least four men to murder Alexander Evans Lloyd, Haroon Qubadi, Louis Lamb, Dr. George Jakes, Gilbert Evans, and Nasdar and Nazneen Qubadi, and many others."

"Look," Haroon pointed to the report from James Wray. "They found evidence that he hired all those guys that tried to get us. Charles Streitheimer, Sandy Pollard, Martin Campbell and Beryl Plinder."

"Lawrence Fafner," Lamb said. "A man with an audience and a wish for power."

Xander shook his head, "Grandpa always says that people become even more desperate when their power is threatened."

Lamb nodded. "When I woke up to his tactics, I took away his radio voice, and his power over his audience. When I put him in a back office, I made him more dangerous."

Xander said, "That probably made him more frantic, but he hired Beryl Plinder long before you took him off the airwaves."

Gary said, "I bet Fafner offered money and a restaurant to Mr. Breiton, so he'd harass Nazneen Qubadi."

"He did just that," Haroon said, pointing to the report. "Mr. Wray says here that Mr. Breiton admitted that to the police this morning."

Soon after news of the arrest of Lawrence Fafner, Louis Lamb called his news crew to dictate stories and an editorial.

CHAPTER FORTY-FOUR

The morning after the explosion came with little rest amidst the freezing cold weather. The families hunkered in Grandpa's living room while Rick's men watched the perimeter. Gulbahar finally rested her tear-stained face. She fell asleep in her brother's arms where he sat on the sofa. Nasdar and Nazneen sat on the carpet near the warm fireplace holding each other, and shivering under the blanket that Aunt Justine had placed over their shoulders.

"Tea for everyone," Aunt Justine said, and she hurried out to the kitchen.

Grandpa and Xander stepped out onto the porch to bring in the *Journal of the Americas* morning news. Gilbert showed Xander that James Wray had produced an article about the trial, the search for evidence, and the exoneration of Nasdar Qubadi.

At the top of the editorial page, they found Mike Halverson's cartoon. It showed two opposing groups holding protest signs and glaring at each other across a great ditch. One group's signs said, "We, the people of the jury, having heard the evidence, find Nasdar Qubadi innocent of all charges." On the other side of his cartoon divide, the signs read, "We, the people of rumor and dread, having heard none of the evidence, believe what we want to believe."

"I wish that were funny," Grandpa said. Xander could only nod in tired agreement.

Security officer, Gary Patton, who'd been on the porch swing all night, said, "Along about four in the morning, I stopped a prowler. Turned out he was trying to hand deliver a copy of this morning's *National Courier*. He was sent by Mr. Lamb."

Grandpa Gilbert took the paper Gary held out and opened it to the editorial page.

"Listen to this, Xan," Grandpa said. "'When boys trust you with their hopes and fears, it is time to listen.'"

They took the paper inside to read with Haroon.

* *

After Xander, Nazneen and Aunt Justine had fed a warm breakfast to the two families and the security team, Xander sat down near Haroon. Mr. Qubadi held his sleeping wife in his arms. Xander reached out and touched Gulbahar's little shoe. She didn't even twitch in her sleep. Her face relaxed against Haroon's chest. Haroon stared at the fire in the hearth.

When all was silent except the crackling fire, Grandpa looked at Xander. He reached into his suit pocket and pulled out three letters. "In Pakistan, Afghanistan, and in Iraq, I took out advertisements hoping to find the boys and your teachers. These letters are the answers. They arrived yesterday, but I didn't know they were in the mail box until Juan and Gary checked our mailbox for bombs."

Xander took the letters and stared at them. *Manzur, Edward, Mr. Bhatti.*

Slowly, he opened and read them.

Manzur wrote. *"We have all survived and are hopeful that you are well. We learned about Mohammed's death and Mr. Din. We feared that you also were in that yard, and not alive. When we saw this advertisement, we could not, at first, believe it. But, Mr. Bhatti and I have heard from your grandfather that it is true. You live, and we are thankful beyond telling."*

In the letters, Xander learned that Edmund now lived with his aunt and uncle on a farm in England. It became clear Edmund needed Xander to write to him. The death of his parents, the days in hiding, the loss of Mohammed, all weighed on the little boy's mind. Xander knew he'd have to write several short letters, see how little Edmund took each idea, and then write again. *Maybe*, he thought, *I should get some advice from Doctor Webster about what to say to him.*

From the rest of Manzur's letter, Xander could see that Manzur put a tough face on his own bad memories, but he, too, needed to hear from Xander. Mr. Bhatti's writing seemed business-like, but Xander sensed that his cool tone masked trauma – his days of worry and terror as he herded the boys from the building and into hiding during the siege and the battle, then days of searching for food and safety. They all needed each other. Xander was grateful they were alive and had been found. He worried about how they would survive the "after".

Through tear-fogged eyes, Xander glanced at his grandfather. "Thank you. I can write to them."

"How are they?" Grandpa asked.

"Like me," Xander said. "Okay sometimes."

Grandpa's face seemed more lined, older, lonely. Xander reached a hand for his grandfather's. Grandpa closed his eyes and leaned slowly back in his chair, relaxing into Xander's shoulder.

"I miss . . . I miss them," Grandpa said, "Your Grandma Elizabeth, Mr. O'Connor, my folks, and that old Max Million, who loved us all. And I hurt every time I think about your dad and mom. Rebecca and Daniel believed in the goodness of people."

Xander thought back over his years in Pakistan, watching his teachers, his parents, their patients, and their fellow doctors. "Mom and Dad were right, you know," he said. "Most people want what is right. They want food, a home, health, and a chance to work. That's all they need."

Grandpa seemed to study the hard knuckles on his hands, then his forehead creased in thought. "For most, that is true. But then we give power to the few – the ones who want to keep us afraid – the Gotamere types, Agent Saurus, the sellers of rumor and hate – those who won't let go of power without a fight."

Haroon awakened from his trance. He glanced at his father. "Dad, did you see it?" he whispered.

His father looked up at him. "See what, son?"

"The flames burning the front wall of the restaurant. The heat rippled the other walls."

Nasdar seemed to hesitate before he answered, then lifted his head and spoke clearly. "Yes, my son. The murals."

"The hounds, the dogs," Haroon said, "the Taziyan, they still hunt the poor goat."

"As they always have, and if we let them, they always will."

QUESTIONS FOR CLASSROOM AND BOOK GROUP DISCUSSION

1. Xander's school in Pakistan was the work of the community and of many religious groups. Why did this seem to function well? What dangers did it face?

2. After the attack on his community, Xander blames himself for being alive when everyone he cares about has died. Do you understand this feeling? Do you have experience with self-blaming? Do any of your friends or family?

3. What moments in his parents' and friends' lives does Xander focus on when he remembers them? Why those moments?

4. Not making friends becomes Xander's first defense against being hurt again. Yet, he finally agrees to join Haroon at soccer practice. What makes him change his mind?

5. How might Nasdar Qubadi have been treated if he were of a different cultural background, say Russian? German? Irish? Swiss?

6. One of the accusations against Nasdar is that he went target practicing. How was this relevant? What were the other accusations? Discuss why they seemed important to the prosecution, and to people like Louis Lamb.

7. The two newspaper men, Louis Lamb and Gilbert Evans, have very different views of how to provide security in the United States. One believes that safety is more important than preserving freedoms guaranteed by the Constitution, the other believes that the Constitution should trump safety fears. Why did each man come to his conclusions? How do their experiences and conclusions match yours? Do you have friends whose beliefs about national safety are at odds with yours? Can you discuss these differences and maintain friendship?

8. Xander's experiences from age seven to seventeen are very different from those of most of us. How do those experiences make his life in the United States un-comfortable? How do his experiences help him make sense of life in the United States?

9. In the United States, a small percentage of citizens speak a second language, or have opportunities to learn about the cultural norms of other countries. Why do we not know more about other cultures? How does that lack of exposure color our view of the world?

10. Xander and Haroon discover that the crowd outside the courthouse is actually a lot smaller than it seemed when they had to walk through angry people. Are there times when

a small group of people can have a big influence on how a situation is understood? What does that tell us about how we should view news reports? What does it tell us about our responsibilities as citizens?

11. Nasdar Qubadi was found not guilty of all the charges, yet, after the trial was over, a crowd formed outside his restaurant to protest that finding. Others were willing to blow up his restaurant. Why could each of these groups not accept the court findings?

12. Grandpa Gilbert gave Xander an assignment. "Look up a history of dissent in the United States, and see what you find." What would Xander have found?

To learn more about the historical considerations behind Xander and Haroon's story, you can begin at my website, www.raerichen. com/USConstitutionSinceNine-One-One

There you will find discussions and suggestions for further reading about our US Constitution, the Patriot Act and court rulings concerning the treatment of terror suspects since the attacks of September 11, 2001.

ACKNOWLEDGEMENTS

Many people made this story possible. Readers of Scapegoat: *The Price of Freedom* have asked what happened to Gilbert Evans afterward. Their interest certainly encouraged me to finish this sequel. Thanks to noted author and teacher Larry Brooks for his insight into storytelling and his suggestion to make Xander's story the focus of a second book.

A big, loving thank you to my writing friends Ken Byers, Jennie Bricker and Jane Carlsen, Cindy Brown and Susan Parman for their brilliant ideas and practical suggestions.

Mrs. Faiza Noor offered invaluable help with my understanding of the Northwest Muslim community and with her gracious commentary on scenes involving the fictional Qubadi family's possible habits of thought, dress and worship. The teachers and students of the Muslim Educational Trust and the women of Bilal Mosque have been very welcoming. I hope to continue growing in understanding of our differences and our similarities in spiritual and cultural matters. Any misrepresentations of Muslim beliefs and cultural ways is my own misunderstanding and not the fault of these generous people.

Thank you to Daniel Ladinsky for his permission to use his translation of important thoughts from the poetry of Shams-u-din Muhammad, Hafiz. Mr. Ladinsky's generosity is much appreciated and serves as an example for me. The poem is in Mr. Ladinsky's *The Gift, Poems by Hafiz the Great Sufi Master.*

Melissa Blumklotz is a wonder in the business of keeping on top of my blogging life and my connections with the wider world of readers. She explains the workings of cyber-space and the true meaning of techno-jargon with humorous and picturesque metaphor. I urge her to take up the pen for herself one day soon.

As ever, Woody Richen has been an encouragement and an inspiration for perseverance and growth in my writing. Margaret Price's consistent interest and encouragement to write my next story, and Owyn Richen's patient help with critical details have kept this project moving forward.

ABOUT THE AUTHOR

Rae Richen's short stories and articles have appeared in anthologies, newspapers and in handbooks for writers and teachers. She has taught middle school, high school students and adults and has always been impressed with the wide-ranging curiosity and the persistent search for answers among her students.

Her novels include the adventure novel, *Uncharted Territory*, and the historical *Scapegoat* series, *The Price of Freedom* and *The Hounded*. She has also written *To Serve Those Most in Need*, a non-fiction history of social services in the Pacific Northwest.

Her novels include questions for book groups dealing with story content and storytelling choices. They are appropriate for interested readers and also for students studying fiction writing.

The author is available for classroom presentations and discussions. She enjoys leading workshops for any age group on the writing of fiction and non-fiction. Contact her through:

Lloyd Court Press www.lloydcourtpress.com Or at www.raerichen.com

OTHER TALES OF ACTION AND ADVENTURE BY RAE RICHEN

For a good read of all first chapters, and the history and back story of these novels, sign in as the author's friendly reader at https://www.raerichen.com/guest-area.

Uncharted Territory – a father-son adventure in the mountains and in learning to accept and love despite the fragility of life. Learn more: https://www.raerichen.com/books.

Scapegoat: The Price of Freedom – a teen and his friends struggle with a culture of easy accusation during the McCarthy Anti-Communist era. Learn more: https://www.raerichen.com/books. This is the prequel to *Scapegoat: The Hounded.*

In Concert – A novel of suspense and romance when a famous musician is stalked by a vicious man who wants to own her and her son. Visit https://www.raerichen.com/in-concert and read the first chapter for free.

Frozen Trust – a novel of espionage and romance within the United States during World War II. Visit https://www.raerichen.com/frozen-trust and read the first chapter for free.

Sentinels of Solitude – a novel of suspense and love during a murderous land grab in the lush Willamette Valley of Oregon. Visit www.raerichen.com/blog for the stories behind the story.

A Fool's Gold – a novel of treachery and romance in the Rocky Mountains of Colorado during the mining fever of the 1880s. Visit www.raerichen.com/books for more information.

Those Who Curse You – A Murder Mystery of Unlikely Bonds and Unrelenting Peril – Can inner-city architect, Sarah Rohann and her client, Abraham Hallowell save their families from the murderous drug gang that threatens all of their lives? www.raerichen.com/books

Without Trace: A Glyn Jones and Grandma Willie Mystery
When Trace Gowan, drummer in Glyn Jones' hip-hop band, goes missing, Glyn and his friends involve Grandma Willie and her connections to prison and police in the search. They find there is a lot more than a kidnapping going on and all of them are in danger. www.raerichen.com/books

Coming Soon: *Calling The Shots, An Anthology of Short Stories* – A confection especially for readers who asked "What happened to Elizabeth in The *Price of Freedom*? To Dick Street of *In Concert* and in *Those Who Curse You*?"

Learn what caused Gryf and his brother Sam to be the targets of a madman even before they came to the United States – the back story of *A Fool's Gold*.

And see what happened to Lewis James's missing brother, Dicken – a follow-up on Lewis's search for Dicken during *In Concert*.

In this and other anthologies soon to be published, Rae Richen has given us short stories to reveal where these characters lives intersected with the stories in the novels and where they went after we last saw them.

At the same time, in other tales, Rae Richen also has brought us whole new worlds and characters that we will want to follow and cheer for as they attempt to untangle their complicated lives.